Churchill County Library
553 S. Maine Street
Fallon, Nevada 89406
(775) 423-7581

HANG HIM
TWICE

Center Point
Large Print

Also by William W. Johnstone with J. A. Johnstone and available from Center Point Large Print:

Brotherhood of Evil
Black Friday
Tyranny
A Stranger in Town
Monahan's Massacre
Twelve Dead Men
The Jensen Brand
The Doomsday Bunker
The Trail West

THE TRAIL WEST:
HANG HIM TWICE

WILLIAM W. JOHNSTONE
WITH J.A. JOHNSTONE

CENTER POINT LARGE PRINT
THORNDIKE, MAINE

This Center Point Large Print edition
is published in the year 2018 by arrangement with
Kensington Publishing Corp.

Following the death of William W. Johnstone, the
Johnstone family is working with a carefully selected writer
to organize and complete Mr. Johnstone's outlines and
many unfinished manuscripts to create additional novels in
all of his series like The Last Gunfighter, Mountain Man,
and Eagles, among others. This novel was inspired by
Mr. Johnstone's superb storytelling.

The text of this Large Print edition is unabridged.
In other aspects, this book may vary
from the original edition.
Printed in the United States of America
on permanent paper.
Set in 16-point Times New Roman type.

ISBN: 978-1-68324-758-6

Library of Congress Cataloging-in-Publication Data

Names: Johnstone, William W., author. | Johnstone, J. A., author.
Title: Hang him twice : the trail west / William W. Johnstone with
    J. A. Johnstone.
Description: Center Point Large Print edition. | Thorndike, Maine :
    Center Point Large Print, 2018.
Identifiers: LCCN 2018000808 | ISBN 9781683247586
    (hardcover : alk. paper)
Subjects: LCSH: Large type books. | GSAFD: Western stories.
Classification: LCC PS3560.O415 H34 2018 | DDC 813/.54—dc23
LC record available at https://lccn.loc.gov/2018000808

HANG HIM
TWICE

CHAPTER ONE

Some things, a man knows, he ought never do.

Like placing your hat on a bed. Or riding a pinto horse—unless you happen to be an Indian. Or borrowing a pocketknife that has the blade open but then returning it with the blade closed. Or not sharpening a straight razor three times on each side. Or removing the ashes from a stove on a Friday. But here sat Dooley Monahan in the Elkhorn Saloon in Denver City, Colorado, about to make the worst move of his life.

Which was saying a lot.

"One card," Dooley told the dealer while tossing his discard onto the center of the table.

The dealer, a pockmarked man with a handlebar mustache, sleeve garters, and shaded spectacles, deftly slid a paste card across the green felt cloth toward Dooley's pile of chips, which happened to be a lot smaller than when he had taken that empty seat four hours earlier.

The stagecoach messenger—the one the size of a grizzly with about as much hair, not the other driver, who was bald and had no teeth—drew three cards. The merchant wearing the bowler hat and plaid sack suit took three as well. The dealer sent the stagecoach driver, the bald one, two cards.

That was it. The dealer had folded on the first bet, and the other chairs had been vacated during the course of the four hours, and no one in the Elkhorn appeared willing to try to bust the stagecoach driver's—the bald one, without any teeth but a massive pile of chips—run of luck.

Dooley watched as the players picked up their cards, shuffled them into the proper places among the cards they held.

"Your bet." The dealer nodded at the toothless stagecoach man, who grinned, wet his lips, and studied his chips.

"Check," the man said.

"Check," said Dooley.

That caused the stagecoach messenger—the one who looked like a grizzly, and smelled like one, too—to use his substantial neck to turn his substantial head at Dooley.

"You ain't even looked at your card, mister," the big cuss said, and tapped a substantial finger on the felt, pointing at the card Dooley had drawn.

Dooley sipped his beer. "I don't have to," he said.

That caused the big man to straighten and study Dooley closer. Then he eyed the dealer, who merely shrugged and said, "Your bet, sir."

The big one looked at his cards, then at Dooley, then at the dealer, then at that double-barreled coach gun, which he used to guard against stagecoach robberies. Dooley did not plan on robbing any stagecoach, and, at this point, he wasn't even sure he planned on sticking in the game once the betting started.

The grizzly bear looked back at Dooley.

"You some kind of clear voyager?" he asked.

Dooley blinked.

"Huh?"

"You heard me."

"I heard you," Dooley said. "I just don't understand what you mean."

"I said either you's some kind of clear voyager or this here's 'bout as crooked a deal as I've ever had—and I've had me a passel of crooked deals."

Dooley's mouth turned to sand, and he had just swallowed about a fifth of his freshly poured beer. He began running those superstitions through his head again as the big man placed his cards on the table and lowered the right hand toward the substantial scattergun that would make even Buffalo Bill Cody or Wild Bill Hickok nervous.

Never place your hat on a bed . . . Always sharpen your straight razor three times on each side . . . Don't ever take ashes out of a stove on a Friday . . . And don't be a danged fool and . . .

The merchant interrupted Dooley's thoughts.

"Do you mean clairvoyant?"

Now the leviathan turned his massive head at the merchant. "That's what I said, gol darn it."

Dooley grinned, shook his head, and said—after

breathing a sigh of relief: "I'm no clairvoyant."

Which turned out to be the wrong thing to say.

Because the stagecoach messenger rose, tipping his chair over. "Then that means this here be a crooked deal."

The man's hand reached for the shotgun, a massive Parker ten-gauge that looked more like a howitzer than a scattergun. And as big as that cannon seemed, the big cuss's hand practically dwarfed it.

The dealer had reached for the much slimmer Colt in a shoulder holster. The merchant simply turned about as pale as Dooley thought his own face must be looking about now. Blue, Dooley's merle hound, growled. A saloon gal bringing drinks toward the neighboring table abruptly took her ryes and bourbons and beers and one glass of champagne toward the other side of the saloon. And the folks sitting at the neighboring table stopped playing cards and quickly cleared out of the way.

That's when the other stagecoach man—the jehu without any teeth—broke into laughter.

"Sit down, you ignorant oaf," he said to the grizzly bear. "He ain't no clear voyager and this ain't no crooked deal."

The grizzly trained his angry eyes at the skinny old man, who downed a shot of rye and smiled a toothless smile.

"He ain't got to see what card he drawed

on account I didn't bet," the jehu said as if explaining a math equation to a bumpkin. "He's waitin' to see how this hand plays out, you fool. So bet, check, or fold."

Those words finally registered, and the giant released his grip on the shotgun. One of the neighboring poker players decided to be a gentleman and lifted the grizzly's chair off the floor, smiled at Blue, who settled back down by Dooley's chair's legs, and the man returned to his own chair at his own table.

Dooley finished his beer.

After the giant settled back into his seat and reexamined his cards, he snorted, gave Dooley a sideways glance, and said, "I still think you might be a clear voyager."

Bet and find out, Dooley started to say, but he had already broken one of the sacred vows of cowboys and poker players and decided now was not the time to push his luck. He shrugged, and nodded at the saloon gal and called out, "Another round for my compatriots."

"Thank you," everyone said except the grizzly, who spit into the sawdust and said, "I wasn't no conned patriot, mister. I wore the blue with the finest artillery regiment in Rosecrans's army."

"What were you?" the slim jehu said, sniggering. "A cannon?"

The grizzly frowned and slid his winnings into the pile in the center.

"It'll cost you my whole pile to find out."

As the dealer eyed the chips, greenbacks, and coins, the merchant tossed his cards onto the deadwood. "I am too drained after this excitement to think clearly," he said, "so I shall fold."

The toothless driver of stages laughed. "On account you didn't draw what you needed."

The merchant did not respond.

Said the dealer: "I make that right at one hundred thirty-seven dollars and fifty-five cents."

"You done all that in your noggin?" the toothless jehu said.

"He's probably one of 'em clear voyagers, too," the grizzly bear growled.

Dooley swallowed down his nerves and looked at the one card he had drawn, still facedown on the felt, but did not lift it . . . yet.

The skinny driver grinned and said as he reached for his chips, "Why don't we make it an even five hundred dollars?" He tossed in some greenbacks and gold coins.

"But you checked," the merchant pointed out.

"There's no law against checking and raising," the dealer said.

"But it's not gentlemanly," the merchant said.

Dooley had to agree with the merchant's assessment, but that didn't matter. The only thing that mattered now was to see what the dealer had delivered him. Since Dooley was neither a clairvoyant nor a clear voyager, he stretched his left hand across the table, put his fingers on the card, and thumbed the corner up just slightly. He left the card on the table and laid the four cards he kept on top of them.

"I guess that's a fold . . ." The sentence stopped in the toothless coot's throat as Dooley picked up his cards and asked the dealer:

"So it's five hundred to me?"

"That's right."

Holding the five cards in his left hand, Dooley began counting what he had left. It amounted to a little more than $230.

"Tell you what, mister," the toothless codger said. "That's a fine dog you got lyin' there by your boots. I mean, if you want to raise."

Dooley grinned. "How much you think old Blue's worth?"

Thin lips cut off the toothless grin.

The merchant's chair legs scraped across the floor, and the man pushed back his bowler and walked around. "I know a few things of dogs." He studied Blue, who did not seem the least interested. "That's an Australian shepherd, I think. Maybe seven, eight years old. Good dog."

"You some dog clear voyager?" the grizzly bear asked.

The merchant smiled. "No. I just know dogs. A dog like that, in Denver, would go for six hundred dollars."

Everyone at the table stared incredulously at

the merchant, who sat down. "Boys," he said, "this is Denver City. You know how much a bath costs. Or an all-night woman. A dog like that is worth a lot of money."

"Last dog I had," said the grizzly bear, "I et for supper."

The barmaid brought over the drinks, and Dooley paid her, and asked the dealer, "Table stakes?"

Once the dealer nodded, Dooley slid the rest of his money into the pot.

"Are you calling, sir, or raising?" the dealer asked.

"Just a call." He leaned over and scratched Blue's ears.

"What I figured," said the toothless gent.

The grizzly bear snorted, and reached inside his greasy buckskin jacket, withdrawing a piece of crumpled yellow paper. "This here is the deed to a mine I gots up in Leadville. You saw the poke I cashed in to sit in this game. That poke come out of my mine. If a damned blue dog is worth six hundred bucks in this town, I reckon my mine is worth five thousand. So that's my bet."

"Hoss," the thin jehu said, the word hissing through his gums. "You can't be bettin' your mine."

"I sure am, Chester. Because I know you's bluffin'."

The dealer reached into the pot and withdrew the paper. His face registered distaste as he smoothed it out and said after a long while, "This looks to be a proper deed, duly registered. But as to the veracity of its value . . ."

"It's worth five thousand," the toothless jehu said. "Ain't the best mine in Leadville, but it's plumb fine. He won't tell nobody where it is, though."

"If you've got a valuable mine," the merchant said, "why are you guarding the Leadville–Denver stage?"

That, Dooley thought, was a mighty intelligent question.

The grizzly bear growled. "Stage runs once a week. When I ain't riding guard fer Chester, I's workin' my mine."

The merchant shook his head. "It's a two-day run to Denver. A two-day run back. And if there's snow, rain, or mud, it can be three days. So you're saying that you work a mine two or three days only, and it's worth five thousand bucks?"

"Yep," the grizzly said. "Ask Chester."

"I tell him," the jehu said before anyone asked him, "that he ought to give up this job and concentrate on the mine. But he don't trust nobody to guard his silver, so he rides shotgun."

Everyone sipped drinks and stared at the grizzly.

"Boys," the jehu said, "if you don't believe it, he puts his money in the First Republican Bank of Denver."

The dealer shrugged. "It's up to you players. The Elkhorn has no money in this hand."

"A thousand dollars to you, Chester," the grizzly told the toothless man.

The lean driver looked at his hand, then at the grizzly bear, and cursed as he tossed in his hand.

"Ha!" The grizzly bear leaned back in his chair. "I knowed you was bluffin'. So I reckon . . ." He reached for the pot, but Dooley cleared his throat.

"It's a thousand to me, then?" he asked.

The front legs to the chair slammed against the hardwood floor, and the giant turned, surprised as Dooley said, "If my dog's worth six hundred dollars, how much would you reckon that horse I tethered to the hitching rail out front is worth?"

"That fine bay gelding?" the merchant asked. The man was sure observant—and he knew a whole lot about the cost of things in Denver City.

"His name's General Grant," Dooley said.

"Two thousand dollars," the merchant said. "This is Denver City, so it's Denver prices. If you were playing in Dodge City, I'd allow it would be worth six hundred, seven hundred."

"Well, I wouldn't sell him in Dodge City for two thousand," Dooley said.

"But you're bettin' him . . . and your dog?" The grizzly bear grunted.

"You got anything else worth betting?" Dooley asked. He turned to the merchant. "How much is that scattergun worth? . . . Denver City prices?

Or maybe you have a mule? A horse? Some more pokes in your saddlebags?"

The grizzly bear tossed his cards onto the table.

"Horatio!" the toothless cur named Chester said. "Don't be a damned fool. At least call the son of a gun. I was bluffin'. So was he. You got him beat. You ain't got to fold, you ignoramus!"

"No. I ain't bettin' ol' Betsy." He rubbed his palm against the shotgun's twin barrels. "And I ain't bettin' Clyde. That's my mule. She's in Leadville."

Clyde, Dooley thought, *is a she?*

"But . . ." Chester whined.

Dooley let out a breath and dragged his winnings toward him, including the filthy deed to some hole in Leadville. As he was doing that, Chester reached across the felt and overturned Dooley's hand.

Nine of spades. Ten of hearts. Queen of spades. King of clubs . . . Jack of diamonds.

"See," Chester said, nodding at Horatio. He turned over his hand, three eights, a deuce, and another jack. "He had me beat."

"Wait a minute," said Chester. "You mind telling me what you drawed?"

Dooley smiled. "The jack."

Chester settled into his chair. "You don't know no better than to try to draw to . . . to . . . to an inside straight?"

"You checked," Dooley said, "and raised?"

Horatio frowned, then grinned, and finally laughed.

A good thing, Dooley thought. His luck had to be changing. He had managed to break every poker player's rule: Never draw to an inside straight. He had won.

"But he could've beat you," the merchant said. "He drew two cards."

"If he had anything better than three of a kind," Dooley said, "he would have bet the mine to begin with. He's no sandbagger."

The grizzly bear put his elbows on the table, rested his big head in his huge hands, and nodded. "Yep," he said glumly. "But at least I didn't lose ol' Betsy . . . or Clyde."

Dooley pushed his winnings to the dealer. "Cash me out, will you. And take a ten for yourself. And another round for the table."

The dealer nodded. And after drinking and talking with the boys, Dooley rose at last, the money belt heavy across his waist.

"Come on, Blue," he said. He looked at the grizzly bear. "How do I get to Leadville, sir?"

"You can ride in my stage," Chester said.

Dooley shook his head. "I'd rather ride my horse."

The big head moved slightly, but the toothless man spoke: "Ride west, mister. Then climb the tallest hill you see and keep on climbing till you reach the moon."

"And how do I find your mine?" Dooley asked.

The grizzly shrugged. "I'll draw you a map tomorrow morn when I's sober. And iffen you still can't find it, I'll show you myself when Chester and me hit Leadville."

Nodding his agreement, Dooley Monahan felt pretty good. Well, who wouldn't with a silver mine and a good dog and a great horse and a lot of money in his belt. He had drawn to an inside straight. He had won more money than he had seen in years. No one had tried to kill him. In fact, everyone here in Denver City seemed right friendly. Things were looking up.

He stepped onto the boardwalk and felt a bullet rip off his hat.

CHAPTER TWO

The long-barreled Colt .45 leaped into Dooley's hand, but Dooley did not leap. He dived, landing against the water trough in front of the saloon as another bullet slammed into the batwing door. Blue growled, barked, and started to charge whoever it was across the street shooting at Dooley, but Dooley reached out with his left hand, gripping the makeshift collar he had affixed—the bouncer at the saloon had told Dooley in no uncertain terms that the Elkhorn did not allow dogs in the establishment unless they were well trained and had a collar. Dooley understood. He had unfastened his bandanna and tied it around the merle-colored dog's neck. Then he had tipped the bouncer a dollar.

He wasn't about to leave Blue outside with General Grant—not in a town like Denver City. He hadn't been crazy about leaving his gelding tied to the hitching rail.

A third shot boomed, and Dooley felt cold water splash on the brim of his hat. He sucked in a deep breath and stared at the doors to the saloon, waiting for somebody to come out, to help, to yell for the constable or marshal or sheriff or army or vigilantes or whoever was responsible for law and order in this rough town.

He could see where the bullet had punched out some tiny planks in the door, which still swung on its hinges. Shouts inside the saloon slowly ceased, replaced by, Dooley thought, whispers. Nobody appeared. Nobody called for the law. Finally, once the door stopped swinging, the big door, the real door, on the left side, closed. Dooley frowned. Blue growled. A second later, the door on the right side shut.

Someone twisted a key in the lock.

"Great," Dooley whispered.

Another bullet splintered the column post to Dooley's left. The horses, including General Grant, began pulling against their tethers, stamping their hooves, snorting, and causing quite the commotion, but Dooley had to give the gunman credit for one thing. The man didn't want to hit a horse, even by accident. He just, for some unknown reason, wanted to shoot down Dooley.

Or did he?

That first shot—the one that had punched two holes, entrance and exit, into Dooley's hat—easily could have taken off the top of Dooley's head. Had the gunman merely wanted to get Dooley's attention?

It was an interesting theory, Dooley allowed, and he might have studied on it a little longer had he not quickly disavowed that notion altogether.

He looked down the boardwalk and darkened

street, at another hitching rail and watering trough that was nowhere nearly as crowded as the one he crouched behind now. He couldn't see the building that clearly for the streetlamp was not burning, but Dooley could make out the design of a star on the window. He had not noticed the lawman's office when he rode up to the saloon, but he had not been thinking much about lawmen . . . just poker . . . and a beer . . . and . . .

Dooley sucked in a deep breath, held it for just a moment, and exhaled. "Stay here," he whispered to Blue, and he came up to his knees, then on the balls of his feet, and exploded through the mud toward the darkened corner and the building with the lawman's badge on the window.

A bullet burned his back and shattered glass in the saloon that was no help, and Dooley dived as another bullet tore a gash across the corner of the trough. Dooley landed behind the safety of the watering spot, came up, and caught his breath.

"Hey!" he shouted to the darkened building.

Then he cursed.

It was darker here than it was in front of the saloon, even after some jerk had closed the main doors, but Dooley had good eyesight and had learned all his letters back at the subscription school and through his mother's instructions and at church back in Iowa.

STARR'S MILLINERY

He had to laugh.

So much for finding safety at a lawman's office. *Well,* he thought, *my own hat's got holes in it now, but I don't know how I'd look in an Orleans turban or some fancy thing of braid, satin, and flowers with a bow tied on the top.* He also wondered:

What kind of town has a ladies' hat shop sitting next to a saloon and gambling parlor?

He stopped thinking when another round pounded against the watering trough. This time, Dooley came up, felt the .45 buck in his hand, and ducked before he got his head blown off. His back burned from where the bullet had torn his shirt, just below where the vest has risen up on him, but he felt no blood, just heat. That also told him that either the man shooting at him had to be the best shot in Denver, Colorado, if not the entire Western frontier of these here United States, or that the man certainly meant to do Dooley Monahan harm.

Blue growled, causing Dooley to panic.

"Stay!" he shouted, and cringed as a bullet ripped into the door of Starr's Millinery.

He looked up and down the street, but nothing came into view except the horses still dancing and snorting and scared in front of the saloon. Dooley started inching toward the corner of the trough nearest the saloon, but stopped, reconsidering, and moved the other way. When he reached the edge, he looked down the darkened street, waited, and came up again, firing the Colt, and this time waiting just long enough to see a shadow disappear. He thumbed back the hammer, aimed this time, and squeezed the trigger. The muzzle flash pained his eyes, as it had done before, but Dooley saw splinters fly from the wooden façade across the street. He dropped down, shoved open the loading gate, pulled the hammer at half cock, and worked the plunger and cylinder until the hot empty casings fell beside him.

His fingers pushed fresh loads from his cartridge belt. One dropped into the mud. He didn't pick it up until he had every chamber filled, the gate shut, and the hammer pulled back to full cock.

One he had wiped the grit, mud, and moisture from the shell, he slipped it into his vest pocket and moved back the other way, toward Blue, closer to the saloon, and stopped at the trough's edge. Blue whined. Dooley tried to give him a smile and wink of encouragement. He wet his lips, pressed his body into the cold dampness of the mud, and inched a bit forward again.

Now that he knew exactly where the assassin was hiding across the street, Dooley figured he had at least a chance of surviving this gunfight.

Providing, he thought, the man hasn't moved to another position.

He looked up at the outline of the building.

The shooter could be on top of the roof.

He looked underneath the bellies of the horses, including General Grant, and through the legs of the steeds at another alley.

Or he could be down there.

He felt his back burning again from the slug the man-killer had fired.

Or he could be behind me.

"Stop thinking!" he whispered to himself. "You've been in scrapes worse than this."

The assassin might be . . .

"Stop it!" he snapped. His voice startled him. He hadn't meant to yell anything.

He told himself: *You'll worry and think yourself into Boot Hill if you keep this up.*

A movement across the street caught his eye. He steadied the heavy Colt in his hand, waited.

So . . . the man shooting at Dooley had not moved after all. Dooley slowed his breathing, steadied himself, refusing to blink or move.

The barrel of a rifle caught the reflection of a street lamp down the street. Dooley squeezed the trigger.

He came up this time, fired again. The rifle dropped into the dirt. A hand reached for it, and Dooley pulled the Colt's trigger.

"Yeee-owww!" The hand disappeared back behind the corner of the building across the street. Dooley sent another round, heard the ricochet as the bullet whined off something in the darkness.

Then he dropped back down into the mud and worked on reloading the pistol one more time.

He had hit the gunman in the arm, maybe the hand. That much Dooley knew, and as long as he could keep that rifle out of the killer's hands, he would be all right. Maybe. For a brief moment, Dooley considered charging across that street, Colt blazing in his right hand, screaming like some wild rebel soldier—even though Dooley had Northern leanings as a farm boy from Iowa—but saving two or three rounds until he reached the corner.

Reasoning did not elude him, however, and he understood that the man with the rifle could very well—indeed, in a town like Denver and in a state like Colorado—most likely had a six-shooter in addition to the rifle he had dropped.

Dooley would stay put.

But the man had been shooting a rifle. He might not be much of a hand with a six-shooter. Most people weren't. Dooley happened to be one of those exceptions, though he always considered himself lucky, not a real marksman.

Besides, a rifle cost a lot more money than a revolver. The killer won't leave it in the mud. *Not if he's as cheap as I am.*

All I have to do, Dooley told himself, *is just keep my eyes open, wait for him to make a play to fetch that rifle back.* He made himself relax, or as much as one could, lying in the cold mud on a wet street in winter in Denver, Colorado. He wet his lips. He did not blink.

Blue began to growl.

"Hush," Dooley told his dog without looking. The dog started barking, and then Blue charged.

"Blue!" Dooley saw the dog run past him, leap onto the boardwalk, and then Dooley understood how serious a mistake he had just committed. He rolled onto his back, bringing the Colt up, firing at the shadow in the alley on the far side of Starr's Millinery. Dooley tugged again on the hammer and found it stuck.

He swore. Pulled harder. But the Colt had jammed.

Blue barked, and Dooley saw the gunman step onto the boardwalk. The man laughed. Dooley saw him bring up the rifle, and he wondered if these were going to be his last thoughts:

How did that son of a gun get his rifle back and get around to this side of the street?

The man quickly turned away from Dooley.

"Don't!" Dooley yelled, fearing that the man would use his gun on Blue. He then threw the Colt in that direction, but all he heard was the gun smash through the painted star symbol on the plate glass window at Starr's Millinery.

All this had happened in mere seconds. Blue remained a good ten feet from the man on the boardwalk as the glass shattered. And in the hours that followed, when Dooley had time to think things clearly, he understood that the man lifted his rifle, not at Blue, not even at Dooley, but down the boardwalk.

That's when Dooley's ears began to ring after an explosion detonated behind him. And the man dropped the rifle he was holding as dust and blood jettisoned from his bib-front shirt. And more splinters flew off the planks on the wall of the millinery, and the man was flying backward, disappearing into the alley, until Dooley could see only his boots, toes upward.

The sulfuric scent of gun smoke reached Dooley, and as Blue skidded to a stop on the damp boardwalk, Dooley spun around to see the man from the poker game, standing on the other corner of the saloon, holding a double-barreled coach gun in his hands.

Now the horses were really pulling, and the hitching rail's post grunted and budged. Dooley saw Blue turn around and find the new assailant, but Dooley said, "It's all right, Blue." He reached across the trough, grabbing the reins to General Grant. "Easy," he said. "Easy."

Two of the horses did not listen. Both broke their tethers and galloped down the street. Another pulled free, too, but seemed to understand the excitement had ended and just backed out into the center of the street.

"Easy," Dooley told his horse again, and looked back at the old messenger as he opened the breech of the Parker ten-gauge, extracted the remnants of the fired shotgun shells, and replaced the loads in the barrels before the shotgun clicked shut.

Dooley looked at the boots in the darkness—they still did not move—and the rifle on the boardwalk, and at Blue, and then at the grizzly bear who had been playing poker.

The grizzly named Horatio yelled at the still-shut front doors.

"It's all right, Chester. Ever'thin's done that needed to get did."

Dooley found his voice. "How?" He couldn't hear himself. He coughed and tried again.

"How . . . I mean . . . why . . . why did you help me out?"

The bear of a man looked at Dooley as if he were the dumbest man in Colorado.

"That cur was gonna shoot you in the back." He spit tobacco juice into the mud. "That ain't right."

The door opened, and light bathed the front of the saloon. Chester, the stagecoach driver, stepped out, followed by a saloon girl, a bouncer, and a man in a silk top hat who swore and said, "Damn, you won the bet, Milton. The guy with the dog's still alive."

Suddenly, Blue growled, and Horatio spun, bringing up the shotgun. Dooley spun, too, and saw the flash of a rifle from across the alley.

Dooley remembered that he had thrown his

revolver through the Starr's window. But the bouncer had a Remington, and he fired from the hip. Once. Twice. The rifle in the far alley roared again. The people in the saloon door screamed and dived back inside, and the horses in the middle of the street stampeded. By then, however, men came riding down the street.

"It's the marshal!" a woman on her knees in the saloon doorway shouted.

"Across the street!" Dooley yelled. "He's in the alley yonder."

The lawman and his deputies ran that way, swallowed by the shadows, and Dooley started to thank the stagecoach guard named Horatio and the bouncer.

The thanks died on his lips.

CHAPTER THREE

"Damnation, Horatio." Chester, the toothless old coot who drove the stagecoach, sniffled and pried the Parker ten-gauge out of Horatio's stiffening hands. Dooley moved over, stepped onto the boardwalk, and looked over Chester's shoulders. The jehu was on his knees, bending over that grizzly bear of a guard's body. Dooley saw the stagecoach guard staring at him, but not seeing a damned thing.

Dooley swore softly under his breath.

The saloon girl on her knees in the doorway sniffed, too, and said, "Oh, that poor, poor, sweet old man. Is he . . . ?"

"He's dead." Chester's knee joints popped as he rose. "I told'm not to come out here, that this weren't none of his nor our business, but you couldn't tell that fool nothin'. Not even to call a tinhorn's bluff."

"But he wasn't bluffing," said the dealer from the poker game that now seemed to have been played centuries, not minutes, ago.

Dooley knelt beside the man named Horatio. He reached over and closed the dead hombre's eyes. He sighed heavily, shook his head, and looked at Chester the stagecoach driver.

"He saved my life," Dooley said.

"Yeah." Chester wiped his eyes. Found a rag in a dirty pocket and blew his nose. "That was Horatio. That's why he rode shotgun with me all these years. That's why he fought for the Union during the late War Between the States. That's why he carted that Parker . . ." He looked at the heavy, still-warm weapon in his hands. ". . . ever'where he went. Poor Horatio. He just always wanted to shoot somebody. Even when it weren't his fight."

"I'm sorry," Dooley said.

"Me, too." The wiry old driver stepped back and leaned against the warped pine planks used to wall the saloon. Dooley heard the sucking sound of boots walking through mud, and he stepped toward the first lawman.

He was a robust man in a red and black mackinaw, with a high-crowned beige hat and a graying mustache that covered his upper lip and curled down past his chin. He did not look happy, but, then, it was cold, and dark, and damp, and a dead man was lying on the boardwalk, another in the alley, and a millinery shot all to pieces. Dooley wasn't happy, either. In fact, he felt a bit on the queasy side.

"What the Sam Hill happened?" the mustached man said. He pushed back his jacket just so everyone could see the six-point star pinned to the lapel of his vest. The other four men, who flanked him, wore stars, too, but theirs were pinned to their coats. They did not look happy, either.

Dooley cleared his throat, but before he could say anything, the big marshal spit out a litany of curses, then spit tobacco juice into the mud. He pointed a stubby finger at the dead stagecoach guard.

"That's Horatio, ain't it? Who the hell shot him down like a dog? Who done it? Why, I'll string that miserable assassin up from the rafters of my brother-in-law's livery stable on Blake Street, have him drawn and quartered, and toss his guts into Cherry Creek. Son of a gun. Horatio cut down in the prime of life. The lousy cur owed me seventeen dollars, too! Who done it?"

Again, Dooley tried to speak, but one of the deputies interrupted him, saying, "Marshal Cavendish." He pointed the barrel of his Sharps buffalo gun toward the millinery.

When Marshal Cavendish saw the destroyed plate glass window and the splintered door and frame wall, he bellowed several more choice cuss words, including many that he had not sang out upon seeing the dead messenger.

"I got a dead man that owed me money and the best ladies' hat shop between San Francisco and St. Louey shot all to pieces. Some low-down snake's gonna get himself in a heap of trouble if I don't get some answers mighty fast. Now, who done it?"

"Marshal . . ." That was all Dooley got to say, because one of the deputies on the lawman's left—the one with the Sharps Big Fifty had been on Marshal Cavendish's right—said:

"Marshal, there's some drunk sleeping in the alley next to Miss Starr's place."

"Denver don't tolerate no vagrants and no drunks sleeping in the streets or our alleys." Marshal Cavendish stormed onto the boardwalk, followed now by his four deputies, and strode past the watering trough and into the darkness, his boots crunching on some of the shards of glass that once had displayed a finely painted star and the word's STARR'S MILLINERY, and he stepped off the boardwalk, into the mud, and stared at the boots with the toes still pointing upward.

"Jason," Marshal Cavendish said.

"Sir," answered the one with the big buffalo gun.

"Strike me a lucifer, son. It's pitch-black here."

The deputy handed his buffalo rifle to another deputy, fished a sulfur-tipped stick from his shirt pocket, and struck it against the splintered corner of the millinery. The match blazed, and the deputy knelt beside the dead man.

"This ain't no drunk," Marshal Cavendish said. "It's Chucky Hart."

"How can you tell, Marshal?" asked the deputy holding his own Winchester carbine and Deputy

Jason's Sharps rifle. "After he done taken two loads of buckshot."

Dooley moved over to get a better look at the man who had almost sent him to the sweet hereafter. He wished he hadn't. He seemed to recall seeing the man's bib-front shirt explode from Horatio's shotgun blast, but that must have been on account that Dooley had been looking at the gun the man held, aimed at Dooley Monahan, and not his face. Now there was not much of a face left. Dooley was thankful when Deputy Jason shook out the match before it burned his fingertips.

"That's his rifle." Marshal Cavendish nodded at the weapon in the mud. "And those are his boots." Because Deputy Jason had fired up another match, Dooley now saw the boots, black and up to the knees, and the aces of spades that had been inlaid into the uppers. He did not look at what was left of Chucky Hart's face.

"All right, Jason." Marshal Cavendish turned away. "Go fetch Mort, the undertaker." The big lawman spit again and stepped back onto the boardwalk. "I reckon I've figured it all out now. Chucky and Horatio got into a fight over cards. That's ruined many a friendship and marriage."

"But," Chester, the old jehu, said, "Chucky and Horatio didn't even know one another. They wasn't no friends."

"And they sure weren't married," said the

saloon girl who no longer was on hands and knees in front of the doorway.

A few men in the saloon laughed. Dooley didn't find it funny. Nor did Marshal Cavendish.

"So why in hell did y'all send me and my boys running yonder way?" His fat finger pointed across the street at the darkened alley and the corner of a vacant building that was splintered, but not in such dire straits as Starr's Millinery.

"Marshal?" Dooley said, and now the lawmen stared coldly at Dooley. So did the three deputies left as Jason had walked down the boardwalk to fetch the undertaker.

"Who are you?" Cavendish asked.

"Dooley Monahan," Dooley said, and steeled himself for what he knew would be coming.

Dooley Monahan! The famous bounty hunter? The gunfighter who killed Dev and Alf Baylor, and their brother Jason, and all their kinfolk and even some who weren't kinfolk. That Dooley Monahan?

Only, the lawman did not say that. He did not even open his mouth. He just glared.

"What do you have to say, Dooley Monahan?"

Dooley sighed.

"I was playing poker," he said. "When I stepped out, some fellow over there . . ." He pointed at the alley, and had to catch his breath. He felt himself shaking now that everything was over, now that the adrenaline had worn off. "Some man took a shot at me." He picked up his hat and poked his fingers through the two holes. "I dived there." He pointed at the water trough with new scars from bullets.

"Un-huh," the lawman grunted.

"I got off a few rounds, and I'm pretty sure I winged the gunman in his left arm." He considered that, and sighed. "Maybe his right."

"You can't tell your right from your left, Dooley Monahan?" the marshal said without any humor.

"Well." Dooley tried to picture what he could remember, see the gunfight again, but he saw mostly darkness, a few muzzle flashes, and a dead stagecoach guard who had saved his life, and a man with fancy boots whose face had taken quite a few rounds of buckshot.

"If he was left-handed, I'd say I winged him in his right hand," Dooley said. "Around here." He tapped his underarm between the wrist and elbow. "But if he shoots right-handed, I think I hit his left arm."

"Did you see him?"

"Just his rifle. Too dark."

"Charley," Marshal Cavendish said to the deputy holding his own Winchester and Jason's Sharps. "Go back there and see if you spot any blood or maybe a left arm, or a right arm, or a Winchester, or anything that might tell me just why the hell some fools decided to shoot up

Denver proper on a night when it's twenty-two degrees and damp."

Deputy Charley handed his Winchester to one deputy and Jason's Sharps to another and jogged across the muddy street.

"So you're shooting at this guy across the street," Marshal Cavendish said. And waited.

"Yes, sir. I got a few rounds off, and then I know I hit him because I heard him yell and drop the rifle. And I thought I had him, but then Blue . . . that's my dog." He stopped, looked around, and let out a sigh of relief when he found the dog back behind the water trough, waiting patiently.

"Shepherd," Marshal Cavendish said. "Good dog. Dog like that'd fetch six hundred dollars in Denver." Dooley blinked. The merchant had not been exaggerating about the prices in Denver. "What's a saddle tramp like you doing with a good dog like that?"

Dooley shrugged. "Lucky. Just lucky. Anyway, I was waiting for the man across the street to try for his rifle he had dropped when Blue started growling, and charged, and I turned around and saw that man." He did not look in the direction of the late dead man with fancy boots and not much of a face anymore, but merely jutted his thumb in the general direction of what remained of Chucky Hart and Starr's Millinery.

"My Colt jammed. I threw it at him, but missed. It . . . um . . . well . . . it went through

38

the millinery window." He paused, but seeing no reaction, continued. "That's when Horatio came from around the corner there. He shot that dead man with the boots."

"Chucky wasn't dead then, was he?" the marshal said.

Dooley studied Cavendish, thinking the man was joking, but then realizing it was a real question.

"No," Dooley said, shaking his head. "No, no, of course not."

"Sixty-five-dollar fine," Cavendish said, "for shooting a corpse in this city."

Dooley couldn't sink his teeth into that. He shook his head. "Well, Blue was charging, Horatio came out, and Hart, the man there, he tried to swing his rifle from me to Horatio, but Horatio shot first."

He seemed to see the whole thing happening again. Dooley leaned against the column, feeling the splintered post scratch his back.

"So," Marshal Cavendish said. "The old coot who owed me money up and killed the turkey trying to kill you, and then the turkey got off his last shot and killed the fellow that killed him. Is that what you're telling me, sonny boy?"

Dooley shook his head.

"No, no, Hart didn't kill Horatio."

"Then who, by thunder, done the dirty deed?"

Dooley looked across the street and saw

39

Deputy Charley jogging back through the mud until he stopped a few paces in front of Marshal Cavendish.

"No rifle, Marshal," the deputy reported, and took his Winchester from the hands of one of the remaining deputies but did not bother to relieve Jason's Sharps from the other. "And the alley's too muddy and it's too dark to see if there's any blood. But beyond the fence and the trash cans, I saw where two horses had been tethered. Some horse apples, right fresh, ground all churned up, and it stunk of horse pee. Found some boot prints. One horse was still there. The other was gone."

"You see all that, but no blood?" Cavendish asked.

"Well, like I said . . ."

"Don't say it again, Charley." Cavendish stared at Dooley again. "Go fetch the horse that was left. I figure it'll be Chucky Hart's, but my figuring ain't been so good this night, so let's make certain of things." Deputy Charley handed his rifle to the deputy not holding another deputy's rifle and, sighing, went back through the mud and slop to the alley again.

"And look for blood this time, Charley!" Cavendish shouted.

"Why don't we come to my office." The marshal was not asking a question. "Have some coffee. Warm our toes by my stove. And see if I

40

can get my head wrapped around what happened here tonight. Ben, go into Miss Starr's store and fetch this jasper's pistol. And maybe one of them fancy hats. My wife, she's partial to those pretty little things."

Which is how Dooley spent the rest of the night. Marshal Cavendish turned out to be quite particular when investigating two killings in his city, because, he explained, Denver had plenty of newspapers and reporters asked plenty of questions. He took statements from all the witnesses and finally came to the conclusion that an unknown assailant had fired on Dooley Monahan, no permanent residence, with deliberate and willful intention to do bodily harm and perhaps even commit murder on said Monahan. Horatio Whitman, guard employed by the Leadville-Denver Transportation Company, then killed Chucky Hart, notorious scoundrel hanging his hat since September at the McAllister Wagon Yard on Broadway, who was attempting to kill the aforementioned Dooley Monahan, and leaden shot willfully fired from two barrels of a Parker ten-gauge shotgun duly dispatched the aforementioned Chucky Hart into Boot Hill by way of Mort's Undertaking Parlor. Moments later, an unknown assailant fired a .44-40 caliber shot from a Winchester rifle or carbine and said .44-40 bullet penetrated the breast and

41

heart of the aforementioned Horatio Whitman, killing the latter dead instantaneously. The assassin fled with the rifle used to dispatch the aforementioned Horatio Whitman and departed for parts unknown.

"Sign there." Marshal Cavendish tapped the paper and handed the pen to Dooley, who signed his name and leaned back in his chair.

"And you got no idea who'd want to kill you?" the marshal asked as he sipped his coffee.

"No, sir."

"Maybe," Chester Motz, the stagecoach driver, said, "it wasn't Dooley the cur wanted to gun down. Maybe he'd taken that shot at Dooley to lure Horatio out into the open. So he could shoot down Horatio, which he done, and get his mine."

"What mine?"

"The one Dooley won offen him."

The marshal stared hard at Dooley, then at Chester, then at his four deputies, then at Mort the undertaker, and finally at Blue, who was gnawing on a steak bone.

"You read too many dime novels," Cavendish said. He slid his coffee cup across the desk, gathered the papers, stacked them into a neat pile, and laid them on top of the city directory.

"I'm fining you, Dooley Monahan, three thousand dollars."

"What for?" Dooley sprang out of his chair so fast, Blue stopped devouring the bone.

"Unlawful discharge of firearms in the city limits." He shook his head. "We got a lot of fixing to do on Miss Starr's store." He stared at the hat he had procured for his wife.

"But I didn't start the fight. I'm a victim."

"All I know is I've got two corpses that didn't have no money on them at all, and a store shot to hell that if it don't get fixed and fixed up good might run off the best lady ever come to Denver for some hellhole like Cheyenne or Deadwood. You want that on your conscience, Dooley Monahan?"

Dooley sat back in the chair. "I don't think I have three thousand dollars," he said.

"What about that mine up in Leadville you won off the late Horatio Whitman?"

Dooley glared. He found his poke and dropped it on the desk. Marshal Cavendish began counting, and adding on other fines he decided Dooley needed to pay. After all, two horses were now missing, scared off from the hitching rail in front of the Elkhorn Saloon, and there were other buildings, including the Elkhorn, that had been damaged.

The marshal returned Dooley's poke with thirty-two cents. Dooley shook his head.

"Get out of town, Dooley Monahan," Marshal Cavendish said. "We got us a city ordinance that doesn't allow no vagrants here."

Dooley smiled. "I still have a mine."

43

"Yep. But I've seen plenty of mines in my day and plenty of broke miners."

Dooley was ready to leave Denver. He turned and saw Chester Motz staring at Dooley.

"Old-timer, how do you get to Leadville again?" Dooley asked.

"You ride the stagecoach with me," the toothless jehu said.

Dooley laughed. "I'm no messenger."

"You are now." Dooley drew in a breath, slowly realizing that Chester Motz was not joking.

"That's another law we have in Denver, boy," Marshal Cavendish said. "If you're responsible for a man's death, you got to fill his job for two or three days."

"But I didn't kill Horatio," Dooley said. "I . . ."

And then it struck Dooley that, indeed, he was responsible for the stagecoach guard's death. That he owed Horatio more than he could ever repay. The chair legs ground across the rough floor as Dooley slid away from the desk and rose.

He shoved his not-so-heavy poke into his pocket.

"Can I tie up my horse behind the stage?" Dooley asked.

"Suits me," Chester said. "I'll only charge him half fare." He handed Dooley the Parker ten-gauge that had once belonged to Horatio Whitman.

CHAPTER FOUR

He woke up in the wagon yard, wondering how his luck had turned. One moment, he had a deed to a mine in Leadville and a small fortune in his poke. Now he was brushing hay off his bedroll and did not have enough money to buy a decent breakfast—not at Denver prices, anyway.

On the other hand, Dooley thought as he rolled up his bedroll, he still had that deed to the mine the late Horatio Whitman—Dooley still found it hard to believe what had happened last night— had signed over to him. After getting most of the hay off his clothes, Dooley saddled General Grant, tied the bedroll behind the cantle, and washed his face in the water bucket outside the stall he had paid to sleep in.

Once Dooley had slipped the bridle onto General Grant, he took the reins and led his horse into the early dawn.

"Come on, Blue," he called out. He saw his breath in what little light the clouds and slowly rising sun allowed. The merle-colored dog lifted its head, yawned, stretched, and slowly followed Dooley and the horse out of the wagon yard.

Slowly, the city began to show life, and by the time Dooley had reached the Queen City Hotel, people began opening their stores, and the aromas of coffee and hotcakes and fried bacon and eggs made Dooley realize that he had not eaten in an eternity. Then he saw the stagecoach, and lost his appetite.

"That's not a Concord," he told Chester Motz, who sat atop the wagon securing a trunk with some rope.

The bald-headed, toothless old man in buckskins finished his knot and gave Dooley a quick glance. "And it ain't no celerity wagon, neither." The driver spit tobacco juice that splattered and steamed on the hard, cold ground. "You ain't never seen no mud wagon before?"

Dooley sighed. "I've seen them, but nothing like that."

Laughing, the old man backed his way back into the driver's box and deftly climbed down, dropping from the cap of the front wheel and into the frozen street.

"I call her For'," the jehu said, and patted the side of the coach.

"Four?" Dooley asked. "As in . . ."

"No," the old man barked. "For'. Short for *Forlorn*." He moved down the six-mule team and gestured toward an open door. "Let's get some coffee, Dooley. I'll tell you about the route we take to Leadville."

Dooley decided he could drink some coffee, so he tethered General Grant to the hitching rail in front of the hotel's side entrance, told Blue to stay, and he entered the kitchen of the hotel. He hoped he didn't have to pay for the coffee. He didn't.

Motz pointed at a map and talked about this and that, but Dooley mostly looked through the open door at the mud wagon.

It was square shaped, with canvas stretched across the top over struts of some wood that Dooley prayed would be strong enough to keep the trunk from falling through and smashing any passengers seated in the back seat. Dooley wasn't sure where the old man had secured the rope, but he understood why the trunk had not been put in the rear boot. That was already packed with crates and barrels and grips and carpetbags. There must be a full load of passengers, and the three benches inside the coach had some blankets and even more luggage. Canvas side curtains—no doors, no wooden sides—had been rolled up, but Dooley expected the passengers to lower them once they rode off, to keep out the wind and cold.

Dooley figured it wouldn't be much colder riding in the box with the old man. From the look of the seat atop the mud wagon, it wouldn't be any less comfortable than riding in the coach.

Otherwise, the wagon looked like any other stagecoach on the frontier—with thoroughbraces that would have the passengers seasick before too long. Yeah, Dooley decided, he would be better off riding up top with Chester Motz.

And the coffee wasn't disgusting.

"For' ain't bad," Motz told Dooley. "Lighter than most coaches. And those mules know my touch. You just keep an eye out for bad men. We'll hit Leadville in two days, plus a few hours. Or three days. Maybe four. What time does that watch of yourn say it is?"

Dooley fished out the old key-wind. "About ten past six."

"Hell's hottest fires, boy, we need to light out." He pulled up his collar, tugged down his old hat, gulped down the rest of the coffee, and stepped outside, yelling in a voice that would raise the dead:

"The stage to Leadville is leavin' in five minutes. Stops at Idaho Springs, Georgetown, Silverthorne, and Frisco along the way. And anywhere else we happen to lose a wheel or break an axle. Get on now or get left behind."

Dooley drank the rest of his own coffee, wiped his mouth, hurriedly tied General Grant behind the mud wagon, and then picked up Blue and handed him to Chester Motz, already in the driver's box and filling his mouth with fresh tobacco.

"What's that fer?" the old man asked, spraying dark, wet tobacco leaves into the wind.

"The passengers won't like a dog riding with them," Dooley said.

Motz frowned.

Dooley smiled. "He's still got his winter coat. It'll keep your feet warm."

That did it. The old man smiled, reached down, and took Blue in his rawhide hands.

"Had a pet coon oncet," Motz said. "Was a good pal. But then come the hard winter and I got hungry."

Dooley tried to forget that statement, and he reached up for a hold, put one foot on the cap, and quickly made his way into the box after Chester slid into his place.

"Horatio's Parker's down in the boot," the old man said. Then he stood up and bellowed, "This wagon's pullin' out. If you ain't on now, you ain't gettin' on till I comes back in about a week or three or four."

No one had gotten on the wagon. Dooley had just brought up the ten-gauge shotgun when Chester Motz released the brake, lashed out with a whip, and began bellowing a string of profanity as the mules bolted, the mud wagon rattled and lost a few parts, and they took off out of Denver and heading west.

"There's nobody on board!"

Dooley had pulled up his bandanna to fight the wind and the cold.

"What?"

Chester Motz leaned forward, whip in one hand, lines to the six mules in the other. He slashed out

49

again with the whip, but Dooley couldn't hear the pop because of the wind roaring past his ears and the creaking and banging of the coach.

Dooley repeated his statement.

"That's right!"

They reached the first hill, which meant the coach slowed, and the wind did not roar so loudly as the team climbed the incline.

"There's a lot of luggage for an empty stagecoach," Dooley observed.

"Cheaper than paying the freightin' cost," Motz said. He spit over the side of the coach.

"Do you ever haul passengers?"

"Oh, sure." He leaned forward again and barked curses at the lead mules, worked the lines, and set the whip back in its holder. "But not this time of year, hardly a-tall."

"Why's that?"

The old man laughed and turned away from the mules and roads and stared at Dooley as if he were an idiot.

"You know anything 'bout Leadville, boy?"

"It's a silver town. Boomtown."

"Yeah, and it happens to be about two miles above sea level. Denver's right at a mile. You feel how cold it is right now?"

Dooley nodded.

"That's summer in Leadville, boy." The whip came out of its holder and the profanity came out of Motz's mouth.

Thirty grueling, bone-jarring, butt-aching miles later, the mud wagon slid this way and that into Clear Creek Canyon and wheeled into Idaho Falls, which, from what Dooley could see, looked like a fine little town, jammed into the canyon, with plenty of saloons and gambling halls. He had read about the town during the Pikes Peak gold rush all those years ago, but he did not get much time to appreciate the city because they were pulling out after dropping off the trunk atop the coach and a barrel inside.

Georgetown looked interesting, too, from what Dooley could see of it, for it was pitch-dark by then, and the old jehu spit and nodded at some flickering lights in the distance. "That's Silver Plume," Motz shouted, "but we don't go there."

Thus went Dooley's tour of Colorado's front range.

He had fallen asleep after the change of mules and slept fitfully, bouncing this way and that, until he felt the wagon lurch to a stop and heard Chester Motz mutter something.

"Come on, you lazy, good-fer-nothin' replacement for ol' Horatio who was just as worthless as you is!"

That was not muttered. Dooley almost tumbled over the side of the coach and wondered if he would ever be able to hear out of his left ear again.

"Get down!"

Dooley blinked the sleep out of his eyes and

slid off the mud wagon, careful not to step on the sleeping Blue.

"What are we doing?" asked Dooley, who still had not awakened completely.

It was dawn, cold, and here patches of ice covered the road and most of the country.

"Grab that log," Chester Motz instructed, and Dooley saw the stripped piece of pine or spruce or whatever. He had to kick it a few times for it had frozen to the ground, but he managed to shove it down the embankment. Motz had moved to the other side of the wagon.

"We're gonna lash this to the coach, brace it against the back wheels," the driver explained. "That way the wheels don't go too fast. Don't go a-tall iffen we's lucky."

"That'll slow us down," Dooley said.

"That, boy, is the gen'ral idear." He pointed. Dooley looked at the mountain they were about to descend.

"C'mon, Dooley, daylight is a-burnin'."

His throat turned dry, and his chest ached from the bitter, frigid air, and his own anxiety. Somehow, they managed to fasten the log to the wheels, and Dooley saw General Grant eyeing him, more like pleading with him.

"Hey, Mr. Motz," Dooley said as he stepped to the off side of the mud wagon.

"Call me Chester, boy, or don't call me nothin' a-tall."

"Well, Chester, maybe I should ride my horse down this slope."

"Maybe you should get your arse back in this seat. I've been down this hill more times than you can count, Dooley, and I ain't wrecked a stagecoach on this route but four or five times. Two of 'em don't count 'cause I was drunk."

Dooley made himself climb back into the box.

"Are you drunk now?" Dooley asked.

"No." The old man released the brake. "But I wish to Sam Hill I was."

He did not use the whip, but merely flicked the lines. The mules began tentatively stepping down the hill. The old man deftly moved his left hand to the brake, and set it. One thin hand gripped the lines to the six mules. The other held the brake, giving it more pressure, then less. By now Dooley could see the ice-coated road clearly, and he could see the twists and turns and the edges that plummeted into a sea of white and rocks and snow-covered trees.

Dooley took in a deep breath. Part of him wanted to jump off the side. But he managed to summon up enough courage, although his fingers practically tore through the rotten, dried, brittle wood on his side of the driver's box.

"What do we do now?" Dooley asked.

Motz answered, "We pray."

CHAPTER FIVE

"You're the best damned jehu I've ever seen," Dooley said after they had removed the log brake at the bottom of the treacherous mountain. "Stephen Foster should write songs about you."

"I ain't half-bad," Chester Motz said. "You're all right, Dooley. Old Horatio, God rest his worthless soul, he wet his britches five or six times we made the run. You done fine. Didn't even puke."

Dooley wondered if his hat would still fit. That is, when he had enough money to buy a new hat. His old one, the one with two bullet holes in the crown, had blown off his head sometime between Georgetown and the Clear Creek crossing.

"Maria should have us a hot meal and some good coffee waitin' at Silverthorne."

Maria did, and Dooley ate with relish after that nightmarish, frigid run. The fat Mexican woman took a liking to Blue and fed him table scraps until he bloated up. There wasn't much to Silverthorne, just a stagecoach station and some fresh mules. There wasn't much to Frisco just down the road, either, though Chester Motz said both towns—if you could call them towns—had plenty of prospectors who were searching for pay dirt and had grown tired of Breckenridge and

Leadville and that once one of those miners found gold, or silver, or maybe even some copper, the towns would pull hard-luck miners away from Leadville and maybe as far away as Denver.

At Frisco, the damnedest thing happened.

A man was waiting to get on the mud wagon and travel to Leadville.

Dooley did not know quite what to make of the man.

Oh, he definitely stood out, with the curly, dark hair pulled behind his ears and hanging well past his shoulders. He sported a well-groomed mustache and long goatee, had dark eyes, a bronzed face, and appeared to be a good two or maybe even four inches taller than Dooley. He wore a low-crowned hat with the brim turned in just about every which way possible, pushed up on one side, down in front, cocked almost at a right angle in the back, and just slightly askew on the other side. A multicolored, braided stampede string of horsehair hung tight against the man's throat. His shirt appeared to be made of red velvet, and the double-breasted coat, unbuttoned and hanging loose, had a fur collar and fur trim down one side, fur cuffs, and fringe along the shoulders and down at the bottom. It was a long coat, too, of buckskin, just like the man's britches, which were stuck inside black boots that gleamed. He wore a gun belt—though the long coat hit whatever holster he donned on a hip—that was held up by the biggest, dad-blasted buckle—silver with some red stones set inside—Dooley had ever seen. The man wore gauntlets, too, fancy and stitched with multiple colors that made the design of a pelican—or maybe an osprey . . . well, a bird of some kind, anyhow.

The man also held a heavy Winchester rifle—not one of those carbines but the new Centennial model that chambered shells that could bring down a buffalo.

"By jingo," the man said in a musical voice that matched his dazzling eyes, "had I known you would be driving the wagon to Leadville, Chester, I would not have shot my horse, but merely put a splint on the poor creature's left forefoot and made him take me into Leadville."

"Willie," Chester Motz said with a nod after bringing the team to a stop and wrapping the lines around the brake. "I thought you'd be playing soldier boy or thespian or just drunk."

"I might be playing thespian, old hoss," the man said, butting his Winchester on the cold ground, "and I have not soldiered in many a year, but I certainly could not play the drunk." He winked. "One cannot play what he truly is. That's real."

"You got money?" Motz asked.

"Waiting for me in Leadville." The man smiled. "Don't you trust me, old hoss?"

"No, but as soon as these jaspers unload some of the boxes in my coach, I'll have need of you for ballast and the likes. You can pay the boss man when we ride into town. And the boss man is me."

"That might not be necessary, old friend." Dooley frowned. Willie—and decked out like some dime-novel hero—was staring with quite the admiring eyes at General Grant.

"If you're thinking about making an offer on that horse," Dooley informed him, "don't. He's not for sale. If you're thinking about stealing him, don't."

The man laughed. "I'm no common horse thief, my dear fellow. But perchance you might be interested in wagering this fine, handsome steed against." He tapped the stock of the Winchester Centennial against the ice pack near the porch to the stagecoach station.

"Even at Denver prices," Dooley said, "that rifle couldn't buy enough hairs from General Grant's tail to braid you a new stampede string."

The man laughed again. "No matter. I have but one cartridge left for this cannon of a rifle."

The burly men at the station got the last luggage out of the wagon. The man with the long hair brought the Centennial up and tucked it underneath his left arm while his right reached toward the driver's box.

"My name's Cody, sir. William F. Cody."

"Most folks call him Buffalo Bill," Chester Motz said, "but I just call'm Willie."

Dooley almost dropped the Parker ten-gauge over the side of the mud wagon. He wiped his hands on his trousers and took the fancy gauntlet worn by William F. Cody into his hand. The man had a firm handshake, but not one that would crush Dooley's bones. He kept the shake brief, too.

"I'm . . . um . . . Dooley," Dooley said. "Dooley Monahan."

Buffalo Bill Cody backed up toward the rough-looking log cabin that served as the stagecoach station in this small little burg.

"Not *the* Dooley Monahan," the famed scout and thespian and hero of many stories and novels and newspaper accounts said.

"Well," Dooley said, uncomfortable, "I am a Dooley Monahan. It ain't that common of a name, but I reckon there's probably at least another one with that handle." He had read back in one of the Denver newspapers that the people who did all the counting expected the population of the United States and her territories to come close to fifty million or maybe even more once they got around to counting for the next census.

"The Dooley Monahan I refer to," Buffalo Bill Cody said, "dispatched the nefarious scoundrels Jason Baylor and his no-account brothers Alf and Dev. He shot dead their cousin in Cheyenne, Wyoming. He ended the reign of terror brought on by the notorious Dobbs-Handley Gang. I have

58

long waited to make this bounty hunter's hand and shake it."

Dooley shuffled his feet. "Well, I reckon you done shook his hand, sir. I'm that Dooley Monahan, but I'm not a bounty hunter. I just happen to . . . get . . . ummm . . . mixed up in things."

"By jingo," Buffalo Bill said, and stepped back. "A man as deadly as Jesse James with the eye of Wild Bill Hickok and the nerves of Sitting Bull. And he's modest, to boot. Well, Chester, you have no need to fear of bandits plundering your worthy conveyance . . . not with the legendary Dooley Monahan riding shotgun on . . ." He stopped suddenly and turned quickly toward the bald-headed coot who crammed his mouth full of chewing tobacco.

"By thunder, where is Horatio?"

"Dead," Chester said. "Kilt in Denver by the bullet fired by some unknown fiend who lacked the courage and scruples to step out of the shadows and face a body man to man."

Now the jehu was sounding just like Buffalo Bill.

"Sad. Old Horatio." Cody removed his hat, bowed his head, closed his eyes. "Struck down in the prime of life."

"He was older than Methuselah, Willie," Motz informed the showman. "If you're comin' with us, say amen and climb aboard. I got a schedule to keep."

"Amen," Buffalo Bill Cody said, and climbed into the coach.

"Give him your dog," Motz ordered Dooley.

"I'll do no such thing," Dooley protested.

"Not for keeps, you dern idiot," Motz said, and shifted his massive bulge of tobacco from one cheek to the other. "For ballast. They've moved my loads around and if you think we've done some crazy turns and gone through some places not fit for a snake to crawl through, wait till you see the road to Leadville from here on up. And I mean *up*."

So Dooley climbed down and let the old coot hand him Blue. He let the workers pet Blue and allowed a rawboned man with a beard to his belly give the dog some jerky. Then Dooley stuck his head through the closed curtain door and introduced Buffalo Bill Cody to Blue, the merle-colored shepherd from somewhere.

"A noble beast like this fine specimen," Buffalo Bill said, and scratched Blue behind the ears, "will make this ride all the more bearable."

"He'll keep your feet warm, too, Colonel Cody," Dooley said. "Be a good dog, Blue."

"We shall get along splendidly," Cody said. "I will see you in Leadville, Dooley."

"Yes, sir."

"If we live to see Leadville," Chester Motz hollered from the box. "Now get back in this box, Dooley Monahan, or you'll be walkin' to Leadville. And that's like walkin' to heaven."

Dooley came back up, and the wagon was barreling out of Frisco before Dooley got his left leg inside the box.

Roughly thirty miles. That's all that separated Frisco from Leadville, and fresh mules could cover that distance in no time. At least, that's what Dooley thought. But the mud wagon was not a crow. And the road was not much of a road.

Up they went, following Tenmile Creek until darkness swallowed them, for night came early this high in the Rocky Mountains. And before long Dooley Monahan wished he had Blue up in the driver's box to keep his feet warm.

Dooley thought he might doze again, but not with the lurching wagon, the biting cold, and the curses and popping of the whip. They turned left. They turned right. They ran over logs knocked down by wind and heavy snow. They sank into the thick mud that had not frozen. They skated over the ice when the creek crossed the road.

He smelled the forest. He saw the outlines of trees, of boulders, of towering mountains that made him feel ever so small. He froze his butt off. They stopped at a rise, woke Cody up, and lashed another log to the back wheels and slid down another terrifying ride, with only the light of two lanterns and the eyes of six mules guiding their way. Dooley had half a mind to take General Grant and leave this insanity behind. But he kept telling himself that he was a man of his word, and, well, it was mighty dark in these hills.

Twice, Motz pulled the mud wagon to a stop and made Dooley and Cody and even the loyal blue-haired dog step out and walk up the steep trail behind the coach. Four times, Cody and Dooley had to push, their boots slipping and sliding, trying to find traction on the ice. Once, Cody slipped and began sliding down the ridge, and Dooley grabbed hold of him and slid a few yards, too, before he managed to find a limb that stopped both of them from going all the way down to Clinton Creek or wherever it was the jehu said they were near. Another time, it was Dooley who slipped and Buffalo Bill Cody who stopped his fall.

By dawn, they made the turn and crossed the East Fork of the Arkansas River.

"It's a piece of cherry pie from here on in to Leadville, boys," Chester Motz exclaimed. "And there's hot coffee and marmot dumplin's waitin' fer us at Sugar's place in Leadville."

"Marmot dumplings?" Dooley thought aloud, and wondered just what he had gotten himself into.

A short—relatively speaking—while later, the mud wagon pulled to a stop at the confluence of Chalk Creek and the East Fork.

"Wake up," Chester Motz said.

Dooley opened his eyes.

"Some shotgun you is. I'd been better off just proppin' Horatio's dead carcass up to be my guard."

Dooley blinked, yawned, and felt his stomach jump up toward his throat.

Six men blocked the road. They all wore masks. They all pointed shotguns at Dooley Monahan and Chester Motz.

"This is a holdup," one of the men said.

"No foolin'." Chester Motz spit tobacco juice into the frozen water.

CHAPTER SIX

"Shotgun," the leader demanded. At least, Dooley assumed he led the road agents, as he had announced that this was a holdup. Dooley knew what he meant, and he wet his lips, considering his options. The odds had to be worse than actually drawing to an inside straight, but he had hired on to protect the stagecoach. Chester Motz, however, showed his wisdom and common sense by whispering, "Son, there ain't nothin' on this haul worth dyin' fer."

Using plenty of caution, and deliberately showing the bandits his movements, Dooley thumbed the lever just below the scattergun's hammers. The barrels tilted forward, and Dooley slowly removed the two loads of buckshot, dropped them between his boots, and then gently laid the shotgun on the top of the canvas roof.

"Pistol, too," the masked man said. "But drop it over the side. We don't have all day to watch you unload that six-shooter."

A few of the men chuckled. At least, Dooley thought they laughed, but it was hard to tell with their masks muffling their voices.

Before Dooley could move to tug the heavy revolver out of his holster, the man with the flour sack for a face waved his pistol and spoke again.

"On second thought, just leave the pistol in the holster, and carefully—and I mean real careful, mister—unbuckle the whole rig and drop it over the side."

"Ain't you the careful one," said a big cuss on a piebald mare and with a yellow bandanna over the bottom of his face.

"That man," the leader said, "is hell with a six-shooter. So, yeah, I aim to be real careful around him."

Dooley carefully rose off the bench, wondering how the man knew his reputation as a gunman, while pushing open his coat and pulling on the belt. He slid the gun belt well over the side, just so no one thought he might try to pull the Colt, and let it fall. It cracked on the ice.

About that time, the canvas door unfurled, and Buffalo Bill Cody stepped out.

"What is the meaning of this?" he demanded, all in a huff.

"The meaning of this," said the leader, "is that if you don't lift them hands, is that Chalk Creek's ice is gonna be red with your blood till the spring thaw."

Dooley looked behind him, relieved to see that the legendary frontiersman had left his Winchester Centennial in the coach. What made him breathe easier was when Cody lifted both hands. He did not look happy, but at least he decided not to be the hero he truly was.

For the time being.

"All right," the leader said. "See what suits you."

Three of the owlhoots slid out of their saddles, holstering their guns and moving delicately across the slippery ground toward the mud wagon. The others kept their guns aimed at Cody, Motz, and Dooley.

Dooley focused on the leader.

He wore black woolen pants, black boots, and a green plaid mackinaw. A flour sack covered his face, with holes cut out near his eyes, and he wore a tan slouch hat with a yellow bandanna tied over the crown, bringing the brim down over his ears and tied underneath his chin. Instant earmuffs, because it was mighty cold. Dooley had done that several times back during his cowpunching years on the Northern Plains. But the man did not look like a cowboy.

First, he didn't have spurs. Second, he didn't carry a lariat. Third, the revolver he held was a nickel-plated Smith & Wesson, far too fancy for a thirty-dollar-a-month-and-found waddie. And his saddle scabbard was empty. Maybe he had loaned his carbine or rifle to one of his colleagues in crime.

Colleagues in crime?

Dooley shook his head.

"I've been reading too many dime novels," he said to himself, "or listening to Buffalo Bill Cody."

"What's that?" the leader said.

"Nothing," Dooley told him.

There was something else about the bandit chieftain. He wore black leather gloves, but the sleeve of his mackinaw and shirt had risen, and Dooley could see a white rag wrapped around his left wrist. The rag appeared to be stained brown, which could have been tobacco juice, but the man was not chewing, and Dooley figured it might be blood.

He wasn't sure what it meant, but that empty scabbard and that makeshift bandage had him thinking about the assassin in the alley back in Denver City.

Dooley shook his head. That was a stretch.

One of the men lifted Buffalo Bill's purse from his coat pocket and the .44 caliber Remington from his holster.

"His gun's almost as pretty as yourn—"

The leader squeezed the trigger, and the bullet slapped into a tree on the side of the road.

The mules jumped in their traces, and one of the outlaws had to dismount and quickly gather the reins to the horses without riders.

"Say my name," the leader said, "and I kill you, you damned fool, and the passengers."

"I wasn't gonna say your name, boss," the man said. His voice quivered with fear.

"Just get their valuables."

On the other side of the mud wagon, another outlaw muttered, "I can't make heads or tails out

67

of all these boxes and stuff in here . . . Hey . . ."

Dooley grimaced. The man had likely spied Buffalo Bill's rifle.

"There's a dog in here."

Inside, Blue growled.

"Nice dog," the bandit said.

Blue's growl intensified.

"Nice dog." Panic filled the outlaw's voice.

"Blue," Dooley called out. "Easy, boy. Easy."

The canvas curtain flapped back, closing the coach, and the outlaw eased away.

"What's the matter, you yeller cur!" one of the outlaws chided. "You scairt of some dog?"

"Wolfhound," the man explained. "Blue. Mean critter."

The men laughed.

Buffalo Bill Cody took a moment to make a speech.

"I assure you boys," he said, "that you think you have the upper hand, but crime never pays. I know. Not that I ever tried my hand at nefarious, evil schemes, but I have lived on the frontier long enough to have witnessed the folly of men who try to make their fortune on ill-gotten gains. Therefore, I suggest that you forgo this poor judgment. Before hell breaks loose."

Hell, Dooley knew, always broke loose when he found himself in a predicament like this one. And he had been in many such predicaments. He wished Buffalo Bill would . . .

"Shut your fool mouth!" The criminal nearest Cody took the words right out of Dooley's mouth.

Buffalo Bill Cody pouted.

The outlaws went about their business.

Dooley tried to make a few mental observations that he hoped he might remember. The horses. He could not see the brands. The saddles. Mostly slick forks, double-rigs, a few with breast collars. But nothing really stood out. And the outlaws themselves seemed pretty much nondescript, with their various masks and standard clothes. The only special weapon, Dooley noticed, was the shiny Smith & Wesson the leader kept aiming at Dooley's chest. He looked down the trail, but saw only more ice, more snow, and woods lining the road.

"Beans," said the man checking the luggage boot in the back. "Nails. Minin' tools. It'll take a month of Sundays to sort through this, and I ain't sure we'd find nothin' of much value. But this here's a real nice hoss that's been ridin' drag."

"Take the mules," the leader said.

That got Chester Motz's hackles up. He reached for the whip in the boot, but now it was Dooley's turn to offer sage advice.

"Those mules aren't worth dying for, either, old man," he said.

"The hell they ain't," Motz said in a deadly whisper.

"You want to be the man history will blame for getting Buffalo Bill killed?" Dooley tried again.

"Because you pull that whip out, and we're all dead."

Motz slipped back onto the hard bench and spit tobacco as some of the boys began unhitching the team.

"How much in that dandy's billfold?" another outlaw asked the one who had stolen Buffalo Bill's purse.

"Two hunnert," the man answered, "maybe more."

"That's more like it," the outlaw searching the boot said.

The other one backed out of the coach and stuck his sawed-off shotgun at Motz. "Strongbox up there, mister?"

"No," Motz said. "Ain't carryin' no mail pouch, neither."

"Then I'll take your poke."

Motz laughed, but lifted his butt off the bench high enough so he could squeeze his fingers into his trousers pocket and pull out a very, very thin pouch, which he tossed down between the outlaw's boots.

"That's it?" the man said after picking up the pouch, pulling open the drawstrings, and staring inside.

"Let that be a lesson to you, boy," Motz said. "Don't play poker."

The other man aimed Cody's Remington .44 at Dooley.

"How 'bout you, shotgun?"

Dooley grinned and found his wallet, which he handed with a gleam in his eyes at the man with the red and white polka-dot wild rag covering the lower part of his face.

"Ain't nothin' in here but some coins," the man said.

"Denver prices," Dooley explained.

The mules were being led away.

"This ain't hardly worth our time, freezin' our arses off all night waitin' for this coach," said the man who had almost called the leader by his name.

"Maybe." But now the leader kicked his horse into a walk and eased the chestnut mare toward Dooley's side of the mud wagon. The fancy pistol lifted toward Dooley's face, and the man said, "A man with a horse like that—he's got to be coming to Leadville with something more than small change."

"Boss," said one of the men looping a lead rope to the mules. "That messenger can't own that horse. That's a fine, fine steed. Horse like that, he has to be owned by the dandy yonder." *Dandy* meaning Buffalo Bill Cody.

"You're hiding out on me, mister," the man with the Smith & Wesson said. And Dooley could see the white rag just above the man's left wrist. It was not stained with tobacco juice. The man held the Smith & Wesson in his right hand.

Right hand. Bullet wound in the left arm. Empty scabbard on his saddle.

This, Dooley knew, was the man who had tried to waylay him in Denver.

"Let's have it," the highwayman said.

"It ain't," Chester Motz whispered, "worth dyin' fer, Dooley."

So Dooley let out a sigh of defeat and eased his left hand inside his coat pocket. He found the deed the late grizzly bear of a shotgun guard named Horatio Whitman had signed over, and withdrew the flimsy piece of paper, and handed it, between his pointer and middle fingers, to the man in the flour sack.

Although he could not see the man's face— just the hard eyes through the holes in the sack—Dooley knew the leader was smiling as he plucked the deed from Dooley's fingers and shoved it into a coat pocket.

"I'll fetch that fine-lookin' hoss," said one of the outlaws.

"I'm a-gonna take that dog," said another. "Always wanted me a cur dog fer a pet."

"Don't be a dad-blasted fool," the leader said, turning his head quickly, away from Dooley, staring at the man who was reaching for the canvas-curtain door.

Dooley braced himself. Started to yell at Blue, to yell at the damn fool outlaw, but he was too late. The curtain was pushed back, and Blue let out a vicious bark. The coach seemed to lunge this way and that, so hard Dooley thought the mud wagon might tip over. The man screamed. A gun roared.

And Dooley dived onto the man with the flour mask, the fancy Smith & Wesson, and the deed to Dooley's mine in Leadville.

Hell broke loose, but Dooley had figured that was bound to happen.

CHAPTER SEVEN

The dumb fool screamed as Blue sank his fangs into the man's arm, as he dropped his weapon between the right wheels on the mud wagon. Dooley saw the man and the blur of Dooley's blue dog. He also saw the leader with the flour sack of a face, swinging that shiny pistol toward Blue. That was just about all Dooley had a chance to see, because he was still standing, and he leaped out of the driver's box.

He caught the gang's leader across the chest, heard and felt the blast from the pistol, but Dooley knew he had knocked the gun arm, spoiling the killer's aim. He felt the pain of contact, felt the leader's horse spinning in a panic, and felt the air whooshing past him as the white ground rushed out to meet him and the leader.

They landed with a thud. The man grunted. Hooves crashed against the road. Another gunshot roared. Curses came here and there, grunts, and gasps for breath. Blue growled, snapped, and attacked. A man cried out.

Dooley came up quickly, sent his right fist into the leader's flour sack. Then he rolled off. His eyes searched the white ground for the silvery Smith & Wesson, or his own revolver. He saw the latter and reached for it, but his boots slipped on the ice and he fell facedown.

Swearing, he put his hands out in front of him and pushed himself up again. The hands slipped on the wet, slick ice, and Dooley planted his face in the hard, cold ground again.

Now he came up, just as a bullet practically parted his hair. He did not know who had fired the shot, only that it had not come from the leader of the road agents. That's because Dooley saw the man, on his knees, eyes behind the flour sack, searching desperately for the revolver he had dropped. Dooley also noticed something else. The man was gripping his left wrist, and dark blood seeped between the black fingers of the leather gloves, dripping onto the snow and ice.

That's when the man saw Dooley, and Dooley realized he was looking in eyes filled with pure hatred. The stare held for barely a second, because the man had also spotted the Smith & Wesson.

Dooley, however, had spotted something else. His Colt, still in the holster, lay just near the front wheel. It was closer to Dooley than the Smith & Wesson, and he leaped for it.

Only to see the entire gun belt and holster disappear as he dived. It happened like a blur— something shiny and black and tan—and only later could Dooley recognize what had happened. He had caught the glimpse of Buffalo Bill Cody's boots and buckskin britches.

Cody kicked the holster with his polished black boot on his left foot, somehow sending the holster and belt up in the air toward the wagon tongue. Yet all the while Buffalo Bill Cody kept moving forward, reaching up with both his hands, securing the holster with his left, and slipping the Colt .45 into his own right hand.

The hand holding the gun belt lowered. The hand with the Colt came up, the gloved thumb pulled the hammer to full cock, and the weapon exploded. Twice. Almost sounding like one shot, but Dooley saw two of the bandits go down. One of them somersaulted over the back of his horse. The other grunted and flew over the wagon tongue, dropping the pistol—Buffalo Bill's Remington .44—which slid next to the whip Chester Motz had dropped on the other side of the mud wagon. Dooley also glimpsed the man with the flour sack of a face, who left his Smith & Wesson on the ice and took off through the woods. That happened to be in the same direction as the outlaw leader's horse had taken off after Dooley's dive. Buffalo Bill Cody sent a shot after the fleeing man, but missed, and quickly turned to fire two more shots.

By then Dooley was sliding underneath the coach.

He slid across the ice and reached out, snatching the handle of the .44. Briefly, he thought about going for the whip, but Dooley had not much practice with a whip, and only a fool would bring a whip into a gunfight.

His hand came up, thumbing back the hammer and finding a target. He saw two. Unfortunately, those two had found him, and Dooley stared into the barrels of a cut-down, sawed-off shotgun in one hand, and the barrel of a Henry rifle in another gunman's arms.

Dooley had the Remington, though, and he pulled the trigger.

The hammer gave an antagonizing click.

He had no time to cock the .44 again.

The outlaw with the shotgun smiled. Then the sack covering his face disappeared in an explosion of carnage, and the one working the lever on the Henry rifle groaned and spun and fell to his knees, stood up, staggered a few paces, and fell to the ground, rolled over, and lay spread-eagled on the bloody snow.

Above Dooley, standing in the driver's box of the mud wagon, Chester Motz laughed.

"Idiots!" Dooley thought he heard the old man singing. "Y'all ferget 'bout the shotgun on the roof or 'em loads Dooley dropped in the box?"

Dooley saw the gunman that Blue had mauled as he ran for one of the horses that had not skedaddled. He thumbed back the hammer on the Remington, carefully aimed, and squeezed the trigger only to hear another click. He tried again. *Click.*

By then, the man with the mauled left arm had caught up a buckskin mare and was trying to pull himself into the saddle as the horse took off at a good lope down the Arkansas River fork. Dooley looked at the jehu.

"Shoot him!" Dooley yelled. "I'm empty."

Chester Motz stared down at Dooley and spit tobacco juice into the ice. "Well, give me some shells, boy. They's in yer coat pocket. I can't shoot nothin' with no empty gun no better'n you can, you cur of a whippersnapper who thinks he knows ever'thing."

Cody had stepped around the wagon, too, and slowly opened the chamber gate to Dooley's Colt and began plunging the empty cartridges onto the ice.

"A bully good show," Cody said.

"But that one's getting away," Dooley said.

"Indeed," Buffalo Bill agreed. "And after the mauling your loyal pooch laid on him, I dare say he might well remember my advice from earlier. That crime never pays, and when men use poor judgment to try their hands at nefarious, evil schemes to make their fortune on ill-gotten gains, hell is bound to break loose."

He began feeding fresh loads into the cylinder and smiled up at Chester Motz.

"A jolly fine show, sir. The way you dispatched those evildoers with the shotgun."

Motz grinned and shrugged in something that

looked like embarrassment. "Well, 'tweren't nothin' much. They was standin' too close to each other, and I give 'em both barrels."

Dooley shook his head, and moved, glanced at General Grant to make sure he was safe and still secured behind the coach, and then picked up the Henry rifle the dead man had dropped and stepped across the wagon tongue on the other side of the road.

"Maybe we can catch the leader. He doesn't have pistol or carbine."

"But," Cody said, "he has a horse. I heard its hooves crashing through the verdant and white forest as he rode away."

Dooley swore, and butted the Henry in the ice.

That's when the adrenaline left him, and he felt himself beginning to shake. He squeezed the barrel of the Henry tighter and looked at the battleground. Buffalo Bill Cody had killed two of the outlaws with pistol shots. Chester Motz had blown away two more with the Parker ten-gauge. The man whose left arm had been ripped had gotten away and ridden down the river. The leader had found his horse in the woods and fled for, as the folks liked to say, parts unknown.

Dooley saw no horses, just General Grant still behind the mud wagon, acting as calm as though this kind of thing was as natural as getting a rubdown in a quality livery stable. Of course, gunfights did seem to follow Dooley Monahan on regular schedules.

"Their horses took off," Dooley said.

"So did my mules."

Dooley spit the bitter taste out of his mouth.

"Undoubtedly, the animals are well on their way to Leadville," Buffalo Bill said. "I suggest that we follow them."

"Walk?" Dooley complained. No self-respecting cowboy would walk across a street if he could ride.

"We do have one horse," Chester Motz said.

"Riding double in this country is unwise," Buffalo Bill said. "Riding triple is insanity."

"No," the old man said. "No, I'll take that fine hoss into Leadville. Tell the law what has happened. Bring back some buckboards and blankets, and maybe even the yellerbacks who calls 'emselves vigilantes will show gumption to get a posse after those bad hombres who got away."

"It's my horse," Dooley said.

"Yeah. But nobody knows you, youngster, in Leadville. They might just shoot you dead. I'll take your hoss, sonny, and you and Buffalo Bill rest here. If it starts a-snowin' agin, well, you can stay warm in the mud wagon. Blue there . . . he'll keep your feet warm."

Dooley frowned.

"Can you bring back a bottle of rye whiskey?" Buffalo Bill asked.

"Sure, Colonel. Sure." Dooley watched the old man as he moved to the rear of the coach. Blue growled again, and General Grant laid his ears back in an aggressive reaction, but Dooley said, "It's all right, gents. It's all right."

After the old man eased into the saddle and backed the horse away from the coach, he leaned forward and smiled. "You boys done good. It was a pleasure to have men of your ilk and backbone riding in ol' For'. Ain't but a hoot an a holler to Leadville from here. I'll be back with the law, grub, blankets and the undertaker—and a bottle or two of rye—before dark comes down again. That I promise you." He shook both hands and kicked General Grant into a trot, moving around the dead bodies, and disappeared around the bend.

Blue whimpered, but Dooley picked up the dog, stroked his back, and eased him into the mud wagon, closing the canvas windows behind him but not before he fetched Buffalo Bill's Winchester rifle off the floor.

"This," he said, "was covered with a blanket. Guess that's why the outlaws did not steal it."

"I put it there," Buffalo Bill said, "when I realized we were being waylaid by ruffians."

Dooley frowned. "Well, you could've opened fire, got the drop on them."

"And gotten you and Chester shot dead in the prime of your manhood." Cody's head shook. "And remember, I have only one round chambered."

Dooley handed Buffalo Bill the Remington.

"And none," he said, "in your revolver."

After Cody took the .44 and shoved it into the holster on his hip, he said, "Silver Plume," he said, "is an expensive town."

Dooley's head bobbed in understanding. "I think the whole state of Colorado is pricey."

"Ah." Cody now turned. "But methinks we might have a way to earn a few dollars."

CHAPTER EIGHT

Buffalo Bill reached the man who had taken most of the blast from Chester Motz's shotgun.

"Well." Cody knelt and did not bother trying to remove what was left of the wheat sack. "Perhaps there will be some sort of identification on his person."

Dooley understood, and he went to the second man. The bandanna covering his face had slid off, but Dooley didn't recognize him.

"I don't know him," he said.

"Did you expect to?" Buffalo Bill Cody asked.

"No . . ." But Dooley stopped and studied on a few things. "Well . . ."

Something troubled him. He decided to talk things out.

"Well, Mr. Cody . . ."

"Call me, Colonel, son," Buffalo Bill said.

"Well, Colonel, the leader of the gang. He had to know something about me. Maybe not my name, but he . . . you might find this hard to believe . . . but, well, sir, he ambushed me in Denver City. I know that because I was certain I winged him in his arm. And that fellow he had a bandage wrapped around his arm. Here. Just above the left wrist. And he dropped his rifle in the alley. In Denver, I mean. And his saddle . . . the one he was forking today . . . well, the scabbard was empty."

What Dooley couldn't figure out was . . .

He figured it out.

"Son of a gun. Now I know. He tried to gun me down outside of the saloon in Denver because he wants the mine I won." He looked down at the dead man again. "First he tried to shoot me down in Denver. He must have been spying on that game the whole time."

He closed his eyes and tried to think, tried to remember those who had been in the saloon. No faces came to him, except that of the saloon girl who kept his drinks coming—she sure was a pretty thing—and then he saw the faces of the men playing poker with him. But those men had been inside the saloon when Dooley had walked out. He tried harder, but the saloon had been fairly crowded and mostly he remembered a bunch of black hats, brown hats, heavy coats, heavy boots, mustaches that were black and red and brown and gray and blond and salt-and-pepper, and suspenders and plaid shirts. No faces. Nothing that looked like the gent lying in front of him, deader than all get-out.

Dooley closed the dead man's eyes. It's one thing to look down at a dead man. It's another altogether to have a dead man staring at you.

He had not recognized anyone he'd seen in Denver. He spit and pushed himself to his feet.

Buffalo Bill Cody had moved to the other man. The colonel sure had a strange way of trying to learn a dead bandit's identity. He pulled out pocket watches and crumpled dollar bills and coins, an ancient pocketknife, and a nice pocketknife . . . and these he shoved into the deep pockets of his fancy coat. Then Buffalo Bill moved to the last corpse.

"You understand what I'm saying?" Dooley said as he squatted near the last dead outlaw and the famous frontiersman.

"I do indeed," Cody said as he shoved a double eagle into another pocket.

"The fellow in charge was after the deed to the mine."

Cody looked up, his dark eyes suddenly focusing on Dooley.

"A mine?"

Dooley nodded.

"In Leadville?"

"Yes, sir. Old Horatio Whitman had it."

"I see," Cody said.

"And the leader of these ruffians knew I had it. That's why he picked this coach to rob." Dooley studied on that and shook his head. "But why didn't he just shoot me and Chester off the stage? Come to us and fetch the deed that way?"

Cody smiled that knowing smile an older man might give his kid. "The shot could have hit the deed. You could have fallen into the coach, and the coach carried you on to Leadville. You could have fallen into a river, cracked through the frozen ice, and swept into the frigid waters of the brutal Rubicon and not been recovered till summer . . . hundreds of miles downstream. You could have . . ."

"I get the general idea, Colonel," Dooley told him.

"There's nothing to identify these men," Cody said as he rose, the coins and knife and odds and ends jingling inside the scout's pockets. "Perhaps the posse members or the undertaker will recognize them when they arrive."

"He's right-handed," Dooley said.

"Who's right-handed?" Buffalo Bill asked.

"The captain of these rogues." Dooley waved his arm over the two nearest corpses. "With a bullet wound in his left arm." Dooley tapped his own forearm. "Here."

Dooley tried to remember other details about the villain, but Buffalo Bill showed that he had a good memory, too. Well, it should not have come as a surprise. After all, the legendary scout had been busy these recent years acting on theater stages across the country, playing himself in action-packed melodramas with Texas Jack and Wild Bill and Captain Jack and Ned Buntline himself.

"A green mackinaw, plaid as most mackinaws,

with leather trim," Cody said. "Tan hat. Yellow wild rag. But he'll dispose of all his clothes. And he shall have no need of the gun rig he wore as he dropped the Smith & Wesson when he fled like the craven coward he truly is." Cody nodded at the silver weapon in the ice.

"There's his horse," Dooley said.

"Which he will sell to an unsuspecting miner far off in the hills, take the money, and buy or steal a new horse."

Dooley frowned.

"The only thing that can identify him, to you," Buffalo Bill explained, "is the bullet wound in his left arm, just above the wrist." Buffalo Bill did the tapping now. "Here."

Dooley sighed. A body couldn't go around Leadville and the Rocky Mountains asking men to tug up their sleeves.

"Well . . ."

Cody rose. "Son, we shall split the reward three ways."

Dooley sighed. He didn't care much about collecting bounties on dead men—none of which he had killed.

"I don't like the idea of having a man I can't identify gunning for me," Dooley said.

Buffalo Bill laughed. "Son," he said, "he has no reason to gun you down. Not anymore. He has the deed to the mine. Remember?"

That didn't make Dooley feel any better.

· · ·

They dragged the bodies underneath the coach. Then they waited.

Noon came, and passed.

They waited.

About the time the sun seemed to be saying it was right around three o'clock, Dooley asked, "How well do you know Mr. Motz?"

Buffalo Bill laughed. "Well, he's not a bosom comrade or blood kin, or a man I would trust my life with, but he is a fine individual, honest as the day is long, and I do trust him. Not with money. Not with a horse."

Dooley did not like that at all. General Grant happened to be the best horse he had ever owned, and, well, he started rehearing that fellow back in Denver telling him—and within Chester Motz's earshot—just how much a horse like that would fetch in Denver.

On the other hand, the old jehu had ridden off in the direction of Leadville—not back to Denver—but then a man of his years probably knew all the trails that a man could follow that would take him back to Denver.

"He won't steal your horse, son," Buffalo Bill said reassuringly.

Dooley did not answer.

"Chester loves this wagon more than life itself. He'll be back for it. Trust me."

Two hours later, Buffalo Bill Cody was not

laughing anymore. He was pacing back and forth, while Dooley sat on the ground, bracing his back against the front wheel, rubbing Blue's winter coat.

"Well, this breaks all bonds," Cody said, and he started walking down the trail, but stopped and came back to the coach. "No. It is too late to start the arduous journey afoot to Leadville. We might freeze to death, caught out in the open, in the elements." He lifted his head and gazed at the sky. "And this weather portends of . . ." Cody shivered.

They spent the night in the coach, canvas curtains and doors closed, huddling together and relying on the warmth of Blue.

It proved to be a miserable night.

The wind blew, moaning through the canvas and cheap wood and nails, bolts and glue that held this contraption Chester Motz called a wagon together. The wind also kept changing directions, popping one canvas curtain and then another. Every now and then a mighty gust would lift the wagon off two wheels, and Dooley's eyes would pop open and he'd brace himself for the mud wagon to be turned over and over and over. Only the gust would die as quickly as it started and the stagecoach would light down and rock like a sickening cradle until finally settling on the ice.

That's when Dooley would relax his muscles

and quit grinding his teeth and learn how to breathe again.

All the while the wind was blowing, the coach teetered on the precipice and Dooley prayed that he would not soil his britches, Blue snored peacefully, and Buffalo Bill Cody snored, too, only not so peacefully.

The famed frontiersmen snorted like a pig, or maybe a locomotive, snorting and chugging and groaning.

Even when the wind didn't blow like a sailor, Buffalo Bill Cody snored. Dooley snapped at him, kicked at him, and elbowed him in the ribs, but it made no difference. He would stop, though, and Dooley would sigh, thinking now he might be able to catch some shut-eye—unless the wind happened to be turning into a regular gale at the time—and Dooley would close his eyes and try to will himself into a deep, peaceful sleep.

Only Cody would start that infernal racket once more.

That was just the noise. The cold was the real killer. Now, Dooley Monahan had cowboyed across the Western frontier, and before that he had farmed in Iowa, and neither the Hawkeye State nor the woolly, wildest West, could match the cold of the Rockies just outside of Leadville, Colorado. Canvas curtains and doors did little to keep out the wind, or that biting, numbing cold.

Blue kept his feet warm, and Buffalo Bill

had that long, fur-trimmed heavy coat—made even heavier from all the plunder the scout had plucked off the dead outlaws—and he seemed to be oblivious to the subzero temperatures. Blue was a dog. Dogs never got cold, in Dooley's estimation. Yet Dooley was no dog and had no fancy thespian's coat. He shivered. He shook. He wondered how a body felt just before he froze to death.

Eventually, after a nightmarish eternity, the winds started to die down, and the temperatures began to warm. The coach stopped rocking. Dooley felt the coming of dawn and realized he had survived the night.

Somehow, his eyes managed to close, and he imagined that the canvas sack of flour to be the most luxurious pillow in the swankiest hotel in San Francisco. His clothes were a downy comforter. Blue's fur was a foot warmer. Bill Cody was two thousand miles away, playing in a Bowery dime theater in New York State. He could dream.

Cody barked, spat, and stamped his boots on the coach's rickety floor to get the blood circulating again. Blue whined and began dreaming that he was running after a rabbit, his paws scratching against the floor. The colonel farted, burped, snorted again, and opened the canvas that served as the mud wagon's door.

"Ah, a glorious morn," Colonel Cody said, and

stepped outside. He did not pull the canvas down as he went, presumably, to answer nature's call.

Dooley sighed. One eyelid lifted. He saw gray, not light, not black, somewhere between dawn and night. But he realized this might be his only chance to actually sleep, so he squeezed that eyelid shut and tried to sleep. Sleep. Sleep. Deeply. Without dreams.

Maybe he did doze, but not for long. Because he happened to wake as the coach lifted off its front wheels, then dropped, then almost turned onto its side. Blue was up, barking, snarling, the hair standing up on all ends. Dooley sat up, as well, and felt himself slammed to the floor as the mud wagon lurched to one side, then another. A strange noise ran through his brain.

It sounded like . . . like . . . like . . .

CHAPTER NINE

. . . Like meat being ripped off a carcass.

Which, Dooley seemed to understand, was exactly what was happening.

Blue growled and began digging furiously at the floor. A sack of rice fell off a keg of nails. Dooley caught the musky odor from underneath the mud wagon, and, though his mind felt heavy after a miserable night without sleep or warmth, he understood what was happening.

"Grizzly," he said.

The bear underneath the wagon, breakfasting on the dead highwaymen, growled.

Blue barked.

Dooley reached over and grabbed the merle-colored hound and pulled him tight against his body. No small dog, Blue scratched and growled like he had the hydrophoby, and the grizzly below did not like the racket. The mud wagon lifted, Blue stopped raising hell and whined, and Dooley felt himself sliding on the floor as the coach tipped to one side and crashed over.

The sack of flour grazed his head. Two bolts of calico smashed his nose. A bag of rice left Blue yelping. Luckily, the keg of nails missed both Dooley and his dog. Dooley slung the cloth off him, saw Blue scrambling to his feet as the mud wagon rocked like a ship in a gale. Holding his breath, Dooley braced for the roaring grizzly to use its brute strength to turn the wagon over again and again. The bear roared. Blue took to barking again, and Dooley lifted the heavy Winchester Centennial.

He spit, and remembered Buffalo Bill mentioning that he had only one round remaining in the rifle. Dooley turned the rifle, worked the lever slightly, and saw it was already chambered. He lowered the lever and thumbed back the hammer. He looked up at the windows and doors.

The curtains hung down, and the early light of morning showed him a sky of gray clouds.

"Hush!" Dooley yelled.

Blue did not obey the command. Nor did the grizzly.

Suddenly, a pistol popped, thudding against the floor of the wagon off toward the rear of the mud wagon. It might have punctured the floor, but so much debris of crates and boxes and barrels and sacks were piled up there, Dooley could not tell.

Another gunshot roared, and Dooley flinched, but that round did not hit the wagon.

Someone's shooting at me! raced through his mind, but he dismissed it immediately.

"No," he said, and came to his feet, tentatively. "It's Buffalo Bill."

Shooting at the grizzly.

The bear yelped now and roared again. Then

Dooley heard the thundering crashes as the bear must have charged. Yes, that's what the grizzly was doing. Because now Dooley heard Buffalo Bill Cody scream like a little girl.

"Stay," Dooley ordered, and stood on an overturned barrel, braced between luggage and crates so that it did not roll too much. He pushed the Winchester through the opening, grunting as he climbed onto the side of the coach. The wind had died down now, but the air remained frigid, prickling Dooley's flesh. He bit his lips, looked until he saw the grizzly.

The bear ran faster than many horses Dooley had bet on in match races. Buffalo Bill Cody certainly wasn't slow.

It looked like the scout had dropped his revolver—but then a .44 round from a pistol was not likely to do anything more than irritate a grizzly. Cody had found a thin tree and scrambled up it. Dooley came down off the side of the coach and tripped over a mangled, partially eaten dead robber.

Inside the coach, Blue barked ferociously, and Dooley could hear the shepherd jumping toward the opening. He realized he had the grizzly to thank. By overturning the coach, the bear had left the dog caged . . . safe. Dooley could focus on the bear now, and the bear had all its attention on Buffalo Bill Cody, who had climbed as high as he could safely ascend the tree.

The bear stood on its hind legs and pawed for Cody, but came only a few inches below Cody's dangling boots.

Dooley brought the Winchester to his shoulder, but held his fire. One shot. That's all he had. Miss, and the bear might kill Cody or might turn its attention and come charging after Dooley. He wet his lips, adjusted the sight, and saw the bear push the tree.

Roots holding firm in the frozen earth, the tree seemed to crack, and did tilt some toward the mountains. That was enough to send Buffalo Bill Cody dropping to the earth. His knees bent, but he did not fall, and he shot forward, away from the bear. He staggered, trying to keep upright, trying to run away from the bear, but it was fruitless.

A man cannot outrun a bear, anyway.

Buffalo Bill slipped and cried out as he slid across the earth.

The bear dropped down to all fours. It charged.

Dooley swung the barrel.

One shot.

That's all he had.

He held his breath, let it out, kept the rifle moving with the bear.

His finger touched the trigger and felt the Centennial kick like a cannon.

"Shouldn't he have been hibernating?" Dooley asked. He kept rubbing his shoulder, for he had fired many a rifle and shotgun over his life, but nothing that packed the wallop of Buffalo Bill's rifle, which he handed to the great frontiersman.

Buffalo Bill Cody circled the dead grizzly and shook his head. "It's spring. Close to it. Something could have disturbed his nap, or he could have just woke up. You never can tell about a griz, sir."

Sir. No longer son or sonny. Buffalo Bill Cody must have finally realized that Dooley was older than the scout. Or now, after Dooley had saved Cody from an agonizingly painful death, the fabled frontiersman had grown to respect the keen eye of Deadwood Dick.

Dooley smiled at the thought. Then he rubbed his shoulder again, and the jovial thoughts left him.

The grizzly was dead. He had never killed an animal so magnificent, so huge, and he regretted that he had to do it—like he often regretted having to kill the men he had killed. But those men had been trying to kill Dooley, and the bear had been trying to kill Buffalo Bill Cody, who now lowered himself to his knees and began praying some Indian prayer, raising his hands skyward, singing in some guttural chant, asking the Great Spirit to take the bear to the happy hunting grounds.

Still trapped inside the stagecoach, Blue barked.

Buffalo Bill finished his prayer and rose, letting out another sigh of frosty breath. "That," he said, "was the finest shot I have ever seen—and I have made many outstanding shots over the years." He moved around the dead animal and extended his hand.

Embarrassed at all the attention, Dooley shook the hand, and the two men walked back to the overturned mud wagon.

"Do we wait for Motz?" Dooley asked.

"No," Cody said. "For I am hungry. And we do not know what has become of the intrepid jehu. Besides . . ." He hooked his thumb toward the graying clouds that hit the mountaintops. "Spring might be near, even here, but you cannot tell that to Old Man Weather."

Dooley handed Cody the heavy, empty rifle and reached out for the nearest wheel. He climbed to the mud wagon's side, slid over, and reached into the ruined coach. "Here, boy," he said. "Jump." After a few tries, he lifted Blue out, and slid down, somehow managing not to step onto a dead outlaw. The dog growled at the dead bear, but seemed to understand that the grizzly no longer posed any threat.

"What now?" Dooley asked.

Buffalo Bill sighed and nodded at the road.

"As much as I detest the thought, we walk." And the frontiersman led the way.

"How far is it?" Dooley asked when they stopped to catch their breath.

"Ten miles," Cody said, his chest heaving. "Perhaps a little less."

The East Fork of the Arkansas River flowed, or froze, to their left. The ruts held ice and snow, as did the forests. Dooley's lungs burned for oxygen.

"I'm usually . . ." Dooley shook his head. "This . . ."

"It's the altitude," Cody explained. "Air's thin. Takes some getting used to."

Dooley made himself walk. Buffalo Bill Cody followed.

Dooley had no idea how far they had traveled, or how often they had stopped to rest and struggle to find more air, but when they rounded a bend and covered a few hundred more yards they came to another bridge where a creek met up with the river.

Blue wagged his tail, then growled. Cody and Dooley drew their six-shooters and cautiously approached the horse, on the side of the path on the other side of the bridge.

Ordinarily, Dooley would be overjoyed to find General Grant, safe and sound, but the dead man on the side of the road near his horse spoiled the reunion.

As Dooley scanned the forest, looking for the sign of any threat, Buffalo Bill unhooked the dead man's foot from the stirrup and rolled the body over.

Dooley, figuring that whoever had committed murder was long gone, slid the Colt into its holster and dropped to a knee beside Chester Motz.

"At least," Cody said, "old Chester did not know what had become of his mud wagon. That would have broken his heart had not a bullet pierced it first."

Dooley frowned. He saw the powder burns on the dead man's chest, and little blood, but the old wagon man had not died so cleanly.

"Look at him," Dooley said. His chest ached, but not only because of the thin air.

"Yes."

The pockets had been pulled inside out and blood had dried or frozen in his busted lips, his broken nose. Another wound had bled significantly in the man's side, where he had been shot.

"Robbery, no doubt," Buffalo Bill said, pointing at the pockets.

"He didn't have anything to steal," Dooley said, "especially after the holdup back yonder."

"The ruffian would not know that."

"I think he did," Dooley said.

Buffalo Bill pushed back the brim of his hat and waited for an explanation.

"The leader of those owlhoots who held up the stage," Dooley said. "He shot him. There." He pointed at the bullet hole and congealed blood in Motz's side. "Came up to him as he was defenseless."

Cody now nodded and pointed at the impressions in the snow and mud. "Yes, yes. Straddled him. Probably slapped him first, then punched him."

"Not for torture," Dooley said.

The frontiersman nodded excitedly. "But for information."

They thought they were onto something now.

"That's why he pulled through Chester's pockets," Cody said.

Dooley said: "He needed something."

"But he already had the deed," Cody said.

Dooley sucked in a deep breath, exhaled. "Wait a minute." He pictured the deed the late messenger had signed over to Dooley. He closed his eyes, wishing he had that perfect memory. Oh, he could count cards well enough while playing blackjack, or remember what cards had been turned up after a few players folded during a round of stud poker.

"The deed," he said.

"That road agent already has the deed," Cody said.

"But it doesn't say exactly where the mine is located."

Cody blinked.

Dooley tried to remember. He had the deed. He had not expected to lose it. Besides, he had

Chester Motz, too, who seemed like a good enough fellow to have helped Dooley find the mine—for a percentage, naturally.

"It said off Halfmoon Creek."

"And . . . ?" Cody waited.

Dooley shook his head. "Horatio Whitman was supposed to give me directions the next morning. But he got killed that night."

"That's it? You accepted a deed that said a mine is 'off Halfmoon Creek.' Off? Which way? North? South? East? West? Past Elbert Creek? Or the Derry Ditch? South Halfmoon? North? By Champion Mill or just a skip and a jump from the Arkansas?"

Dooley shrugged.

"Confound it, sir." Buffalo Bill shook his head. "You accepted a deed like that . . . in a poker game . . . in Denver City?"

"Well . . ." That's all Dooley could manage.

Buffalo Bill rose. "Well, the killer did not take your horse."

"That would have been hard to explain in Leadville," Dooley said.

"Agreed."

Dooley looked down at the dead man. He shook his head. "I guess Chester told the killer what he needed to know and then died anyway. Shot in the heart. At close range."

"No," Buffalo Bill said. "Chester Motz would have taken the secret to the grave, knowing he would die anyway. And Horatio Whitman would not have told Motz where his mine was anyway. He trusted no one."

Dooley tried to think about that. He thought of something else.

"The killer had another gun," he said. "Remember. He dropped the Smith & Wesson during the ruckus we started."

"Derringer," Cody said. "From the size of the bullet holes and the powder burns on his shirtfront."

"Well," Cody said, "at least we now have a horse."

Dooley was stepping away from the body and General Grant. Blue was growling again.

"We also have company," Dooley said, and pointed down the road.

CHAPTER TEN

Well, Dooley thought, *at least these men aren't wearing flour and wheat sacks and bandannas pulled up over their noses.* There were about a dozen of them, wearing coats and winter hats, and carrying shotguns and rifles, which, after reining their horses to a stop, they all aimed in the general direction of Dooley, Blue, and Buffalo Bill Cody.

"Road agents!" one yelled.

Another shouted. "Foul murder! Foul murder!"

But the third voice showed good reason. "Shut up, you dad-blamed fools. That's Buffalo Bill Cody there. Howdy, Colonel!"

"Good day, old hoss," Buffalo Bill said, rather cheerfully, and tipped his hat. "A good day to you all." He lowered his gaze at Chester Motz's body and removed his hat. "But it has not been good for my fellow man of buckskin here."

Most of the men eased their horses forward, and Dooley knelt and took hold of Blue's bandanna collar to keep him from lashing out at the strangers.

"Nice dog," said one man, which caused another rider, a young man with a cheery face and wearing striped trousers, to stare at the dog, then at Dooley.

"By thunder," said the oldest of the lot, a thin, lean man with a rawboned face and handlebar gray mustache, "that's old Chester Motz, struck down by murder most foul."

"Where's the shotgun?" asked another. "Whitman?"

"Dead," Dooley answered. "Killed in Denver."

"This young man," Buffalo Bill explained, "took Horatio's place riding guard. But alas we were waylaid just up the road there, at the crossing near Chalk Creek. Four of the scoundrels are dead, one of which has been now half-digested by a silvertip griz. Two fled. One wounded. And the leader, alas, we suspicion has murdered Chester for ill-gotten gains. It is a long story."

Someone had the foresight to bring a jug of whiskey. The cork was pulled, and the miner with a black beard nudged his horse forward, took a snootful, and lowered the jug toward Buffalo Bill.

Excitedly, Cody took the offering, drank several swallows, wiped his mouth, and began to recite the story of the ambush, which led to a side story about the attack of the Mormon train in Utah Territory back in the '50s when Cody was but a mere boy, the sending of Chester Motz to bring help, which led to a side story about the time Cody had ridden 267 miles for the Pony Express to deliver Lincoln's inaugural address to the readers in Sacramento, California, the attack of the grizzly bear, which deviated into a side story about the time a griz had left Cody's dearest pard Wild Bill Hickok—God rest his soul—grievously wounded and was why he was in Rock Creek Station that time back in '61 when Dave McCanles and his brood of badmen came to the Express station and got killed for insulting a woman and drawing down on Wild Bill, which deviated into a story about an attack of Sioux Indians over in Kansas but near the Colorado line or might have actually taken place inside the territory, for Colorado was not a state then as it is now, which finally came back to the discovery of Chester Motz, shot dead in the prime of life, beaten before he expired, and dealt a mean bullet into the heart after torture and maligning.

Which led to a round of applause and the passing of the jug, which finally came to Dooley.

"Where's the griz?" someone asked.

"Where's the wagon?"

"Where's the dead outlaws?"

Cody nodded up the road, and a few riders loped off in the direction indicated. Most stayed with Cody, and Dooley, and the second jug of whiskey since the first had been depleted during Cody's story about Wild Bill and Dave McCanles and had been tossed on the other side of the road.

"And who's this feller again?" asked a man in plaid britches and a green bib-front shirt and a sheepskin-lined coat.

"He," Cody introduced, "is the man who saved my life. Were it not for his keen eye, resolve, and expert touch on the trigger of a Winchester Centennial in .45-75 caliber, I would not be here to regale you with these stories, which may sound like brag but are just the true, unadorned facts. He lost the deed to a rich and wonderful mine, perhaps, to the nefarious scoundrels and cold-blooded killers who waylaid us and took the lives of a good man, noble and true, and stole two hundred dollars and change from my person."

"Welcome, mister."

Some men cheered. A few nudged their horses closer and leaned out of their saddles to shake Dooley's hand.

Buffalo Bill Cody then asked someone, "Now, what brings you fine men, heavily armed, out on this road so early in the morn?"

The leader answered. "We knew Chester was due yesterday. As road agents have been plaguing the road between here and Denver, we called our vigilance committee to investigate. Alas, we should have ridden out yesterday."

"Then," Cody said, "I would not have a new fine story to tell . . . or be indebted to this fine, upstanding young American frontiersman for the rest of my life."

They were staring at Dooley once again.

"Don't mean to be rude, mister," said a short man with spectacles and a muffler around his throat. "But I'm editor of the *Leadville Ledger*. Might I have your name and permission to print this story in next week's edition?"

Dooley shrugged, shook the journalist's hand, and said, "Reckon I can't stop a free press. Just tell the story factual, if you could. My name's Dooley. That's D-o-o-l-e-y. Monahan." He spelled that, too.

"Hello, Dooley," said the waddie who had been staring at him all the while when most eyes had been upon Buffalo Bill Cody.

Dooley looked at the youngster. He had red hair, almost as long as Buffalo Bill Cody's, practically down to his shoulder. But it was winter. And hair did keep a fellow's ears warm, Dooley figured.

"Remember me?" The boy smiled. "Howdy, Blue," the redheaded waddie said.

Blue wagged his tail.

"Been a long time," the cowhand said.

Dooley remembered. Then he grinned widely.

He had first worked with the boy years back, too many to count, Dooley almost figured. That had been on the Circle D up in Utah. Dooley had barely said hello to the cowhand that time and had then stopped the boy from getting his head stoved in by the hooves of a mean bronc. They might have become saddle pals then, but that had to wait because Dooley was going up to a line shack for the winter, and come spring, the boy had moseyed off down the trail to find another job.

Years later, probably three, maybe four, their paths had crossed again. That had been just after Dooley had found poor Blue, his family waylaid by Indians, and the kid had arrived with the sheriff out of Tempe . . . Yes, that's right. That had been in Arizona Territory, back when Dooley had found that clipping and was bound and determined to get to that gold camp in Alaska.

After the Indian attack, the redheaded cowhand and Dooley had drifted across the territory, with Blue tagging along, and the Baylor boys—not, Jason, the one Dooley had killed, or the cousin he would kill sometime later, but Dev and Alf, as low-down curs as the West had ever seen—were hot on Dooley's trail.

The boy had been with Dooley when they came to that old Indian hideout, a cave in the foothills, and had fetched that little girl, a pretty little thing, and she had joined the troop, too.

"Butch Sweeney," Dooley said. That was the redheaded cowhand's name, not the girl's. She was . . . Dooley had to remember. Julia Alice Cooperman. He wondered what she had grown up to become. He could tell Butch Sweeney had not gotten cowboying out of his blood.

They shook hands.

"You know this man, Butch?" asked the journalist.

"Indeed, I do." Butch Sweeney straightened in the saddle. "He saved my life many years ago."

109

Dooley shook his head. "Wasn't nothing," he said, embarrassed at all the attention now on him.

"That means you and I have something in common," Buffalo Bill said, "for he saved my life, as well."

Somebody handed Dooley the jug of whiskey, but he shook his head.

Sweeney swung out of the saddle and handed the reins to a man with a mustache and goatee and some furry, dead animal on his head as a hat.

Dooley took his hand, shook it hard, then pulled the youngster—though Butch Sweeney had done a lot of growing up in the years—into a warm embrace.

"What the heck happened to you?" Sweeney asked. "I mean, we were in San Francisco and you just up and disappeared. So what happened?"

Dooley's head began to ache.

"Gentleman," Buffalo Bill said, "I proposition that we move our reunion and reconvene our tales at the closest saloon in Leadville."

That motion was unanimously approved.

The First Chance Saloon was not the fanciest watering hole in Leadville, but it was, as its name implied, the first chance a man had to get liquored up once he turned the corner and entered the bustling town.

Dooley sat at the corner table near the fireplace—he wondered if he would ever warm up—

as Butch Sweeney brought a bottle of red-eye and two glasses from the bar, his boots crunching the peanut shells that carpeted the floor. Buffalo Bill Cody stood at the corner of the long bar, one boot on the brass rail, the other on the floor, waving his hands and using all sorts of movements to enhance his story of the grizzly bear attack, again.

After Sweeney filled the glasses and sat down, Dooley told him what little he could remember about that incident in San Francisco.

They were supposed to be boarding a ship the next morning and taking out for Alaska—Dooley, Butch, Julia, and George Miller, another old acquaintance of Dooley's—and find their fortunes in the gold mines in that wonderful, wild north country.

"Well?" Sweeney asked after toasting and downing his shot in a swift, burning gulp.

"Butch," Dooley said. "I don't know what happened."

Oh, he explained, he remembered some of it now. He could even still taste the chocolate mousse he had eaten for dessert after the scrumptious meal at Morgan's Fine Dining. He had gone to the livery to check on General Grant.

"The lights went out," Dooley said, and touched the back of his head that still ached hard and painfully just from the memory.

CHAPTER ELEVEN

"When I came to," Dooley said, and refilled the empty glasses on the table, "I didn't know who I was, where I was, or anything else."

"Amnesia." Buffalo Bill Cody had joined the table. He was eating peanuts he had taken from the bar. "I have heard of it, read about cases in various journals, but I don't believe I have ever met someone who ever suffered from it."

"Oh." Dooley tossed a peanut into his mouth, threw the shells on the floor as appeared to be the custom at the First Chance Saloon, and sipped his whiskey. "I certainly suffered."

He remembered waking up with the most miserable headache he had ever known, or thought he had known. He brushed hay off his clothes and saw General Grant in the stall staring at him.

"For the craziest reason, I recognized my horse," Dooley said. "I knew him, and he knew me."

"Robbery?" Cody asked. "You seem to have a knack for getting robbed."

"Wasn't robbery." Dooley shook his head. "I opened my billfold, hoping I might find some clue as to who I was, but I found only one thousand dollars." He smiled. "I remember thinking that I must have been a rancher who had just sold a fortune in livestock."

He ate another peanut.

"And I also thought that maybe I was a gambler. Somehow, I must have let that notion take over, and I pretty much became a gambler."

He hoped in retelling the story that he might remember a few things, like why somebody had tried to bash in his brains. Maybe he had seen the cur, though the way his head hurt and where it hurt, he knew he had been clubbed from behind.

"I knew General Grant's name was General Grant. But I couldn't tell you my own name. Then I heard a dog barking, and here came Blue, wiggling his butt and his bobtail, and I remember asking the dog, 'You mine?' and Blue seemed excited, and licked my face, and wagged his tail more, and I recall saying something silly like here I was in a barn, awake for maybe ten minutes, and I had a lot of money, a good horse, and a good dog."

"A man with a good horse and a good dog and a lot of money is a lucky man indeed," Colonel Cody said.

Butch amened that. Dooley nodded his agreement.

"I threw my traps onto General Grant and rode out of town. Didn't even know I was in San Francisco until I saw a few signs. I just thought..."
He rubbed his head again. "... thought that, well,

I needed all these cobwebs to clear till I could think straight again. So I rode east."

"Did you know your dog's name?" Butch Sweeney asked.

"Not till I found his food bowl," Dooley said. "His name was carved in that."

"So how come," Sweeney asked, "do you reckon you knew General Grant's name?"

"It was the last thing he saw before he suffered that horrendous blow to his skull," Buffalo Bill said, and explained. "As I've already mentioned, I have read about such things in medical journals and newspapers and magazines."

Dooley nodded. Butch refilled the glasses.

"When did you regain your faculties?" Buffalo Bill asked.

Dooley studied, decided what Cody meant by faculties, or guessed at it, and said, "Bits and pieces came back over time. Out of the thin air, sometimes. Then it all come back to me in Cheyenne up in Wyoming where I sat down to play some poker."

Vanwy's Gaming House on Fifteenth Street happened to have room at the hitching rail for Dooley to tether General Grant, and he had walked inside, had a whiskey at the bar, and made his way to the poker tables. This cowpuncher at the table had stared at Dooley and peppered him with questions like, Did you ever work in

114

Arizona? to which Dooley had answered: "I don't know."

Around midnight, after Dooley beat the cowhand for a nice pot, the waddie asked Dooley if he would mind telling him his name. Since that was one thing Dooley could remember, he did.

The rest of the scene replayed through his mind like some nightmare.

"You the same Dooley Monahan who killed all the Baylor boys?"

"I don't know."

"They was cousins of mine. FIRST cousins."

And Dooley had remembered how to survive a gunfight.

"Everything came back to me as I kept fanning that hammer," Dooley said, and made himself eat another peanut.

Shaking his head, Butch Sweeney sighed. "My, oh, my, Dooley, and here Julia was, probably while you lay in that livery with your brains all a-twisted, saying that you was probably just out doin' Dooley stuff."

Dooley swallowed the peanut. "Dooley stuff?" he asked.

Sweeney grinned. "I asked Julia the same thing. She said it was doing things you figured we were too green to handle, or none of our business, or"—he shook his head—"as she put it, 'too hard on our tender eyes or ears.' "

Dooley sipped another whiskey and decided this would be his last one. He could usually hold a lot more liquor than this, but he had eaten little except peanuts and the jerky one of the townsmen had given him, and being two miles above sea level also, he was learning, affected not only your breathing but how much red-eye you could hold.

"Well, a fine story, Dooley," Cody said, and scraped his chair legs across the floor as he polished off his drink. "I am hanging my hat at the Hotel Tabor. You will do me a favor by dining with me in the hotel tomorrow morning. Say one thirty?"

"In the morning?" Dooley asked.

"Afternoon, my good man. But it's morning for me after a night on the town. Right early, at that, too." He grinned, shook hands, and left Dooley alone with the redheaded cowhand.

Dooley found the pause awkward. He wanted to ask about Julia, what had become of her, and tried to imagine her all grown up now after, what, four years or so, maybe five. Yet he couldn't bring himself to ask anything. Not even about Alaska.

That had been his dream. See the goldfields of Alaska. Strike it rich. Most cowboys always wanted to see the elephant, as they called it. It meant see what's over on the far side of the hill. Something new. Different. Something adventurous.

Alaska.

Spilt whiskey.

"Where you staying, Dooley?" Butch asked, and corked the bottle, even though they had polished off all the whiskey.

Dooley laughed. "Well . . ." He wondered how cold it would be to sleep in a wagon yard or livery again.

Butch Sweeney had grown up in those years. He wasn't the greenhorn cowpuncher anymore. He understood Dooley's predicament.

"Come on, Dooley. My digs ain't gonna be as fancy as where Colonel Cody's sleeping in over at the Tabor, but the bed ain't ticky, and it's fairly quiet—by Leadville standards. Besides, there's a café right next door. We can take our supper there. It is getting late. And you need to find a livery that ain't full up for General Grant."

The fresh air—now filled with gently falling flakes of snow—seemed to do Dooley some good. Oh, the cold and the altitude would take some getting used to, but Dooley swung into the saddle and followed Butch Sweeney down Poplar Street, turned on Seventh, then down Harrison, and finally to Front Street.

It struck Dooley then that he did not need to have seen Alaska. All these years he had dreamed of finally hanging his hat in some gold town, but he seldom had gotten to experience that. He had been bound for Deadwood, up in Dakota Territory, just a short while back. He hadn't made it to Deadwood, either. But here he was . . . in Leadville, two miles high and full of riches and noise and all the wonders of a wealthy gold camp.

The Silver Saloon was crowded.

The Silver Palace was rowdy.

The Silver Café was packed.

The Silver, Gold, Lead and Dead Funeral Parlor was busy, too, with the bodies of four dead outlaws and one heroic old stagecoach driver to prepare for burial and funeral at Evergreen Cemetery on the other side of town up north.

The Silver Assay Office was the only place closed.

Which caused Dooley to remember. He wasn't in a gold town. Silver was king in Leadville.

That didn't matter. He was here. Granted, with no money, but he had been reunited with a good friend who had ridden with him across Arizona and all the way to northern California. He had his horse, his health, his dog.

They were lynching two men at the Silver Carpentry Shop.

Yes, this was some town.

At the edge of town, they found space at the Loomis Livery for General Grant. Butch Sweeney paid the fee for a week.

"I'll pay you back," Dooley promised.

"Pard," Butch told him, "you don't owe me a thing after all you've done for me."

"I'll pay you back," Dooley told him.

This time, Butch nodded, as he led his own mount into the stall.

"Stay here, Blue," Dooley told his dog, who went into the stall with General Grant.

Dooley and Butch walked just across the street and found another café and grabbed a table. Dooley ate his ham and eggs and drank his milk watching out the window at all the commotion. The clock on the wall told him it was four thirty in the afternoon, but it looked like . . . well . . . Dooley had no idea. Snow kept falling, men and women bustled about on the boardwalks on both sides of Front Street. Wagons came by. Men rode horses. A whistle blew at some mine, signaling the end of a shift. He could hear banjos being clawed and the ivories and ebonies of pianos being banged at the hundreds of saloons they had passed since the First Chance on Poplar Street. All that noise, that wonderful noise, and yet Dooley had not heard one gunshot.

Despite the road agents that had spoiled their entrance into this fair city, Dooley found it peaceful. The two men being lynched down the street had deserved it, Dooley knew, because even the widow woman with her gray hair in a bun had said so before she had begun leading the Maple Street Methodist Church Choir in a song to send the wrongdoers to their just reward and then to the Silver, Gold, Lead and Dead Funeral Parlor for even more business.

The waitress brought dessert, even though Dooley had not ordered any dessert, and when Dooley saw what was put on a plate before him, he could not believe it.

He looked up at Butch, who grinned and thanked the young waitress.

"Chocolate mousse?" Dooley asked.

"Remember?" Butch said.

"Of course." Sweeney had wolfed down strawberry shortcake on that last night in San Francisco, and Julia had eaten some ice cream. Old George Miller had managed to finish off his lemon meringue pie. That had been after beef tenderloin and lobster. Lobster. How rich that had been. How rich Dooley had been.

He sighed, and ate. Butch Sweeney just had a lemon cookie for dessert.

"Full?" Butch asked.

"Yeah." Dooley shook his head.

"Hotel's just down the street. It's the Georgia Gulch Inn."

They walked there, crossing the street in the snow, raking the mud off their boots on the first step, then stamping off the rest on the mat in front of the main door, and walked inside.

Dooley looked up, expecting to find Julia Alice Cooperman standing there, looking lovely and much older, more mature, a real woman instead of just a girl. Instead, he saw a burly man with a twisted mustache and slicked-back hair.

"Good evening," the man said in a most unpleasant voice.

"This is Dooley Monahan," Butch Sweeney said. "He'll be bunking with me for a spell."

"Then I shall adjust your bill," the man said. "And . . ." His eyes widened. His face paled.

"*The* Dooley Monahan?" the man said. "The famed gunman and bounty hunter who has rid the West of some of the foulest killers on the frontier?"

CHAPTER TWELVE

"You want to what?" Dooley managed to get out of his mouth after finally swallowing the bit of bacon that had been stuck in his throat. It was good bacon, too, not burned, not raw, with a hint of maple-wood smoke and apple to it. And a thick slice, as well. He had never tasted bacon so good.

"Grubstake you," Buffalo Bill Cody said.

It was a bit early in the morning—well, afternoon, really—and Dooley had not known the colonel long enough for Cody to start funning him, or play some practical joke on him. Yet the more Dooley stared across the table in this fancy café the more it seemed to him that William Frederick Cody was not funning, not joking, and not playing Dooley for a fool. But Dooley had to be certain.

"You're not fooling?"

Cody roared with laughter, disturbing the other ladies and gentlemen who were eating their dinner, not breakfast, but no waiter came over to shush Buffalo Bill, and most of the gents merely smiled or patted the hands of their companions in petticoats.

"Fooling! Hah. You make me laugh, sir, you make me laugh." Cody retrieved a silver-plated flask from the inside pocket of his frock coat, unscrewed the lid, and sweetened his coffee. He held the container toward Dooley, who, while tempted, shook his head politely. The flask soon disappeared, and Cody leaned forward after taking two or three swallows.

"You saved my life, sir, and Buffalo Bill Cody is a man who always pays his debts in full."

"I didn't do anything, really," Dooley protested.

"There's a dead grizzly over at the Silver Queen Taxidermy Shop that is being stuffed as we speak that says otherwise, Dooley. If the bear could talk, I mean, after you place a shot—one shot—perfectly before I became a snack for a silvertip."

Dooley wiped his mouth with his napkin, stared at the big slice of bacon staring at him, and looked again at Buffalo Bill.

Indeed, the frontiersman was serious.

"Well . . ." Dooley just couldn't digest all this.

"Sir, this is not charity. I am not giving you money to go out and find your fortune in silver in these hills. There are barons aplenty who likely have all the valuable ore locked up with their claims. A grubstake is like a partner. If—and this, you must know, is a mighty big if—you find pay dirt, then you pay me back with an interest of twelve percent. That might strike you as high, but, well, this is Leadville."

Thank the Lord we're not in Denver, Dooley thought.

"How much money are we talking about?" Dooley asked.

Cody grinned again, set the cup of coffee and rye on the table, and reached inside another pocket. Once he pulled out his wallet, he opened it and fished out several greenbacks and yellow-backs. He started counting out bills, bills that from where Dooley sat had a couple of zeros on the end. Dooley listened as the scout and showman counted. His eyes widened as the stack piled up.

Dooley wet his lips. He thought: *And Cody was robbed of a couple hundred bucks just two days back.*

Absently, he picked up the piece of bacon and stuck it in his mouth. He chewed, and stared, and washed down the bacon with the last of his coffee. Finally, as Buffalo Bill stopped counting and closed his wallet—which Dooley could tell still had plenty of currency in it—Dooley looked across the table and saw the frontiersman grinning from ear to ear.

"What do you say, pardner?" Cody asked.

Dooley said, "Uhhhh."

Disturbing the diners again with a roaring, table-rattling belly laugh, Buffalo Bill stuck out his hand. "You're a man of my style, Dooley. I'm proud to grubstake you and know you'll do us both proud."

What else could Dooley do? He shook hands with Cody and finished his breakfast.

• • •

He hurried back to the hotel, hoping to find Butch Sweeney, keeping his right hand in his pocket so none of the bills would come flying out. A million thoughts raced through his mind.

Has Butch ever done any mining? Of course he has. Maybe. I mean, what else would he be doing in Leadville, Colorado? This certainly isn't cattle country. Maybe Butch learned a lot about mining up in Alaska. Did he actually mine in Alaska? Well, it doesn't matter. But will he want to be my partner? . . . What exactly does a miner need? Shovel? Pan? Beans and coffee for certain . . . Man, I sure wish Horatio and Chester had not gotten killed. I could use some help in this mining venture . . . Maybe Buffalo Bill would know something. No. Don't be silly. Buffalo Bill's just up here visiting before going back to fighting Indians on the Plains, and guiding rich dignitaries from foreign countries on wild hunts in the West, and starring as himself while treading the boards across the United States back East. I'll need to file a claim. I'll need to find a place that has not been claimed. Wait a minute. I won a deed in a poker game from Horatio Whitman. A deed. A deed has to be filed. A claim has to be recorded or it's up for any takers. That I know for certain. I read it in the Police Gazette. *Now where . . . ?*

He stopped on the boardwalk and stared across the street.

COUNTY CLERK

That seemed like a likely place to start. Dooley let three heavy freight wagons trudge on past before he crossed the muddy street, wiped his boots, and opened the door.

"Lode claim, naturally," the clerk said. He was a nice-enough gent, bald headed with thick spectacles and a skinny tie and suspenders. He wore sleeve garters to keep his sleeves bunched up on his upper arms, and hung his coat and hat on hooks on the wall behind his desk.

"How's that?" Dooley asked.

"Placer claims give you rights to what you can find on the surface," the man said. "If you were panning for gold, that's all you'd need. But we're silver country, so I think you mean lode claim. That grants you rights to what you dig out. Unless you want to pan for gold. I'm not saying you won't find gold here. It's just we've found silver here. Tons of it. Millions of dollars' worth."

"Well . . ."

You would think that a clerk who handled filing silver-mining claims in a town like Leadville would get his fill of talking, but not this guy.

"Once you stake your claim—you stake it by

setting up a monument at least three inches in diameter and six inches out of the ground. This has to be in the northeastern corner of your land."

"But . . ."

"And then you have no more than twenty acres. Once you've staked your claim, you have thirty days to file your claim with me. Now . . ."

Dooley took advantage of the man's pause to sing out: "I'm wondering about a claim filed by a man named Horatio Whitman."

The man's eyes widened.

"Did I say something wrong?"

"No. You're just the third man who has asked about a claim filed by that old geezer."

Dooley straightened. He sucked in a deep breath, held it a moment, and exhaled. "Do you know the other two men?"

"Not personally. One said he was a newspaper man from Cheyenne. The other was Buffalo Bill Cody. He came in just yesterday."

"Buffalo Bill?"

"Yes. You have heard of him, no doubt."

"No doubt." Dooley pulled his hand out of the pocket that held all of that money.

His mind did some calculating.

So Cody came here yesterday. Wanting to find the location of Horatio's mine. And when he couldn't . . . he decided to grubstake me. Or maybe he did find it and decided to grubstake me to keep me in those big-arse mountains till summer.

"But as I told the honorable colonel and the newspaper scribe and as I am telling you, Horatio Whitman never filed a legal claim."

"Nothing?" Dooley asked.

"Nada. Zilch. *Cero.* The old goose egg. Oh, son, don't look so disappointed. Many miners don't file claims. Some just don't understand the law. Some might be breaking the law. I did not know the late Mr. Whitman personally, merely saw him from time to time when he was guarding the stagecoach, or drunk, or trying to sell game he killed. That said, I don't think he was dishonest. If he found silver, or gold, or lead, or copper, or, by grab, walnuts, he thought he had an honest claim. But it would not have held up in a court of law."

"And if he had a deed?" Dooley asked.

"A deed and a claim are not the same thing, sir. Mr. Cody, when he inquired about the claim, he said he had never seen this mysterious deed the late Mr. Whitman was purported to have on his person."

"And the inkslinger from Cheyenne?" Dooley asked.

"He made no mention of it one way or the other. Merely said he had heard that the late Mr. Whitman claimed to have a deed to a mining claim off Halfmoon Creek."

Dooley stepped closer and put his shaking hands on the counter.

"When did he come in?" Dooley asked. He felt his heart pounding against his chest.

"Day before yesterday."

Dooley tried to picture the man. He shot out a piecemeal description: "Black pants, green mackinaw, tan hat, yellow kerchief?"

The clerk shook his head as he laughed. "No. He was dressed like a gentleman reporter."

"Oh."

"But I had my suspicions," the clerk said, and Dooley's heart raced again. "You see, for a reporter—and in a town like Leadville, I have been interviewed by reporters from Denver and national magazines doing feature articles on our lovely, booming town, but this man did not take one single note. Most reporters write down everything I say, but he wrote nothing. He said he had an ironclad memory. But once I told him that Mr. Whitman had filed no legal claim, he lost interest."

"Did he favor his left wrist?"

"Sir, I cannot remember. Many people come here every day. Even reporters. If he was one."

"What makes you think he wasn't? Other than the fact he did not take any notes?"

"I did not doubt him at the time, but you must understand, sir, that I had not learned of the late Mr. Whitman's untimely death. When that news swept through town yesterday, I thought back. Then Buffalo Bill Cody came by. And now you. You were the hero that saved Cody's life, aren't you?"

Dooley shrugged.

"Yes, Mr. Cody mentioned you, said you were a man to ride the river with." He shook his head. "But he did not say which river. Are you a riverman?"

Dooley shook his head. "It's just a saying, is all."

"Well, I do not understand all this Western lingo."

Dooley felt a little better about Buffalo Bill. He wasn't trying to cheat him, he decided, if he mentioned him while asking about Horatio Whitman's claim that had never been filed.

"Oh, Whitman came in here once and almost filed the claim," the clerk said. "He pointed to this disgustingly horrendous map he had and said he was filing it here. I looked, laughed, and said, *'Oof Halfmoon Creek? You mean Off Halfmoon Creek.'* And I corrected it on his map and then asked, *'But how far off Halfmoon Creek and what direction and did you stake the claim properly?'* And Whitman, he ripped the paper from my hands. Gave me a wicked paper cut on my finger. Here. Right there. Hurt like Hades. And do you know what that old man said? He said he would file no claim with an idiot like me and that I might regret my actions one day."

Dooley blinked. He had tried to stop listening after the paper cut and had only half listened before that.

"Is there anything else I can do for you?"

Dooley started to shake his head, but then he thought of something.

"Could you show me what hasn't been claimed along Halfmoon Creek?"

CHAPTER THIRTEEN

The clerk handled a few other claims and questions about claims while Dooley studied the map. Halfmoon Creek went a long ways, divided into separate creeks, and had several claims nearby. Dooley saw the initials and numbers marking the spots that had been filed, legally, as proper claims in the county.

After a while, Dooley decided that he had been hoodwinked by an old reprobate who found some silver somewhere and filled out a bogus deed. Flimsy paper. Shoot, now that Dooley had spent a couple of hours in the county clerk's office and seen actual claim forms filled out and registered, he knew what they looked like—and they certainly did not look like that piece of trash old Whitman had signed over to him.

Then again, Dooley thought, the old man had plenty of money that he could not have been earning riding shotgun on the late Chester Motz's mud wagon. He had been mining somewhere, and the late Chester Motz had said that he mined when he wasn't working.

But where?

"Sir?"

Dooley looked up at the clerk, who had put on his coat and put on his hat and held a key in his hand. Dooley glanced out the window, only to see the curtains had been drawn. The regulator clock on the top of the cabinet behind the counter began to chime.

"Closing time, eh?" Dooley gave the man a warm grin, which the clerk did not return.

"I appreciate your help and your time and your wisdom," Dooley told him as he gathered his own hat and coat and stepped out the door with nothing to show for better than two hours spent in the clerk's office but eyes aching from poring over various maps and plots and lines and all sorts of things written in tiny, tiny print. At least the clerk's office had been warm, though.

Outside, it was snowing again.

He returned to the livery to check on General Grant and make sure Blue got something to eat. Now that Dooley had a pocket full of money, he bought some jerky and a ham bone, which he gave to Blue in the stall. He ought to buy Butch Sweeney some chow, he thought, which reminded him that he needed to see if Butch wanted to partner with him in a mining venture grubstaked by Buffalo Bill Cody.

Then he headed for his hotel, thinking something about justice. Sure, he did not have a claim to a mine, but nor did the man who had stolen it from Dooley. Only Dooley was a bit ahead as he had been grubstaked by Buffalo Bill

Cody. He wondered what Butch Sweeney would tell him when Dooley proposed that they go into the mining business together. Or at least go into the looking-for-an-actual-mine-that-might-be-worth-something business together.

He entered the hotel, removed his hat, and walked to the clerk, who recognized him and fetched his key.

"Is Mr. Sweeney in?" Dooley asked.

The clerk titled his jaw toward the attached dining room, and Dooley thanked him and headed toward the smell of beef and bread. He almost ran over a woman who was coming out of the dining room.

Dooley did a stutter step, moved to his side, put out his arms, but the woman did the same thing, and they kind of did a dance in a circle, then she broke out laughing. Dooley did the same.

"Dooley," the woman said.

Dooley stopped laughing. His mouth fell open. He just stared.

"Don't you recognize me, Dooley?" the woman asked.

Dooley did. Well, not really. After all, a few years had passed, and Julia had just been a kid way back in Arizona Territory and San Francisco, California.

"Julia," he said. "I mean . . . Miss Julia. Or . . ." He got so tongue-tied he did not know what to do.

Julia smiled. "I was just going to ask the clerk to send you into the dining room when you came back. Come on." She took his elbow and guided him past the counter and weaved between patrons and waiters and waitresses, around tables, and chairs, and came to a table in a corner near a fireplace. For a hotel that wasn't fancy, this dining room seemed better than most. Well, it wasn't Morgan's Fine Dining in San Francisco, but it wasn't a chuckwagon, either.

Butch Sweeney rose from his seat. So did another fellow in a plaid sack suit. Dooley stared at the other, who held out his hand, smiled, and said, "Hello, Dooley. It has been a long, long time."

Dooley's hand reached out. They shook. Recognition came slowly, but it came, and Dooley nodded.

"George."

George Miller sat down. So did Butch Sweeney. Dooley remembered his manners and pulled out the chair for Miss Julia, who settled into it and allowed Dooley to push her closer to the table. Dooley found his chair opposite Julia.

His stomach did all sorts of flopping.

"Where you been?" Butch Sweeney asked. "Ain't seen hide or hair of you all day."

"Oh . . ." The weight of Buffalo Bill Cody's many dollars felt like lead in his pocket. "Around. Seeing the town."

"All day?" Sweeney shook his head. "You sure you just didn't go off drinking with Buffalo Bill?"

Dooley shook his head. "I haven't had anything but coffee. And haven't had that in a long time."

"Well," George Miller said, "let's see if we can't rectify that situation." He held up his hand and waved at a waiter. The burly man with the blond mustache and slicked-back hair came over, nodded when George Miller asked for champagne, and hurried away.

"We have some catching up to do," George Miller said.

Stories? Dooley wondered. *Or drinking?*

Mostly stories. Dooley never could get used to all those bubbles and how that sparkling French wine tasted.

Alaska had been a bust. Any pay dirt that had been found had long been hauled out of the earth, as far as George Miller and Butch Sweeney had been concerned. Oh, people in that frozen country said they would find gold one of these years, or maybe up in the Klondike in the Canadian territories, but it wasn't for them.

They had stayed two years.

"It took us that long to earn enough money to pay for our way back to Seattle," Julia explained.

"Oh." Dooley thought: *Seattle. That's in Washington. Maybe Oregon. Two states I don't*

136

recollect ever setting foot in. Maybe one of these days . . .

Dooley had to repeat his story about what had happened to him, about amnesia but that he eventually recalled everything he had forgotten. For Miss Julia's sake, he did not say how he had regained his memory while killing a no-good owlhoot who happened to be kin to some other no-good owlhoots he had sent to Boot Hill.

At length, George Miller excused himself, but it was George Miller who paid for the meal, even though Dooley tried to pull out one of the big notes Buffalo Bill had grubstaked him. Then Butch Sweeney said he needed to go, and he smiled across the table at Julia and shook Dooley's hand and headed through the main doors before Dooley could even proposition him about becoming a miner somewhere down Halfmoon Creek.

"What are you thinking, Dooley?"

He looked up and could not stop staring into Julia's eyes.

"Uhhh."

She smiled, but the smile faded quickly and it looked as though tears formed in her eyes.

"I never should have boarded that boat, Dooley. Butch didn't want to. We made him, George and me. No, I made him. I figured you'd just suffered from another case of wanderlust. Or maybe you just didn't want to be saddled with a bunch of kids."

"Well," he said. He was just a wizard when it came to talking to a girl. He thought of something to add. "You didn't know." *Say something else,* he told himself, and he did, which sort of surprised him. "Besides, you and Butch and the half the population of San Francisco could have turned that city inside out and never would have found me. General Grant, Blue, and I were miles and miles from town by the time you would have formed a search party."

That seemed to make her feel better. The tears disappeared anyway. "You still have that dog?"

"Yes. Didn't Butch tell you?"

"No." The way she said it gave Dooley pause. Butch was a tad older that Julia, Dooley had figured, but nowhere near the difference in age as that kid and Dooley himself. He started to ask about George Miller, but stopped. A man did not pry into the affairs of a woman.

Affairs. He almost blushed from the thought.

Woman. He leaned back.

What was that Butch Sweeney had mentioned? *"You figured we were too green to handle, or none of our business, or . . . too hard on our tender eyes or ears."* Butch had often complained, he now remembered, that Miss Julia had a mouth that went off like a Gatling gun, and he had called her Little Miss Loudmouth. Stuff like that. She and Butch were kids. At least, they had been all those years ago in Arizona and California.

138

He made himself drink some of the water in the glass before him.

She wore a tailor-made suit of garnet cashmere—skirt with thin, knife-plaiting along the bottom, two panels on each side of the blouse with buttons and green, yellow, and black stitching, and long drapery of a rich green and gold in the front and looped at the side. The hat was elegant, and she had removed her white gloves while she ate. It was a far cry from the rags she had been wearing when Butch and Dooley had found her in that miserable cave.

Her hair was tucked up underneath that hat, showing off her cute little ears, with a few strands of hair—darker now that he remembered—showing on her forehead. The collar was one of those stand-up types, black with garnet stripes, hiding most of her throat.

He had to keep telling himself that Leadville might be two miles high and a grueling, numbingly cold, miserable, multiday stagecoach ride from Denver City. And that there might not be any railroad service here, but this town was mighty rich, filled with silver barons and famous folks like Buffalo Bill Cody. It was a place of wealth. And Julia Alice Cooperman sure looked to be filling that bill.

Kid?

Her eyes were soulful, haunting, and her face unblemished. She reminded Dooley of those dolls

139

he saw in stores in good, proper towns like . . . well
. . . Des Moines, maybe. But not Council Bluffs.
Not the raw, savage towns he had seen in Denver,
Julesburg, Omaha, Yankton, Tucson, Tempe.

The nose turned up just enough, and her lips
shone a deep red. But Dooley knew she wore
no paint on her face. No rouge. No lipstick. She
was a natural beauty. Little Miss Loudmouth had
grown up to be someone any red-blooded man
would be staring at. And Dooley realized that
he certainly was staring. He looked at the open
doorway, at the folks passing by the dining hall
on their way to the opera house in Leadville or
upstairs to their rooms.

"You always thought of me as a snot-nosed kid,
Dooley," Julia Alice Cooperman told him.

Dooley swallowed.

"You sure aren't a kid anymore, Julia," he told
her, and rose. He held out his hand—didn't know
why, but it seemed to be the proper thing you did
when you were in the presence of a lady, and she
rose, pulled those skinny little gloves onto her
hands, and took Dooley's into one of hers. Her
arm fitted in nicely in the crook of his elbow as
he escorted her through the entrance and into the
lobby. He was heading her to the staircase when
George Miller came down, grinning like a fellow
who had just hit blackjack on a sizable bet.

"Hello, Dooley," George said, and he took Julia
from Dooley.

"Hello, dear," Julia told George Miller.

"I trust you had a pleasant evening," George Miller told Dooley.

"Yeah."

"Well, good night to you. It's good to reunite. I'm sure I'll see you plenty over time in Leadville. It's a fast-growing metropolis, a wonderful boomtown, but it is not . . . say . . . San Francisco."

That's when Dooley noticed the linen wrapping around George Miller's wrist. He also noticed something else.

"Let's retire to our room, dearest," George Miller said, and he escorted Julia Cooperman up those stairs, leaving Dooley just standing there like an oaf.

Just staring . . .

CHAPTER FOURTEEN

. . . just staring at that slim gold band on Julia Cooperman's finger.

"Son of a gun," Dooley said. "They're married."

So here was Dooley Monahan, finally in a boomtown—not a ghost town—with money in his pocket and a chance to do some real mining. He had been reunited with old friends Julia and Butch and an old colleague, George Miller, whom Dooley certainly wasn't going to call a friend now that he knew he was married to Julia, no matter how many bottles of champagne he bought. Hell, Dooley didn't even like that bubbly booze. Besides, Dooley had noticed that bandage on Miller's arm. George Miller, good old George Miller, was the man who had led those road agents. George Miller was the ornery hombre who had murdered Chester Motz and had stolen Dooley's deed, not that the deed meant anything. There was some justice to that.

So here Dooley sat in that fancy café with the swell-tasting doughnuts he had just discovered, and laid out his plan to Butch Sweeney. Dooley was even buying breakfast.

Butch sipped his coffee, set down the cup, and ran his fingers through his hands.

"Well, Dooley," the young cowboy said, "I appreciate the offer. And I surely wish you luck finding all the silver that ain't already been plucked out of the ground. But I got me an idea. It ain't as hard on the hands as a pick and shovel, though it might make my butt sore."

Dooley let out a long breath. He felt so lucky, and now, not so lucky. Yet he was curious.

"What do you mean?"

Leaning forward, Butch began a conspiratorial whisper. "It's like this, Dooley. I'm going to get back to that stagecoach that those badmen robbed. I'm gonna buy the mules from the livery man. They're not his mules anyway, but he found them, laid claim to them, and I already checked. Motz didn't have no kin. And he was the sole proprietor of the Leadville-Denver Transportation Company. Well, Horatio Whitman was his partner, too, but he's dead, you know."

"I know," Dooley said regretfully.

Butch leaned back and grinned. "I figured it would sure beat riding herd on doggies. Easier on my thighs if not my hindquarters." He found his doughnut, dunked it, and shoved the rest in his mouth. As he chewed he said, sort of regretfully, as if he knew how Dooley would answer already: "I was sort of hoping that you might come in with me."

"Riding shotgun?" Dooley asked.

"As my pard," Butch said.

Dooley frowned.

"And ride shotgun, too," Butch said. "Though we could switch if you ever got bored. I mean . . ." He started speaking faster, the words running together. "You could drive some. Have you ever driven a team? Oh, knock my head off. Of course you have. I'm not asking you to ride shotgun because of your reputation. I mean, that didn't stop those badmen . . . Oh. That came out wrong. And it's not that I'm trying to step on Chester Motz's grave or nothing. You know. I just thought . . . well . . . I guess . . . you don't want to do it, do you?"

Dooley stared at the doughnut, which did not look so appetizing anymore. With a sigh, he explained, "It's not that I don't want to do it, Butch. It's just that . . . well . . . for years I've wanted to try my hand at mining. I've cowboyed. I've gambled. I've led a dad-blasted wagon train, sort of. I've been trying to get to a boomtown for as long as I can remember, and now I have. Now . . ." He made himself smile. "I think you likely have the right idea. That stage line will make you a profit, or at least a decent living. And I suspect it's real pretty and a little bit warmer once summer arrives. So I wish you luck. And maybe, when I don't strike it rich, I'll look you up for a job."

"Would you?" Butch perked up.

"You bet."

They shook hands across the table.

Dooley felt better until Butch said, "I reckon I'll have to ask George Miller to ride shotgun."

Dooley had been about to eat that doughnut but now his hand stopped, and he stared, feeling his ears start to burn in anger. "He'll likely tell me no, too," Butch was saying, "but he probably could get someone to do it for me."

He saw Dooley's face, and his red ears, and mistook the anger as being directed toward him. "Not that I'd make George or somebody he knowed a pard, Dooley. He'd just be on for . . . wa—"

"I wouldn't do it, Butch."

Butch Sweeney swallowed. "You know he married Julia, don't you?"

Dooley nodded.

"Happened up in Alaska. I was looking for some rubber boots to buy in this store in Skagway and . . . well . . . he found a preacher. It struck me in the gut like bad whiskey, but . . . well, I heard tell that Kit Carson married this gal who weren't no older than fourteen, but that was Kit Carson. And that was in New Mexico. Or someplace like that. And . . . well . . . Julia always had a mind of her own. You know that."

"I'm not jealous," Dooley lied.

"Well, of course not, Dooley. I ain't jea—" Butch couldn't finish.

Dooley started to talk, stopped to let the

waitress refill their coffee cups and collect Butch's empty plate. She left Dooley's, though Dooley wasn't certain he could finish the doughnut now.

He stared at the steaming coffee, which matched, he thought, his steaming head. He leaned forward and said, "Butch, George Miller robbed that mud wagon. George Miller murdered Chester Motz." And he told the kid everything he could remember. Afterward, he thought of something else.

"I also think that George Miller was the one who clobbered me with a pistol butt from behind in that livery in San Francisco. It was George Miller who give me the amnesia."

That got Dooley to thinking and steaming some more.

Then Butch asked, "Can you prove any of that?"

Dooley frowned. He made himself drink some coffee just to keep his hands busy. Afterward, he shook his head. "Probably not. My word against his. He wore a mask, flour sack pulled up over his face. Couldn't see him. And a hole in a man's arm doesn't mean nothing."

Outside, as if to prove a point, a gunshot boomed, and moments later, a man's voice cried out, "Harley Boone has kilt Cheater Norris!"

A few patrons got up. Some stared out the window, whispering to one another. Others opened the door—ringing the little bell and letting in the cold—and stepped onto the plank boardwalk to get a better look. Most, of course, kept right on eating, as murders and shootings happened quite often in Leadville.

Dooley saw that Butch Sweeney was a mite skeptical, so he said. "The county clerk saw George, Butch, I'm certain of it. He told me that a fellow came in, said he was a newspaper reporter from Cheyenne, and that he asked the same questions that I did. About that claim on Halfmoon Creek. Was George gone recently?"

Butch frowned, but nodded. "Said he wanted to check some things in Silver Plume."

Ears getting redder with each fact, Dooley squeezed his hands into fists that trembled. "He was in Denver. Waylaid me. Killed Horatio Whitman. He must have seen me win that hand, and the deed. I'm sure he knew about the deed. He's a low-down, murdering, back-shooting coyote . . . even if he hasn't shot anyone in the back. He would." Then he got excited. "Butch," he said, "the county clerk . . . he could identify George. That would give me the proof."

He felt good, slightly. The clerk would identify George Miller as the man posing as a newspaper reporter. Which might not be enough to get a man tried legally and then legally hanged in a civilized place, or semicivilized, like Denver or Cheyenne or Georgetown or Omaha, but certainly that and the hole in his arm would be enough proof for the vigilance committee to string George Miller up.

"Dooley."

He saw that look on Butch's face.

"Did you hear that fellow outside? Cheater Norris. The one Harley Boone just killed? Cheater Norris—that wasn't his real name, don't recall his real name, just what folks called him . . . Cheater Norris is, I mean *was* the county clerk."

Dooley swore again. And to think of all the prospects he had just a few days ago.

"Dooley?"

Frowning, the coffee in his stomach rocking the one doughnut he had managed to get down before his breakfast and morning soured, Dooley looked again across the table at his old pal, young Butch Sweeney, whose face, never bronzed like Dooley's, was turning paler with each falling snowflake outside.

"You ain't gonna shoot down George Miller?" Butch measured each word. "Are you?"

Not without a call, Dooley thought to say, and started to say, but stopped.

"Because . . . well . . . you just can't do it, Dooley," Butch said. "No matter how many men he has murdered or how many claims he has jumped, or how many men he has paid Harley Boone to gun down. You just can't do it."

But Dooley was thinking that, well, he would be doing the world a favor, bringing at least a wee bit of justice to this lawless city of silver and wealth and greed and cold. He had killed men in self-defense. It would be better, he wanted to make himself to believe, to kill someone for the betterment of the United States of America and her Western territories.

"Dooley." Butch Sweeney had summoned his resolve. "I know George Miller's a mean, contrary, no-good person. But if you kill him, well, just think what it would do to Julia."

It would make her a widow, Dooley thought angrily. *It would make her a hell of a lot better off than she is now.*

But the anger, the hatred, left him, almost immediately. Julia Alice Cooperman had done a lot of growing up over those years since San Francisco. So had Butch Sweeney. Hell, now Dooley realized that he needed to grow up, too. He made himself smile, even though he was a million miles from happiness. He made his head bob up and down as though he agreed with Butch's assessment of the situation.

"You're right," he said softly. "You're right, Butch."

He made himself look out the window, mostly so that Butch wouldn't see those tears welling his eyes. The snow kept coming down harder, wet snow, heavy flakes, and people walking by breathed out frosty air like a locomotive's smokestack as it tried to climb a high grade.

Folks in Leadville kept saying this was spring, but it sure still looked like winter to Dooley, and Dooley had spent some time in high country. He knew about cold. He watched two men in duck trousers and winter coats haul the late Cheater Norris down the boardwalk across the street, taking the recently departed county clerk to the Silver, Gold, Lead and Dead Funeral Parlor.

"I wish you luck with that stage line, Butch," Dooley heard himself say. "You keep yourself safe, old pard. And . . . well . . . you tell Little Miss Loudmouth I said good-bye. I'll see you after the snowmelt."

CHAPTER FIFTEEN

The wind blew hard, rustling through the trees, dumping snow from the limbs and branches. Yet Dooley found himself comfortable in the little dugout he had managed to dig.

Mining, he learned, was mighty hard work. And this time of year, cold work at that.

Now he understood why most miners gave up during the winter, moved down to lower, more manageable, elevations, where March really did mean spring. But the dugout was deep and big enough for Blue, General Grant, and a toasty little fire. The pack mule, of course, could not fit in completely, but he was a tough old bird, used to the elements, the man at the livery had said, and now he did not seem to mind blocking the wind. Dooley had enough food to last till true spring arrived, and for the most part, he had Halfmoon Creek and all of the rough country around it to himself.

Using the crude map he had copied from the detailed maps in the office of Cheater Harris, the late county clerk, Dooley had ridden his horse, pulling the loaded-down mule behind him, with Blue trudging along in the snow. They rode southwest out of town until they hit the Arkansas River, then rode along it till it intersected with

Lake Fork. They had crossed the freezing, slow-moving river at the crossing there, and rode up Lake Fork, on the left bank, and a short while later came to Halfmoon Creek. They only made it to Derry Ditch that first day. That's how tough and rough and hard on everything this country happened to be.

The next day proved a mite easier. They made it to the abandoned old cave somewhere between a mountain stream and Ebert Creek, and Dooley figured this place would make a good base camp until he got too far to come back to it. He worked six days a week, ice fishing in the pond on Sundays, or what he thought might have been Sundays, mostly to save up his strength.

He did not shave. He brought no whiskey and certainly not any bottle of champagne.

At the Tabor Book Shop, he spent $2.17 of Buffalo Bill Cody's grubstake on a book, and he read it on Sundays as the fish fried in his skillet, before the sun sank and it became too dark to read. The sun disappeared really early in these rugged mountains and did not rise in any hurry, either.

SILVER MINING: A Primer
How to make your fortune in the rugged
Western Frontier!
What to look for . . . What to bring . . .
Stories of men JUST LIKE YOU, *wanting*
to find their FORTUNE—

152

On the fifth day, he explored the mountainous ridges on the far bank of the creek. He caused a small avalanche, and, after digging himself out, he went back to the dugout to warm himself and dry his clothes. That was the night he burned J. K. L. O'Brien's book.

Eventually, he realized he needed to move camp, for he had explored the mountains all around him and found a few mines with NO TRESPASSING signs posted. Some had a few friendly notes.

BACK COME JUNE
HELP YOURSELF TO CRACKERS
IN THE LINE SHACK
BUT TAKE <u>ANY</u> SILVER
& IT'LL BE
R. I. P.

Others weren't so friendly.

CLAIM JUMPERS
WILL BE SHOT
ON SIGHT

He even found a few graves. He also saw the markings some people had posted as a site of a

153

claim, and Dooley did not want to be mistaken for a claim jumper. He was honest.

Down Halfmoon Creek, he passed a few other mines, some still working but left during the winter, a few with actual miners, some boarded up and left. One of these he decided might as well serve him as his home for the next few weeks. Even the mule would fit inside it.

A wet storm dumped two feet of snow on the mountains one night, and Dooley wondered if somebody had given him a bum calendar. According to his X's, it was March 29, but it sure felt like January 2. Still, he had enough kindling and enough matches and plenty of coffee and beans, plus grain for his horse and mule.

A week or two later, after the snow had melted mostly, or at least turned to ice, he moved on to where Halfmoon Creek split. South Halfmoon Creek went down like a straight line, and Dooley wondered about that, but decided that "Off Halfmoon Creek" meant the real creek, not that cold, mean-looking tributary or whatever it was.

On the sixth week, maybe eighth, he met a miner whose eyes were so sunk back in his head and whose beard was crawling with lice that Dooley did not want to get too close to the old man. But the fellow asked for jerky, and Dooley had plenty, so he brought some out of the saddlebag and tossed a good-sized one to the man whose mule looked as bony and decrepit as the old man did.

General Grant lowered his head to drink the cold water from Halfmoon Creek, and Dooley kicked one boot out of the stirrup, lifted his leg, and hooked it over the saddle horn.

"Obliged," the man said in a voice as dead as he looked. "Nice horse."

"Good-looking mule," Dooley lied.

"I et the other mule," the man said. "Was a hard winter."

"Find anything?" Dooley asked after digesting the dirty old-timer's statement. He wondered if it was proper to ask a miner if he had found anything. Would that be like asking a man his name in this country? And what did mule meat taste like? Chicken? Marmot?

"Just enough," the man said, "to get me a ticket on Chester Motz's stage and get my bones down to Georgetown where I can see my ma."

Dooley lacked the heart to tell the old-timer about Chester Motz, but sure hoped Butch Sweeney would give the man a ride down to Georgetown—and that no passengers, or even Butch, would get bitten by the bugs crawling all over this guy.

It had warmed up. Thirty degrees would feel like sixty these days, and Dooley felt like it was hotter. That's why the bugs had thawed out.

The man worked the jerky with what few teeth remained in his mouth. "Where you camped?" he asked.

Dooley hooked his thumb down the creek. "Spot abandoned about half a mile yonder." He wanted to sound like he was a friendly miner. "There's some beans. Little coffee in the pot that'll be cold by now. But you're welcome to it. Only I got a dog. And he can be touchy with strangers. But I'll go back with you if you want. I'm kind of played out. This mining . . . it's . . . well . . ." He laughed. "It sure ain't cowboying."

"Course it's hard, youngster. Real hard. Unless you're one of them silver barons who just sits in his mansion countin' his dollars. But you're a smart one. Comin' up before most folks figure it's warm enough to look for silver. You might find some, but I figure most of the stuff's already claimed."

Well, Dooley thought, at least he had tried mining. He thought maybe he would drift to Texas. Or even Mexico. Cowboy down there. Thaw out. It would only take him about three or four summers in that country and he might feel warm again.

"I thank ya fer the jerky, an' fer the offerin' of what you gots in that mine. That'd be Ol' Ole Finkle's claim. Not that Ol' Ole ever claimed nothin'."

"I thought it was abandoned," Dooley said, suddenly terrified that for all his caution he had actually jumped some honest miner's claim, even if he had not even looked for silver or even overturned a stone inside that miserable pit.

"It is. Ol' Ole got hisself kilt 'bout a year ago. Or . . ." He stopped chewing. Stopped moving, except for the critters on his person. "What year is it, youngster?"

Dooley told him.

The chewing resumed. "Yep. 'Bout a year ago. Harley Boone shot him dead on Hemlock and Seventh. That's about as abandoned as a mine can get."

Dooley paled even more. "Harley Boone doesn't think he has claim to that hole, does he?"

The man snorted. "Harley Boone wouldn't work a claim for nothin'. He don't work nothin' 'cept his trigger finger. Nah. Ever'body in Colorado, Wyoming, and Utah knowed Ol' Ole Finkle never struck nothin' but a hard time. And he never filed no papers on that miserable hole, neither. No point. Ol' Ole never struck nothin'. His luck was lousier than mine. Especially once he got kilt by Harley Boone."

"Oh." Dooley thought, turned his head this way, then asked, "Old Old Finkle? How old was he?"

"Not Old Old, boy. Ol' Ole. He was a Swede. Or Finnish. Norwegian. Somethin' 'long those lines. Ol' as in Old. Ole as in . . . hell . . . I ain't from no frozen tundra. I've just tried to mine in one. You know."

"I know," Dooley said. "I understand."

"Thirty-two years," the old-timer said. "That'd

be my best guess at his age. Yes, sir. He'd lived a long life in these mountains. Poor Ol' Ole. Thirty-two and struck dead by a bullet from Harley Boone's pistol. A year older than I am. Be seein' you, youngster."

The old, decrepit miner—who, if he wasn't touched in his head and indeed was thirty-one years old, was a good many years younger than Dooley—went on down Halfmoon Creek.

Dooley reached up and scratched his beard. Maybe he would wash tonight.

Another thought hit him: *Maybe I'll just head back to Leadville and quit this blame foolishness.*

But he trudged on, sweating now, for indeed the sun had come out. The creeks flowed faster now, more turbulent, and finally he came to another branch. One went southeast, the other northward. He pulled his makeshift map from his pocket and realized he had come to the end of his map. Halfmoon Creek flowed southeast, and as far as he knew, the other branch did not have a name. That tempted him, but he knew it was too late in the day to start up that creek. So he turned around and rode back down Halfmoon Creek toward Ol' Ole Finkle's old claim.

"Well." Dooley smiled.

Right before Dooley had pulled out to find his fortune in these mountains, Buffalo Bill had told him that mining was a lot like poker and that he doubted he would see anything from the grubstake he had handed Dooley, but that was how mining went.

So Cody would not be surprised when Dooley returned to Leadville with no silver, nothing but stinking clothes and a beard that needed shaving off and hair that needed a good washing and trimming. It was time, he knew, to quit this folly and get back to punching cows. Or he could always go home to his farm near Des Moines.

Oddly enough, he felt content, satisfied, happy. So what if he had not found any riches, even any traces of silver? He had lived his dream. Since discovering that old, old clipping from some newspaper about a gold strike in Alaska, Dooley had dreamed of finding his fortune, panning for gold or digging for silver. Doing something that did not involve branding steers with a hot iron, roping an ornery longhorn, riding line camps in the loneliest of winters, or planting taters in Iowa. And he had done it. He had lived out his dream. Sure, he had nothing to show for it but calloused hands, an itchy beard, worn-out clothes, and a belly button that was just about to rub up against his backbone. But, by thunder, he had done it. He had lived his dream. My, what stories he could tell . . .

He frowned. He was about to say *Julia*.

Well, Butch might enjoy a story or two. Like the avalanche that had almost buried Dooley. Maybe he would take that job offer, ride shotgun for Butch's wagon. Maybe . . . or he'd just do what most cowboys did.

Drift.

That's what he did now. Drifted. Back along Halfmoon Creek toward his temporary digs of Ol' Ole Finkle's hole in the ground. He came to the spot, saw Blue standing in the opening, wagging his tail. He saw the mule grazing on grain Dooley had spread out before he had saddled General Grant and ridden off on one last adventure, one last look for a fortune in silver.

He crossed Halfmoon Creek, and Blue barked with excitement, as if he knew he would be leaving these dark woods for sunlight and Leadville and maybe something different.

Apparently, the ancient thirty-one-year-old prospector had not stopped for food or water. Dooley dismounted and led General Grant to the mine. He removed the saddle and blanket, set both out to dry in what little sunlight made it through the forest, slipped off the bridle, and rubbed the horse's neck.

Next, he fetched a piece of jerky and tossed it to Blue, who swallowed it without tasting or doing much chewing.

Dooley found his washbasin and splashed frigid water across his face, drying off with his dingy bandanna. He told Blue, "Let's get a good night's sleep, Blue, and we'll see what civilization looks like tomorrow."

160

He stared at Halfmoon Creek, shook his head, and turned around to look at the mine.

He blinked.

He turned back and looked again at the rapidly swelling stream.

He wet his lips and slowly craned his neck, moved his body, and gazed at the worthless hole in the ground.

Back he looked at the creek.

Back he studied the mine.

Creek.

Mine.

Creek.

Mine.

Creek.

Mine.

Creek.

Mine.

Then he swore.

CHAPTER SIXTEEN

"Oof Halfmoon Creek," Dooley said, as he lighted the lantern and turned it up.

He remembered what Cheater Norris, the county clerk, had said when Horatio Whitman had come into the office and almost filed a claim. *"Oof Halfmoon Creek?"* the now recently deceased clerk had said he had admonished Whitman. *"You mean Off Halfmoon Creek."* Dooley remembered it clearly now. Norris saying that he had corrected the crude map Whitman had brought in. The old messenger had gotten angry, taken the map back—rendering Norris with one wicked paper cut—and left the office.

Dooley thought things out. When Whitman had made up his own deed, he had kept Cheater Norris's spelling. OFF Halfmoon Creek. Not OOF. But OOF was right.

Halfmoon Creek.

OOF.

O.O.F.

Ol' Ole Finkle.

He moved deeper into the hole, with Blue following nervously. He came past mounds of guano, but saw no sleeping bats, no flying bats, no bats at all. He remembered the grizzly that had almost done in Buffalo Bill Cody, Dooley, and Blue, and hoped nothing was hibernating now. He wondered why he had not thought about bears before.

The hole went deeper than he figured, but eventually he came to a dead end. He held the lantern high and looked but saw dark, damp rocks. He studied the ground, but found not footprints left by Ol' Ole Finkle or Horatio Whitman. He moved back and, suddenly exhausted from the altitude, the stress, the excitement, the grueling weeks he had spent in these mountains, he rested on a boulder.

He was warm, but a cool breeze prickled his neck.

It soothed Dooley. Then he turned, lowered the lantern, and lifted his hand. He could feel the soft blowing of wind. It was coming from the wall. He rose, grabbed the lantern, and held it higher. He moved back, almost tripping over Blue, who skedaddled and moved out of the way.

Once the lantern was set down opposite the wall, Dooley came back and grabbed a stone. He moved it. He looked, studying the wall closely, realizing that this was no natural rock formation, no rockslide. His heart pounded and he moved back, grabbed another stone. He moved back and forth, working up a sweat, straining his muscles. Eventually, he shed his coat. Then his vest. Then his shirt and bandanna. He moved until he could not work anymore, and curled up into a ball, and slept with Blue beside him, guarding the wall.

He did not bother cooking breakfast, just drank the cold coffee, although he did make sure Blue had something to eat, and the horse and mule were grained. He also remembered something else and stepped outside, still in his long-handle underwear and woolen pants. It did not feel so cold this morning. He drank water and wished he had not burned J. K. L. O'Brien's *Silver Mining: A Primer*. But he could remember his meeting with the late county clerk, Cheater Norris.

He found a piece of wood, sat down, carved a point, measured it against his Colt revolver, and moved off.

The words of the late Cheater Norris rang through his brain:

"Once you stake your claim—you stake it by setting up a monument at least three inches in diameter and six inches out of the ground. This has to be in the northeastern corner of your land."

Northeast. He found the sun, just now appearing. He thought about the direction the mine went, the shaft that Dooley was convinced Horatio Whitman had sealed off by moving boulders to hide the entrance. That made sense. It had to be.

Horatio Whitman was not like that old thirty-one-year-old coot Dooley had met coming out of the mountains yesterday. Whitman was like

164

most miners. He would get out of these hills in the winter, ride shotgun for Chester Motz. And he was somewhere between the miners whose properties Dooley had passed during his mining misadventures this spring.

Horatio Whitman would not invite any passersby in to help themselves to crackers whilst Horatio Whitman was maybe better than a hundred miles away in Denver. He wouldn't threaten to shoot anyone on sight, either, but Horatio Whitman was smart enough to hide what he had found. Horatio Whitman had sealed the entrance to the tunnel or trap or room he had found in the late Ol' Ole Finkle's claim that had never been claimed.

The hidden entrance would go off that way, Dooley said to himself, and he took off that way. He did not pace off too much, though, but enough to cover the hole. Besides, he could always go back and move the claim marker if the tunnel appeared to stretch deeper.

He used the Colt's butt to hammer the stake into the ground, and measured again, making sure it was three inches in diameter and at least six inches above the ground.

The county clerk's voice whispered again in the morning wind:

"Once you've staked your claim, you have thirty days to file your claim with me."

Thirty days. Dooley wrote his name on a piece

of paper and set it beside the marker, covering it with a good-sized stone.

Then he ran back to Ol' Ole Finkle's far-from-worthless worthless mine.

It took him half that day to get the top of the makeshift wall down, but that was all he needed. He climbed up, and through the hole, bringing the lantern with him. Blue barked, the noise bouncing off the walls, and then the dog sprang up the makeshift stairway of rocks and boulders and entered the room with Dooley.

At first he didn't see much of anything, just more rocks. Silver, he remembered somebody once telling him, can be black. Black as coal. It might fool a person.

He moved back, loving the steadiness of the temperature, how relaxing it felt. Despite being bottled up from Horatio Whitman's wall of rocks, it did not feel or smell stuffy or stagnant. He still felt the breeze, and knew there had to be shafts sending fresh air into this chamber. He also knew that this chamber went deeper and deeper than he had figured.

"I might," he told Blue, "have to move that stake back a few hundred yards."

Blue barked, which echoed across the dark room, and wagged his tail.

They went on. In the darkness where the glow from the lantern did not reach, he saw the beams of light shining from the ceiling. Air holes. Natural or otherwise. But a good sign. A man could breathe here. He stopped and looked back, glad to see a light from the opening he had managed. He sighed with relief, knowing that the light there would provide a beacon, so he would not get lost in this chamber. He recalled all those stories he had read in the *Police Gazette* and *Frank Leslie's Illustrated* about men getting lost in mines, eating candles until they died.

Just don't go too far, he told himself. *Don't stay in here till the sun goes down.*

His boots and Blue's paws splashed through puddles of water, and now Dooley heard, above his own pounding heart and heavy breathing, water dripping.

He passed the sunbeams, past a little trickle of water coming from the roof and puddling on the floor. He came to a division in the mine, one chamber going off to the northeast, the other going northwest.

"That's right, isn't it?" he asked Blue. Suddenly, he wasn't sure of his directions. He moved to the left, northeast, but quickly stopped. That way was blocked by another wall of boulders.

Dooley cursed Horatio Whitman for being that untrusting. He didn't have the time or energy to move another mountain of rocks. Something peppered the brim of his hat, and he stepped back. More soft pebbles fell from the ceiling onto the floor. Now Dooley was certain that he did not want to be moving any rocks. He waited until the drizzle—a far cry from a cave-in—passed, and afterward he moved back into the closet, held the lantern as high as he could, and breathed a little easier.

This wasn't the act of a paranoid miner hiding his treasure. It was solid stone. Just what he had called it in his mind, a closet. So he backed up and took the other opening.

It was much larger than a closet, and, thankfully, no drizzle of dirt or rocks or even water fell from the ceiling. Ahead of him, he saw other beams of light, revealing openings that would provide air, fresh air, and life. He turned to his right and held the lantern upward.

Blue barked, backed up quickly, and Dooley quickly lowered his lantern and shielded his eyes from the violent reflection.

His eyes burned. He blinked, sucked in another breath, and looked again.

The light from the lantern, and the holes in the ceiling, reflected off the wall Dooley stared at. A wall that might not have been completely papered with gleaming silver, but had to be pretty damn close to it.

Unbelievable.

"My goodness," he told Blue. "We're rich."

CHAPTER SEVENTEEN

Two weeks later, Dooley Monahan rode into Leadville, Blue trotting alongside him, the pack mule sinking in the thick mud of spring—which had slowed Dooley down considerably. His heavy winter coat was rolled up and strapped behind the cantle with his saddlebags, for it was warm . . . well, warmer than he had felt in ages after a couple of months along Halfmoon Creek.

What made him grin was seeing all the miners, freshly duded up and freshly shaved, that he met heading into the mountains as he came to town. Most of them pointed at him, and plenty of them whispered, but Dooley did not mind. A few of them noticed how slowly the mule moved, but no one said anything to him other than a "Howdy" or a joking "You're heading the wrong way, mister. This is when we start mining."

Oh, Dooley would think and grin underneath his untrimmed beard, *you're right. I haven't even started mining just yet.*

The streets, a quagmire, remained packed, with wagons and horsemen going both ways, and the boardwalks were equally crowded. Leadville had always seemed a vibrant city that might have rivaled *Harper's Weekly* woodcut impressions of New York City or Chicago or old Charleston as she had been before the Civil War. Now it might have even outmatched those images Dooley had imagined. It was a bustling, wild city, full of people—and only two men were hanging from a telegraph pole on the edge of town.

He passed the county clerk's office, but saw a line out the door, so rode on, trying to think about where he should go first. One thing he knew for certain was that he needed a bath and a shave, and the way he smelled, that might take him all day before he ever felt clean. He looked for the late Chester Motz's mud wagon, but didn't see it, or any stagecoach, or even Butch Sweeney.

It just so happened that a man left the bank on the corner of Harrison and Third, mounting his horse, backing it out, and taking off toward one of the forks or tributaries of the Arkansas River, and since space in front of any building came at a premium, Dooley guided General Grant to it and dismounted. He managed to bring the mule to his horse's side, and went to the packsaddle and brought out one sack.

He grunted and felt his boots sink deeper into the mud underneath the weight, but adjusted the sack over his shoulder and stepped onto the boardwalk. People gave him a mighty wide berth, allowing Dooley to move across the creaking planks of the boardwalk and to the entrance to the bank. A businessman in spectacles and a sack suit opened the door, gasped at the sight of Dooley, and almost fell back inside.

Dooley thanked him for holding the door open and stood like a dumb oaf watching the commotion of bees as men and women went to cashiers, and other folks sat in desks talking to men with frowns etched permanently across their faces and eyes glazed over with boredom. People leaving the bank swung a wide arc around Dooley. People coming into the bank did the same.

After the longest while, a timid soul wearing sleeve garters came up to Dooley and made himself try to grin. He didn't completely succeed, but it was enough to let Dooley know that the boy tried to be civil.

"Can I . . . er . . . be of assistance?" the fellow asked.

Dooley nodded. It had been two weeks since he had actually spoken to a living human being, and the last person he had spoken to had been that old miner who was younger than Dooley. He said, "Yeah." Then, louder: "Yes, sir. I want . . ."

He glanced around him and made sure no one was listening.

"Want to open an account. Make a deposit."

"I see." The clerk sounded and looked ever so skeptical. He looked around for help, found none, and realized what kindness and generosity and civility had netted him. So he moved back and pushed open a rickety little gate and motioned toward his desk.

"This way, sir."

Once the fellow sat down, and Dooley laid his sack on the desktop and found himself sitting in an actual chair for the first time in ages, Dooley stared. He looked up at the ceiling, made of tin and full of all sorts of designs. He studied the chandelier that had to have come from St. Louis or maybe even down Mexico way. The roof fascinated him. He hadn't seen one since . . .

"How much cash do you wish to deposit with us, Mr. . . . ummmmmm . . ."

"Monahan," Dooley said. "Dooley Monahan." He spelled both names and watched the clerk write the letters in a cheery cursive.

"Very good, sir," the clerk said, lowered his pencil, and stared across the desk. "How much currency?"

Dooley shook his head. "No currency. It's . . . umm . . ." Again he looked over his shoulder, then leaned forward and whispered, "Silver."

"Silver." The clerk did not sound as though he believed him.

So Dooley reached into the sack and pulled out a chunk of ore.

"Where on earth did you find this?" The president of the bank, Tim Lake, twisted his mustache and refilled the snifter Dooley held with French brandy. They had moved away from the clerk's little desk to the private office of Mr. Lake. Dooley had a cigar in his mouth, two more in a greasy pocket, and a snifter of brandy in his hand. The clerk and an assayer called in from a business two blocks down were busy working on the samples Dooley had brought in in his sack.

"A ways from here," Dooley said.

"A ways," the bank president repeated.

"A ways." Dooley brought the glass to his lips but just brushed them against the liquor. It had been so long since he had taken a snoot, he wasn't sure he wanted to do this yet . . . not on an empty stomach.

"A ways." Mr. Lake frowned.

After a while, the clerk and the assayer came over, and the assayer, who had his sleeves rolled up and appeared to be sweating, rubbed his bald head and looked at Dooley.

"You have staked your claim, haven't you, sir?"

Dooley did not answer. "Listen," he said, and set the cigar in the ashtray, the liquor on the desktop, and cleared his throat. "All I want is some cash money to get myself cleaned up. And enough to pay back Buffalo Bill Cody what he grubstaked me."

"Colonel Cody grubstaked you?" President Lake asked.

"That's why I want to pay him back," Dooley said, speaking to the president as if he were an

173

idiot. "Now, I appreciate the brandy and the cigars and the loan of your chair, but I'm itching as all get-out, and I can tell by how that little jasper of a clerk you have keeps holding his nose and wiping his eyes with his silk handkerchief that I don't smell too good anymore. I'd like to rectify that. But if you can't help me, just tell me and I'll find me another bank in this here town."

That was probably more words than he had spoken since he had ridden down Halfmoon Creek.

"We will be delighted to handle your account, Mr. Monahan," President Lake said, and he looked at the assayer. "Am I correct?"

"I'd think so," the clerk said.

"Is it good ore?" Dooley asked.

The man stared at him, rubbed the slick top of his bald head again, and looked over at President Lake.

"It's good," he said, and looked at his notes. "It's gray silver, Mr. Lake, with ruby silver, and gray copper on quartz."

"And?" Now the banker was starting to sweat.

"Well, by my estimation, if the rest of his claim is like what he has brought in, this would assay in silver per ton of two thousand pounds to be . . ." He checked his figures, swallowed, and looked at Dooley as he answered.

"Six thousand two hundred thirteen dollars and eighty-nine cents."

Denver prices didn't trouble Dooley that much anymore.

But something troubled him. "I don't think I brought in a ton," he said.

"Not in that sack," the assayer said.

"How much is that worth? What I brought in?"

It was the clerk who answered. "From the weight, I'd say three hundred ninety-five dollars and sixty-one, no, I mean sixty-two cents."

Dooley frowned. "Buffalo Bill give me a sizable more money than that."

"Well."

But Dooley was already standing, walking out of the president's private office, and moving across the lobby to the front door. All three men chased after him, calling him Mr. Monahan, but Dooley left the bank, let a nice old lady in a bonnet pass, and moved to the side of the hitching rail. The banker, the assayer, and the clerk slid to a stop. Dooley pulled another sack and swung it over his shoulder and stepped back onto the boardwalk. He nodded at the three men.

"Could y'all bring in those three other bags for me? I'll leave this one on your desk and come back to fetch the last one."

When Dooley left the office, the clerk—the one who had started it all with an act of kindness, or business, or guilt—opened the door for Dooley. He whispered, "Sir, if I were you, if you have not already filed on your claim, you should do so immediately." He pointed. "That's the county clerk's office. That's where . . ."

"Y'all got a new clerk?" Dooley asked. "To replace Cheater Norris?"

"Yes."

"Fine, fine. Do you know if Miss Julia . . . I mean . . . Missus Julia . . . Miller . . . Is she in town?"

"I . . . I don't . . . Miller?"

"And did Butch Sweeney start up old Chester Motz's stage line to Denver and those other cities?"

"Um . . . yes. Yes. The stage should be coming in sometime today, I think."

"Fine. Fine. And is Buffalo Bill Cody still in town?"

"Yes. But I think the *Ledger* reported that he was leaving when Mr. Sweeney takes off again for Denver."

"Good, good." Dooley pulled up his money belt and held out his hand. He shook with the clerk and gathered the reins to General Grant and the lead rope to the mule.

The clerk watched him swing into the saddle, then slowly, numbly, he returned to the bank, closing the door behind him.

After two months, would Miss . . . Mrs. Julia Miller still be living in that hotel? And would Butch Sweeney have a place of his own, or be sleeping in the wagon yard or livery stable? The clerk said that Buffalo Bill was staying at the Tabor, but Dooley did not think the gentlemen in the lobby would let a man who looked like Dooley did just now inside without a ruckus. No matter how many double eagles he had in his money belt to tip those rascals.

First, he thought, he ought to find that bath. Get his hair shorn and the beard and dirt removed from his face. He remembered that clothing emporium he had passed when he had first ridden into Leadville what seemed like a million years ago. He could buy clothes there. But first he needed that bath. No. No. He thought about when he had first made that claim. Two weeks. So he had about two more weeks to file, legally, his claim. Yet he did not want to wait. Silver had a way of bringing out the worst in people, especially silver that graded out as much as Dooley's had.

He rode back down to Front Street and found the county clerk. The door was no longer packed with people, and the hitching rail was practically empty. Dooley swung out of his saddle, brought the pack mule in, told Blue to stay, and fetched his map out of the saddlebag on his right-hand side.

Once he pushed through the door, he saw the clerk shoving some maps back into a sliding cabinet. Cheater Norris's replacement turned around and grimaced at the sight of Dooley.

But it was Dooley who felt as if he had just been kicked in his belly.

CHAPTER EIGHTEEN

"What do you want, old man?" George Miller demanded.

An eternity passed.

"Well." Miller was not happy at all. "I haven't got all day."

Another figure, a pockmarked boy with a pale face, slowly rose from beneath the counter, holding more bundles of paper that needed filing. The boy made a face at Dooley and cringed when Miller cut loose with another blast of profanity directed at Dooley.

Only it wasn't aimed at Dooley, at least, not Dooley Monahan.

It slowly dawned on Dooley that the murdering, woman-stealing, stagecoach-robbing claim-jumper did not recognize Dooley. He thought he was just some flea-bitten, miserable miner who needed a bath and a shave. Dooley started doing some mental figuring.

"Well," Miller barked. "I haven't got all day. God, you stink."

"Want to file a claim," Dooley said, and waited for recognition to cross the new county clerk's face. It didn't happen. Instead, he shook his head, slid some maps back into place, and told the kid who still held those papers,

"See to this, Homer. I'll be in the back."

Dooley watched Miller move toward the rear office, his broad back making a mighty inviting target for a .45 caliber chunk of lead Dooley could fire. But that was just a dream, a fleeting thought. A fun joke. Dooley was not a back-shooter. Besides, would Julia Cooperman—no, that's Julia Miller—wear black and mourn the loss, small that it was, of her husband?

With the boy depositing his papers and fetching a pencil and a ledger, Dooley walked over and leaned against the counter.

The kid's eyes watered at the stink coming off Dooley's clothes and Dooley's body. He couldn't blame the boy. Dooley could smell, too.

"Ummm." The boy looked up. "Do you know the location of the claim you wish to file?"

Dooley nodded, and the kid turned the ledger around. Dooley studied the map, flipped the page over to where the map continued, and found Halfmoon Creek, which he traced with his dirty finger until he found the spot. The boy nodded.

The boy jotted down something on his pad and asked, "Have you marked it?"

"Yes," Dooley said.

"Well, good. Nobody else has filed for this, either. So it's available. Lode or placer?"

"Lode," Dooley answered quickly.

The boy smiled. "I figured. But I got to ask."

Dooley grinned at the kid. He was all right.

179

When Dooley was that age, he couldn't be particular about what outfits he signed on to, either.

As they finished with the paperwork, George Miller came out and stared over the boy's shoulder. Dooley hunched down lower so that Miller could see only the filthy hat and his long, greasy hair.

Miller put a finger on the map, looked up, did some mental thinking, and finally laughed. "Isn't that the cave old man Finkle worked?"

"It's not registered, Mr. Miller," the kid said.

"Course not. That old coot didn't know anything about mining. Worthless hole in the ground was all it was." He laughed. "I wish you luck, mister." Still chuckling, he walked back to his office.

The kid handed Dooley a pen, which he dipped in the inkwell and signed his name, then printed it on the line above. The boy tore out a receipt and handed that to him while he waited for his signature to dry. "This gives you twenty acres . . ." Dooley only half listened as the boy explained the particulars of what he could mine.

"I wish you luck," the boy said. He didn't offer to shake Dooley's hand, but Dooley understood. If he happened to be on the other side of the counter, he might not have wanted to shake hands with a greasy, buggy, filthy hombre who happened to be sitting on a fortune in silver that only he and the boys down at the bank knew about.

At least he was legal. He studied the registration of his claim, paid the filing fee, and headed toward the door.

"I wish you luck . . ." George Miller had returned from the rear office. "That hole in the ground at least will keep the rain off you, Mr. . . ." Dooley turned around to watch the miserable reprobate look down and read the signature and the name printed in the registration book.

Dooley grinned as George Miller's face paled. The new county clerk looked up, and the cigarette topped from his lips, bounced on the counter, fell to the floor as he stared across the cramped little office.

"Dooley?" Miller sounded skeptical.

"George."

Miller sucked in a deep breath, recognizing at last Dooley's voice.

The clerk tried to smile while the boy did some sort of dance to snub out the cigarette on the floor behind the counter. Miller moved around, swung through the gate, and tried to paint a happy picture on his face. He almost even held out his hand, but stopped, either not wanting to touch a man who might have bugs crawling all over him,

Dooley would bet even money on the some-thing else, because George Miller gave the

Colt .45 on Dooley's right hip a quick glance. And George Miller's arm came back, so he could make a pull for the hideaway gun in the shoulder holster if Dooley decided to start the ball.

"Well, Dooley, we wondered what had happened to you, Julia and I." He spoke so syrupy; Dooley figured he could have been accidentally tapped by a maple fellow in Vermont. "You'd been gone for two months, and I was just telling Julia that maybe we should get up a search party. Of course, I didn't tell Julia that I thought we'd be searching for your body . . ."

Dooley thought, *If you were leading the party, George, you'd make damn sure what you brought back was my body.*

". . . but it's so great to see you, Dooley." He found a cigar in his jacket pocket and slowed his movements when Dooley moved his right hand to the butt of the revolver. Pretending not to notice Dooley's actions, Miller handed the cigar to Dooley, but Dooley did not take it or reject it. He just stared, and kept the right hand where it was.

George Miller could play that game of pretending not to notice things, too. He ignored Dooley's hand and ignored Dooley's ignoring the cigar, which he put into his own mouth, and said, "That mine. Well . . . that hole in the earth . . . is worthless, Dooley. Don't you know that?"

A gentle shrug served as his answer.

"I wish you luck, Dooley," Miller said, beaming. "But you should know something, Dooley. That's just a hole in the ground. Worthless. An old man dug that hole sometime back."

"Ol' Ole Finkle," Dooley said. "Who never filed a legal claim."

"That's right." George Miller's head bobbed.

Dooley wanted to see how Miller would react, so he said, "Then Horatio Whitman decided to try mining it."

Miller nodded, then quit, and his eyebrows knotted. He was no longer pale, as his ears started to redden.

"Whitman did not file claim to that worthless hole in the ground, either," Dooley said. "But I have. Duly noted and registered." The friendliness left his face. "You look like someone just punched you in your stomach, George." Dooley's grin held little humor. "Oof."

Eyes narrowing into slits, Dooley backed toward the door, taking the knob with his left hand, keeping his right on the Colt's walnut butt, and moving out into the boardwalk. He closed the door and stepped quickly away from the window of the county clerk's office.

After standing against the wall for a while, he backed off the boardwalk, keeping his hand on the butt of the pistol, and eased toward his horse and mule. He could see in the window, see that the clerk was busy filing those papers and George

Miller had his back to the window, face buried in the plats of mining claims along Halfmoon Creek. Dooley gathered the reins to General Grant and the lead rope to the mule and eased them from the hitching post and down the street until he felt safe enough that Miller wouldn't accidentally spot him. Dooley thought he had time to find that emporium where he could buy some new duds, and then a place for a bath and a shave, but as he rode past the *Leadville Ledger*, he began to think that maybe he should take some necessary precautions. It wouldn't take George Miller that long to figure out what Dooley had meant when he had said, *"Oof."* O.O.F. Not O-f-f.

O.O.F., Halfmoon Creek.

"Can you get that in the next paper?" Dooley asked.

The editor at the *Ledger* frowned. "No, I'm afraid not. I'd have to rip up . . ."

He saw the gold piece appear in Dooley's palm. The editor, a thin man with a thick graying mustache and goatee, adjusted his spectacles.

"Well, I supposed it's newsworthy." The editor took the coin from Dooley's palm, and dropped it in his desk drawer.

"So this is merely an ad saying that you have filed and registered a claim on Halfmoon Creek, once mined by the late Old Old Finkle and the late Horatio Whitman, who never filed legal claim on said property. And that you are hiring miners with experience at top wages."

"Ol' Ole," Dooley corrected.

"Sir?"

Dooley pointed at the yellow paper in front of the editor. "Ol' Ole, not Old-comma-Old. O-l-apostrophe. O-l-e." He smiled. "He was Scandinavian or something like that."

"I see." The editor was impressed with Dooley's spelling and that he knew what an apostrophe was. "I have need of a tramp printer if you are familiar with the trade."

Dooley grinned. "I'm just a cowboy, sir, turned miner."

"It will be in tomorrow's paper, sir. We thank you for your business and wish you all the luck in your mine." Dooley could tell the editor figured him to be a complete idiot, but that would change. The bank down the street could not keep a secret for that long.

Another printer came over with the placards Dooley had just commissioned, and paid Leadville prices for, and showed one to Dooley.

"That looks just dandy," Dooley said. "And you've made copies of that claim?"

"It's being done as we speak. You'll need to get it notarized, of course, but Mr. Filmore here happens to be a notary."

"That's a fact," the editor said.

185

Dooley fished out another gold piece. "Could you mail those copies for me?"

"Well, sir, surely . . ." Dooley fished out a greenback from his money belt, and the editor flipped the page in his notepad, licked the point of his pencil, and asked, "Who would you like these to go to, sir?"

"The state recorder's office in Denver," Dooley said. "But I don't have an address."

"We can get that easy enough."

"What's the biggest paper in this state?"

The editor shrugged. "I'd say the *Denver Telegram* . . . but we are not far behind."

"Mail one to the editor of the *Telegram*."

"You have three other copies," the clerk said.

"Right. I'll take two, and . . ." He gave them the address of the farmer looking after his place in Iowa.

The remaining copies he shoved in his pocket, paid the editor a tip, and started for the door. Then he remembered something, and turned around to ask:

"Now, is there an honest lawyer hanging his shingle in this burg?"

CHAPTER NINETEEN

Lawyer Jonah Terrance Cohen sat across his desk nodding at what he figured to be the appropriate pauses, jotting down a few notes on the pad in front of him, and trying his best not to cough or cringe from the stink seeping through every one of Dooley's pores. His eyes watered, but Dooley didn't mind. By thunder, Dooley was hankering to get rid of these duds and soak in a hot tub filled with suds for about a month of Sundays.

"Now, let me get this straight, Mr. Monahan." Once Dooley had finished explaining his needs for a lawyer, Jonah Terrance Cohen—J. T. for short, he had said, after Dooley paid the retainer in double eagles—tapped his pencil on the pad.

"You want to record your will, have me keep a duly notarized deed to your mine in my office, and mail the other to the United States marshal in Denver?"

"That should cover it," Dooley said. He handed him the envelope he had borrowed from the *Leadville Ledger*. "And you keep this with my last will and testament. It's to be opened upon my untimely demise."

"Which," the lawyer said, "we hope will not come anytime soon." He grinned. Dooley didn't.

"Very well," attorney J. T. Cohen said, and

reached into a desk drawer to find the proper forms. "A will is a good thing to have, young man. It saves your heirs much grief. It will aid and comfort them, oddly enough, when your time comes."

Dooley smiled. "Oddly enough," he said, "it might keep that time from coming anytime soon."

"Beneficiaries?" the lawyer asked without catching what Dooley had just told him.

"The Cahills," Dooley said. "And Missus Julia *Cooperman* Miller." He stressed the Cooperman part of the name. "Equal partners, or however you put it. And write in there, if you could, that they are to take real good care of Blue, my dog, and General Grant, my horse."

"Your generosity knows no bounds."

"I'm alive," Dooley said. But he was thinking:

But I need to stay that way until that newspaper gets published and folks, George Miller in particular, know that I've protected my interest . . . and my well-being.

He made one other stop before heading to the emporium to buy some new duds, and that was at the miners hanging out in front of one of the buildings, hoping to land some work. He hired the two stoutest sorts, after they passed the right qualifications. They were the only two men in the group who owned shotguns, a single-shot twelve-gauge, and a double-barreled Greener. He gave them enough money to buy some buckshot, and gave them directions to his mine.

"If anyone who shows up and is not me and wants to get in," Dooley ordered, "you know what to do."

The burly men did not need to nod their agreement. They had that look about them.

The clerks at the emporium did not look like they really wanted Dooley inside their store, until he pulled out some greenbacks and silver from his money belt. Then they practically had to beat off two other employees who wanted a piece of the action.

Dooley bought work duds and dress duds, shirts and long-handle underwear and socks, wool and cotton, a dress vest and a working vest, bandannas and skinny ties and ribbon ties, and paper collars of various fashions. He even bought jeans because he was a miner now and while working cowboys did not care much for those blue pants, miners knew they were solid work duds. He found a good pair of boots, and some more shirts and pants, and finally wound up in the hat department.

He found a good Stetson, and tried it on his head, and saw the four clerks cringe when it did not fit, and he placed it back on the hanger. Dooley frowned, feeling the pain of those clerks. Would they be able to sell anything that had touched his filthy hair? Well, he determined that he would be more careful then, and looked for hats that seemed just about right.

He bought a slouch hat to wear while working in the mine, and then he found a good Stetson that did fit and might even fit better once he got his hair washed and cut, and he did not even blink over how much a Stetson cost in a town like Leadville. He thought he had enough clothes for the time being, but then he saw a top hat, silk, black, shiny, and just like the kind Abraham Lincoln might have worn all those years ago. He started to buy it but then he stopped himself and set it back on the wooden head of the dummy on the counter.

You need to remember your roots, he thought.

He said it out loud then just so he might hear himself.

"You're an old cowboy, Dooley," he said, and the clerks backed away to give him a moment of privacy in his conversation with himself. "Don't let all this money go to your head. Fame and wealth are like poker. They can be fleeting."

That made him remember that he was Dooley Monahan, late of Iowa and parts unknown, and he was the son of hardworking farmers and not some uppity silver baron like those dandified gents who ate in Leadville's fanciest restaurants with . . .

He frowned with pain.

. . . with Mrs. Julia Miller.

"Put those back," he told one of the clerks. "And that shirt, too. I don't need that. That's way too fancy for an old cowboy like me. No, no, keep the boots. I need those. Three pairs of socks are enough. No, I'll keep the frock coat and the winter coat. You never know when summer's here to stay at this altitude. The duck trousers are good. The blue jeans . . . well . . . yeah, I guess I can keep them."

That seemed to be all he needed.

"Oh," he said, and the clerks forgot their disappointment. "I need some oil to clean my guns, and a couple of boxes of .45 caliber shells for a single-action Colt. While you're at it, give me two double-barrel shotguns and four boxes of double-ought buckshot." He had to tell himself that he was a miner now, and not every guard he could hire would own a shotgun. Not that he would be like some ranchers he had been forced to work with, that the ranch would supply all horses and that cowboys riding for that brand could not own their own horses. No, he just wanted to be prepared, and if a guard did not happen to have a shotgun, he could use one of Dooley's . . . no . . . one of . . . the *Monahan Mining Company's* Parker twelve-gauges.

While he was at it, he got a new saddle and saddle blanket and bridle for General Grant, and some jerky he figured he would feed Blue.

"What's that?" he said when he reached the register with his load of plunder.

"A box of chocolate from Switzerland," the mustached clerk said.

Dooley reached for it, but stopped himself and slid the box back on top of the others. His heart pained him, and he had to blink his eyes, but not from the stink permeating from his rancid body.

"Oh . . ." he whispered. "Oh, poor Little Miss Loudmouth."

He made himself smile, thinking of better days.

Then the clerk, as he kept tapping on those buttons on the register and making things ring and ring, asked, "Where do you wish to have these delivered?"

That stumped Dooley. He had been living in a hole in the ground along Halfmoon Creek for the past two months. It wasn't like he was still bunking with Butch Sweeney anymore.

"Well . . ." Dooley thought. He wet his lips. "I don't think you boys want to be hauling that stuff into the mountains."

"Take it to my room," a voice said, and Dooley turned around to see a redheaded jasper holding the late Chester Motz's whip and smiling a huge smile that made his new mustache bob.

Dooley laughed, slapped some dust off his pants, and started toward Butch Sweeney, but quickly stopped before he could hold out his hand or pull Butch into a bear hug.

Butch Sweeney's wide grin showed how much he appreciated it.

Sweeney gave the cashier the address of his new lodge in town, and Dooley went back to pay the bill.

As the clerks hurried off with Dooley's plunder toward the southwest side of town, where Butch Sweeney must be living, Dooley and Butch stepped onto the boardwalk.

"Mining must pay a lot better than stage-coaching," Butch said.

Dooley grinned. "Yeah, but you get to bathe regular."

"Do you ever intend to wash again?"

Dooley laughed.

"I mean," Butch said, "Chester Motz and Horatio Whitman, God rest their souls, weren't the most pristine of gents to drive a mud wagon, but, well . . . I mean . . . there are some boys in town who stink worse than you do."

"I sure don't want to meet those boys," Dooley said.

"I need to get some dust and mud off me, too," Butch said.

Dooley grinned. "Shall we?"

Outside, Dooley marveled at the mud wagon Butch had fixed up. It was parked just a few stores down, and Dooley could tell the boy had a good hand with the lines and did not overwork the mules that pulled the stagecoach.

"Who's riding shotgun for you?" Dooley asked.

"Don't need one," Butch said. "For one reason, I can't afford one . . . not yet . . . anyway. For another, I haven't been hauling any passengers or anything of much value."

"Chester Motz wasn't hauling anything valuable when those owlhoots robbed us," Dooley told him.

Butch Sweeney grinned. "From the looks of things now, pard, I'd say they had a good reason to rob you. They just did it too early. Did you earn that money you just forked over at that place mining the past month or two? Or did you try another hand at poker?"

Dooley shrugged. "We'll see how long it lasts."

"A run of luck."

"In a mine," Dooley said. "Not cards."

"Well, I'll be damned."

Dooley changed the subject. "You mentioned a bathhouse."

It wasn't Leadville's fanciest bathhouse, Butch Sweeney explained to Dooley as they moved down the street, dodging traffic and horses and even a few pigs.

"But it has plenty of water," Butch said as they stopped.

It was also a barbershop. CHIN LU'S, the sign read, BATHS . . . SHAVES . . . HAIRCUTS . . .

Underneath was another sign.

Open 24 Hours

"An all-night bathhouse?" Dooley was skeptical. He figured this might be a front for something else that Butch Sweeney might have in mind.

"For the miners," Butch explained. "They work in shifts all day, all night, a few mines even stay open Sundays." Butch grinned. "You ain't in Kansas no more, you know."

"Iowa," Dooley corrected.

The proprietor, on the other hand, had to be persuaded to let Dooley into the facilities. Dooley did that persuading with a half eagle coin.

He bit the coin, decided it was real, and stepped aside of the doorway to the bathhouse, barking in Chinese orders to his workers.

Then Harley Boone stepped onto the boardwalk.

"You're Dooley Monahan, ain't you?" The man smoked a cheroot cigar, which he pulled from his mouth with his gloved left hand. His right hand rested on the out-turned butt of a Colt revolver on his left hip. That wasn't his only gun, either, for on his right hip another gun, this one with the butt facing the back, hung in a black leather holster decorated with pewter conchos.

A lean man with a pale face pitted with pockmarks and the coldest eyes Dooley had ever seen, Harley Boone wore a black hat with a flat crown, a ribbon tie of purple with yellow polka dots over a crimson shirt of silk, a vest of black leather, tan britches with thin black stripes tucked inside black boots that came up to his knees. The gloves he wore were leather, and his teeth were yellowed from tobacco, although one of the front top ones sparkled from the silver filling.

Dooley could tell when a man was sick, and Harley Boone was a sick, sick man, probably from consumption, the way his lips and eyes looked, maybe something else. He was the kind of man, Dooley figured, who hoped to meet someone faster on the draw than he was.

Of course, Dooley did not want to find out if he was faster.

"I'm Dooley Monahan," he said.

The man wheezed . . . consumption, Dooley figured . . . and flipped the cigar into the muddy street.

"You insulted my mother, Dooley," the gunman lied. "So make your play. I aim to kill you."

Dooley slowly raised his left hand and thumbed toward the door of the bathhouse and barbershop.

"You don't mind if I get a bath and shave first, do you, Mr. Boone?"

Harley Boone stared at Dooley, then at Chin Lu, then at Butch Sweeney, at the sign hanging over the door, and then back at Dooley.

That's when he laughed, and nodded.

"Sure, Dooley. I never want to send a man to hell till he's had a chance to clean himself up."

CHAPTER TWENTY

"It might take a while," Dooley told him. "But I'll be out."

"I'll be here," Harley Boone said.

"You might get tired," Dooley said. "Be back here by seven in the morn. I should be clean by then."

Harley Boone had lost his good humor, but he did read the sign, and saw the Chinese barber nodding hopefully at the hired killer.

"You try to run away from me, you gutless coward . . ." Harley Boone paused, waiting for Dooley to go for his Colt at such an insult, but Dooley just scratched his left side that itched like crazy. "You run . . . I'll track you down. A man who insults another man's mother ain't worth spit and don't deserve the fair fight I'm offering him. You got that, Dooley Monahan?"

Dooley stopped scratching. "I don't believe I ever insulted your mother."

The killer straightened. "So now you're calling me a liar. Make your play, clean or not."

Dooley smiled, which caused the gunman to step back, bewildered. "Seven o'clock," Dooley said. "I'll be clean by then. You might not even recognize me. Have a good breakfast. They have real good doughnuts in this town. And the bacon tastes like the hog bathed in maple syrup."

197

He slipped inside the door, followed quickly by Butch Sweeney and Chin Lu, who slammed the door closed.

"What are you doing, Butch?" Dooley asked as he sank into the steaming water and bubbling suds. Man, that felt like paradise.

Butch Sweeney peered through the crack in the door he had opened in the back of Chin Lu's bathhouse and barbershop. "I don't think that's Boone, but someone's definitely watching the alley here to make sure you . . . we . . . don't skedaddle."

"Man," Dooley said as he sank underneath the foam and water and came up quickly shaking his wet hair and grinning. "Never knew a bath could make a man feel so good."

One of Chin Lu's workers came over and drenched Dooley with fresh water.

Dooley motioned at the empty tub near him. "Better fill this one, boys. This one will be pitch-black in a short while, and I want to be real clean."

The door slammed, and Butch Sweeney whirled. "Confound it, man, that's Harley Boone out yonder waiting to gun you down. How come you'd insult a man's mother?"

Dooley grinned. "I never met Harley Boone till just now, Butch. Certainly never said anything bad about his mother, or anyone's mother—if Harley Boone ever had a mother."

Butch came over to the bench in front of Dooley's tub and sat down. One of the Chinese servants offered him a flask, and he accepted, drinking heartily.

"Harley Boone has killed thirty men," Butch said.

"Including Cheater Norris," Dooley said.

"Yeah. I think that's right."

"And Ol' Ole Finkle."

"Well, yeah, but I remember when that happened. Didn't see it. Ol' Ole called Harley Boone a liar, and Harley wouldn't take no insult. Ol' Ole reached for his pistol in his waistband, and Boone shot him down."

"Sounds familiar," Dooley said. "I wonder if Cheater Norris insulted Boone's mother."

"Don't start cracking jokes, Dooley. This is serious. I'd fetch the marshal, but we ain't got no marshal in town no more."

"Did the marshal insult Boone's mother?"

"No, damn it. Quit funning. Cheater Norris didn't even carry a gun." The workers busied themselves filling another tub for Dooley, as his was turning the color of crude oil by then. When they were gone to refill their buckets, Dooley moved to the other tub.

"He didn't carry a gun? And no one thought to file a complaint against Boone? Last I heard, shooting an unarmed man was something like a felony."

199

Butch drank more from the flask.

"Why doesn't this town have a marshal?" Dooley asked.

"I dunno. I hear folks talkin' 'bout it, but they got the vigilance committee, although that guy who writes those articles for the *Ledger*, he keeps writing that it's time for the law, and not hemp justice, to come to Leadville."

The workers came by and dumped more water on Dooley, who nodded with satisfaction and pointed at the tub he had just vacated, now filled with filthy water. "Drain that one, boys, and refill it. I think I'll sleep in that one for a while." They nodded, and Chin Lu translated Dooley's orders.

"Your bathwater's getting cold, Butch." Dooley motioned at the tub that was starting to lose its steam. Then Dooley leaned over and yelled at Chin Lu, "Hey, could you order some supper for Butch and me? Maybe some whiskey for Butch? And get some supper and drinks for yourselves, too. That sound fine?"

"Fine," Chin Lu said as Dooley pointed at his money belt hanging on a hook near the new duds he had brought with him from the clothing emporium.

"Get in the water, Butch," Dooley said. "It'll make you feel better. There's nothing to worry about." He paused, suddenly uncertain. "What time does the *Ledger* come out?"

"What?"

"The *Ledger*. The newspaper. What time can a person buy a copy?"

Butch Sweeney stared at his friend as if he had gone daft. "I dunno. I see them carting bundles to the stores and places when I'm hitching up the team. That's right around daybreak. Before the six o'clock whistle sounds for the mines."

The answer appeared to satisfy Dooley, who dunked his head underneath the fresh water again.

When he came up, smiling again, he motioned at the tub. "Come on, Butch. I'm paying for this, and if I'm clean and smelling sweet, you should be, too, else you might spoil my appetite. Don't fret, pard. Harley Boone won't kill me."

"How can you be so sure?" Butch Sweeney worked the bar of soap furiously underneath his left arm.

"Sure about what?" Dooley was lathering up his untrimmed beard for the fifth time.

"About Boone? He gunned down that old miner. He shot the county clerk deader than a dog. And he has shot four or five others in town, and I don't know how many more before he got here shortly after we got here."

"Thirty men," Dooley said. "I assume that includes Ol' Ole Finkle and Cheater Norris."

"Confound it, man!" Water slopped over the sides of Butch Sweeney's tub as the young

201

cowboy turned stagecoach operator lost his cool again. "This ain't nothin' to laugh at, pard. That's a cold-blooded killer out there. Waitin' to gun you down like a sick dog."

"He won't kill me," Dooley said.

"How can you be so sure of yourself, Dooley? I know you did in Jason Baylor and a bunch of other gunmen, and I know you ended the reign of that bunch of bad hombres up in Nebraska or Wyoming or wherever that was . . . but . . ."

Chin Lu came in with the food. Dooley rinsed his beard.

"As long as the *Ledger* comes out in time," Dooley said, "we don't have anything to worry about." He looked at the clock on the wall. "But we do have plenty of time to kill before morning comes. I might take a nap in some fresh water, Chin Lu, after we eat. And then . . . do you happen to have a deck of cards we can borrow to pass the time?"

It was a façade. Dooley had learned that word while in Abilene, Kansas. Someone had pointed at all those false-front buildings down Front Street, years ago, back when Wild Bill was still marshaling in that cow town. Dooley never considered himself a man of letters, but he did like the word.

Façade.

It had a nice ring to it.

Of course, Dooley was showing big, like the false fronts in Abilene, Ogallala, Dodge City, Julesburg—well, maybe not Julesburg, or Julesburg as Dooley had seen it—and even Leadville. Inside, he knew a million things could go wrong and leave him dead.

He did not want to face Harley Boone, but he knew he would if he had to . . . and if things did not go as planned, he would. But he also knew he did not want Butch Sweeney to get killed on his account. And Butch, loyal as Blue and General Grant, would try something if Dooley didn't act like he was as calm and relaxed and manly and heroic as Buffalo Bill Cody.

A few things he had managed to figure out. Harley Boone had killed Ol' Ole Finkle, but Dooley wasn't sure what had caused that crime. Killing Cheater Norris was much easier to solve. That was to give George Miller a job to fill, to let George Miller get the appointment as county clerk and have access to mining claims and all sorts of official documents. George Miller had a worthless deed that lacked any legal standing in the state of Colorado—or so the attorney Cohen had told Dooley, and charged Dooley Leadville prices for his time and wisdom—and George Miller had turned out to be a greedy criminal.

Dooley just had to live through tomorrow morning. He kept his Colt .45 close, never out of reach, just in case Boone lost his composure and came charging in, unwilling and unable to wait until morning to earn whatever George Miller had offered the cold-blooded assassin to do in Dooley Monahan. And he had to keep Butch Sweeney's mind off making some damn fool play that would get the kid killed.

Six baths later, Dooley dried himself off and pulled on his new long-handle underwear and retired to the barber chair as Chin Lu prepared to cut off his beard and mustache and then give him a close shave. Dooley kept his Colt in his right hand, resting on his belly, as the barber worked his magic.

That came after supper. Chinese food. Spicy noodles with bits of chicken and all sorts of vegetables and things Dooley did not know what anyone called them or where they grew, but they had a fantastic flavor.

The tonic the barber slapped on Dooley's fine face tingled but smelled sweet, and then Dooley asked for another bath, a warm one. He removed his long-handle underwear and sank into the soothing waters again.

"It sure is nice," Dooley said.

"What?" Butch asked. "The water?"

"Being rich," Dooley said, and winked.

"I'll carve that on your tombstone, pard," Butch Sweeney said. He looked at the clock on the wall. "In about eight hours from now."

CHAPTER TWENTY-ONE

Eight hours. That kind of wait would make even the best gunmen a tad jumpy, on edge. Harley Boone would be awake all night, wondering, fretting, knowing that if Dooley managed to slip away during the night, and get out of Leadville, then Harley Boone would not get paid whatever George Miller was offering to pay him for willful and premeditated murder made to look like just another gunfight on some Western boomtown's streets.

Dooley, on the other hand, slept like a baby.

"It time. It time. You go now. You go."

Dooley's heavy eyes opened and he saw Chin Lu staring at him. The barber and bather did not look happy.

"Morning," the Chinese man said, and gestured angrily at the streets starting to show signs of life in the early-morning light. "Morning. You here all night. No one else come. Me need miners to pay rent. No pay you here all night."

Dooley rose from the cot he had slept on, cursing himself for sleeping at all. Harley Boone could have come in during the night and shot Dooley full of holes.

"I think," Dooley said as he yawned and set

the Colt .45 on the bench, "that you were paid pretty well." He adjusted his long-handle underwear and moved to the clothes still hanging on the hooks by the bathtubs. Butch Sweeney sat in one of the tubs—all of the tubs had been emptied of water during the night—with his hat for a pillow and some towels over his body for a blanket. He snored contentedly. The half-empty bottle of whiskey on the floor near the tub must have served as mighty fine sleeping medicine.

Dooley found his money belt and pulled out a greenback. "I want you to do me a favor, sir," he said, and handed the note with two zeros after a one at the owner of the barbershop and bathhouse. "Buy two of today's *Ledgers*. Take one to George Miller's office. Give it to him. Not the kid working for him. To your county clerk. Do you understand that?"

Chin Lu looked skeptical. "He no be in."

"He'll be in. He might not have to open his office for"—Dooley glanced at the clock—"two more hours, but I'll guarantee you he'll be inside and looking out the window." He waited.

Mr. Chin Lu took the note.

"Bring the other paper here. With some coffee." He thought that, should things not go the way he expected, maybe he should treat this morning as though it was his last on earth. There still were even odds that it might be. "And some doughnuts and that really good bacon that has a sweetness to it like candy."

The man looked at Dooley as though his brain might have been damaged by all the bathwater and suds last night.

"Or just bacon," Dooley said.

The man left, closing the door behind him, and Butch Sweeny stirred in the tub, lowered his hat, and opened his eyes sleepily.

Dooley busied himself getting dressed. New socks. New boots, kind of stiff, but the leather would break in after a few months in a saddle. Fine pants with nice suspenders, a real silk shirt—sort of like the one Harley Boone was wearing yesterday, only blue, not crimson—and a double-breasted vest, a silver pocket watch and chain, to stick into one of the many pockets, a good paper collar, a black string tie, and a brand-spanking-new hat that fit even better now that Dooley's hair had been cut to a manageable length.

He looked mighty fine, he had to admit as he stared at the mirror behind the barber's chair in the haircutting portion of Chin Lu's business.

"Mighty fine," Dooley said to himself, and added, just so he wouldn't feel so cocksure on a morning that could be his last. "For a façade."

"Damn it!"

Dooley tightened the buckle on his gun belt

and moved to the bathhouse part of Chin Lu's building, tugging on the Colt in the holster.

The back door slammed, the lock was bolted, and Butch Sweeney, still in his clothes he had put back on after his one bath last night, stomped his boots on the floor.

"What's the matter?" Dooley asked.

"That guard. That fellow out back watching the alley."

Dooley waited.

"He's still out there." Butch slammed a fist into his palm. "Hoped he might have fallen asleep at least."

Dooley smiled. "It's all right," he said. "You'll feel better. I sent Chin Lu to fetch us some coffee and breakfast."

"I'd feel better," Butch said, "if you'd sent him to fetch the soldier boys at Fort Garland."

"They wouldn't get here in time, Butch," Dooley told him. "That fort's a far piece from Leadville."

Butch found his hat, pulled it on his head, and started toward Dooley, but stopped, frowning, staring out the window.

"He's out there," Butch said. "On the board-walk. Smoking a cigar. Looks real sure of himself."

He did not have to tell Dooley who he was talking about, and Dooley did not want to look out that window and see Harley Boone waiting for him. That might be just enough to crumble this façade.

That's when the door opened, and Dooley smelled coffee and hot doughnuts.

"You must be hungry, Butch," Dooley said, and he moved into the barbershop portion of Chin Lu's business. But in that room, with his nerves starting to prick him and trouble him, and last night's Chinese supper rocking harshly in his stomach, Dooley felt his voice crack as he asked, "I don't see a newspaper, Chin Lu."

The man set the bags and the pot of coffee on the table filled with tonics and potions and razors and shaving mugs. His left hand disappeared around his back and drew out a *Leadville Ledger* from his back pocket.

Dooley couldn't hold his nerves in check. He stepped forward, practically tore the paper from the Chinese barber's hand, and folded it open.

He could breathe again.

He lowered the paper and watched Chin Lu fill a mug with coffee, and then another. But Dooley wasn't sure he could drink coffee and he certainly didn't trust maple-cured bacon and sweet doughnuts in his stomach just now.

"The county clerk?" Dooley managed.

Chin Lu lifted a second mug, and Dooley felt Butch Sweeney behind him.

"Yes," Chin Lu said. "He there. I give paper."

Dooley's appetite returned, but only slightly.

• • •

"Dooley Monahan, you low-down yeller dog. I'm calling you out!" Harley Boone must have gotten up on the wrong side of the bed this morning. "And if you don't step out on the street in five minutes, I'm coming in with revolvers in both hands, and I'm blasting you to hell, your pard with the red hair to hell, that Chinaman to wherever it is men of his skin go, and then I'm burning the building and everyone in it to the ground. Do you hear me?"

Dooley was stepping out the door before Harley Boone had finished.

He had read about times like this, in dime novels and newspapers that printed more falsehoods than facts, but until this morning in Leadville, he had never seen anything like this except in his mind when he read those wild blood-and-thunders.

Harley Boone stepped off the boardwalk and into the mud. The notorious killer had not slept last night. At least, he had not changed his clothes.

Same leather gloves. Same two gun belts bulked over each other, one Colt's gun butt facing out front, the other toward the back. Same fancy holsters that advertised both a leather shop and a silversmith. Same flat-crowned hat. Same purple ribbon tie with yellow polka dots, only the tie had been loosened, and the paper collar unbuttoned. The crimson silk shirt was ruffled and stained with sweat and beer or whiskey or something. The pants looked less pressed than they had yesterday, and the boots were caked with mud, some fresh, a lot dried. Dooley wanted to think that Harley Boone had done quite a bit of pacing over the night.

Of course, his face remained pale, the eyes held no humor, and the silver filling sparkled as the sun cleared the mountaintops.

He had crushed the cheroot underneath his boot heel on the boardwalk before stepping into the street and crossing about halfway before stopping and smiling at Dooley Monahan. The eyes were dead. The smile held no humor.

Dooley grimaced as his brand-new boots sank into mud on his side of the street.

"You called my mama a bad name, Dooley Monahan," Harley Boone called out as though anyone was listening other than Dooley Monahan in Leadville that morning.

It was too early for most businesses to open. The cafés and hotels were farther down the street. Here most buildings remained shuttered. No one roamed the streets, on the boardwalks or on the muddy roads. Even Chin Lu had closed the door and drawn the shade as soon as Dooley had stepped outside. Whoever had been watching in the alley probably was there, but Dooley was not a greenhorn. He would not turn to see if that killer was there. That's the chance a man like Harley Boone would be waiting for.

Besides, Dooley knew Butch Sweeney would be watching that man, if he indeed remained in the alley.

If anyone had seen Leadville this day, at least on this street, they would have figured they were in a ghost town. That's what Dooley had meant. You read about things like this in showdowns in dime novels. You didn't think they actually happened this way, but Dooley's folks had always told him that you learned something new every day.

And Dooley's pa had opined: *"If you live long enough, you'll see it for yourself."*

Dooley wet his lips.

"I said," Harley Boone repeated, "that you called my mama a filthy name. I won't abide that. Go for your gun."

"I don't think I said anything about your mother, Mr. Boone," Dooley said.

"Now you're calling me a liar. No man calls me a liar."

A door slammed. Dooley thought he might be able to breathe again. For a moment, he thought it would happen just like this, on a deserted street in a deserted town, two gunfighters facing each other, both drawing their guns, two shots sounding like one, and one of the gunmen falling dead in the mud with a bullet straight through his heart.

Even money that Dooley would have been the dead one.

But Dooley had lived long enough to see it himself.

"Wait a minute, Boone!"

Dooley dared not breathe, and certainly would not look down the boardwalk, even though he heard the boots pounding on the planks, slugging through the mud on the street and thundering against the wooden planks on the next block.

The voice rose into almost a panic: "I said, wait. Wait. Don't go for your guns, boys!"

"What the hell . . ." Boone snarled.

Dooley let out a short breath, but did not move his hand from the Colt holstered on his hip.

The footsteps halted. The door to the Chinese bathhouse and barbershop opened. Dooley figured that would be Butch Sweeney stepping outside, just in case George Miller had come along to shoot Dooley in his back.

"I think," Dooley heard George Miller say as he gasped for breath. "I . . . think . . ."

It seemed like ten months limped past before Miller could finish.

". . . there's been . . . a . . . mistake."

"Mistake?" Harley Boone looked as though he had just been poleaxed.

CHAPTER TWENTY-TWO

The sucking sound told Dooley that George Miller had just stepped off the boardwalk into the muddy street. The noise came closer to Dooley's right, and he tensed, ready to draw the .45 and start blasting at George Miller, Harley Boone, whoever it was still hiding in that alley on the side of Chin Lu's place, and George Miller again . . . if he had enough time. Yet he breathed a little easier as Miller slogged through the mud and stopped at the gunfighter's side. This morning's copy of the *Leadville Ledger*, which Miller held in his left hand, came up.

Speaking in whispers, the two men talked for a few minutes, the newspaper coming up a bit, Miller pointing to it with his right hand, Harley Boone grimacing and snarling and not understanding hardly anything, Dooley figured, that Miller tried to explain.

The sun crept higher. A dog—not Blue, it wasn't his bark—let out a racket somewhere to the north. A rooster crowed. Yet nobody came down this street, although Dooley glanced behind him quickly to see that Chin Lu had stepped outside, staring with a face filled with bewilderment.

Butch Sweeney had the same expression on his face.

At length, Harley Boone shook his head, stepped back, spit in the dirt, and glared at Dooley. His mouth opened, but quickly snapped shut, and then he turned and glared at George Miller.

"Do it." Dooley could read George Miller's lips.

The gunman faced Dooley again, spit again, and said in a tone as icy as the previous winter's winds: "Reckon I mistook you for somebody else, pilgrim. My mistake." The last two words came out like a bitter cough, and Boone wheeled around, moving quickly back to the boardwalk, where he stuck another cheroot into his mouth and struck a match on the rough-hewn column and lit his cigar as he walked hurriedly to the nearest saloon.

It wasn't open, either, but Boone smashed open the door with a solid kick and stormed inside. Dooley could hear the chairs and maybe even tables overturning as the hired killer made his way to the bar.

Only then did Dooley feel the pressure in his brain begin to recede. He felt as if he could breathe again, but he stood there, waiting for his muscles to relax, to cooperate, and watched George Miller walk past him. Miller did not make eye contact, and his face showed pure rage.

"You're a dead man, Dooley," he whispered as he passed. "Mark my words. You're dead."

The county clerk made it to the boardwalk, wadded up the newspaper, and tossed it in the mud as he stormed back toward his office.

When Dooley breathed again, he stood in the mud, staring down the street, watching George Miller move down the walk, huffing like a locomotive climbing a hard grade. A door opened on the other side of the street, and a man poked his head out. A window cracked open. He thought he could hear hushed conversations. Looking farther down the streets, he caught a glimpse of a curtain moving in the top story of the Hotel Tabor. He made himself believe that was Julia Cooperman—he decided to forget that she was married to that scoundrel Miller—and that she was relieved to see Dooley wasn't lying dead in the mud.

It didn't make him feel that much better, but he moved back toward the barbershop and bathhouse, where Butch Sweeney took off his hat, scratched his head, and asked:

"What the Sam Hill just happened there, pard?"

"I still don't understand," Butch said as he pushed his scrambled eggs around his plate with a fork.

They sat in the busy restaurant that served those tasty doughnuts. Dooley was on his second dozen. It's a wonder, he thought, how hungry you can feel after feeling you might puke your guts out and then learn that you're going to live through this day, at least.

Dooley washed down the last of the pastry that was filled with apples and cinnamon and set the coffee cup on the table.

He pointed at the *Ledger*.

"That's a notice of my filing claim on the mine," Dooley said, and tapped at the woodcut image.

"I understand that." Butch kept pushing the eggs around. He had hardly taken a bite.

"The story also says that I have sent notices to the United States marshal in Denver, the *Denver Telegram*, and that I have even filed a will with an attorney." Dooley sipped the last of the coffee. "I didn't say which attorney. Figured that would be wise." Harley Boone might decide that J. T. Cohen had insulted his mother and called him a liar, too.

"So?"

Dooley grinned. "They can't kill me to get the mine. That's what this means. Miller knows that. If I die, the *Denver Telegram* will start reporting on things, causing a ruckus, and the U.S. marshal will come here to investigate. Plus, I have filed a last will and testament—"

The redheaded cowboy quit playing with his fork and food and pretending to eat. "Don't you think that's dangerous?"

"What . . . making out a will?"

Butch Sweeney nodded. "It's bad luck."

"It's keeping me alive."

Sweeney shook his head. "It'll jinx you. Man I knowed, old cowboy up in Utah. Pat Powell. You recollect him? No, no, I think that wasn't at the ranch where you saved my bacon. Well, anyway, he once stepped on a rusty nail. And took a fever. He had the old cookie, Jasper Gibson, make out his last will and testament." Butch snapped his fingers. "That's all it took. Come down with the lockjaw and croaked."

"You're one superstitious kid, Butch."

"Damn right. And I'm still alive."

Dooley grinned. "So am I."

"For now." Butch slid his plate to the other side of the table, leaned forward, and, setting his elbows on the tablecloth, clasped his hands with the thumbs sticking out and rested his chin on the thumbs.

"It ain't just Miller and Harley Boone you got to worry about, chum," Sweeney whispered. "If that mine is as rich as you say it is, what it assays out to a ton, you'll have every silver baron in town after that hole in the ground. And that means they'll be after you."

Dooley laughed and reached for the last doughnut, waiting as the waitress refilled the two coffee cups and took away Butch's plate of half-eaten breakfast.

"I'm not a fool, Dooley," Butch said, and

Dooley lost that smile. "I've been in this burg longer than you have. So has Julia. I've seen things. I've seen how those barons can take over a mine, one with a legal claim to it. They got lawyers, too, and they don't need no hired gun like Harley Boone. They ain't low-down cutthroats like George Miller. They don't use guns to get what they want. They use power. And they got plenty of power."

Dooley did not finish that last doughnut.

Although Butch Sweeney offered him a place to bunk in his shack, Dooley declined. Just in case Sweeney was right about the silver barons, Dooley didn't want his old pard to wind up getting hurt, or even killed. He decided that he should not flaunt his newfound wealth by taking a room at one of the fanciest hotels, so he found that hotel where he had stayed when he first arrived in Leadville— the one with the really good bacon in the café next door. It wasn't that fancy, but a good hotel with a good reputation. The Millers had checked out, Dooley knew, after George was appointed county clerk. They now stayed in the Hotel Tabor with all the silver barons and powerful players in Colorado mining ventures.

He had to hire a bookkeeper. He had to hire a foreman. He let the foreman hire the miners, but Dooley kept the two guards on the payroll. It was interesting, he decided, being a real man of capital. Blue could grow old and fat. So could General Grant, but Dooley took them to the mine every day. Sometimes, he even left the offices the carpenters had built—at Leadville prices, mind you—and went back into the mine. He had always had a curious nature, and he wanted to see how miners—real miners—did their jobs.

The miners seemed to appreciate this, that an owner, a rich, rich man by their standards, would take a drill or hammer in his hand, or even tap sticks of dynamite into a hole and light the fuse. Dooley also paid them a nickel more than most of the mining companies in town. He didn't want to become an evil silver baron.

Actually, what he wanted was to go back to punching cattle. That was more his nature, but, this was his dream. Not being stuck in an office, signing checks and drafts and legal things, or talking things over with his foreman or his bookkeeper, although half the time Dooley didn't have any idea what they were saying to him or what he was saying back to them.

Being rich wasn't all it was cracked up to be.

Owning a silver mine was even worse.

Then there were the nights. He attended one ball at the opera house, and another highfalutin party at the Hotel Tabor. George Miller and Julia were at both events, and seeing them dance at the hotel soiree made Dooley nauseous. He decided not to attend any other parties, unless maybe the miners invited him to a poker game or to join them for a beer at one of the many saloons in town.

Every day, at his hotel, when he was eating bacon and eggs at the dining room or taking his supper, or when he was at the office being bored and not doing actual work in the mines, the silver barons would bring him offers. Oh, not personally. Silver barons were too big to handle trifling affairs like meeting with this lucky son of a gun who had been a cowboy and bounty hunter all his life and just happened to land on one of the richest claims in the Rockies. But they would send their minions, men in plaid sack suits with carpetbags filled with paperwork and cash.

They would make Dooley an offer for the mine.

It was rather tempting, seeing all that cash money, but Dooley had to explain to them, at least once a day, sometimes more. Sometimes the same man in the plaid sack suit would see Dooley at breakfast, get dismissed and rejected, and return that afternoon with another bid before the six o'clock whistle sounded.

"You need to understand," Dooley tried to explain. He had said this so often he had the thing memorized. "Tell Mr. So-and-So that I appreciate the offer. I truly do. It's a mighty fine offer, and generous, befitting Mr. So-and-So's reputation as a generous and wonderful man. But it's like this, you see, I just always dreamed of mining. I missed my chance in Alaska. I missed my chance in Deadwood. I'm not saying that I want to do this all my life, but, well, you see, it's just something that I want to do. See me again later, though, but let me enjoy this adventure for a spell."

They would see him again later. Usually later in the week, or maybe early the next week, and sometimes even later in that very same afternoon.

So here sat Dooley in his office, flexing his fingers after signing so many papers that morning. He looked down at Blue, who was curled up on the bed Dooley had bought for him—not a real bed, but a bed, more like a cushion, that the really fancy emporium sold for dogs and cats—snoring away. Dooley thought about leaving the office, once his fingers did not ache again from clutching that ink pen, maybe planting some dynamite in the hole, or even joining the workers as they took their dinner break. Being one of the boys again, and not just some silver baron.

The bookkeeper tapped on the door and opened it. Blue did not stir.

"Yes?" Dooley said with a heavy sigh.

"Someone to see you, Mr. Monahan."

Dooley sighed even heavier. "I've told you, Jarvis, that you need to call me Dooley. Not Mr. Monahan. Dooley."

"Yes, sir." Jarvis looked impatient.

"Show him in." Dooley sighed again.

"It is not a man, Mr. Monahan, but a woman," Jarvis said.

CHAPTER TWENTY-THREE

She took his breath away.

Dooley blinked, wondering if he were dreaming, then realized he just gawked, might have even been drooling, and he shut his mouth and sat up quickly. Blue awakened from his slumbers, barked, and hurried off his plush pillow, tail wagging. Blue indeed was drooling. Yet Julia Alice Cooperman Miller laughed, and knelt, putting her knees and that fine dress on the dirty floor of Dooley's office.

"Blue," Julia said, scratching the merle-colored shepherd's ears, laughing as he rolled onto his back and Julia rubbed the dog's stomach. She laughed until tears flowed down her cheeks, and Blue looked so contented that he probably wished Julia would have kept that up the rest of the day.

Recovering, Dooley looked at his clerk, staring in disbelief, and Dooley pushed himself out of his desk and said, "That will be all, Jarvis. Close the door behind you."

The clerk hurried, but as he pulled the door shut, Dooley called out, "And, Jarvis . . ."

As the door stopped, the clerk raised his eyes over his spectacles.

"Keep your damned mouth shut," Dooley said. The door closed.

Dooley found the pitcher of water and filled a glass, realized that glass was filthy, and found another. He had only two glasses on the table in the corner, but, thankfully, that one was clean. He filled it and held it in his hands, watching his hands tremble so much that he thought he would spill the water before Miss Julia . . . Mrs. Julia, damn it . . . finished rubbing the dog's stomach.

She did, though, and looked up at Dooley. He started to offer her the glass, then realized he ought to help her up first, so he set the glass on the edge of his desk and stepped toward her, extending both hands.

When she accepted his hands, he felt the electricity shoot through his body. His heart ached as it pounded against his chest.

Her gloves were white satin, and her dress a pretty cambric suit of blue and gray, the skirt knife-plaited, the top featuring a cutaway basque with a striped vest. Her hair was curled, and diamond earrings hung from her ears. He could not believe just how beautiful she was as he lifted her to her feet and reluctantly released his hold on those trembling fingers.

Dooley gestured at the chair across from his desk, and Julia sat and looked for something to wipe the tears off her face. He stared for a moment, trying to believe that this was the loudmouthed wild hellion he had found in a cave in Arizona Territory. He could not believe how much she had grown up, or how beautiful she had become, over those few years. Then he quickly moved to the coatrack behind his desk and fished a handkerchief out of the pocket of his Prince Albert that he never liked to wear except when he was outside or at some formal party.

He handed her the white cotton, and she reached for it, muttering an apology, and tried not to look at him. She focused on the handkerchief, which Dooley involuntarily pulled away from her fingers.

He stared.

She looked at him in surprise.

He stared harder.

It had never really been like Julia to apply rouge on her face, but she had. Only the tears of joy from playing with Blue had caused the makeup to run with streaks, and now he understood why she had applied the creamy stuff underneath her eyes.

Realizing that sweet Julia was trying to hide a wicked bruise, Dooley swore under his breath.

She looked down, and Dooley realized his mistake and extended his hand and the offering to her.

"Here," he said.

She took it and held it under her eyes, then began wiping away the makeup. He took the handkerchief when she was finished, tossed it onto his desktop, and helped her to her feet, and guided her toward the chair. Next he found the water, in the relatively clean glass, and slipped that into her hands. She sipped, thanked him in a hollow voice, and Dooley stood there like a knot on a log, before realizing he was acting the fool. He told Blue to go back to the bed, but the dog lay down at Miss . . . Mrs. . . . Julia's feet, and Dooley returned to his desk.

His throat was parched, and he downed the water in his not-as-clean glass in a few gulps. His knees began to buckle, so Dooley sank into his desk.

He stared.

She looked at her feet and at Blue.

He tried to find some papers to move from one pile to another.

Refusing to look at Dooley, Julia asked, "How old is Blue now?"

"I don't know." Dooley moved the pile of papers back to where the pile had been when Julia first entered his office. "Ummm . . . I don't know how old he was when I first met him."

"There are gray hairs on his coat now," she observed.

Dooley ran his fingers through his hair. "I've got more than he has nowadays."

She laughed, not really a hard laugh, more like a sigh. A real sigh followed, and she looked up, sipped water, set the glass on the floor, and finally just looked deeply into Dooley's eyes.

"Oh, Dooley," she said.

He had no response.

She filled her lungs with air, exhaled, and at last raised her head to look Dooley eye to eye.

When she did not say anything, Dooley tried, "How did you get here?"

"I rented a horse at one of the liveries."

"A horse?"

"Sidesaddle," she said.

"Sidesaddle?"

Her head tilted. "I mean . . ." It was Dooley's turn to draw in a deep breath, hold it, let it out, and try to sound like he still retained all of his faculties. "We're working on grading a road, clearing some of the forests and rocks, basically following the creek . . . but . . . well, it's rough country for anybody."

"No rougher than Arizona Territory," she said.

He made himself smile, to take her mind off whatever was troubling her. But he had good inclination of what her problems were, what had brought her all the way from the Hotel Tabor to Dooley's mine. He thought he might break every bone in George Miller's body for giving sweet, innocent Julia a black eye that she had to hide with rouge like some two-bit . . . He stopped the mean thoughts, and remembered that he was trying to cheer her up. "But sidesaddle?"

He grinned, and felt his heart skip when she grinned back and sipped more of the water he had poured.

"Have you seen Butch?" Dooley asked. "I haven't seen him in a spell."

She shrugged. "Not much. I think he's in Denver now, or on his way, maybe on his way back. He stays busy with the stage line."

"And you?"

She shrugged. "Oh, you know. I . . . ." The gentleness left her eyes. "I stay in the hotel room and stare at the paintings, the china, the silver. And when needed, I accompany George to balls and to the theater and the opera house, and a dinner or a supper and sometimes even a breakfast with some of the silver barons in Leadville."

"Well," Dooley said, "I reckon I'm a silver baron." He found his sack in the bottom left-hand drawer and brought it out, cringing at the wet spot of grease on the bottom. "You can dine with me." He frowned. "It's only a roast beef sandwich and some taters, fried in bacon grease." He stared at the sack, saw Julia shaking her head, and dropped it back into the drawer, which he slammed shut.

"I reckon you eat a mite better than that."

That pained her, and made Dooley curse himself.

"Dooley," she said. "That's not it. I came here . . ." She caught her breath. "I came here because . . ."

He wanted to leap out of his chair and over the

desk and sweep her into his arms and kiss the tears off her damaged cheek and swear to her that she would be all right, that he would protect her.

What stopped him was when she said, "Dooley, you just have to sell this mine."

He felt as if he had been kneed in the groin. She must have seen the color drain from his face, and he felt he had trouble even stopping the tears from welling in his own eyes. He hated the first thoughts that raced through his mind.

So that's how George Miller is playing this game. He and his filthy-rich pals in the silver-mining business can't buy my mine, so he sends Julia to do his bidding.

"Dooley," Julia cried. "They'll kill you if you don't sell this to them."

"Oh."

Now he despised himself for thinking that even a scoundrel like George Miller could persuade his wife, a beautiful, honest lass like Julia, to do his evil bidding.

He tried to ease her fears. "Julia. They can't kill me. That's why Harley Boone and I didn't shoot it out those weeks, or maybe months, ago. They know that if they kill me, the United States marshal and the *Denver Telegram* and my lawyer will be visiting them and making them pay. I've got what amounts to the best life insurance out there." He wanted her to know how smart he was. "I figured that out myself. And that made Harley

Boone back down. And that's why I'm still here and doing what I always wanted to be doing."

That wasn't entirely true. What Dooley had dreamed of doing was panning for gold, not paying other men to blow up the insides of caves and haul out silver to be taken to the smelter and turned into greenback dollars and double eagle gold pieces to pay off miners and clerks and wagon masters and road builders and carpenters and guards armed with shotguns. When he had taken off for Alaska, and when he had lit out for Deadwood in the Dakota Territory, he had envisioned himself as a grubby old miner, not that far removed from being a bone-weary dirty-outfitted, thirty-a-month-and-found cowhand. Instead, he wore silk shirts and Prince Alberts most of the time and sat behind a desk being bored out of his mind listening to what his clerk and his assistant and his foreman and his accountant and everyone else told him what to do.

It wasn't a hell of a lot of fun being rich. Or being the boss man.

"Dooley," Julia pleaded.

He waved his hand. "I'm safe, Julia." He wanted to add that he could take her with him when he did decide to sell—once he thought he had had enough of mining and once silver prices reached what the accountant and the foreman and his conscience told him was likely to be as

230

good as things would ever get. Or maybe right now. If she'd just ask him to help save her from a scoundrel like George Miller and from a lousy, doomed-from-the-start marriage.

"Dooley." Her voice lost its gentleness, its entreating. Julia's eyes turned as hard as they used to be back in Arizona . . . and San Francisco . . . back when she had been a corncob-rough hellion in her teens and not the genteel wife of a county clerk who aimed to control all of Leadville for himself.

"You need to grow up."

Now she sounded just like Little Miss Loudmouth.

"Quit being a damned fool."

CHAPTER TWENTY-FOUR

Now she sounded more like Butch Sweeney, or the old Dooley Monahan when he was trying to keep him and Butch and Julia alive.

"Do you know who you're up against? This isn't some twenty-dollar gunman like Jackson Taylor or whatever his name was, or his brothers, or anyone else you've gunned down on the streets in defense of your person and just happened to collect a nice bounty for staying alive."

Blue whined.

Dooley felt like joining him.

"These are silver barons. This is George Miller, who isn't just some corrupt clerk who does the biddings of rich, filthy, evil men. Harley Boone is an ant compared to the men out to crush you, Dooley."

"But I've got the U.S. marshal—"

"Damn it, Dooley, listen to me. I'm not the stupid kid you always thought I was. Thought Butch was. A United States marshal can be bought. Do you understand what I'm saying? Any reporter in Denver can be bribed. So can your pettifogging lawyer. You've got to get the hell out of Leadville, Dooley, or they're going to bury you here. And that would kill me. And it would get Butch Sweeney killed, too."

· · ·

"I'm sorry," Julia said after she finally dammed the tears.

"It's all right." At least, he thought he said something, and that was what he had meant to say. *It's all right.* He shook his head. What a stupid thing to say. He stared at the bruise on Julia's cute little face and felt the blood rushing to his head one more time. He wanted to march out of his office, saddle up General Grant, and gallop down the road they were trying to finish grading all the way into Leadville and trash George Miller, just kick him up and down the street and finally out of town.

"You'll do what you always do, Dooley," Julia said, and she pushed herself out of the chair. She meant that Dooley would dismiss her notions and do what he had planned on doing.

Dooley told her: "What I do, is stay alive."

She stared at him, and Dooley grinned. "I've gotten to be pretty good at it."

He waited. He knew it was coming. It had to come. If it didn't, his heart would break right then and there, and he'd be worthless. Harley Boone would have no trouble gunning him down.

There it came. Dooley's heart leaped and he felt ten years younger.

Julia smiled at him. She shook her head, but could not shake off that look.

"You are incorrigible, Dooley Monahan," she

233

told him. The smile left, and she whispered, "You will take care of yourself, won't you?"

"I will," he affirmed. "Now that you've warned me, I'll know what to look out for. Do you need an escort back to Leadville?"

Her head shook.

"You sure? That's barely even a road right now."

"No. I still know how to ride. I still know how to look after myself. And . . ."—her head shook sadly as she frowned and sighed—". . . well . . . it just wouldn't be proper for me to be seen with you, Dooley." Her head lifted, but he saw no tears.

"Do you understand?" she asked.

"Of course," he said. He opened the door, and Julia knelt to pat Blue and whisper a string of pet names at the shepherd, then she held out her right hand. Dooley shook it, then thought: *Was I supposed to kiss it? Would that have been proper had Jarvis saw me do that?*

It was too late. Julia was out of his office and made a beeline for the door. When that door closed, Dooley looked at Jarvis, who busied himself shuffling papers from one side of the desk to the other. Dooley closed the door to his office and moved to the filing cabinet behind the desk. He pulled it open and withdrew the Colt .45 and shell belt, which he usually deposited there every morning when he got to work. This time, he buckled it on, opened the chamber gate, and rotated the cylinder to check the loads. Briefly, he thought about filling the empty chamber—the one underneath the hammer, kept empty as a safety measure—but decided that would be silly. He did not holster the Colt, though, but left it on the top of his desk in plain view.

Then he sat down and tried to focus on some of the papers the clerk said he needed to look at, but Dooley could not make heads or tails out of those things. So he leaned back, stared at the wall, then at Blue, and kept thinking about those days in Arizona and even California.

At some point, Jarvis tapped lightly on the door, opened it, and came in with more papers for Dooley to sign. His face paled at the sight of the Colt, but he swallowed down that fear and told Dooley what he was signing and why and a few other things Dooley did not understand. Dooley answered with a nod, and the clerk left the office. Dooley read the papers, read them carefully, before he signed them.

When the six o'clock whistle blew, Jarvis again opened the door. This time he brought in a tin box and not more papers with figures and legalese and stuff only an attorney-at-law could figure out. The clerk set the box in front of Dooley and stepped back. Sighing, Dooley opened the lid and stared at more gold coins than he had ever seen, not to mention greenbacks stacked to the lip of the box.

"What's this for?" Dooley asked.

"Payday is tomorrow, sir," the little runt said.

"Oh." Dooley nodded as if he understood. "Well, see that the boys get paid."

Jarvis cleared his throat. "Sir, I have already put the payroll into the safe for tomorrow. This is yours, sir."

Dooley blinked. He found it hard to comprehend, especially when Jarvis kept talking.

"Naturally, there is much more money from the silver we have mined over the past month, sir, but that went into the mine's account, a reinvestment, so to speak, sir. You understand, I am sure."

"Well . . ."

"If I were you, sir, I would take that money to the bank and deposit it quickly. Rogues have been known to . . . well . . . you know."

Dooley thanked the clerk and watched him leave, shutting the door behind him. Then Dooley kept staring at the tin box. At length, he counted out thirty dollars in scrip and shoved those bills into his trousers pocket. He also took a twenty-dollar gold piece and slipped it in, as well.

He waited until he heard Jarvis leave, heard the commotion as most of the miners left, waited until darkness came and the only ones left at the mine were Dooley and the two guards with the shotguns. That's when Dooley opened the door and went to the toolshed, fetched a shovel, and paced off twenty yards behind the shed and started to dig.

Banks? Dooley already had what he considered a sizable sum in that bank in town. He saw no need to risk any more, because Dooley remembered a time—not that long ago—when the Dobbs-Handley Gang had robbed the bank in Omaha, Nebraska, and then at another bank in some other town in that state. He remembered hearing about the James-Younger boys robbing that bank in his own home state of Iowa, over in Corydon, and he had read about that bank robbery back in '66 down in Liberty, Missouri—and how that place went out of business a short while after the robbery.

Banks got robbed. People lost their life savings because banks got robbed. Dooley remembered his father, that hardworking farmer who never trusted any bank and always put what little hard money he ever owned in a jar and stuck it back by the pigpens because nobody was going to go digging around near a pigpen if he didn't have to.

There were some pigpens in Leadville, but Dooley figured somebody would see him digging there, as busy as that town was. So he dug here. Then he leaned the shovel against a tree and walked back to his office.

He closed the lid and lifted the box, strained, and let the box slide safely back onto the desktop. That timid little Jarvis, a runt of the litter if Dooley had ever saw one, had managed to get that box from his desk to Dooley's, and here was Dooley straining like a weakling.

Blue yipped, ready to go home. Dooley frowned. "I'm getting soft sitting behind a desk, Blue," he said, "lifting nothing but a pencil or pen all day." An idea struck him, and made him feel good. He went outside and counted the number of miners on the payroll, came back into the office and counted out that number of five-dollar coins. He thought about the guards and Jarvis, and counted out three more. And the foreman. There was another. These, he slid into the big drawer of his desk, and thought the boys would be right pleased at getting a bonus from their boss after work tomorrow.

After sneaking back to the hole, he deposited the tin box. Of course, Jarvis would probably want the tin box back, so he returned to the office, found a couple of sacks, and then hurried back to the hole, careful to make sure he didn't arouse the suspicion of the shotgun-wielding guards. That appeared unlikely as the guards stayed in the mine, keeping any silver thieves out. Which reminded Dooley that maybe he ought to talk to the foreman and Jarvis about having another guard, one to patrol the perimeter of the mine. The safe, for one thing, was in the office. Equipment like shovels and picks did not come cheap at Leadville prices.

Dooley loaded the paper currency into one sack and the coins into another. He started shoveling and pondered on another thought.

But if I hired a guard and he walked around outside, would he see that a hole had been dug here? Mightn't he do some investigating, perhaps digging? And wouldn't two sacks filled with a fortune be more tempting than whatever we paid him, even at Leadville prices?

Dooley kept shoveling, cursing himself. Oh, boy, how he wished he were just that thirty-a-month cowboy again, with no worries except the caring of the boss man's cattle and horses.

He arrived to town late—not that Leadville was asleep—found a café he had never been to, and took his supper there. Dooley told himself he was just seeing if this Chinese joint was worth taking any friends to, but he failed to convince himself of the lie. What Julia had told him stuck with him, and he figured he shouldn't make his moves a pattern.

He did not board General Grant at the livery, but tied him up in the alley that ran behind the hotel. He even took the rear staircase to his room, and drew his Colt before unlocking the door.

"You're being paranoid," he told himself.

"You're being safe," he argued.

He slept that night with a chair hooked under the doorknob, woke before sunbreak, and left Blue in the room.

It was too early to pay a visit to his lawyer or the bank, so he rode out of town and back to the mine.

The boys sure were happy at the bonus they got, and that made Dooley feel better. He mentioned the idea about an extra guard, and the foreman and Jarvis said they would put together some figures and see what it would cost and if it was worth it, the two old skinflints. Again, he worked late, not that he was actually working, and waited till everyone had left after the last shift. He checked on the hole he had dug, saw nothing to make him fear his hiding place had been discovered, and went back to his office. He slept there that night, thinking that he had left Blue enough water and some food and several copies of the *Leadville Ledger* on the floor so the shepherd could do his business.

On Sunday, he went fishing, but took Blue with him. Of course, the water was running too fast to catch any trout, but he felt relaxed, soothed by the rushing water, being out in the woods alone. Of course, his mother had always warned his father about fishing on the Sabbath. It went against her religion. Bad things happened to those who fished on Sunday. But nothing bad happened to Dooley that Sunday. God waited till Monday to punish him.

CHAPTER TWENTY-FIVE

The office of Jonah Terrance Cohen, attorney-at-law, was upstairs of one of Leadville's banks in which Dooley had no deposits. After taking breakfast in the restaurant next to the hotel, Dooley walked down the street, turned the corner, and climbed the rickety staircase that led to the upstairs offices. Jonah Terrance Cohen, J. T. to his pals, had the corner office on the left side of the hallway.

At least, he had.

Oh, his name was still stenciled onto the fancy glass, but tacked to the door was a crudely written note.

FOR RENT
SEE John Price
at Bank
(downstairs)

Dooley felt his breakfast teetering in his stomach, and he caught his breath and hurried back outside, down the stairs, around the corner, and into the bank. He looked around—that early in the morning, the bank had few customers—and walked to the first teller he saw.

"Is John Price in?" Dooley asked.

The teller shook his head. "Should be in—oh, there he is now."

Dooley turned and saw a portly gent with two chins close the door and use a cane as he made his way through one of those banker's gates and toward an office that had a door to it. Hurrying toward the big man, Dooley called out his name. The man turned, smiled, and said, "Yes, sir, what may I do for you this fine morning?"

"It's about the lawyer, Mr. Cohen, upstairs."

"Ah. Do you wish to lease it? It is fine, a good view, and I'm sure you'll find our rates reasonable—for Leadville prices. Come in, sir, come in." He pulled open the office door, but stopped when Dooley said he wasn't here about renting space.

"He was my attorney," Dooley said.

"Oh." The man looked Dooley over, but found him to be a respectable-looking man in his striped britches and coat and ribbon tie and all.

"Do you know where he happened to move to?"

The fat man shook his head. "No. He came in last week, said he was bound for the Sandwich Islands. I guess one of his clients must have won a gigantic lawsuit for Mr. Cohen to be sailing across the Pacific. He certainly was dressed quite prosperous when he came in, and smiling as though he had found the golden goose. He closed his account and left."

The fat head shook again. "But I am certain he will write you when he resettles, or perhaps he has turned his business over to another attorney here in town. I'm sure that is the case . . ."

"Yeah," Dooley said, but he knew better. He thanked the banker and the teller and walked out the door.

Julia had been right. The silver barons could get to an attorney after all. At least he still had his letter with the U.S. marshal in Denver, and with that inkslinger at the *Denver Telegram.*

"Hey, Dooley."

Across the street, George Miller waved him over. "I want you to meet some folks," Miller called out.

Dooley saw two men, one lean and hard, the other fat and pale, standing outside the door to the county clerk's office. They did not look like gunmen, which made Dooley look across the street at the roofs of the buildings. No sunlight reflected off a rifle barrel. He did not see Harley Boone anywhere, and nothing looked out of the ordinary in the alleys. Some riders, about six, wearing dusters, were riding slowly down the street, but did not look to be keeping their horses under a strong rein and ready to give them their head and run over Dooley if he crossed the street. "You're going to worry yourself to death, Dooley Monahan," he told himself, laughed off his paranoia, only to realize that, in his excitement to check in with his lawyer, he had made a mistake. Blue was upstairs again in his hotel room. So was Dooley's gun belt and .45.

After all, respectable mine owners did not go heeled when visiting lawyers.

"Well," Dooley told himself, once he saw how crowded the streets were becoming. "They won't ambush me now. And it's not like those two gents with that scoundrel are the U.S. marshal and the editor at the *Telegram*."

He let a freight wagon cross, then stepped onto the street—dry now, but rutted from all the traffic during the muddy season—and found his way to the clerk's office. Miller and the two strangers remained outside. All were smoking fine cigars.

"Dooley Monahan," George Miller said after removing his cigar, "allow me to introduce you to Richard Blue, deputy U.S. marshal out of Denver. And this, I'm sure you know, is Paul Pinkerton of the *Denver Telegram*."

The lean one was, to Dooley's surprise, the journalist. The fat one was the marshal. Yeah, Dooley thought, fat from taking bribes and living off other folks' misfortune.

Neither made a move to shake Dooley's hand. Dooley unbuttoned his coat. Let them think I am heeled, Dooley figured. That might get me through this day.

"Maybe we can talk again, Dooley, about a business deal." Miller gestured with his cigar in the general direction of Dooley's silver mine. "A lot of things can happen in a town like this."

But, Dooley thought, they can't just gun me down on the streets. The *Leadville Ledger* is an honest newspaper—especially since I've paid them money for advertisements and even pay the $2.50 annual subscription. If I'm killed, murdered most foully, or come to some unfortunate accident, they will investigate.

Not that that'd do me any good, being dead and all.

"What do you think, Dooley?" George Miller asked. "Want to step inside and work out a deal that favors us both?"

You get rich. I stay alive.

Dooley shook his head.

"Suit yourself," Miller said, and stepped into his office. The low-down, bribe-taking federal deputy and scribe for that horrible little rag of a newspaper in Denver followed him. The door closed behind them. The shades remained closed.

Again, Dooley looked up and down the street. Nothing seemed out of the ordinary—no gunmen looking to kill him, no strangers on the rooftops, no Harley Boone anywhere to be found. Dooley decided that maybe, before heading to the livery to get his horse and ride to work—if you could call being a boss work—maybe he would check with the postmaster inside the Wells Fargo station and see, on the very off chance, if lawyer J. T. Cohen had left a forwarding address.

That's where he was going when, halfway across the street, someone sang out:

"The bank's being robbed!"

Dooley froze. He saw the six mounts, remembering those men in the linen dusters from just moments earlier. They were tethered to the hitching rail in front of the bank where J. T. Cohen leased an upstairs office.

When he later found time to think, he realized that the warning about the bank robbery came from behind him. How could that person have known the bank was being robbed? Six horses tethered in front of the bank wasn't out of the ordinary. The shades remained closed inside, so nobody could see what was happening. No guards had been posted outside the bank, drawing attention to himself. And later, Mr. John Price of that very bank reported himself that the bandits did not make off with one single bank note.

Dooley did not freeze long, because the doors of the bank were being pushed open, and a man in a linen duster raised a sawed-off shotgun at Dooley.

He ran, ducking, feeling the whistle of buckshot over his head. One of the horses reared, pulled free of its tether, and crashed into the boardwalk. That gave Dooley a chance because the robber couldn't—at least, he didn't—fire over the horse and try to kill Dooley with his second barrel. Out of the corner of his eye, Dooley saw him dropping the scattergun and moving desperately to catch up the reins to the frightened bay gelding.

Another outlaw came out of the building and fired a shot that tore off a chunk of wood as Dooley rounded that corner. His plan was to keep right on running. Hell, he didn't have a gun, couldn't put up a fight. Another man in a linen duster came around the other corner of the bank and sent a slug that burned Dooley's left ear. He shifted directions and came up the stairs. Gun smoke attacked his nostrils. Gunshots rang in his ears. He heard the wood splintering the wooden steps Dooley climbed three at a time as the man with the six-shooters blazed away. How he managed to reach the top had to be a miracle. He grabbed the knob and turned.

"Oh, hell!"

The door was open just a few minutes earlier when he had discovered J. T. Cohen's office was being rented out. Now some fool had locked the damned thing.

More gunshots sounded. Dooley hoped one of those guns being fired came from that deputy marshal out of Denver. Another bullet smashed the door Dooley was trying to open. He ducked, saw the linen duster–wearing hombre with the six-shooter had reloaded. Then he saw another bank robber in a duster coming around the corner, carrying two pistols. Dooley ran as hard as he could and threw himself against the door, feeling the heat of a bullet tear through his frock coat, and another rip off his fancy hat. Yet the door splintered, a hinge broke off, and Dooley tumbled inside. He landed hard against the floor, rolled over, kicked the door shut, knowing: a lot of good that'll do.

There was no time to catch his breath. He came up and ran, only to catch a shout from outside.

"He's upstairs, Clint!"

Only then did Dooley remember the staircase that led to the offices from the bank lobby.

Footsteps sounded from downstairs on the bank floor. Dooley stopped. Footsteps sounded on the bullet-riddled staircase outside, too. Inside, he saw the shadow, and heard a hammer being clicked.

There were only two exits, and men in linen dusters were coming up those steps. He wanted to think that surely Richard Blue, deputy United States marshal out of Denver, had some honor. That as a duly sworn officer of the law he would try to stop a bank robbery. That he was shooting at men in linen dusters right this very second.

The steps sounded closer outside.

Of all the times to leave my Colt in my room! Dooley thought.

He was a dead man. Because he had not taken precautions. Hell, Julia had warned him.

Damn it all, he thought, *I really need a gun.*

The bad men climbing the stairs certainly wouldn't be loaning him any of theirs.

That's when he saw the office to his left, next door to the vacant office of J. T. Cohen, attorney-at-law.

It had a fancy glass window with stenciling on it, too, and no FOR RENT sign tacked to the door.

Just as the man in the linen duster from the inside staircase jumped into the second-story hallway, and just as two men wearing dusters crashed through the already-broken door to the outside corner staircase, Dooley hurled himself against the pretty cursive stenciling on the door's window.

The pretty glass and the words—O'BRIAN'S GUN SHOP—disintegrated underneath Dooley's weight.

CHAPTER TWENTY-SIX

He ignored the blood on his cheeks and hands, but couldn't block out the pain as he pushed himself up quickly with his left hand, and a shard of glass ripped through his palm. Groaning, Dooley came up to the left side of the door and reached with his right hand for whatever he could grab to defend himself.

There was no time. The man from the inside staircase rammed his Colt through the opening Dooley had made through what once had been a window of fancy glass. Dooley saw the revolver. The man saw Dooley, and tried to turn his hand. Only, an instant later, the man had no hand at all.

Dooley saw the heavy bowie knife, with the D-shaped bronze guard, in his right hand. He saw the man stagger away, spraying blood against the ruined door and into the hallway outside.

A knife? Someone had left a big bowie knife on the counter in a place that repaired guns?

Curses came from the other two gunmen in the upstairs hallway, but could not drown out the cries of the man whose hand Dooley had just chopped off. Another shot rammed against the door's frame, and Dooley dropped below the shattered glass. The man with two pistols appeared first, his revolvers already cocked, his face masked with grim determination as he trained the two barrels on Dooley.

"Take this!" the outlaw shouted.

He took it instead, took that knife Dooley threw through the opening. The blade drilled him plumb center, moving through ribs and muscle and into the badman's heart. That impact was enough to force his two hands to move slightly. Both guns roared, filling O'Brian's office with smoke, but both .44-40 slugs whistled past Dooley's ears. Dooley couldn't see the man because of the thick smoke from his two pistols, but despite the ringing in his ears from the close range of the .44-40's reports, he heard the man with the bowie knife in his chest hit the floor.

As a cowboy, Dooley had seen many a waddie who got a finger sliced off trying to dally his lariat around the saddle horn. A few times Dooley had come close to losing a digit himself. But he had never seen a bloody hand cut off with a bowie knife. It was enough to make a body sick.

Dooley had no time to be sick.

He pried the Colt from the sticky fingers of the cleaved-off hand. The gun came up—it was already cocked by Clint, or whoever it was who was still yelping out in the hallway—and he touched the trigger as the third man, the one who had cut loose with Dooley and shot up the doorsteps outside, tried to gun down Dooley.

The man in the duster probably would have

killed Dooley, but he must have slipped on the blood spraying out of the arm of the first bank robber. That spoiled his aim. Dooley's shot missed, too, but only because the gunman went crashing to the floor. He heard the man try to rise, but his boots went out again from under him, and he rocked the floor. By that time, Dooley had risen, thumbed back the hammer of the Colt, and quickly pushed his torso through the ruined window.

There was a saying Dooley remembered that went something along the lines of: You never kick a man when he's down.

Dooley did not kick the man, but he sure shot that low-down snake lying on the floor.

It was not cold-blooded butchery or revenge. The killer in the now-bloodstained linen duster was bringing up his Colt, about to try to blow off Dooley's head, when Dooley shot him dead center and killed the bank robber instantly. His gun hand crashed against the door, and slid down.

Kicking the bloody hand across the gun shop, Dooley pulled open the door. He glanced at the staircases, and at the man with the bloody mess of a right arm, and came outside. Quickly, he knelt, trying to keep his new boots out of the pools of blood on the floor—although his own leaking left palm did its share of bloodying his duds—and pried the Colt from the hand of the dead man on the floor.

Something clicked, and Dooley spun, seeing the recently one-handed killer in a linen duster bring up a Remington over-and-under derringer in his left hand. The little pistol popped, but the man was in a lot of pain and was likely not good with both hands. Besides, even at close range, a derringer wasn't always reliable.

Grimacing, the man tried to shoot the second barrel, but Dooley pulled the trigger. The man spun, dropped the derringer, and tumbled down the stairs, leaving a trail of blood on the wooden steps.

Again, Dooley looked out the busted-open door that led to the outside stairs. He moved over dead bodies and more bloody ponds, braced himself against the wall, and inched his way to the edge of the opening to the stairs.

Whispers sounded downstairs. No guns barked outside, although Dooley could make out the barking of dogs.

He hollered, "Downstairs in the bank?"

A few gasps answered.

"It's me! Dooley Monahan. Owner of the Blue Grant mine." He had named the strike after his two loyal companions.

More whispers. Dooley again looked at the opening outside.

"Any of the robbers still downstairs?"

"No." That was a woman's voice. Dooley thought about this. Three outlaws were dead at Dooley's hand. *Hand.* He shook off the image of

253

the hand he had hacked off with a D-ring bowie and then kicked across the floor of a gun shop. That meant three were left. But if just one of them was downstairs, wouldn't that be enough for anyone to lie, to say no one was down there?

A floorboard squeaked outside, and Dooley turned, dropped to his knees, and brought up the Colt in his right hand. Almost immediately, a figure in a linen duster kicked through the already kicked-in door, saw Dooley, and also the bloody carnage surrounding Dooley. Still, he tried to touch the trigger, but Dooley fired first. The man went backward, pulling his trigger but only puncturing the FOR RENT sign and the door itself to lawyer J. T. Cohen's office. He backed up, onto the landing outside, and tried to fire again.

Dooley gut-shot him, and the man groaned, leaned against the railing, but again refused to die. He died, though, as Dooley put a third round into his chest. Then the man was gone, falling over the railing and landing in the street.

Dooley grimaced at the sickening thud outside.

Four men, he counted. Two left. He checked the loads to the Colts he had procured, dropped one, replaced it with another, and pried a few cartridges from the holster of one of the recently deceased duster-wearers. Once he held two fully loaded six-shooters in his hands, he moved toward the opening outside, but kept listening to the commotion downstairs.

He heard what he wanted. Downstairs, the front door opened. Dooley stopped walking and now eased his way, gently, so no one could hear his movements downstairs, until he reached the edge of the doorway. He came down cautiously, seeing the main doors still open, and watched the ashen-faced tellers and the sweating, trembling John Price stare at him as he came down the stairs.

The woman teller, a buxom redhead, pointed out the window. "Two men!" she said. "They just ran out!" He could tell she felt sorry for having lied to him earlier. Of course, he wished she had not yelled. Now he ran, just in case the linen duster–wearing hombres came back toward the bank, down the stairs and across the floor, stopping at the door.

Six horses remained tethered out front. The two killers left had not fled. He shot a glance across the street. The shades to the county clerk's office remained closed, the door shut. Inwardly, Dooley cursed every deputy marshal in Colorado. He looked down the streets.

Nobody rode down the road. No one stood on the boardwalk, behind a water trough or column or in the corner of an alley. He had read all sorts of newspaper and magazine articles about towns whose residents rose up in defense when ruffians tried to pull off a raid or robbery of some kind. But not here in Leadville.

Dooley stared down the boardwalk. "Which

way?" he asked the redheaded teller, figuring she would still feel guilty about having lied to him earlier. Not that Dooley blamed her any.

Her head tilted toward the corner. Which made sense. They would be waiting for Dooley to step onto the landing. Instead, Dooley stepped out the door, ducked underneath the hitching rail, and began unfastening the reins to the bank robbers' horses. The one at the far end, the one that one of the outlaws had had to stop from running away when the shooting commenced, was now tied to the column. That was fine with Dooley. After releasing the last from the rail, he grabbed the reins around the column, pulled them free, and swung into the outlaw's saddle, firing a shot into the ground that sent the other horses screaming and galloping down the street from whence they had come.

"The horses!" someone screamed, or maybe, most likely, Dooley just imagined it. After all, the thundering of hooves, the ringing in his ears again, and the commotion all around him practically made hearing voices impossible.

The horse Dooley had mounted, reared, and wanted to follow his comrades, but Dooley pulled hard on the reins, kept his seat, and forced the gelding around the corner.

He leaned low in the saddle, practically hanging over the horse's neck, and saw the two linen-duster men. One was halfway up the stairs to the office of the lawyer, the gunsmith, and whoever else rented from the bank. The other was on the corner. Dooley fired at the one on the corner, but missed. Then he lost his grip and came crashing to the ground, rolling free from any hooves that might crack bone, and coming up to his knees.

It had been a foolish play, Dooley realized. And here is where he paid the price and the piper.

But he told himself that he would die game.

The gun in his left hand pointed at the duster-wearing owlhoot on the corner. The gun in his right hand aimed, more or less, at the duster-wearing killer halfway up the stairs. He had never been much of a hand at shooting two guns. His left hand always failed him, and—especially given that his left palm bled like the dickens from that shard of glass from the window of the gunsmith's office—failed him now. That bullet went nowhere near the killer, nowhere, in fact, even near the corner. The Colt in his right hand might have hit the wall to the bank. On the other hand, it might have missed the bank completely.

Yet Dooley could not believe what he saw.

The man on the corner spun around, discharging both barrels from his scattergun into the boardwalk, blowing a hole through the planks, and then crashing into the hole he had just made. He did not stir.

The killer on the stairs slammed against the wall, blood suddenly drenching the front of his pale-colored muslin shirt that he wore underneath his tan-colored duster. Still, that man, grimacing, brought up the Remington he still gripped in his right hand. He aimed, but not at Dooley, at something that must have been behind Dooley.

Dooley just stared at his own guns and quickly brought both up to shoot the man on the stairs. Before he could pull a trigger on either gun, though, another shot barked, more blood erupted from that muslin shirt, and this time the robber tumbled down the stairs and rolled off the corner into the dusty street.

CHAPTER TWENTY-SEVEN

Quickly, Dooley spun around, and somehow he managed to smile. Butch Sweeney stood on the corner of the boardwalk across the street, and quickly jacked another round into his .44-40 carbine. From that angle, Dooley knew that Butch had shot down the bank robber who had rolled down the stairs. But the one with the shotgun? He looked the other way, and the frown quickly became a grim frown. Shoving one revolver into his waistband and dropping the other from his bleeding left hand, Dooley hurried across the street to the corner of the grocery store. Butch Sweeney's boots pounded on that boardwalk as he ran, too.

Dooley reached Julia Cooperman Miller first, and took the Henry rifle she held. Her face had gone stark white, and those eyes, so vacant, unfocusing, scared Dooley out of about ten years. She stepped back, and Dooley reached for her, dropping the rifle into the ground, but Butch Sweeney got to her first, taking her in his arms as she fainted dead away.

Butch shouted something. He looked like he might faint, too.

A few doors began to open, and the rushed talk of excited Leadville citizens reached Dooley's ears. He stepped back, stared down the alley behind the grocery. There was no time to think things through, and Dooley pointed down that alley, speaking to Butch in rapid-fire sentences, while staring at the corner to the bank building. So far, no body had poked a nosy head around the corner.

"Get her out of here, Butch," Dooley said.

"But . . . where . . . ummmm . . . ?"

"Just get her out of here. Before someone sees her. No telling what that no-account husband of hers will do to her if he finds out she saved my bacon." It struck him later that there was no telling what George Miller would do to Butch Sweeney. Then, moments later, he realized he could tell exactly what George Miller would do to Butch.

He pointed down the alley. "Now, damn it!" he barked, and the color returned to Butch's face. He scooped up Julia's legs—er, limbs—letting his Winchester bounce on the ground. Butch moved quickly now, and rounded the corner and took off at an awkward, bowlegged gait just before Mr. John Price's sweaty, pale face appeared at the corner.

First, Dooley picked up the Henry that Julia had dropped, and he leaned it against the window-less wall of the grocery store. Next, he found a handkerchief in his trousers pocket and pressed it against the cut in his left palm. He loosened the string tie around his paper collar, pulled the tie free, and used it to tie the handkerchief as tight as he could make it against his palm. By that time, several other heads had dared to show their petrified faces, and even a few, including bank president John Price, had managed to force their entire bodies out onto the street.

Dooley picked up Butch's Winchester with his left hand—it wasn't as heavy as the Henry, which he lifted with his right, and walked toward the gathering group of concerned citizens. He did not dare stay too close to the alley, fearing some busybody might see Butch and the sickly Julia before they had found a place to disappear.

"Goodness gracious," the fat banker said, staring at the dead men—the two killed by Butch and Julia, and the third Dooley had blown off the landing. "That's four of the robbers accounted for."

"Six," Dooley said.

The faces stared at him with no comprehension. He tilted his head toward the upstairs. "Two more are up yonder."

"Goodness," said a man in a white collarless shirt with brown stockings protecting the clean sleeves. "You killed all six."

"Nah," said a miner in overalls and a slouch hat. "Nah. Some redheaded gent must've gunned down one of them." He spit tobacco juice onto the dust. "I seen him leverin' that Winchester he's a-holdin' and firin' away."

261

The eyes searched for Butch Sweeney.

Dooley cleared his throat. "That was Butch Sweeney." Dooley nodded at the dead man nearest the staircase. "Saved my hide, Butch did. Got this one before he could drill me. You all know Butch Sweeney. He runs the stage line to Denver, the one the late Chester Motz used to own. Good man, Butch. Saved my hide. Saved the bank's money." Although, by now Dooley figured those six men had not come to Leadville to rob any bank.

He searched the faces as more and more appeared, but he did not see the deputy U.S. marshal, the *Denver Telegram* scribe, or George Miller.

"But . . ." a minister asked, "where is the stagecoach driver?"

"Ummmm."

"Where are the vigilance committee?" the grocer said as he made his way from the other side of the street. "What good is paying for a vigilance committee when they do nothing until after a crime has been committed?"

Dooley saw this as a way to give Butch Sweeney more time.

"You mean to tell me you pay those boys on that vigilance committee?"

"Certainly," banker John Price answered.

"Well, wouldn't it make better sense to have a town marshal to enforce the law?" Dooley asked.

"Marshals don't last long in this town," the grocer said.

"But I have preached many a sermon that hemp is not the answer," the parson said. "If we are to have law and order in Leadville, we need a real man, a real officer of the court, a real man to combat the evil that comes to silver towns such as ours."

"Jim Trader was a real man, a real officer of the court," said another merchant, "and he's buried in Evergreen Cemetery with his deputy."

The miner spit again. "So where did that red-headed feller run off to?"

Dooley gestured vaguely behind him.

"I sent him to make sure there were no other robbers in that gang," he lied.

They stared at him.

"It just made sense to me that when a gang robs a bank, they have some lookouts posted in the town."

They stared at one another, and a few made comments, some heads bobbed, and none shook.

Dooley figured he had bought Butch Sweeney all the time he could, because the miner and the grocer were walking down the street, the miner having to step over the dead men, which meant the grocer reached the end of his building and glanced down the alley.

"Which way did he go?" the grocer asked as he turned around. That gave Dooley time to breathe again. Butch and Julia had gotten somewhere. He didn't know where, but at least they were safe for now. No one would suspect Julia of having killed the fifth of the six men.

He exhaled.

"You're wounded," a woman cried out.

Dooley started to look at his left hand, but somewhere from down the street, another voice sang out sharply:

"The other bank's bein' robbed!"

That got Dooley's attention. There were two banks in Leadville, and Dooley's money was in the other bank, Tim Shaw's bank, the one being robbed now. Despite his still bleeding, and really hurting, left hand, he hurried, carrying both rifles, and rounded the corner of the grocery. Two men, mounted on brown horses rearing and spinning around in the street in front of the bank, fired pistol shots in the air, yelling and cursing.

"Get off the street, ya sons-a-dogs!"

"Show yer face again, and I'll blow it off!"

Another man stood in the street, holding three horses.

Doors closed. Women screamed. Men yelled for the vigilance committee.

Dooley took one quick glance at the county clerk's office, but seeing the door still shut and the curtains still closed, he cursed and offered the Henry to the miner.

"Not me." The big man raised his hands. "I

ain't got no money in that bank. Hell, I ain't got no money in no bank, not even more than . . ."

Dooley did not listen to the rest, but scanned the crowd for someone willing to help. The preacher prayed. Mr. John Price, bank president, only started sweating more. The other people— the few who had not fled when the bank robbers started shooting in front of Leadville's other bank—either ran up the stairs and hid in the bloody, bullet-riddled floor above the bank, or hurried into the alley down which Butch Sweeney had carried Julia, or fell on their bodies and covered their ears and heads.

Swearing underneath his breath, Dooley moved down the boardwalk, past the grocery store, looking inside to see the grocer pull down the shades on the plate glass window. He should have taken time to close the shutters before running inside the store, because one of the brown-horse riders noticed Dooley, got his horse under control, and started cutting loose at Dooley.

One bullet buzzed past Dooley's ear before punching a hole in the glass and the green shade. Dooley dived into the little entryway, braced his back against the wood, and lowered the Winchester carbine. Another bullet from the outlaw clipped the wood above Dooley's head. He dropped to a knee, worked the lever of the Henry, and came around quickly, squeezing the trigger, not bothering to aim, working the lever.

One shot. Two. Three. Four. Then he came back to his hiding place as three or four more bullets—he couldn't count the shots, could barely hear or see from all the bitter smoke the .44 caliber rifle had just belched and that infernal ringing again in his ears.

Glass shattered again, and Dooley levered another round into the Henry. He stopped, trying to remember how many shots Julia had fired, how many he had just wasted at the robbers in the street, and, even more important, how many rounds did a rimfire Henry rifle hold.

Sixteen, he seemed to recall. At least, that sounded right. That is, of course, providing the .44 caliber rifle had been fully loaded when the ruckus all started. He could check the tubular magazine, or he could just decide to go with the Winchester, but he didn't know how many shots were left in that weapon, either.

There was no time. The ringing left his ears, and he heard the thunder of hooves. One of the robbers had spurred his brown horse. A bullet sent splinters flying from the boardwalk just inches from Dooley's feet.

He raced backward to the other side, bringing the Henry up. Smoke and flame belched from the hard-charging rider's Colt. The man rode with his teeth clenching the reins, pistols in both hands, the smoke from the bucking weapons obscuring his black-bearded face. A bullet grazed the inside of Dooley's right thigh. Ignoring that, he told himself to take his time, draw a clear bead, don't panic . . .

Don't panic.

Like that was impossible with a man riding a horse hell-bent for leather trying to fill you with holes.

The rifle roared, slamming the stock against Dooley's shoulder, and Dooley stepped out of the smoke, levering another shell—or so he hoped—into the Henry. He swung the rifle around, taking aim, as the horse thundered past him, but quickly leaped back. That was just in time. Another bullet whistled and slammed into the wood. The horse went galloping down the street, past the county clerk's office—shades still down, door still closed—and out of town.

The horse carried no rider. Dooley turned, saw the man lying spread-eagled in the street, still clutching pistols in both hands.

He let out a sigh and wiped sweat from his brow.

But this soiree was far from finished.

One rider lay dying, probably dead, maybe just seriously injured, maybe just playing possum. Dooley looked at the man again. No, he was most definitely dead. And he wasn't bearded at all. That was just powder smoke darkening his face.

Five horses. That likely meant five riders. One dead. Dooley figured four were left.

Unless, he thought, he had been right and that the gangs—either one or both, or maybe they were working on this together—had posted lookouts down the street, as he had suggested to the crowd earlier.

Hooves sounded again, and Dooley figured he was right. Because this time the sound did not come from Leadville's other bank, but down the street from whence the dead robber's horse had taken off.

A bullet roared, and Dooley knew he was about to be caught in a cross fire.

CHAPTER TWENTY-EIGHT

The man coming from the road that led out of town rode a strong palomino steed, reins in his teeth, too. His right hand held a long single-shot rifle, his left a Remington .44. The handgun roared, and Dooley blinked. He wasn't shooting at Dooley at all, but aiming at the robbers.

It would be an image Dooley would remember for the rest of his life, mainly because it happened to be on the cover, a few years later, of one of those dime novels.

Lead and Dead in Leadville;
Or, Buffalo Bill's Duel with Death

My, how magnificent Buffalo Bill Cody looked that morning, long hair blowing in the wind, the front brim of his hat turned upward, determination etched in his face, murderous intent in his eyes, charging like a brave lancer in one of those novels by Sir Walter Scott, not that Dooley Monahan had ever read any of those. In fact, he never would really read *Lead and Dead in Leadville*, either, just skim the pages hoping to find his name somewhere in the account.

Which he never did.

Another pistol barked, but that one came

from down the street, and the sound of another galloping horse reached Dooley's ears. He stepped around the corner, to see the bad man on the other brown horse charging, too, just like two knights charging each other in a scene from one of those medieval stories Dooley had heard about, but never read, and certainly never seen.

Both the outlaw on the brown horse and Buffalo Bill on the palomino fired at the same time, Cody shooting his pistol, the bank robber one of his two six-shooters. Dooley fought back a shriek and grimaced as the splendid gelding Buffalo Bill rode fell onto its front knees, sending its rider flying off the horse, which somersaulted down the street but somehow, miraculously, avoid crushing Buffalo Bill into the dirt. While that was happening, the rider of the brown horse jerked, and fell from his saddle, bouncing in the dirt as the horse turned sharply to avoid being cannonballed by the somersaulting palomino. The brown horse never slowed, just changed its course and took off down the road out of town, just as the other brown horse had done.

The palomino rose quickly, stunned, and just stood in the middle of the street.

Buffalo Bill Cody sat up, his hat off his head, blood flowing from a cut across his forehead, the Remington lying in the dust far out of his reach. Somehow, the famed scout still held the Springfield rifle in his left hand. The outlaw

Cody had shot off his horse sat up. He still held one of his pistols. The two men were perhaps fifteen feet from each other.

"Cody!" Dooley yelled, and stepped toward him. "Look out!"

Dooley had to look out himself, because the man who had been holding those three horses had abandoned that post and now took a shot at Dooley. The slug practically parted Dooley's hair.

Dropping to a knee, Dooley turned his attention away from Buffalo Bill, brought the Henry up, and fired as he dived behind a water trough. The gunman also shot wildly this time, and he took cover behind the barber pole.

Coming up, Dooley jacked the Henry's lever, came up, and fired again, hitting one of the pole's white stripes. Out of the corner of his eye, Dooley saw the outlaw in the street rush his shot. Dirt flew up between Buffalo Bill's outstretched legs as the scout swung the Springfield rifle and pulled the trigger. The gun roared like a cannon and the outlaw flew backward, landing on his back and practically carving a ditch as the momentum of the .45-70 bullet drove him a few feet toward a doctor's office.

"Dooley!" Buffalo Bill shouted. The living legend tossed away the empty rifle and rose. "I'm empty!" He held out both hands.

Ignoring the man behind the barbershop pole,

271

forgetting about the two other cutthroats likely still inside the other Leadville bank, Dooley stood. He tossed the Henry to Buffalo Bill and tried to make it back to the grocery to snag that Winchester carbine. Out of the corner of his eye, Dooley saw Buffalo Bill catch the rifle expertly, and the killer behind the barbershop step out with his six-shooter.

Dooley had no chance to make it to the entryway and the Winchester carbine, but that's when he remembered the revolver stuck in his waistband. He jerked it out, thumbed back the hammer.

The killer fired.

Buffalo Bill's Henry rifle spoke.

The pistol bucked in Dooley's hand.

The outlaw spun around like a ballet dancer, sending the pistol in his hand crashing through one window to the barbershop while he smashed into the other. Glass rained down upon him, the upper part of his body inside the building, his legs hanging out, his boots dragging on the boardwalk and glass.

About that time, the two outlaws came out of the bank.

"Where the hell are the horses?" one yelled.

Dooley noticed that the horses the man now halfway in the barbershop had been holding had taken off, but had not followed the two brown horses out of town. One was about three blocks down the street. Another was in an alleyway, and the third one had found shelter in a livery.

Seeing their dead colleagues—two in the street, the third not getting a shave or a trim—they dropped the sacks of the other bank's money.

Both men took shots at Dooley, and Dooley's pistol roared, too, but they were far out of effective pistol range. Buffalo Bill's shot from the Henry took off one of the outlaw's black hats. He worked the lever, aiming as the two men ran down the street, both for the horse that could still be found. The .44 slug whined off the metal rim of a parked freight wagon. Cody jacked another load into the chamber, or at least thought he had, and pulled the trigger. The hammer clicked.

"Empty!" Cody yelled.

Dooley reacted and tossed him the pistol in his hand, which again the frontiersman caught as though he had rehearsed this scene for one of his stage plays. Dooley took time to snag the Winchester carbine.

The hatless outlaw reached the horse, first, which, somehow, despite all the roaring gunfire and bullets shooting this street to pieces, remained calm.

"Bill!" cried the man still with a hat, and still carrying a sack of money. "Bill! Don't leave me, Bill!"

Bill, without a hat, without any money, but with a horse and a pistol, did not listen. He spurred the horse and took off down the street, popping away with his pistol at Dooley and Buffalo Bill.

Once again, Dooley and Buffalo Bill pulled triggers simultaneously, and Bill flew out of the saddle, dropping his six-shooter and crashing against a water trough on the other side of the street. He did not splash in the water, but smashed against the hard wood. His boots touched the dirt. His right arm and his neck hung over the side, near the apothecary shop. His left hand, the one still holding the pistol, pointed upward, and then it fell into the water trough. It was probably his imagination, but Dooley thought he heard the barrel of the pistol sizzle as it dropped into the water.

The horse, naturally, avoided Buffalo Bill's palomino and followed the other horses out of town.

That left one remaining bank robber, and he ran into the Silver Palace Saloon, kicked open the door. Dooley heard a few tables overturning from inside. The outlaw had dropped the bag of money, but he still had that pistol.

Dooley gave Buffalo Bill Cody a glance. The man checked the loads in the Colt, shucking out the empty casings as he moved to the man he had shot off his horse. Dooley crossed the street and worked the lever on the .44-40 carbine.

"Dooley," Buffalo Bill said grimly.

"Bill," said Dooley.

Cody stopped, and dropped to the dirt by the dead outlaw. He thumbed fresh loads from the outlaw's shell belt and fed those into the weapon he held. Laying the pistol he had just reloaded on the dead man's chest, Cody kept pushing more cartridges out of the belt.

"That's a .44-40, ain't it, Dooley?" Cody asked, meaning the carbine Dooley held.

"Yep."

Cody held out a fistful of cartridges, which Dooley gathered and began feeding into the Winchester's loading gate.

After collecting the pistol from the outlaw's bloody chest, Buffalo Bill rose.

"I'm thirsty, Dooley," Cody said. "Want a morning bracer?"

Dooley thumbed back the Colt's hammer.

"I'll buy," he said.

And the two men walked down the street toward the one-story Silver Palace Saloon.

The shutters had been closed, and Cody and Dooley stopped at the side street, out of view from the door the lone surviving bank robber had kicked off its hinges.

"Back entrance to this place?" Cody asked.

"I don't know," Dooley said. There was no entrance leading to the side street, no windows, either, and the other side butted up against a dance hall. That much Dooley could see. "Probably in the back."

Cody nodded. "All right. I'll take the back door. You take the front. If there ain't no back door, I'll come join you in the front. Don't shoot my head off."

Dooley's mouth was quickly losing any moisture, so he nodded, worked up just enough spit, and said, "Bill?"

"Yeah."

"I'd like to take this fellow alive."

Cody stared.

"For talking," Dooley explained.

Cody gave a curt nod. "I'd like to hear some squealin' myself. Like how come two gangs would try to rob two banks on the same day."

"When one gang didn't even bother taking any money," Dooley said, and that was about all his mouth could muster, for the time being.

Cody started down the alley. "But," he called out to Dooley in a deadly whisper, "I ain't makin' no promises."

I ain't, either, Dooley thought.

"Give me about two minutes," Cody said. "See you at the bar." He winked. "If you get there first, I'll have rye with a beer chaser."

Once Buffalo Bill reached the corner of the saloon, he turned back, nodding that there was a door that led to the alley. Then Cody disappeared around the corner.

Even though the shutters remained tight against the big window, Dooley dropped below and crawled down the boardwalk till he reached the entryway. He looked down streets, but found only dead men and Buffalo Bill's palomino gelding in the street. Up the street, he saw some curtains moving, which told him people were looking from the safety of their homes or businesses, waiting till they knew for certain that it was safe to step outside.

"Some vigilance committee," Dooley whispered. Then he inched his way to the door. He stopped, listening, looking through the crack. The saloon was dark. Having the shutters closed didn't help matters. He could see an overturned table and some chairs knocked onto the floor. Other chairs remained stacked on the tables that had not been knocked over.

Two minutes had to have passed by now, Dooley told himself. His throat felt parched. His left hand still bled and throbbed. He sucked in a deep breath, balanced himself on his knees, and launched himself up and forward, toward the busted door of the Silver Palace Saloon.

CHAPTER TWENTY-NINE

His shoulder slammed into the edge of the door, knocking it completely off the hinges that the last of the bank robbers had loosened, and Dooley hit the floor and rolled over, stopping behind the overturned table. A bullet thudded against the table, but the Silver Palace wasn't any run-of-the-mill watering hole. These tables were pure mahogany, not pine, not cheaply made. The bullet the robber had fired didn't punch through the wood. It didn't even make the round table wobble.

The din from the shot reverberated in the darkened saloon. Dooley managed to catch his breath, and rubbed his sweating right palm on his britches. He didn't bother with the left palm and tried not to look at how ugly his handkerchief and ribbon tie looked now. That makeshift bandage had been on his left hand for what seemed like an eternity.

Light slipped through the doorway, casting a glow on the fancy floors of the saloon, but only for a few feet, and some sunlight filtered in through shutter slats in the large window. Toward the bar, however, where the last of the gunmen was hiding—Dooley could tell from where the gunshot had hit the table—the saloon remained not completely black, but plenty dark.

Eventually, saliva reappeared in Dooley's

mouth and throat, and he could hear now that the gunshot's echoes had faded. Acrid gun smoke assaulted his nostrils. He was inside the saloon, but had nowhere really to run to. The robber had knocked over just one table, as far as Dooley could tell. And he was fairly safe here.

For now.

Thump.

Dooley straightened, listening intently.

Thump.

Thump.

A muffled voice somehow reached Dooley's ears. Then:

Thump.

Thump.

Thump.

"Hell," Dooley whispered to himself as the source of the muffled voice—undoubtedly a curse—and that odd thumping noise became clear to him.

Buffalo Bill Cody had found the rear entrance to the saloon, but the owners of the Silver Palace did not just splurge on quality furniture, but on rear doors, locks, and wooden bars, as well. At least for the back door. The front ones had been for decorative purposes only. The back was to keep out riffraff. Right now, it was keeping Buffalo Bill from getting into the saloon.

So Dooley cursed again, a little more vilely, a little louder.

The robber answered with another pistol shot, which again thudded against the thick table. Grimacing, even though the table still did not feel weakened by another slug, Dooley looked out the door. Still, no one appeared. Inwardly, Dooley cursed that good-for-nothing vigilance committee.

This wasn't quite the Mexican standoff, but Dooley couldn't sit here on the floor all day. Although the wound in his palm didn't bleed as much as it had, it still had not congealed. He would need some stitches, and Dooley hated stitches. Another bullet grazed the top of the table. Of course, Dooley thought, if that owlhoot kills me, I won't need any stitches or medicine.

He decided to move. Coming up to his knees, bending his head down to keep it from getting shot off, Dooley peered around the table. Then he bolted to his right, firing at the bar, seeing his reflection in the fancy mirror on the fancy back bar shatter into a million pieces. Dooley worked the lever, touched the trigger, and started to slide, pushing over another table, sending those chairs clattering against the floor, and then taking cover behind the table, which rolled this way and that.

The man behind the bar did not return fire.

Dooley sucked in air, blew it out, sucked in air, blew it out, and felt his heart racing faster than the speed of the bank robbers' two brown horses as they galloped out of town. When he regained control of his breathing, Dooley looked at the doorway, and the overturned table where he had first taken cover. He estimated how much of the saloon floor he had covered, and how close he was to the bar.

Again, a gunshot roared in the darkened saloon. This time, Dooley moved to his left, aimed, fired, and heard whiskey bottles shatter. What a waste. His shot had come nowhere near the last robber, because Dooley saw the muzzle flash about ten feet down the bar. The light blinded him, and the shot sounded like a bee as it buzzed past his ear. Dooley had already jacked the hammer, and he touched the trigger again as he aimed from the feel. Then he quickly returned to the safety of the heavy table, hearing another shot from the gunman thud against the wood. Had the owner of this joint been a little cheaper with his tables, that bullet would have shattered Dooley's spine or pierced his heart.

He waited, sweating, bleeding, and scared as a greenhorn cowboy in his first stampede. Yet he fought back the nerves, worked the lever again, and rubbed the sweat and residue of gunpowder from his eyes.

Which only burned his eyes even more.

Slowly, the sound of the reports faded. A moment later, his eyes stopped hurting. He blinked several times until he felt certain he could see—as clearly as anyone could see in a saloon this dark.

Where the hell is Buffalo Bill? Dooley thought. Outside, a dog began to bark.

Dooley listened, but the thumping and cursing from the rear of the saloon had stopped. Had Buffalo Bill managed to get inside the saloon while Dooley and the gunman hiding behind the bar had been exchanging shots?

Obviously, the last of the robbers had plenty of ammunition. As far as Dooley could tell, the bandit had entered the saloon with only one weapon, a six-shooter, and he definitely had fired more than six bullets. That caused Dooley to wonder how many shots he had fired. Granted, the Winchester held more rounds than a Colt revolver, but . . . still . . .

You count cards, he told himself, *so why can't you count shots when you're in a game where the stakes are much higher?*

He almost turned to look out the door again, but this time stopped himself. The light shining through the door, dim as it was, still strained his vision when he looked back toward the bar. Those gun flashes certainly hadn't helped his vision, either.

With the Winchester carbine cocked and ready, Dooley moved again, firing, levering another round, squeezing the trigger, and sliding against the front of the bar. The brass boot rail felt cold against his cheek. Now he just had to decide which way to go: To the nearest edge of the bar?

Or sneak down the floor to the far side? Or just stand up, hurtle himself over the bar, and hope he fired in the right direction?

Slowly, he came to his knees. He wet his lips and began inching his way toward the far side of the bar.

The bank robber must have had a similar notion. Dooley happened to be looking down toward that side when the outlaw stuck his head around the corner. Dooley could have sworn, even in the darkness, that he saw the man's eyes widen in fright. But Dooley wasn't ready for the man. He started to bring the Winchester up, and came up to his knees, but the outlaw dropped onto his belly and squeezed the trigger of his revolver. Dooley felt his hands wring with pain as the bullet from the robber's .45 flattened and whined off the case-hardened receiver. The Winchester flew from Dooley's grip and crashed somewhere to his right. The gunman turned his Colt in that direction, but Dooley sprang up and dived up and over the bar—the opposite direction. Still, he barely made it, and felt the bank robber's bullet—after he had corrected his error—tear off the heel of Dooley's right boot.

And those boots he had bought here in town . . . at Leadville prices.

He crashed against the floor, feeling glass shards from busted whiskey bottles bite into his back, feeling the wetness of liquor burn his cuts and scrapes. Yet he knew he had no time to moan, or whine, or just lie here and try to get his lungs to work again. He was behind the bar, and his Winchester was on the other side.

The bank robber must have realized this, too, for Dooley heard the miserable cur start to laugh.

"Well, well, well," the bandit said. "Appears to me that you ain't got no gun no more. But I still got mine."

Dooley rolled over onto his hands and knees. He looked at the bar. He swallowed. Shells began clattering against the floor as the robber still chuckled and began feeding fresh rounds into the cylinder. "I reckon," the varmint said, "I'll just have to gun you down and be on my way. Don't look like nobody in this town wants to stop me. Exceptin' you and that pard of yourn who must've realized the errors of his ways." The man laughed again. Another empty brass casing bounced across the floor.

That's when Dooley sprang up.

The bank robber was about to snap the loading gate to the .45 shut. The barrel pointed at the floor. The outlaw started to bring up the revolver, but froze.

Dooley held the sawed-off Greener ten-gauge, the scattergun the bartenders kept behind the bar in case customers got out of control. And Dooley trained those massive barrels at the gunman's belly. Even though the man was silhouetted by the sun coming through the doorway, Dooley clearly saw the man's smile vanish. Shotguns at this range would have that effect on even a brave legend like Buffalo Bill Cody, wherever the hell he was.

The outlaw backed up, dropped his weapon, raised his hands, and spun around. In blind fear, he ran for the door. Dooley brought the stock of the Greener to his shoulder, and his fingers touched the twin triggers, but he stopped, remembering his own words to Buffalo Bill:

"I'd like to take this fellow alive."

Holding his fire, Dooley laid the sawed-off cannon on the bar and leaped back across it. He grabbed the weapon and started to run after the shooter, cursing himself as the man pushed through the broken doorway.

Then, a sickening crunch sounded, the doorway seemed to go dark, and the outlaw came stumbling back into the saloon, bouncing into another table, knocking the chairs off, although this table remained upright. The man rolled over, fell to the floor, and came up slowly to his hands and knees, bawling like a newborn calf.

Another silhouette came into the bar.

"How 'bout that drink, Dooley?" Buffalo Bill Cody said.

Dooley just stood there as the scout holstered the Colt and walked into the darkened saloon. He jerked the groaning, bleeding outlaw to his feet

285

and shoved him toward the bar. Dooley lowered the hammers of the Greener and leaned against the bar.

It felt good, Dooley realized, mighty good. He was still alive. The last of the outlaws remained alive. Buffalo Bill Cody rounded the bar, his tall boots crunching broken glass as he found three glasses and a bottle of something that Dooley hoped would be better than anything he ever had tasted.

It burned. But it did make Dooley feel a mite better.

"Have a drink, pard." Buffalo Bill motioned at the shot glass in front of the last of the robbers, whose nose gushed blood.

"I can't." He sounded like a croaking frog.

"Very well." Cody downed that shot, too.

Dooley realized he could talk again. The whiskey must have helped. "I don't think," Dooley said, "that you really came to Leadville to rob a bank."

The man looked up. Blood seeped through his fingers that tried to keep his nose from sliding off his face.

To Dooley, it made a lot of sense. If Dooley happened to disappear, if he happened to be found dead by knife or gunshot or an ax to the back of his skull, folks might start thinking about that. But to be killed in a bank robbery— or two bank robberies . . . well, that would just be written off as a tragic crime. Not murder. Not conspiracy.

"Talk," Buffalo Bill demanded.

"I can't," the man managed to croak out.

"Who hired you?" Dooley asked.

"I never seen him," the man managed to say. "Bill just told us 'bout it. 'Bout him, I mean."

Bill was one of the dead outlaws lying in the dust outside.

"My nose hurts," the man whined.

Dooley said, "Then just nod or shake your head." The man lifted his bloody face. Tears of pain ran down his cheeks onto his bloody chin.

"You boys were robbing the bank. That was part of your pay. The others were supposed to kill me. Because they weren't taking any money."

Dooley waited.

"Your head's not moving." Buffalo Bill touched the barrel of his Colt against the outlaw's head.

The head nodded.

"If things somehow didn't work out," Dooley said, "then you were to kill me."

This time, the head bobbed without any encouragement from Buffalo Bill Cody's six-shooter.

That had been a wild stab in the dark from Dooley. To see the gunman's head confirming what Dooley had suggested made his stomach queasy.

"Well?" Buffalo Bill asked.

"Let's get him to jail," Dooley said. He thought: *This town does have a jail.*

Cody nodded. The last of the outlaws turned slowly and, shuffling his feet, moved toward the busted door and Front Street in Leadville. Dooley and Cody followed, Cody still holding the Colt, and Dooley the bartender's shotgun.

The surviving outlaw stepped outside. Then Dooley's ears started ringing again from a pistol shot that was fired outside. The next thing Dooley knew, the last surviving outlaw was slamming against Buffalo Bill Cody and Dooley, and falling dead to the floor.

CHAPTER THIRTY

After digesting what had just happened, seeing the last bank robber lying on an overturned chair, sightless eyes staring up at the punched-tin ceiling, Dooley shot a glance at Buffalo Bill. The frontiersman saw Dooley out of the corner of his eye, but did not look away from the doorway. He kept his weapon trained in that general direction, but answered Dooley's stare with a shrug.

Dooley kept the sawed-off scattergun trained at that busted door, too.

Eventually, a voice from outside called out in an uncertain tone: "Cody? Are you in there?"

As the bile rose in Dooley's throat, he fought back the urge to step through that door and give county clerk George Miller the business end of the double-barrel he held in his now-shaking hands. They shook not from fear, but anger.

"Yeah," Buffalo Bill answered. "Who's out there?"

"George Miller," the little weasel answered.

His next words tore at Dooley's gut. "I'm out here with Richard Blue, a deputy United States marshal from Denver. And a reporter from the *Telegram* of Denver."

Which would be Paul Pinkerton, if Dooley

remembered that poor excuse for an honest journalist's name right.

Still, neither Cody nor Dooley lowered their weapons.

Asked Cody: "Why did you shoot this owlhoot we had captured?"

"I didn't shoot him," George Miller said. "Marshal Blue did."

Dooley groaned.

"We thought he had killed you, Colonel Cody," George Miller lied.

"He was unarmed," Cody announced.

"No . . ." This came from the crooked lawman. "He had a derringer. He was turning around to gun you down when I shot him."

"Liar," Dooley whispered.

George Miller called out in a hopeful voice: "Is that other fellow . . . did the outlaw kill him?"

"No," Dooley and Cody said at the same time.

By then, Dooley could see bank executive John Price, bank president Tim Shaw of Denver's other bank, the editor of the *Leadville Ledger*, and a few other local citizens of prestige and power standing on the streets. Not to mention plenty of men and women whom Dooley did not know. Too many witnesses now, Dooley figured.

Realizing the same thing, Buffalo Bill Cody walked through the busted doorway, and Dooley, reluctantly, followed.

The lawman was kneeling behind the water

trough and smiled an unfriendly grin at both Dooley and Buffalo Bill when they stepped onto the boardwalk. Slowly, Deputy Marshal Richard Blue lifted a Remington over-and-under derringer with his left hand, high above the water trough, so the spectators could see.

Of course, Dooley thought. *They can see you show off that pocket pistol. But they couldn't see you plant the dang thing.*

The blood started rushing to his head again, and he had to tell himself over and over again to calm down or he'd drop dead of a stroke right here and there. Then who would look after Julia?

Which reminded him. He scanned the faces, and the boardwalk and storefronts across the street. No Butch Sweeney. No Julia.

"Thanks," Buffalo Bill told Marshal Blue, but the tone told Dooley that the great scout did not mean it.

"You're a hero, Mr. Cody," the *Denver Telegram* scribe said, laying it on thick. "You saved the honest citizens of Leadville all of their hard-earned money by shooting down these notorious scoundrels who dared to try robbing two banks at the same time. The story I write, sir, will be picked up across the nation, by the *New-York Tribune,* the *Omaha World-Herald,* every newspaper of substance, and many lesser publications."

"I didn't do a damned thing," Buffalo Bill said,

291

and finally shoved the pistol into his holster, even though that Colt wasn't really Cody's. His thumb bent toward Dooley. "It was Dooley Monahan here," Cody said. "He did all the work. Saved my bacon, if you ask me. He's the hero."

Dooley shuffled his feet and stared at the shotgun he still wanted to use on Miller, Blue, and Pinkerton—but he had only two rounds in the shotgun, and those three finaglers were spread out too far to kill three with two blasts. That wasn't the way Dooley recalled things. In his mind, Buffalo Bill had saved his hide.

"Well . . ." George Miller began, but the banker, Mr. Price, interrupted the no-account clerk.

"Buffalo Bill Cody's right. It was this man . . . this Dooley Monahan . . . who stopped the brigands at my bank. He shot them all. Two dead upstairs. One in our lobby. Three on the side street."

That was a lie, too, which the miner who had decided that he had no money to protect, pointed out.

"No, no, no. No, sir. It was another fella that killed one of those hombres. Redheaded boy."

"That's right," said the grocer. "Ummmmm. The gent who took over Chester and Horatio's stage line. Sweeney. Butch Sweeney."

Now Dooley held his breath.

"Well," the banker said, "that is right. But Dooley here sure laid the other five outlaws low."

"Three cheers!" someone yelled. "Three cheers for Dooley Monahan!"

They cheered. Once. Twice. Three times.

Dooley at last lowered the shotgun. "Buffalo Bill," he said, "deserves those cheers, too."

"Three cheers for Buffalo Bill Cody!" a woman shouted, which pleased the frontiersman immensely.

"Hip hip, hurrah!"

"Hip hip, hurrah!"

"Hip hip, hurrah!"

Cody bowed like the showman he was.

Dooley managed to speak once the cheering stopped. "Are any of those robbers alive?"

Heads shook. Too much to wish for, Dooley figured.

Clearing his throat, George Miller stepped onto the boardwalk, to make himself look a little taller, although he was nowhere near as tall or as handsome—or as honest, loosely speaking—as William F. Cody. The crowd gave him the floor.

"Let's not forget," he said, and tilted his head at that dishonest federal lawman, Richard Blue, "that the deputy from Denver gunned down the last of the badmen—just before he was about to do in both Cody and this . . . this . . . this old *bounty hunter*." The final two words came out the way a Lawrence, Kansas, man would call a Missouri bushwhacker or a Missouri farmer would call a Kansas Redleg.

Dooley thought about pointing out the little fact that while most of the shooting was happening, Miller, Blue, and Pinkerton had been inside the clerk's office, door closed, shades pulled down. He didn't have to.

Mr. John Price, banker, pointed that out.

George Miller turned a bit green, but the *Telegram* reporter thought up a lie and thought it up quickly.

"That was my fault," he said. "For while Mr. Blue and Mr. Miller were heading for the door—to bring assistance sooner—I informed them that the shots were likely nothing more than blanks, for the *Telegram* had reported that a circus was coming to Denver next week." He shrugged and looked like an idiot instead of a liar. "I merely assumed that this same circus had stopped in Leadville first, you see. Do not blame our gallant lawman or your valiant clerk. Do not blame the *Denver Telegram*, either, for it is the greatest newspaper for all of Colorado."

It did its job, Pinkerton's speech.

By that time, a few members of Leadville's vigilance committee had shown up and began telling people to clear the streets, to let the undertakers—too many for just one—to start gathering the dead. To let the Silver Palace owners bring in some carpenters and handymen to fix up the joint so they could open for business later that afternoon. And to let Marshal Blue send telegraph descriptions to the Denver office and see if there might be any rewards offered on the dead robbers.

"That would suit you, wouldn't it, Dooley?" Miller asked, and gave Dooley a cold, evil grin.

Someone offered to buy Buffalo Bill a drink. A liveryman said he would certainly look after Buffalo Bill's palomino. Buffalo Bill Cody moved off toward another saloon—one of those that never really closed in Leadville—and the *Denver Telegram* scoundrel and plenty of other Leadville citizens followed.

The reporter for the *Leadville Ledger*, however, remained in front of the Silver Palace. So did one of the vigilance committee's brass, a lean man in a black broadcloth suit and green satin tie.

"Is it true, sir," the reporter asked, "that you are a bounty hunter?"

Dooley was about to answer that he was an honest, hardworking cowboy who happened to have recently lucked into a silver mine. But George Miller stepped in front of Dooley and answered the question.

"Fletcher," he said. "Check the morgue for any papers you have from Arizona Territory from a few years back. You'll see how my good pard Dooley Monahan got rid of the last of the Baylor gang. Go back even earlier, say to autumn of '69, and you'll see how Dooley Monahan gunned down the infamous Jason Baylor up Dakota way.

295

And just last year or so, he rid the West of the Dobbs-Handley Gang. Isn't that right, Dooley?"

Dooley did not answer. He should have just gone directly to the mine this morning.

"Is that true, Mr. Monahan?" the reporter named Fletcher asked.

"Ask the clerk here," Dooley said. "He seems to know about my career better'n me."

"And," George Miller said, "I'll be happy to tell you all you need to know, Fletcher. After all, I was with Dooley for quite a while down Arizona way back in '72." Then Miller handed the reporter a cigar, put an arm over the naïve inkslinger's shoulder, and steered him to the county clerk's office.

The man in the black broadcloth suit just stared at Dooley. He didn't say anything, so Dooley walked down the street to get his belongings and maybe wash up back in the hotel before heading to the mine.

Butch Sweeney stopped him in the lobby of his hotel.

CHAPTER THIRTY-ONE

"What the hell! Where's—" Dooley stopped himself and turned rapidly on his heels. The desk clerk, who had just given Dooley his room key, stood staring, all ears. Dooley lowered his voice, but managed to get only a few incoherent words out before Butch said, "It's all right. Let's go upstairs to your room."

That's what they did, and inside, after Dooley and Butch managed to get the overly excited merle-colored shepherd settled down, Dooley found a bottle of rye in the top drawer of his dresser. He did not bother looking for any glasses, but simply pulled the cork and took a short sip. He tossed the bottle to Butch and filled the basin with water from the pitcher.

But he did not start washing his face . . . yet.

Instead, he made his way back to the door, cracked it open, and peered up and down the hallway. It was empty, and Dooley had to figure most guests and residents would be at work by now, or out on the street to gawk at the dead bank robbers.

When the door shut, Dooley found Butch holding the bottle with both hands.

"She's all right," Butch said.

Dooley snapped, "I told you to . . ." He fought

back the panic, the anger, and tried to calm himself. "Where is she?"

"At her place."

That caused Dooley's face to flush with anger.

"Her servants—that's right, she has servants—they're good ladies. They said they'd take care of her, Dooley, and they also said it wouldn't look good—and certainly wouldn't help Julia—if her husband came around and found me at that place with her."

Butch was sitting in the creaky chair. The cowboy turned stagecoach owner and jehu scratched Blue behind the ears. Dooley took a seat on the edge of his bed. Butch held up the bottle of rye as an offering. Dooley shook his head.

"Is she all right?" Dooley managed.

"Yeah. Beatrice, that's her personal servant, she said she would come around . . ."

Dooley cursed. "Goodness, do they know what she did?"

Butch's head shook rapidly. "No, no, I told them that she just saw most of the gunplay. I wasn't even halfway to her place when more gunfire started up. I wanted to go back, help you, figured you could use another gun—but, damn it, Dooley, I'd already given you my rifle. I didn't have nothin' to fight with. And I just had to get Julia out of there. Out of harm's way."

Nodding, Dooley leaned forward and held out

his right hand. Butch handed him the bottle, even though Dooley was trying to shake his old saddle pard's hand. He couldn't laugh, but since the bottle was in his hand, he lifted it and took a quick shot. He coughed. How could men, even cowboys, drink whiskey at this time of day?

Then he thought: *What time is it?*

"Somebody told me another gang was trying to rob Leadville's other bank?" Butch's head shook. "That don't make no sense."

Dooley set the bottle on the floor, away from his boots so he couldn't knock it over. He started to explain his theory, but held back.

"Did they catch the boys?" Butch asked.

Dooley's head shook. "They're all dead."

Butch again shook his head. "Man, when the papers write up that Julia kilt one of those hombres, that's gonna . . ."

"They're not going to write that up, Butch. They think I killed most of them. That Buffalo Bill killed some others. And a U.S. marshal murdered . . . shot, hell, the last one." He paused, and looked Butch directly in his widening eyes. "And they know you killed one of them, too."

"I did. I shot that cur before he gunned you down. And Julia . . ."

"Julia wasn't there," Dooley told him. "I killed the other one."

"With George Miller's Henry," Butch said.

Dooley nodded. "With George Miller's Hen—"

He stopped. He felt sick again, but did not reach for the whiskey bottle.

He asked in a hollow voice, "George Miller's Henry rifle?"

Butch's head bobbed.

"Aw, hell," Dooley said.

"Well, I figured if you could get me that rifle, I could get it back to Julia's house. Even clean it and reload it so nobody's the wiser, Dooley."

It was time for another drink. Not that Dooley wanted to, but he found the bottle and brought it to his mouth and took more than a little sip this time. The whiskey burned his throat, and he stifled a cough. He thought back to all he had seen as he left the Silver Palace Saloon for his hotel.

People were picking up shell casings and anything else that looked promising for souvenirs— one kid ran onto the street and swiped the hat off a dead bank robber. The photographer in town was busy setting up his big box of a camera and yelling at people to stand still or get out of his way, that he was preserving history. Someone ran to a body with a pair of scissors and snipped off a lock of hair from one of the dead outlaws.

Now, to be clear, no one tried to take any of the money from the sacks the bandits had taken from Leadville's other bank. And some even tried to stay out of the vigilance committee members' and that rascal of a deputy marshal's way—and even the newspaper reporter's way—who tried to document all that had happened this morning.

And then there were all those weapons lying on the street and in the bank where Dooley had been and on the boardwalks. Men and a few boys and even a couple of saloon harlots picked up those guns. He tried to remember where he had last seen the Henry .44 caliber rifle.

Then he pictured it clearly. It wasn't a saloon girl or a kid or a banker or miner or anyone like that who had been picking up that rimfire rifle. That might have been a good thing. But the person Dooley recalled lifting that rifle and studying it with serious intent . . . well, it wasn't Deputy Marshal Richard Blue or George Miller himself or even that scalawag of a *Denver Telegram* reporter. It was the man in the black broadcloth suit who happened to be major brass for Leadville's vigilance committee.

"Oh," Dooley said, "hell."

He had corked the bottle and dropped it back into the drawer—out of sight, far from temptation, that sort of thing. The rye he had consumed had little effect on him, or on Butch, but Dooley stressed the story Butch would have to tell over and over again.

"You shot one man. I gunned down the other. Got that? Julia was nowhere around. You didn't see her. She wasn't there. You shot one man. I shot the other. Then I sent you to find help. That's all there is to it. Got that?"

"Sure," Butch said.

"We have to keep her out of this. No one can ever know what happened. This is for her protection."

"Damn it, Dooley, stop treating me like a greenhorn on his first cattle drive. I know what I'm doing. I'm not about to put Julia in something uncomfortable."

Damn, he could use another hit of whiskey about now, but Dooley nodded. After sighing, he forced a wide grin. The smile did not last long at all.

"What about Miller's rifle?" Butch asked after a moment. "How do we explain that?"

"We don't," Dooley answered. "She wasn't there—Julia, I mean. All we saw were bank robbers. They must've broken into Julia's . . . no . . . George Miller's place first. Got that rifle there. I took it off a dead bank robber. That's all I know." He liked that idea. Nodding his head at his own plan, he repeated it to Butch. "I took the Henry off a man I shot. That's all we know about that big ol' .44. Got it?"

Butch nodded.

"Repeat it."

Butch repeated it, verbatim, and went back to petting Blue, who had rolled over on his back and gave Butch a fine opportunity to rub the shepherd's belly.

Dooley took that moment to head back to the door. Silently turning the knob, he then pushed the door open and looked into the hall. It remained empty, and Dooley listened but heard nothing out of the ordinary from the hotel lobby.

"All right," he said, and heard Butch Sweeney rise, tell Blue to stay, and cross the room. Sweeney pulled on his hat, took a deep breath and exhaled, and stepped into the hall.

"Butch," Dooley called out after the young cowboy took a few steps toward the stairs. The kid turned around, and Dooley made himself smile. He extended his hand.

"Thanks for all you did for . . . her," Dooley said.

They shook, and Dooley added:

"And thanks for saving my hide."

Butch nodded grimly, saying, "You'd have done the same for me, pard."

Which made Dooley feel a hell of a lot better.

He wasn't certain exactly what he had accomplished, though. Helped stop two bank robberies, maybe, if those vermin actually wanted to rob two banks. Gotten sweet young Julia into a compromising situation. Had her kill a man in Dooley's defense. Had almost gotten Buffalo Bill Cody killed. The leaders of Leadville would not have enjoyed having that blight on the mining metropolis's record.

When they made it downstairs, the Leadville reporter saw Dooley and snagged him, to lead him to the hotel café for a private interview. Better him than that lying reprobate from the *Denver Telegram*, Mr. Pinkerton. Dooley made it outside, shook a few hands with some citizens, rushing past them, trying to ignore their compliments.

Hell, he had just killed or helped kill ten human beings. Granted, they were scum and would gladly have done him in, but shooting a man to death just never set well in Dooley's gut. And he had gunned down far too many humans in his time.

Outside, he breathed a little easier. The dead were off the street. The town tried to fall back into its standard routine. Dooley made it to the livery without running into George Miller, the deputy marshal, the *Denver Telegram* scoundrel, or even Harley Boone. He told the liveryman that he would saddle General Grant himself, and that's what Dooley did, trying to keep his mind off all that had happened this morning.

One of Leadville's church's bells began to ring. It was noon.

Eventually, he made it to his mine, where Jarvis told him what needed to be done, what needed to be signed, what he needed to know. The foreman then came in and told him what also needed to be done, and what he might want to know, and what he probably didn't want to know but needed to know.

Mostly, Dooley thought about Julia. He sure hoped she was all right, and that maybe, just maybe, she might be able to block out what had happened on the town's streets that morning. He wanted to see her. But that, he knew, was impossible.

He cursed George Miller. Then Jarvis brought in more papers that he needed to sign, and when the door had closed and Dooley found himself alone in his office, he leaned back in his chair, closed his eyes, and dreamed about how great it would be if he were back riding the ranges for some half-arse cattle outfit in the Texas Panhandle, or up in Wyoming, or along those rolling plains of western Nebraska. Where a man had only to do his work, and had no worries about much of anything.

He did not wait around after the last whistle blew. Instead, he pulled on his coat and hat and was out of the office before even Jarvis was ready to call it a day. Dooley resaddled General Grant and put the fine horse into a lively clip as he rode back into Leadville. He had to fight the urge to run and check on Julia. Instead, he returned General Grant to the livery, grabbed a bite to eat at the Chinese eatery, took the side streets and alleys and even the back staircase to his room in the hotel.

It didn't help.

A man was waiting for him in the darkened hallway. He held a rifle in his hands.

CHAPTER THIRTY-TWO

"Mr. Monahan," the man said, "might I have a moment of your time?"

Dooley's right hand had a hard grip on the butt of his revolver, but the Colt remained holstered. He recognized the rifle first, that big Henry .44 that Julia had brought to save Dooley's hide. He also recognized the green satin tie the man in the black broadcloth suit wore.

The rifle's barrel pointed at the floor, and the man did not even have his hand in the lever or a finger on the trigger as he lowered the Henry. His left hand, which had been gripping the long rifle, now hung against the black trousers.

As he fished the key to his room out of his vest pocket with his left hand, Dooley studied the big *segundo* for Leadville's vigilance committee. He wasn't about to take his eyes off him, and he backed his way to the door.

"The rifle's empty, Mr. Monahan," the vigilance committee member said.

It certainly was unloaded when Dooley had shucked it what seemed like a lifetime ago. But that didn't mean the man in the black had not reloaded it.

"I mean you no harm," the man said.

Dooley had turned the key, now held the

doorknob, and he nodded at the man and said, "I'm about to open this door. I have a dog inside. And when he sees that Henry, he's likely to rip your jugular with his fangs. Were I you, mister, I'd put that weapon on the floor and keep your hands spread out far from your body."

He did not wait. Dooley jerked the door open and learned how to breathe again when the Henry clattered hard on the hallway and the man's hands went not far from his body but high over his head.

"That's your dog?" the man asked.

Blue managed to rise off his bed, but he merely stretched and wagged his tail.

"Blue's a good dog," Dooley said as he turned up the kerosene lamp on the wall. "And just be glad you weren't holding this . . ." He tossed the rifle he had picked up onto the bed and closed the door behind him.

The man managed to choke out a laugh as Dooley gestured at the chair Butch Sweeney had taken earlier in the day.

He removed his hat, laying it atop the dresser, and Dooley took off his coat and hat and hung both on the rack in the corner. He kept his gun belt on, but he did motion at the dresser. "I can offer you a drink," Dooley said, and wondered why he had offered a stranger whiskey.

"Will you have one?" the man asked, being sociable.

Shaking his head, Dooley remembered how much of a dent he and Butch Sweeney had put into that bottle earlier in the day. Gunfights tended to lead to hefty consumption of rye. And, typically, a hefty consumption of rye, or bourbon, or Scotch, or gin, or moonshine, led to gunfights.

The man sat down. "Then I shall decline your generous offer."

Dooley struck a match on his thumb and lighted two candles and then sat on the corner of the bed, using the pillows as a backrest. Blue jumped up onto the bed and demanded to be petted, but Dooley refused, told the dog to get back to his spot, and Blue obeyed.

"Good dog," the man said.

In no mood for politeness, Dooley said, "Why do you want to see me?"

"The name's Wolfe," the man said. "Adam Wolfe. I own several properties here in Leadville, including the livery on the north side, some lots heading toward the cemetery, and the Silver Palace Saloon."

Dooley nodded. For a minute, he thought the man might demand that Dooley, as a wealthy silver baron, pay for all the damages done to his grog shop.

Instead, Mr. Adam Wolfe said, "And I'm chief alderman for the vigilance committee."

Dooley did not know vigilantes had aldermen. He said nothing and absently began tapping the fingers on his left hand against the stock of the Henry rifle.

"I assume that is your rifle, Mr. Monahan," Wolfe said.

Dooley stopped tapping. He studied the man gravely. There was a plate on the stock, nickel, maybe silver, with cursive engraving on that stock that spelled out George Miller's name on one line and Skagway, Alaska Territory, on the second line. The man knew damn well this was not Dooley's rifle, so Dooley kept his right hand close to the butt of his Colt.

"No," Dooley said. "I never saw it before I took it off one of the men I'd killed in that robbery." To drive the point home, he gripped the Henry with his left hand, dragged it over the blankets, and sat the rifle on his lap. Pretending to read the engraving, he told Alderman Adam Wolfe: "This must be George Miller's gun. The robbers must have broken into their place before they tried to rob the two banks."

"Indeed," said Alderman Wolfe.

Dooley found an opening, and he took it. "Maybe you ought to return it to that . . . county clerk."

"Perhaps you would enjoy those honors," said the alderman.

Dooley felt his stomach twist and he ground some enamel off his teeth. "No," he said after getting a solid grip on his composure. "No, that's not the job for me. That's a job for the vigilance committee."

"I see." The man nodded at the Henry and held out his hands.

After starting to toss the rifle across the room, Dooley stopped himself and worked the lever three times. No rimfire shells were ejected, so the gun indeed wasn't loaded. Only then, after lowering the hammer, did Dooley toss the heavy rifle back at Mr. Wolfe, who caught the heavy weapon and laid it across his lap. "You, sir, are a careful man."

Dooley did not reply.

Now Adam Wolfe got to the point.

"The vigilance committee met a few hours ago with the town council and the mayor." He shifted in his seat, recrossed his legs, and finally leaned forward. "We've decided that something must be done to combat the lawless element in Leadville."

"Isn't that your job?" Dooley asked.

"After the fact," the man explained. He crossed his legs again. "When we discover undesirables amongst us, we take action." Dooley had seen such results of that action: men hanging from rafters, wagon tongues, tree limbs, or balconies. "But there are no peacekeepers in Leadville. That is something we need to rectify."

Dooley felt his stomach twisting and turning, so now he crossed his legs one way, then the other, and wet his lips and said, "You're not thinking about hiring that deputy marshal from Denver, are you?"

The man spit into the spittoon. "Hardly. A man who thinks a raging gun battle is a circus charade wouldn't last one night in Leadville."

He felt better. Then became squeamish again. "And . . . um . . . George . . . Miller?" Dooley nodded at the Henry.

The man blinked. Thought. Blinked again. "Oh, no . . . Miller . . . yes . . ." He saw the name on the plate on the rifle's stock. "He wasn't at the meeting. He's a county clerk. We're talking about the city proper. Leadville, and the mining district to, say, Chalk Creek. What happens outside that jurisdiction is the county's concern or the state of Colorado's. The sheriff in Granite can take care of that . . . for now. We have high hopes that Leadville will, perhaps soon, become the seat for Lake County. But . . ." He frowned and shook his head. "Not without law and order. Having nine outlaws shot down in the streets while trying to rob two banks is not the kind of publicity we need." He made himself smile. "Not that I'm saying it would be better had we let those bandits escape with our silver and currency. But we need to establish the presence of law in our grand city. What we need is not vigilantes stringing the riffraff up in the dead of night. We need a lawman. A marshal. A man who knows how to handle a gun and shows nerve and complete

312

resolve in the direst of circumstances. A legend. A brave marksman."

Dooley found himself nodding. To his surprise, he happened to agree with everything Alderman Adam Wolfe was saying. High time somebody said this.

When Wolfe stopped, Dooley said, "Buffalo Bill Cody's definitely your man."

"Cody?" The alderman looked as if he had been poleaxed.

"Yeah."

"Well . . ." Wolfe appeared to be considering that, but quickly shook his head. "I suppose Cody would make a marvelous lawman, but he is leaving to join his theatrical troupe in San Francisco tomorrow."

"What?"

"Yes, he had planned on leaving earlier, but found himself winning at poker. The investment on his grubstake of you allowed him to stay longer than he anticipated. However, he says now that he definitely plans to ride out for Denver tomorrow, take a stagecoach to Cheyenne, where he shall catch the westbound train and return to treading the boards, as they say in the business."

Dooley frowned. He would miss that great scout.

"He is drinking now in my saloon."

"I'll have to pay him a visit, shake his hand, say good-bye."

"He would certainly enjoy that."

"A great man, Buffalo Bill."

"The best."

"Yes," Dooley said, "he most certainly is. Well, then maybe Butch Sweeney could pin on that tin star."

"Sweeney?" The man shook his head. "You mean the stagecoach driver?"

"Absolutely. He killed one of those men this morning when he was about to do me in. I'd say Butch Sweeney is your man."

"Then who would drive Butch's stagecoach?"

Dooley glanced at the chest of drawers. Maybe he could tolerate another shot of rye.

"Mr. Monahan," the alderman said. "The mayor, the city councilmen, and the aldermen on the vigilance committee were in complete and total agreement that you, sir, yes, you, you would be the perfect man to become the first town marshal of Leadville."

Dooley went numb. Surely he had misheard. Or maybe Adam Wolfe had gone around the bend, as the saying went. Dooley worked his jaw, his tongue, and his brain, and said, "Me?"

"Don't act modest, sir," Wolfe said. "You have a reputation across the frontier territories and states as a man who knows his business."

But, Dooley wanted to tell him, *my business is cowboying . . . or was . . . till I found all that damned silver.*

"Your reputation as a bounty hunter has no equal. Confound it, sir, you are the man who rid the West of Jason Baylor and his evil brothers, not to mention Hubert Dobbs, Frank Handley, and Doc Watson. I hear that you single-handedly saved a wagon train from cutthroat Sioux warriors in eastern Wyoming Territory. Aren't you that Dooley Monahan?"

He exhaled a long sigh. "But . . . I'm . . . um . . ."

"We all saw what you did today. Yes, yes, I know, yes, Buffalo Bill Cody came through with grand heroics, and Butch Sweeney managed to gun down one of those robbers. But you killed the rest of them, didn't you? Except for that one Marshal Price gunned down . . . a man unarmed and likely no threat and, were he not a federal lawman, would likely be getting hemped around midnight by our vigilance committee."

Dooley thought sadly about Julia.

"You stopped them from bankrupting this town."

Dooley had a hard time believing that Leadville, as rich as it was, would ever go broke no matter how many banks would be robbed.

"Well . . ." Dooley said.

The man rose suddenly. He grabbed his hat and put it on. "Why don't you talk this over with Buffalo Bill Cody? Maybe he can persuade you to come to this town's rescue . . . again. Come with me, sir. The Silver Palace Saloon will buy your drinks."

Well, Dooley told himself, *I sure could use another drink right about now.*

CHAPTER THIRTY-THREE

"I'd bring you with me, Dooley, to San Francisco for our California tour, and wherever the hell else we're bound for this summer. But I got no part for you in the play." Buffalo Bill smiled at Blue, who sat at Dooley's side at the poker table in the corner of the Silver Palace Saloon. "Can your dog act?"

"I don't think so." Dooley had to make himself smile. He knew what Buffalo Bill was doing, trying to make Dooley feel better, comfortable, and take his mind off what had happened in Leadville that morning. It wouldn't work, of course, but Dooley was glad to call Cody a friend.

Cody splashed amber liquor into Dooley's glass, and his own. There were no cards on the table, and nobody sat there right now except Cody and Dooley. There had been several men there when Dooley, Blue, and Alderman Wolfe entered the place—which did not look hardly like the final scene of a bank robbery that day— but Wolfe had enticed them away from Cody's spotlight for free drinks at the bar.

"Well." Cody downed his liquor. "I can't act, either. But it's quite the life. Best hotels. Comfortable beds. Sure beats sleeping on cold, hard ground. Good food. Maître d's putting you in the best seats and seeing that you get the best waiters. Sure beats hardtack and beans or nothing but jerky. Folks who love you and don't want to kill you."

"It sounds a lot better than marshaling," Dooley told him.

After refilling his shot glass, the great scout leaned across the table. "It's not. It's important to me, Dooley, because I'm a showman at heart. I have great ambition. Great ideas. I hope to make the Western ways something the entire world will know and remember. That's me. Not you. But you could do something almost as important."

"What's that?"

"I save the West, or the image of the West, for generations, to preserve this for history. You . . ." He held the shot glass toward Dooley, then downed it. "You save actual lives. You save actual towns. You are the hero, not some playactor."

"You killed Tall Bull," Dooley reminded him. "You saved actual lives . . . a lot more than I have."

Shrugging, Cody pushed back his chair and pulled his hat down. "Maybe. But here's the long and short of things, Dooley. I'm pulling out. Stayed here longer than I intended to in the first place. Leadville's a fine town, Dooley, but I've seen many fine towns. It doesn't hold me like North Platte, Nebraska, or even Denver. Or even

New York City or San Francisco or Chicago. What I'm saying, pard, is this. I got nothing for me in Leadville, other than my grubstaking you, which you have paid in full. And our friendship, which shall endure till my dying breath. Nothing to hold me to this burg, though. Nothing that I honestly think is worth saving. It's a good town, and those miners can't play poker worth a dang, so I can make myself a bit of money and move on. But it ain't a town I truly love because there's nothing in it, or no one, that I really love. Don't get me wrong, Dooley. I like you a whole lot. You're one to ride the river with. But you ain't kin. You ain't my children. You ain't my wife. I like you fine. I just don't love you. And I don't love Leadville. Because there's no one here for me."

The chair scraped on the floor as Cody stood. He grinned down at Dooley, who drew a deep breath, held it, and let it out before he looked at Cody.

"I reckon," Dooley said, "I can't say I love Leadville, either."

"It's just a town," Cody said. "Not much to love, except silver and whiskey. But I don't think you can tell me that there ain't nobody in this town that you can just walk away from."

Dooley stared. Buffalo Bill did not blink. After a moment, the grin on the scout's face widened, and he stretched out his hand.

As they shook, Buffalo Bill Cody said, "Some things are worth fighting for, Dooley. You just got to make sure you're fighting for the right things. And I know for a fact that you are."

Dooley watched the tall man walk out of the Silver Palace, shaking hands with miners and vagrants and hurdy-gurdy girls, businessmen and professional gamblers. He was certainly the showman, Dooley realized, but Buffalo Bill was also a scout who lived up to his reputation. He could read the signs. He could read men.

The legend of the West disappeared, and Dooley stood staring at the doorway, then through the window at bustling, booming Leadville. Across the street, Adam Wolfe, alderman, saloon owner, vigilante, sat on a cracker barrel talking to banker John Price and smoking cigars.

"You want another drink, hon?"

Dooley looked up at the barmaid, a tired woman with a painted face and red-rimmed eyes.

"No thanks." Dooley tossed her a nickel tip as he stood, adjusted his hat, and walked out the door.

The banker and the alderman stopped chatting and kept staring. Dooley waited for a farm wagon and a freight wagon to pass, then he strode across the street, stepped onto the boardwalk, tipped his hat as a lady walked past, and stared at the banker and the vigilante.

"When do I start?" Dooley asked.

Both men grinned at each other.

"Let's go find the mayor and the judge and get you sworn in," Mr. Wolfe said.

The contract Dooley signed made him town marshal for six months. He would be paid $200 a month, but Dooley insisted that $170 would be put into a fund to build a schoolhouse and pay for a schoolmistress.

"There ain't but ten kids in this town, son," the mayor said, "and eight of 'em is orphans."

"Families will come once this town settles down," Dooley said.

"I like the idea of a schoolmistress," said one of the councilmen, and the other councilmen sniggered and elbowed one another.

Dooley kept telling himself that they were not the reason he was taking this stupid job that likely would get him killed.

The judge said that was mighty generous of Dooley, and Dooley said that he made more money from his mine than he knew what to do with anyway.

The contract also said that Dooley would collect half of every fine the judge collected. That gave the judge, naturally, reason to make those fines higher, which suited Dooley fine, too, because he knew that, yes, he did make a passel of money from silver, but now that he would not be working at the mine six days a week he would have to hire a manager and an assistant manager, and a fellow never did know when a mine might go bust. His pa had always tried to save a little bit of hard money when he got some, for those dark days when locusts ate all the money crops or droughts or floods left barely enough food for the family. Besides, Dooley figured he might need some money for poker, when he wasn't working, of course.

The council would have to figure out a way to get money to build Dooley an office, but banker John Price, who was also on the town council, agreed to let Dooley have the office vacated by attorney Jonah Terrance Cohen in his rented spot upstairs. That was fine enough with Dooley, although he figured the carpenters and painters would be making quite a racket down the hall fixing the gun shop and painting over the blood on the walls and floor for about a week or so.

Still, Dooley pointed out, "There's no room in Cohen's office for a jail."

But that did not matter because another board member pointed out that there was a big hardwood tree on a vacant lot just two streets over, and most of the men on the council knew of that tree, especially those who served on the vigilance committee, for they had hanged about six or seven no-accounts from those limbs over the past eight or nine months.

The blacksmith named Hans Schultz, also a

councilman, said he would be willing to donate chains and leg irons to hold the prisoners as they awaited their fines from the judge, John R. Ottinger, to be levied. For small crimes. Bigger ones would require the circuit-riding judge's prudence when he came to town. It would be good for business, and Schultz said he would charge the town only one dollar for every culprit he had to put in leg irons. The secretary and treasurer would get together, the mayor decreed, and order some handcuffs for Dooley from Denver, which, with luck, would arrive on Butch Sweeney's next stagecoach run.

Which brought up something Dooley had not considered until the mayor mentioned Butch's stagecoach.

"What about deputies?"

"The vigilance committee will be at your disposal should you need extra guns," Adam Wolfe said. "Perhaps at the end of the month when the mines pay off their men."

"I was thinking about someone maybe part-time permanent," Dooley said, knowing that Butch would be on the stage a lot of the time, though maybe he could hire a jehu.

"Do you mean Butch Sweeney?" Wolfe asked. After all, Dooley had suggested that Sweeney become Leadville's marshal.

"Then who'd drive the stagecoach to Denver and back?" asked a sleepy-eyed councilman.

Dooley opened his mouth to answer, but shut it. How stupid could he be, trying to pin a badge on his young pard Butch Sweeney? Badges made mighty inviting targets for drunks or outlaws packing iron.

"No. No, not Butch. Butch Sweeney has a job, and he's good at it. I'm sure Mr. Wolfe is right. I'll just get some of the vigilantes . . ."

"Vigilance committee," Mr. Wolfe corrected. *Vigilantes* had a bad connotation, it appeared.

"Vigilance committee," Dooley said. "Whenever the need arises."

"Harley Boone would make a good deputy, though," said the blacksmith.

Dooley stared at Schultz as though he were dirt. "I don't think so," Dooley said.

"I just meant he's a good man with a gun," the blacksmith said.

"Too good," banker Price said, and a lot of the other men in the banker's office seemed to agree with the banker's—and Dooley's—assessment.

A storeowner laughed and said, "I think, once word reaches Denver and Georgetown and Cheyenne about what Marshal Monahan did this morning, no one will be venturing into Leadville to do ill will."

So the meeting was adjourned. Handshakes, cigars, and pats on the back made their rounds, and Dooley left with a silver-plated six-point star pinned onto his shirtfront. The silver came from Leadville's mines, donated by some of the big barons. Mr. Wolfe walked Dooley out of the bank. Summer nights at ten thousand feet still did not feel like summer to Dooley.

"Well," the saloonkeeper and alderman said, "would you like to celebrate your new appointment as town marshal with a drink of my private stock at my very own saloon?"

Dooley shook his head. "I've got some work to do, but I thank you for your offer."

"And I, and everyone in Leadville, thank you for your service, sir. And let me know whenever you need deputies. We are at your disposal. And remember: It's just like our mayor said. You have a free rein to do what needs to be done to keep the peace in Leadville."

Which is another reason Dooley had decided to take that job.

Wolfe went one way, and Dooley walked the other toward the hotel. He wondered what he had gotten himself into, but he also knew he had made the right decision by not recommending Butch Sweeney for a deputy's job. Not that Butch would have accepted the offer anyway. He had a stagecoach to drive, a business to run, and no matter how old he was, he would always be a kid in Dooley's mind. Which seemed a bit odd, now that Dooley considered that. Butch was a kid. Would always be a kid.

But Julia was now a woman.

Dooley stopped and stared across the street. The shades to the county clerk's office remained closed, but yellow light from lanterns seeped through the cracks. George Miller, and likely those no-account *Telegram* scribe and deputy federal peace officer, were inside, burning the midnight oil and probably planning a way to get rid of Leadville's new lawman—permanently.

Which is why Dooley decided not to have Butch for a deputy, and why he was so happy the alderman named Wolfe had pretty much dismissed Dooley's original idea to have Butch Sweeney become Leadville's lawman.

Deputy marshals could get killed just as quickly as town marshals.

CHAPTER THIRTY-FOUR

Dooley spent little time in town on his first day as marshal, but he had warned the mayor and the councilmen and the vigilance committee aldermen that he would certainly need some policemen at least for a day or so as he settled his affairs.

That meant spending the first half of the morning with Jarvis at his office at the mine, getting things squared away, but before he set out for the mine on Halfmoon Creek, riding General Grant with Blue tagging along, he stopped in at the shop of Joe McCutcheon, the sign-maker and an alderman on the vigilance committee, and told him what he wanted and when he needed it.

Joe McCutcheon was a cigarette-smoking, always-coughing, grizzled old man whose face was harder than sandpaper. He wore a carpenter's apron tied around his waist, a pencil stuck atop an ear, and his fingers were splotched with paints of various colors and hues, and yellow stains from a life of smoking cigarettes.

After hacking up half a lung, McCutcheon spit phlegm into an empty tin can and stared at Dooley in disbelief.

"Just do it," Dooley said, and dropped a few gold coins by the tin can.

"You sure?"

"Yep."

The sign-maker shrugged.

"You get much business?" Dooley asked.

"Well," he said, and spit again into the can, "there's a lot of signs needin' replacin' after yesterday's ruckus."

"But you can have this done by the end of the day?"

The man stared at the coins and nodded. "You're the marshal."

Dooley nodded. "And if somebody happens to come in, you'll keep your mouth shut and the signs out of sight."

The man plucked a cigarette on the top of his other ear, lighted it with the end of the butt he was finishing smoking, and stuck it in his mouth. He answered, the cigarette bobbing on his lower lip. "Like I said, you're the marshal."

So Dooley left McCutcheon to his smoke and paint and signs, grabbed a coffee and a doughnut at the bakery, and rode out of Leadville.

He had to hire a new bookkeeper, and left that to Jarvis. He had to hire a manager and an assistant, but he promoted his foreman to the main job, and the foreman-now-manager recommended a good hand at the Empire to become an assistant. Dooley figured that the foreman-now-manager knew about such things and such men a whole lot better than he did, so he gave permission for the hire. They then promoted Good Touch Tim, so called because he never blew up anyone tapping dynamite sticks into the drill holes, to a third assistant, and left the hiring of a new miner to Jarvis.

That went pretty good, Dooley figured, and Jarvis said he would make sure that Dooley got his money on time. Which made Dooley wonder when he would have time to sneak back to his mine and dig up all that money he had buried. But, he resigned himself to thinking, it probably wouldn't matter because George Miller would likely figure out a way to get the new marshal of Leadville shot down in a week, if that.

When he got back to town, he left his horse and the blue shepherd in the livery and strode over to the hotel where Butch Sweeney was loading passengers and getting ready to ride out of town.

Butch smiled and walked up to Dooley, removed his bandanna, and pretended to wipe the dust off Dooley's silver-plated star and give it a good shining.

"That's right pretty," Butch said.

"Thanks." Dooley was not amused.

Dooley glanced inside the coach. "You got a lot of passengers this trip," he said.

"That ruckus yesterday made some folks decide to leave town."

That made Dooley frown. Maybe Leadville did need a town lawman. Maybe it was time law and order came to Leadville. But why did he have to bring law and order to Leadville?

"And," Butch said, "this might be my last run?"

Dooley cocked his head.

Shrugging, Butch said, "Word is that there's another company forming in Georgetown, and a new outfit has this omnibus that they plan on running from Breckenridge to here. And ol' Jarrod Dickinson is starting one up to make runs to Silver Plume and back."

"Town's growing," Dooley said, just to say something as some carpenters worked on replacing doors and windows and patching up bullet holes in the town's many façades. He also saw Joe McCutcheon hanging a freshly painted sign on Front Street.

"Yep." Butch shook Dooley's hand, reached up to grab hold of the driver's box, and climbed up the front wheel and into his seat.

"Be back in a few days," Butch said, smiled, and reached for his whip. The smile faded and he said, "If you can, it wouldn't hurt to check on . . ." Julia's name went unsaid, and Dooley nodded grimly and looked across the street at the county clerk's office. The shades were open this time, and a figure—undoubtedly George Miller himself—stood staring at Dooley and Butch.

"Be careful," Dooley told Butch as he looked back at his young pard.

"You be careful," Butch said, and he released

the brake and snapped the whip over the lead mule's left ear.

He wondered how that kid had learned to handle a whip so well. The kid Dooley remembered from that ranch up in Utah was too green to have even known how to pick up a whip, let alone use one to perfection.

The stage rumbled out of Leadville, and Dooley felt like a man alone.

Of course, when he sat down at the little café to grab a bite to eat, he was not alone for long. The bell on the door chimed, and four men entered the restaurant that smelled of fried potatoes, burned bacon, and coffee so powerful it could float not just a horseshoe, but an entire horse. This wasn't the normal place those four men would take a late dinner or an early supper.

Their wardrobe was fancy, and not Joseph and Lyman G. Bloomingdale fancy, but really, really expensive. Silk top hats; tailor-made Prince Alberts; silk cravats with diamond and silver and gold stickpins; velvet-lined, double-breasted, pearl-button vests; black leather shoes shined to a gleam that reflected the late-afternoon sun and the dim lanterns hanging in this greasy dining hall. One carried an ebony cane with a carved-ivory handle that resembled a lion's head. Another's cane was silver-plated. They did not remove their hats. They did not sit at any of the vacant tables. They walked directly to Dooley.

330

The two cane-toters pulled up the empty chairs and deposited themselves in the rickety seats. The bald one with the monocle disgustedly retrieved a handkerchief from an inside coat pocket and pulled out the other chair. He dropped the piece of white silk on the floor on purpose because, Dooley figured, once his hanky had touched this filth it was no longer fitting for him to keep. The last one waited, turned, and demanded that the nice, skinny waitress fetch him a chair immediately.

Dooley wanted to punch that sorry cur in his big, bulbous nose, but the waitress hurriedly obeyed and asked if any of the gents wanted coffee.

They turned up their noses and did not answer.

Dooley sipped his coffee and picked up a copy of the *Leadville Ledger*. He did not ask the men what they wanted. They'd get around to telling him, which they did.

Quickly.

The silver baron with the monocle spoke.

"Marshal?"

Dooley finished reading a paragraph, although he could not have told anyone what he had just read, folded the newspaper, deliberately took his time laying it on the table, took another sip of coffee and did not grimace, and stared at the one-glass man with that perfectly coiffured gray handlebar mustache and pointed beard.

"Yeah?"

The one with the ivory lion's–head cane spoke. "What are your plans?"

Dooley shrugged. He thought about answering, *Trying to stay alive.* Instead, he said, "Protecting the citizens of Leadville."

The silver-plated cane slammed against the table, and the silver baron with those cold gray eyes and long whiskers down his chin, bellowed, "That is not what we mean!"

"Well, pardon me, but you'll have to tell me exactly what you mean, mister." Dooley's eyes made those cold gray ones staring at him widen in surprise. Silver barons weren't that used to having men speak curtly to them.

"About your mine, Monahan?" said the last one, the rude one who could drop three-dollar handkerchiefs like Ol' Dude Dvorak used to drop lice back when Dooley was working at that outfit in the Texas Panhandle.

That took Dooley by surprise. "What about my mine?"

"Well," said the monocle wearer, "certainly a man with a silver mine as profitable as yours cannot lower himself to wear a badge."

"Even," added the rude one, "if the badge is silver."

"But just plated," said the ivory lion's head dude. "Not solid."

"Like Jim's cane," he then added, and

snickered while the silver-plated cane slammer's face reddened and he clenched his fists till his knuckles whitened.

"Dooley," said the last one, finally, the one with the heavy gold-chained watch and spectacles—not just a monocle—and just a steel gray mustache. He had a pleasant voice, but Dooley figured he wasn't a pleasant man to be in business with, or sit at a table with. "It is not fitting for a man of your wealth to wear a badge." He shook his head. "To be a mere lawman. It does not look right."

"Did it look right when Buffalo Bill and I shot down those vermin who were about to take your money out of those banks?"

The eyes behind the spectacles blinked. He straightened and looked across the table at the one-glass man, who popped his monocle out and stared at Dooley as if he were the dumbest person at the table, which, Dooley would have conceded, he likely was.

The silver-plated cane smasher stopped grimacing and trying to stop his head from exploding and actually laughed. Well, it wasn't quite a laugh, but more like an absurd snigger. The rude one's jaw hung open to draw flies, which were plentiful at this time of day in this type of eatery in Leadville.

The best dressed of the finely attired silver barons recovered first.

"Marshal," he said with a sly grin, "we certainly don't keep our moneys in Leadville."

"Denver," said the silver-plated cane whacker.

"Geneva," said the rude one.

"New York," said the ivory lion's head.

The pleasant-enough one kept his bank a secret.

Dooley wondered what these distinguished gentlemen would say if he told them he buried his money out by his mine. "My mistake," Dooley said. "But I bet the miners who risk their lives to make you all that fortune, they're glad their life's savings wasn't taken." Although he knew those dead robbers did not come to rob a bank, at least, not really. That was just a bonus. They had been paid to kill Dooley Monahan.

But Dooley did not suspect the silver barons of being a part of that scheme. That was all George Miller.

"We'd like to make you an offer for your property," said the pleasant one. And he did. Immediately. Which caused Dooley's mouth to hang open like an idiot and invite the flies.

The rude one topped that offer considerably.

The one with the ivory lion's head cane tip whispered an insanely higher number.

Silver-plated cane smasher cleared his throat, raised his hand, and started to say something, but quickly shut his trap and stared at his fancy cane. Dooley figured that a man who put his money in a Denver bank was out of his league when he was up against barons with banks in Chicago and New York and some unnamed city.

The pleasant one grinned, leaned forward, and made another bid.

No one topped that one. They waited for Dooley to recover.

Which he did.

"I'd like to keep my mine," he said, "at least for a little while."

The rude one snorted and rose. "You might have only a little while to keep your mine, friend. To keep your mine and your life."

CHAPTER THIRTY-FIVE

That next morning was his first day on the job as Leadville's town marshal. He ate at the hotel's dining room, walked to the livery to fetch Blue, and ambled down the boardwalks to the bank, took the outside staircase, and saw that new sign hanging above the entranceway.

Towm Marshal

Dooley wondered if Joe McCutcheon misspelled *Town* on purpose, but it was a rushed job, and, well, he doubted if most people could notice in a town like Leadville. The five-point star would probably let the illiterate know that the local peace officer did business upstairs, even if Dooley's silver-plated badge had six points, instead of five. Besides, that sign wasn't the most important one.

The door was already open, and Dooley stepped inside, catching a whiff of fresh paint and all sorts of cleaning soap, sawdust, and the usual smells when folks are in a hurry to clean up after a bloody gun battle. A few carpenters busied themselves as they tried to patch up the gun shop. Dooley greeted them with a wave and a "Good morning," and unlocked the office and let Blue go inside.

He sat at the desk that had been lawyer Jonah Terrance Cohen's, and as Blue sniffed every nook and cranny of the office, Dooley got an idea. He jerked open one drawer and sighed. It was empty. He moved to one of the filing cabinets. Those drawers were empty, too.

Well, when a man leaves a town, he usually takes his property, Dooley thought, files and letters and all that kind of stuff.

Yet, now he stared at the items hanging on the wall, items he had not really paid much attention to until this morning.

Now a man leaving for a new opportunity might have no need of a portrait of Abraham Lincoln, or one of George Washington, and since he was leaving Colorado, he probably did not need a map of the state. But wouldn't a lawyer want to take his diploma with him? Dooley looked at the desk and picked up a tintype.

The woman staring back at him in the photograph was white haired and wrinkly, with a brooch pinned on a dark dress. Dooley found a bit of resemblance between her and J. T. Cohen. He couldn't prove anything, but it just struck him odd that a man leaving town for a new career in a new town wouldn't take a tintype of his mother, or grandmother, with him.

Wouldn't he?

He went through another desk drawer, found some coins, trash, stationery, even postage stamps. He started to close that drawer, but stopped. He pushed away the stamps and stationery and stared at the brown stain. Another brown stain had run down from the desktop into the drawer. Dooley touched it. It wasn't sticky. It was dried. And Dooley tried to remember if he had seen such a stain when he had sat on the other side of this desk and talked to the attorney-at-law.

Blood, he knew, dried brown. Of course, he couldn't prove that this was blood, and certainly he could not prove that this was a lawyer's blood. He went back to the cabinets and looked through every drawer, closer this time, and then saw Blue sniffing and scratching at the floor underneath the desk . . . where a man's legs would be when he was sitting and doing his lawyering.

"Blue," Dooley said impatiently, and grew impatient himself. He slammed the empty cabinet drawer shut and raced to the desk, pulled Blue away, and found himself under the desk. He plucked up some hairs that his dog had clawed away from other brown stains.

"Son of a—" He didn't finish his curse because he lifted his head and hit it against the desk. Then he did finish his curse as he backed out of the cavernous hole in the desk, rubbed his head.

Remembering all those articles he had read in the *Police Gazette* and *Frank Leslie's Illustrated*, Dooley rose, found the chair, and positioned himself at the desk as if he were working, maybe talking to a client. Then someone clubbed him on the head, Dooley imagined, and he planted his face carefully where the biggest brown stain on the desk happened to be. He kicked the chair out from under him and dragged his nose across the brown stain that led to the drawer that held more brown stains.

Of course, the drawer would have been shut then, but the blood could have run down as the fiends who had clubbed a harmless lawyer—if any attorneys could be called harmless—as they went through the desk drawers looking for . . . ?

"For what?" Dooley asked out loud, and then remembered what he was supposed to be doing. His knees came to the floor, and Dooley laid his hands on the floor, then looking at the stains underneath the desk, put his head down there.

He blinked. He came up, carefully this time, and fingered another stain. This one had a hole in it, but the hole had been packed with something. Dooley pulled out his knife and removed the filler. Dried tobacco mostly. Specifically, dried chewing tobacco. Of a low grade, Dooley figured, because he had read many, many articles at line camps from old and sometimes fairly new *Police Gazettes*. He put the blade deeper into the hole, but felt nothing. After closing the blade, he leaned closer and looked at the hole. He struck a match. He brought the match closer and saw the marks of a blade along the rim and edges of the hole. He put his finger on the hole and remembered that the *Police Gazette* had explained how a good lawman, a fine detective, could determine the caliber of a bullet by the size of a hole.

This one appeared to be from a .44, not a .45, but someone had dug out the bullet from the hole.

Dooley sat up, and Blue came over to be petted.

It made sense, Dooley thought. It made a lot of sense. He just couldn't prove it.

Yet.

The banker had said Cohen had given notice, looked happy, and dressed wealthy. So Cohen and Miller had reached an agreement. But . . . Cohen must have gotten greedy. George Miller had come in here. He . . . No . . . No . . . Dooley shook his head. That's not what had happened at all. George Miller and somebody else . . . Harley Boone, most likely, had come in to talk to lawyer J. T. Cohen. One of the miserable swine—it had to be Harley Boone—had come around behind the attorney. The lawyer had taken money from Miller, and planned on leaving town, but likely wanted more money now before turning over Dooley's will. So Boone had laid the barrel or the butt of his revolver on Cohen's head, which had slammed across the desktop.

Cohen then kicked the desk out from under him, fell to the floor, tried to stand or rise or maybe crawl away, and then collapsed on the floor, his head and chest underneath the desk. He had rolled over. That made sense. Dooley wasn't the best tracker in the world, but those brown stains seemed to confirm Dooley's suspicions. And Harley Boone or George Miller had asked the lawyer once more to tell them what they wanted to know. When the lawyer had refused, Harley Boone had put a bullet here . . . right through Cohen's chest. At that range, a .44 slug would have gone right through the body, and the killers had dragged Cohen's body out, probably rolled it in a bedroll, and taken him to some obscure burying ground.

Then they had taken all of the papers, everything they could carry, out of the drawers, tried to take everything. They had burned the papers— maybe including Dooley's letter and will, or maybe not.

It was a strange feeling, Dooley thought. On one hand, he was quite pleased with himself. He was Dooley Monahan, a farm boy from Iowa who had become a thirty-dollar-a-month cowboy, a kid with not much of an education who had grown into a stove-up cowhand with a massive silver mine. And he had solved, sadly, a murder. But he had no way of proving it.

The door opened, and Dooley reached for his holstered Colt .45 as he looked above the desk.

Cigarette smoke reached him first, then the

noise of a hacking cough. Joe McCutcheon, not bothering to take the half-smoked cigarette from his lips, said, "I got them other signs you wanted me to fix up fer you."

"Good." Dooley stood up. Blue wagged his tail. Dooley tried to make it obvious that he had good reason for hiding on the floor behind his desk on his first real day as Leadville marshal. "Put them up."

McCutcheon reacted. For the first time since Dooley had known the man, he reached up and removed an unfinished cigarette from his lips, and not to light the smoke he had already rolled and tucked up above his ear.

"You want me to what?"

"Put the signs up," Dooley said. "One at each road entering town. North. South. East. West. And the other right here, dead center of Front Street."

"Like hell I will," the old man said defiantly.

Dooley fished out some greenbacks.

"That'll pay for my coffin," McCutcheon said.

A double eagle dropped onto the paper money.

The cigarette returned to McCutcheon's lips, and he moved to the desk, scooped up the money, and walked out of the office.

Dooley brushed the dust off his trousers, told Blue to stay, and walked out the door into the hallway. He could hear the pleasant chitchat downstairs in the bank, and the carpenters had gone, their work finished. Dooley walked to the gun shop. The door was open. The proprietor was inside, working on the mainspring of an old Colt cap-and-ball pistol. He did not smile when Dooley entered.

Of course, the man had good reason. Dooley had practically wiped out his office, which must have cost the merchant a passel of money—at Leadville prices, mind you.

Still, Dooley figured he would earn the merchant's trust and maybe not friendship, but a bit of respect.

"Howdy," said Dooley.

"What do you want?" the man said, putting the .36 caliber Navy and a screwdriver on the counter.

Dooley pointed. "That Parker twelve-gauge there, but I want you to saw down the barrel to about here." He motioned with his hands. "Ten boxes of double-ought buckshot. Do you have that many?"

The man was beginning to take notice. "I think so," he said.

"Ten boxes of .45s for my Colt. Ten boxes of .44-40s for my Winchester. I need another Colt, too, in .45 caliber, even though I never was much for packing two pistols. And I was thinking that maybe a couple more pistols. That double-action there. Ain't that one of those new Colts?"

"A Lightning," the merchant said. "Thirty-eight caliber."

"Good. Yeah. I'll take that one. But only six boxes of .38s. And that little Sharps derringer. But only two boxes of ammunition."

The man suddenly grew suspicious.

"I suppose, Marshal," he said, "that I'll be billing the town council for all this."

Dooley was already bringing out his wallet.

"Not at all, sir. I pay my own way."

CHAPTER THIRTY-SIX

A crowd had gathered around the sign that had just been put up on Front Street. Two businessmen nodded their heads approvingly, another shook his head and whispered something, a woman holding a basket of eggs said, "It's about time," and a gambler drew his six-shooter, thumbed back the hammer, and drew a bead on the center of the sign.

"I'd like to see that star-packer take away my Smith & Wesson, that stupid little son of a—"

He didn't finish.

Dooley slammed the stock of the double-barrel shotgun against the man's silk hat, and he dropped without completing his curse. The woman gasped, the approvers-of and condemners-of backed away and stared now in silence as Dooley bent down and picked up the unconscious gambler's .44.

"When he wakes up," Dooley told the nearest merchant, "tell him he can collect this . . ."—Dooley shoved the long-barreled thumb-busting pistol into his waistband—". . . at my office, after he pays the ten-dollar fine, and just before he leaves town."

The duly appointed town marshal walked away, leaving one man sprawled in the dirt and other transients and locals leaving the boardwalks to stare at the gambler but mostly at the sign.

NOTICE
The Carrying of FIREARMS,
Concealed or In View,
and the Discharge of ANY WEAPON
are **PROHIBITED** *in the City Limits.*

Below that, in smaller type, read:

Subject to FINES OF $10 *or higher*
and as much as 60 DAYS' INCARCERATION
chained to our Tree Jail.

And in the smallest of type:

By Order of **Dooley Monahan,**
Leadville City Marshal.

"Ten dollars," Dooley told the gambler, who could not wear his silk hat on account of the thickness of the white bandages wrapped around his skull. Dooley hadn't meant to hit the fellow that hard, but the tinhorn had it coming so Dooley didn't feel bad.

"Or sixty days."

The gambler grimaced.

"Sixty days? Outside? Shackled to a tree? That ain't rightly fair."

346

"Downright cruel and unreasonable," Dooley said, "but it's the law of the land."

"How do I . . . you know . . . ?"

"Slop bucket."

The gambler shook his head, then regretted that move, and fished out his coin purse from the yellow brocade vest.

He dropped a ten-dollar coin on Dooley's desk.

"Now I get my .44 back," the gambler said.

"On your way out of town," Dooley said.

The man gestured toward the side street. "My horse and grip are outside. Hell of a town. I'm going to Georgetown where the law's more reasonable and tolerant of men trying to earn an honest living."

Dooley rolled his eyes, but jerked open the drawer, grabbed the pearl-handled butt of the revolver, and dropped the heavy Smith & Wesson on the table. The gambler quickly picked it up and thumbed back the hammer, an evil grin stretching across his face as he aimed the giant barrel at Dooley's chest.

Calmly, Dooley stood up and dropped six brass cartridges onto the desk. They rolled around, one fell back into the drawer, and the malicious grin faded, the .44 barrel lowered, and the gambler's face went suddenly pale as Dooley drew his . . . loaded . . . pistol.

Dooley had a heart, so he didn't coldcock the cardsharper again, but merely took the empty

Smith & Wesson from him and marched him to the Jail Tree. He noticed that there was no horse and grip on the side street, and figured that served the gambler right. That sneaky little tinhorn would also have to pay for a hotel room he wouldn't be using for the next two months. Dooley and the judge also decided it would be fitting to up the fine from $10 to $250, Leadville prices and all, and threatening a peace officer was a much more serious charge than carrying a weapon unlawfully. Especially since the judge also got a share of any fines levied and collected.

Dooley still owned a silver mine, but he figured he could live off his salary and percentage of fines pretty well, even in Leadville. It took a while for the residents and visitors to grow accustomed to the new firearms law, but Dooley had explained it fairly well to the mayor, the judge, the Committee of Concerned Citizens, the vigilance committee, and an assorted ragtag group of saloon bouncers, visiting gamblers, and one or two gunfighters who might have been wanted outside of Colorado but hadn't committed anything wrong in the city.

"Listen," Dooley had said, "I cowboyed a long time. I've been into quite a few cow towns and mining camps, and the thing is this: You can't carry a gun in a town like Tombstone. You can't carry a gun in Dodge City . . . at least not in the town proper. The red-light districts, the no-man's-lands, the Nauchvilles and the Hell's Half Acres, those might be different. But we don't have those in Leadville. The best way to keep the peace is to keep guns where they belong. And that's not strapped to a fellow drinking whiskey or playing poker or blackjack."

So a stranger riding into Leadville wouldn't be arrested, slapped with manacles, and chained to that infernal tree just because he rode into town. He could go to the hotel, where the clerk would explain the local ordinance, and the stranger could leave his pistol in the room. He could ride straight to the Silver Palace or any of the other hundreds of watering holes, and check his pistol and/or rifle with the bartender. Most folks in Leadville were honest, and they wouldn't charge a stranger to hold a gun. This was the West, and Westerners were known for their hospitality.

They could even carry their guns to Dooley's office, or drop them off at the gun shop next door upstairs and get them cleaned and oiled, have the trigger pulls tightened or loosened, get them resighted, and they'd be all ready and practically just like brand-new when they rode out of town.

Everybody seemed happy.

Except a few, and those were already chained to the tree with the tinhorn gambler, or they had paid their fines and left Leadville with strict instructions that they were not to return.

The roar of gunfire soon faded, and Leadville

349

nights became known for the soothing sound of the rustling of tree limbs in the evening breeze, roulette wheels spinning, dancers doing their kicks, the howling of wolves in the mountains, and the whistles blowing at the various mines.

Still, Dooley had to change his ways. He slept late in the morning, because he had to patrol the streets at night. Most of the arrests he made were for drunks, and the majority of those stumbled along peacefully to the Jail Tree, where Dooley often didn't even bother chaining them. He wrote them a ticket, stuffed it in the pocket of their jeans or vest or shirt, and knew they would be good for it. Come their next payday, they would head over to the judge's chambers, a corner table in the Silver Palace Saloon or in the parlor at one of the more respectable brothels in town, and pay the fine. The judge, in turn, would give Dooley his share and the town treasurer the rest.

After three weeks, Leadville had lost a lot of its roughness. A theatrical troupe came to the opera house and performed three nights of various Shakespearean plays. A troubadour came and sang some songs. Dooley felt generous and turned loose the first gambler he had coldcocked and arrested, although he did not reduce the gent's fine and he made sure the man paid his hotel bill, and then Dooley mounted General Grant and escorted the sharper out of town to see him off to Georgetown.

It was on the first month's anniversary of Dooley's new job, when this fat lady was planning on performing some opera songs at the actual opera house, that Dooley walked into his office on the second floor of the bank, removed his hat, and stared at the person sitting at his desk and petting Blue.

"Dooley," Julia said, and Blue barked an excited yelp. Not to greet Dooley, of course, but to plead with Julia to keep scratching his ears.

Dooley glanced down the hallway, and shut the door. He opened his mouth, but no words came out.

She looked wonderful, a million times better than the frightful girl Dooley remembered after she had just saved his life. That seemed like a billion years ago. She was dressed in a stunning evening gown, and Dooley figured she must have told that cad she was married to that she was bound to the opera house. Dooley figured a man like George Miller had no interest in listening to fat ladies belt out Italian or German songs that made no sense to him. They made no sense to Dooley, either, which is one reason Dooley had not paid for one of those two-dollar tickets.

"Jul . . ." Dooley stopped. "Miss . . ." He stopped again. "Missus . . ."

"Julia is fine, Dooley." Julia smiled.

Dooley's heart melted.

"Have you seen Butch?" Julia asked.

Shaking his head, Dooley tried to figure out what he should do. Sit down? Stand? Pace? Be still? Ask her if she wanted some coffee? Whiskey? He decided to expand on his head-shaking. "He's on the stage, I imagine. Should be back tomorrow if the roads are all right."

"Did you see him before he left?" she asked.

Dooley nodded. After changing his mind about Butch's safety, he had given Butch a deputy marshal's badge, told him that the badge would mean he could tote his shotgun or even pack a revolver when in town. It wasn't that Dooley needed a deputy—yet—but he figured it might give Butch a chance. Boone and Miller, not to mention that bribe-taking deputy marshal from Denver, were still around, and likely not taking kindly to the fact that Butch Sweeney was a friend of Dooley's and had saved his life. Besides, Butch's stagecoach line had plenty of competition these days, and Dooley figured the fifty-dollar-a-month deputy marshal's salary would come in handy. The town could afford it. Twenty-two folks were chained to the Jail Tree this very minute.

He said, "You look well."

That caused her to stop petting and scratching Blue, who did not object, but curled up on his bed and stared at Dooley. His tail wagged a bit, then Blue closed his eyes. Smiling a sad smile, Julia said, "Better . . . I guess . . . than the last time."

You damned fool, Dooley thought to himself. *There you go up and reminding her of that dreadful, bloody day.*

"You look well," she told him.

An awkward silence filled the room. The regulator clock on Dooley's wall chimed.

She rose, found her purse, and wet her lips.

"I need to go. I'm meeting some ladies to take in the performance tonight."

Dooley nodded. "It should be a good show," he told her. He had no clue, if the fat lady were famous or some charlatan, if she could sing. Hell, he didn't even know if Julia liked opera. She certainly hadn't been one to mention operas during those days in Arizona Territory a few years ago.

She held out a gloved hand. Dooley shook it, and then wondered if he was supposed to kiss it. Too late. He could smell Julia's perfume, or soap, or something.

"You and Butch need to be careful, Dooley," she whispered as Dooley opened the door for her and checked the hallway to make sure nobody was around. At this time of evening, no one would be around, but he wanted to be safe.

Dooley froze, and gave Julia a hard stare.

"What's up?" he asked.

Stepping into the hallway, she answered. "I don't know. But George is up to something. Watch yourself." She kissed his cheek, which

353

made Dooley wish he had shaved before heading over to do his marshaling this evening. He watched her hurry out the side door and disappear in the darkness as she turned to head down the stairs.

She left Dooley standing there, rubbing his cheek where she had kissed him, listening to Blue snore contentedly on his bed on the floor.

What, he thought once he had settled behind his desk, would George Miller be planning?

The next afternoon, at exactly 2:37 p.m., he found out.

CHAPTER THIRTY-SEVEN

He had just come back to his office above the bank, after a late dinner in which he had discussed the operations at his mine (actually, he had just agreed with everything the bookkeeper, Jarvis, had said). The butcher across the street had given Dooley some bones to bring to Blue, and that's what Dooley was doing when the first shot rang out.

Squatting while teasing Blue with the steak bone, Dooley looked up, letting the shepherd take the bone and run off to the corner to do some serious gnawing. The gunfire was close, and it did not stop with just one shot. He rose to his feet, drew the .45, and spun the cylinder to check the loads. Then he grabbed the shotgun and walked to the door.

Blue showed no interest in the gunfire, Dooley's leaving, or the sound of footsteps on the inside and outside staircases.

Closing the door behind him, Dooley stood in the hallway. The owner of the gun shop had stepped out of his door and stared wordlessly at Dooley. A grizzled miner whose eyes beamed brightly from John Barleycorn came through the staircase that led outside. A timid teller came up the inside stairs.

"There's a feller shootin' up yer sign," the miner said.

"It's not just any 'feller,' " the clerk managed to choke out. "It's . . ."

A gunshot roared outside.

"Hey, Marshal Do-Nothin'!" called a voice that even with the echoes of the pistol's reports and the thickness of the bank building's walls, Dooley recognized.

He thumbed back the hammers of the shotgun and walked toward the teller.

"Stay here," he told the miner, hearing the door squeak as the old drunk pulled open the door. "All of you."

Dooley came down the inside stairs, and all business stopped. That is, if any business was going on since the shooting started outside. A woman in a bonnet clutched the rosary beads hanging from her neck. A merchant wiped his sweaty brow with a handkerchief. Other bank employees, and the bank president himself, merely stared in silence as Dooley came to the floor and moved toward the front door.

He repeated his order: "Stay here." And thought of a new one: "Stay away from the windows."

People began dropping to a crouch.

Dooley grabbed the knob with his free hand, opened the door, and stepped onto the boardwalk.

The street, which had been crowded just a few minutes earlier when Dooley had returned from his dinner, resembled a ghost town. The shades, naturally, to the county clerk's office were pulled tight. Dooley stepped off the boardwalk and approached the sign he had erected in the center of the street. The man standing in front of the bullet-riddled sign reloaded his pistol.

He had made his shots count.

By Order of D**ley M*n*h*n, Leadville City Marshal.

Once the last bullet had slipped into the empty chamber, the man holstered his revolver and grinned at Dooley.

"I don't like your sign," Harley Boone said.

The gunman spread his legs apart, and his smile vanished as his right hand began hovering over the butt of the heavy revolver on his right hip.

So it was finally about to happen, Dooley thought, but he kept walking toward the ruined sign and the determined gunfighter. Something wasn't right. Harley Boone kept smiling, unafraid. Dooley stopped forty feet from the killer, and Boone's grin never wavered.

Dooley wet his lips. He held a shotgun filled with buckshot that would blow Harley Boone apart. Gunfighters had nerves of steel, sure, but this was ridiculous. Even if Harley could draw his pistol and put a bullet in Dooley's gut, a touch on the triggers, or just one trigger, and Harley Boone's remains would be scattered across Front Street.

The saying across the Western frontier went that *God did not create all men equal—Colonel Samuel Colt did*. But to Dooley's way of thinking, the sawed-off shotgun was the true equalizer, and Dooley had two barrels of Damascus steel trained right on Harley Boone's middle. Dooley had loaded the shotgun himself, with his own shells, and he had just cleaned the double-barrel so he knew it was loaded, and ready to fire.

Harley Boone never struck Dooley as the type of guy who wanted to kill himself, and, even if he had, most folks could pick a better way of doing themselves in, and a whole lot less messy, than catching twin barrels of double-ought buckshot at forty feet.

"You're under arrest, Harley," Dooley said, amazed that his voice didn't choke on fear. "For destruction of city property."

That stupid little grin flattened. Boone shook his head. His eyes narrowed. His fingers above the holstered piece twitched.

"I don't think so."

A door squeaked open behind him. The drunk miner, Dooley figured, stepping out to watch the show. Dooley wouldn't be surprised if George Miller had raised the shades to watch this one. Still, Dooley couldn't figure out what Harley Boone was trying to prove.

Then he saw it.

A man stepped out behind the alley down the street, bringing a rifle's stock to his shoulder. Dooley had no chance of gunning that man down. He was too far out of range for the shotgun. Dooley started to swing the barrel in that direction anyway. The barrels went back to Boone. And Dooley dropped to a knee.

Keeping the shotgun in his right hand, he reached across his body with his left and tried to jerk the .45 from the holster. That was ridiculous, too, because while he might be able to hit a man—if incredibly lucky—at that distance, Dooley knew he'd likely just hit dirt or mud or his own foot shooting with his left hand.

He had the Colt out, started to thumb back the trigger, watched Harley Boone dive behind the sign. Bringing the pistol up, Dooley stopped. Something else caught his eye. A man on the roof of the store across from the bank. That man had a rifle, too. He fell backward, just as he noticed something peculiar about the first man he had spotted, the one down the street with the rifle.

The rifle was swinging up, not at Dooley, and not at the man on the roof.

That man seemed surprised, too, because his head jerked at the sight of the guy with the rifle, stepping onto the boardwalk. Then he swung the barrel down toward Dooley, just as Dooley touched one trigger on the shotgun.

The explosion roared, leaving Dooley's ears

ringing and his eyes burning with smoke. The kick of the gun also hurt. Despite the noise, Dooley heard the rifle down the street speak, and a man screamed behind Dooley.

Dooley came up, picking up the shotgun he had dropped from the savage kick—most men, he had learned, did not shoot shotguns charged with buckshot with one hand for a very good reason.

It was happening practically too fast for Dooley's mind to register, but it seemed to go like this.

The man on the roof screamed, dropping his Winchester that fell through the new awning on the store to Dooley's right. He grabbed his face, staggered back against the chimney, then stepped forward and toppled over the façade—there was that wonderful word again—falling heels over head and making a bigger hole in the awning and slamming atop the Winchester he had just dropped.

All this while, the man who had fired the rifle was running down the boardwalk, working the lever, stopping and firing again. The man, Dooley suddenly realized, was Butch Sweeney.

The man Butch was shooting at was standing on the landing on the staircase that led from the outside of the bank to the second story where Dooley had his office, where Blue was likely still gnawing on the bone, and where the owner of the gun shop and the grizzled miner were likely still standing in the hallway, trying to summon up enough nerve to step outside.

No. No, that wasn't right. Because the man on the landing was slamming against the door, closing it shut, blood spurting from his dingy shirt. He was dropping a revolver and trying to pull another pistol from his waistband in his back. But more blood erupted from his sternum, and he groaned and stepped forward, and then—just like the fellow Dooley had shot off the roof of the store—he cascaded over the railing and crashed hard and ugly on the ground.

Dooley got a good look at the man's bearded face. He realized that it was the very same fellow who had come up the stairs to tell Dooley a man was shooting holes in this sign that proclaimed the carrying of firearms was illegal within the city limits of Leadville.

Butch kept running, levering the Winchester, and shooting down the street. Dooley started to turn, and shoot, too, but thought better of it. Because he saw the barrel of Harley Boone's revolver poke around the sign he had shot up. Dooley grabbed the shotgun and touched the second trigger. The buckshot blew out the

are **PROHIBITED**

and the top of *City* below that.

The revolver barrel disappeared, and Dooley saw Harley Boone falling onto the street.

Another bullet zipped past Dooley's ear, and he

jumped to the ground. He left the empty shotgun in the dirt, but brought the Colt .45 to his right hand.

Butch was taking care of the men behind Dooley, leaving Harley Boone for Dooley himself.

Boone came up, found his revolver, and swung it to Dooley. The smile was gone, replaced by a mask of hatred, and grim determination.

The .45 kicked in Dooley's hand. The shot tore off the black hat still somehow seated atop Boone's head. That caused Boone to flinch and his bullet just punched another hole in the sign, but this time the lead struck no letters, just ruined more of the painter's job.

Boone dropped to the ground, rolled over, and Dooley squeezed the trigger again. A bullet from behind him tore through his vest. That one caused Dooley to drop into the dirt, but he kept his Colt in front of him, thumbed back the hammer, and sent another round that tore a small ditch in the ground where Harley Boone had been just a moment before. Dooley saw Boone's boots as the gunman sprinted across the street. The .45 swung to his right, lifted, then stopped.

"Dooley!" Butch Sweeney yelled.

Dooley had to let Harley go. Hooves thundered behind him, so Dooley rolled onto his back. Two riders, bandannas pulled up over their faces, spurred a couple of paint horses down the street. Both had put reins into their mouths. One held a Henry rifle, the other a self-cocking revolver.

Dooley tried to remember how many rounds he had fired in his Colt.

A bullet spit up dirt right between his legs.

Dooley shot the man out of the saddle.

Butch worked his Winchester and sent a slug that caught the man in his face. Somehow, he just leaned back in the saddle, his boots still in the stirrups, and his arms flapping against the saddlebags as the horse carried his lifeless body down the street toward Leadville's other bank.

Two more men came running down the streets, working their rifles.

The firing of guns reminded Dooley of Gettysburg. At least, the stories a bunch of old veterans, those who had worn the blue and those who had fought in the Confederacy, had told Dooley over the years.

Dooley went back onto the ground, rolled underneath the sign, and sprinted toward Butch, who had taken cover behind a water trough. He felt one slug clip his hair above his collar, and another sliced off the front of his hat brim. How the shot had managed to do that—clean as if a pair of scissors had done the job—Dooley could never figure out.

For that matter, he couldn't figure out how he had managed to dive behind the water trough alive.

A bullet sent water splashing up and back into the trough.

Dooley had just enough time to catch his breath.

CHAPTER THIRTY-EIGHT

And reload his Colt.

Sweating, Dooley used the ejector rod to push out the hot, smoking brass casings. Beside him, Butch Sweeney kept fishing cartridges out of his pants pockets and feeding those into the Winchester. Dooley thumbed in the last fresh shell, snapped the loading gate shut, and eared back the hammer on the Colt just as Butch worked the lever and pushed a live round into the carbine's chamber.

"Four men down the street," Butch said softly. "Plus that hard-rock in the store."

Dooley was staring at the front door Harley Boone had kicked open. People streamed out of the store as if it were ablaze and ran down the boardwalk toward Leadville's other bank, hands over their heads, screaming out in petrified voices: "Don't shoot." "We're unarmed." "Lord have mercy!" "For God's sake, don't gun us down!"

The last to leave was the owner, who glared at Dooley as he went the other way, turned the corner, and hurried down the street between the store and the bank, and the dead body near the stairs that led to Dooley's office.

"You reckon Boone's still in that store?" Butch asked.

Dooley shrugged.

Then out of Dooley's view, but near the rear of the store, a shotgun roared. A voice followed: "That'll teach you to shoot up my sign, you illiterate, art-hatin' rogue!"

Dooley didn't recognize the voice, but he knew who had fired that shotgun. Joe McCutcheon, that old sign-painter. But that was all McCutcheon planned on participating in this gunfight.

A moment later, a corner of the store's new plate glass window smashed, a pistol roared, smoke and flame belched, and a bullet slammed in the hitching rain by the water trough, sending a few splinters into the air.

"Yeah," Dooley said. "He's still there."

"Where's the damned vigilantes when you need 'em?" Butch said.

That caused Dooley to turn to look at his young friend. "How in hell did you wind up in this fracas?" he asked.

Butch shrugged. He pressed his back against the trough and pulled up his legs, trying to make as small a target as possible. As far as Dooley could tell, they were all right for now. The four men down the street didn't have a clear shot. Nor did Harley Boone from inside the general store.

At length, Butch sighed. "She come up to me this morning," he said. Immediately, Dooley knew who she was. Julia Cooperman, married to that conniving, cheating, miserable cur George

Miller. "Said she overheard George and Boone plotting something. She didn't know what. Just asked me if I could get the vigilantes."

"Did you?"

Butch grinned without any humor.

"Didn't try. For all I knew, the vigilantes want you dead, too. Stage isn't due to pull out till tomorrow, so I figured I had all morning to kill." He laughed. "Kill. Didn't mean it that way."

"I know."

Butch let out an even heavier sigh.

"You should've kept your nose clean, Butch," Dooley said. "Stayed out of this. It wasn't your fight."

"You give me that deputy's badge. And if I'd stayed out of this," Butch said, "you'd be lying dead on this street."

Another bullet punched a hole into the water trough. That shot came from down the street, and water began gurgling and pouring out the hole.

Dooley also let out a mirthless chuckle. "There's still a pretty good chance I will be."

"Will be what?"

Dooley shook his head and moved to the side of the trough. "Lying dead," he explained, "on this street."

Butch laughed. "Yeah. With company."

Dooley saw a man in a big brown hat running down the street, crouched, carrying something that Dooley couldn't quite place. Dooley rolled out, away from the trough, aimed, and let the Colt roar four times. Then he was rolling back behind the cover of the trough as bullets dug up holes where he had been just moments before. Those shots came from overhead. Butch Sweeney recognized that, and he pushed himself away from the trough, found the man atop a hotel, and the Winchester roared. The man turned sideways, slinging the rifle across the roof, and then Butch shot him again, and he crumpled over, fell to his knees, then across the roof, his legs out of view, his torso hanging down from the façade, arms dangling.

The man Dooley had shot at dived behind a cracker barrel. Dooley chanced a shot at him, knew he couldn't hit him, but thought maybe it would make that fellow think long and hard before he tried to get around. Another man fired, and his slug tore off Butch's hat. Dooley came up, trying to find the gunman, but Butch, unfazed by the rifle shot, found the killer first, and put him down with a bullet plumb center.

Both Dooley and Butch braced themselves against the water trough as bullets riddled the heavy wood. Shots came from the gent behind the cracker barrel, Harley Boone inside the general store, and the last man with the Winchester down the street. More water gurgled. Butch and Dooley caught their breath.

"How did you learn to shoot like that?"

Dooley asked as both men began reloading their weapons.

"You taught me," Butch answered.

"Liar," Dooley said.

Butch cocked the rifle. He swallowed what little he could and wiped his brow, then brushed away his sweaty bangs. His hat lay crown down on the boardwalk, ruined by a bullet.

"Well," Butch said after a bit, "I just keep telling myself that this ain't no different than shooting wolves."

"Yeah." Dooley wondered if that could work for him. He bit his bottom lip, pulled back the hammer. "Only the ranches—meaning the good ones—they pay bounties for a wolf hide."

"Might be some bounties on these wolves," Butch said.

Dooley fought down the bile and shook his head. "Trust me, Butch. You don't want to go down that path. Bounty hunting ain't no life."

"No offense."

Dooley made himself smile. "None taken, pard."

"Do you know where the last one with the rifle is?" Butch asked.

"Ironically," Dooley told him, "he's in the doorway to the county clerk's office."

"County clerk?"

"Yep."

Butch worked the lever again. "Wouldn't it

be poetic if the county clerk caught an errant bullet?"

Dooley did not answer. "Miller's probably givin' that two-bit gunman instructions."

He was mistaken. Because the instructions suddenly belted out from Harley Boone inside the store.

"Travis!" Boone yelled. "Get up and get 'em. Tom and me'll cover ya!"

Bullets roared. A splinter nicked Dooley's cheek. Dooley tried to rise up, chance a shot, or just catch a glimpse at whatever Harley Boone and the two hired killers named Travis and Tom had planned, but the gunfire was withering. Boone must have taken time to load all the Winchester, Henry, and Spencer rifles for sale in that store.

Butch made an attempt to stand, too, but a bullet grazed the upper part of his right arm. He groaned and fell, but he had seen enough.

"Dooley!" He pointed. "Guy behind the cracker barrel . . . He's got . . . dynamite!"

Ignoring the bleeding arm, Butch grabbed the Winchester. Dooley rose, fired a shot that shattered more of the store's plate glass window, and he saw the man, Travis, running from the corner of the bank toward Dooley, Butch, and the shot-all-to-pieces trough.

He didn't know why he did it. Didn't think about it. Didn't even consider any other options.

He just ran. In the open. Straight at the man carrying what appeared to be four sticks of dynamite in his right hand, the fuse hissing and humming and showering sparks that left black spots on Travis's pink shirt.

Dooley shot again at the store, and fired toward the county clerk's office. The man named Travis had just reached the shot-all-to-pieces sign. His mouth dropped open. He forgot about the dynamite he was carrying in his right hand and reached for his belted six-shooter with his left.

Dooley shot him in the chest. The dynamite dropped and he fell against the sign, the shards of wood ripping the back of his shirt as he landed with a thud on his hindquarters and rolled heavily onto his side.

A bullet from the store window burned the back of Dooley's neck. A slug from the man with the rifle in the doorway to George Miller's office grazed his left hand. Dooley dived, breaking his fall with his arms, rolled to his side, and sent another shot at the gunman down the street. He came up, and cut loose at Harley Boone, shattering more glass. Leaving the pistol in the dirt, he extended himself toward the dynamite, the fuse's sparks drawing closer and closer to those deadly sticks.

The man with the rifle stepped out and drew a bead on Dooley. That's when Butch Sweeney came up and let his Winchester roar. Two bullets caught the man in the side, and the rifle pitched from his side, as he staggered a few paces and dropped into a heap in the center of the street. Butch had turned now, bracing the Winchester's stock against his hip and firing, levering, firing, levering, firing. He appeared to be yelling something, some primordial scream, that Dooley could not hear. The plate glass shattered like diamonds, and Dooley had come to his knees. He picked up the dynamite. He stood. He ran. And Dooley's mouth had opened, and somewhere deep inside him, he answered or echoed or imitated Butch Sweeney's rage-filled scream. He kept running, the dynamite in his hand, the burning fuse sounding louder and louder and louder.

He could see Harley Boone standing up now. His face whitening. His mouth open but no words coming out. The gunman recovered and brought up his revolver. Dooley saw the hammer fall, but no smoke, no flame exploded from the barrel. Dooley kept running. The fuse kept burning.

Inside the store, Harley Boone dropped the empty revolver. He reached for a rifle nearby, but must have remembered that he had shot that gun dry just moments ago.

All noise stopped. Dooley no longer screamed. Butch no longer screamed. His Winchester no longer fired, for it was empty, too. Even the burning fuse no longer reached Dooley's ears.

Harley Boone turned to run, but tripped over

something, stumbling to his knees. He tried to stand, but must have become frozen by fear. He looked through the ruined window of the general store. He stared in horror.

At last Dooley's sense of hearing returned. From behind him, he heard Butch yelling at him. The words took an eternity to register.

"Dooley! Throw that damned bomb!"

Dooley did, just as he tripped over the shotgun he had dropped earlier in this gunfight from hell. He saw the smoking package, could make out each individual spark from the fuse, could even see the threads from the torn, ragged bandanna that had been used to tie the sticks together. He could see the frozen face of Harley Boone. The bomb sailed in slow motion, in perfect flight, at a perfect angle, through the hole in the front of the general store that once had been a new plate glass window.

Dooley heard Harley Boone's scream.

Then he heard the blast, as heat and chunks of wood and parts of ax handles, and brass, and nails, and burning bolts of cotton rained all around him.

And, most likely, parts of Harley Boone, too.

CHAPTER THIRTY-NINE

Leadville's fire department volunteers, turned out, proved to be a lot more reliable than the town's vigilance committee.

Oh, the store was a total loss, but fires in towns like Leadville had been known to completely wipe out towns like Leadville. The bucket brigade and that fine, handsome fire engine arrived on the scene almost before Dooley had been helped to his feet by Butch Sweeney, who beat the smoldering clothes each wore and then watched the firemen in action before regaining their faculties and joining in to help combat the conflagration.

Hoses and handheld buckets splashed the sides of the neighboring buildings, including the bank across the street. Miners off work came with axes and shovels, and chopped at the burning structure or shoveled dirt into the inferno.

The neighboring building was lost, too, and the next two down the block were damaged, but the mayor, town council, and Dooley himself all bought the firefighters and the miners and the other volunteers whiskey and beer at the Silver Palace Saloon that night.

It took three baths for Dooley to get all the soot and gunpowder off him.

The next morning, however, Dooley found himself standing before the mayor, the vigilantes, and the town council. George Miller was there, too. So were the deputy U.S. marshal from Denver, Richard Blue, and the Denver *Telegram* lying little inkslinger, Paul Pinkerton.

" 'Murders on the Streets of Leadville,' " Paul Pinkerton said. "That's what my headline will say in tomorrow's *Telegram.*"

"It wasn't murder," Dooley said.

"Why wasn't this man"—George Miller angrily pointed a finger at Butch Sweeney—"arrested for violating the town ordinance against carrying weapons in the city limits?"

"Butch?" Dooley shook his head. "He's my deputy." Now, he was so thankful he had given Butch that deputy's badge—but warned him not to go around wearing it or showing it to most people—and had let the town council know he had hired Butch, at fifty bucks a month, which the council had reduced to twenty. The cheapskates.

"Since when?" Miller demanded.

"Mr. Sweeney," the mayor said, "has been drawing a salary since late spring, I believe."

"Which is a waste of our taxpaying citizens' money," Miller said. "Especially when we have a deputy federal lawman residing here for the time being." Here, Miller waved his arm at the impressively dressed Richard Blue, who bowed and gave the gentlemen a slight smile.

Which vanished when Mr. Adam Wolfe, chief alderman for the vigilance committee, said: "I didn't see Marshal Blue or you, sir, Mr. Miller, combating those brigands who launched an assault on our great city yesterday."

It took a while for Miller to recover, but he did. "I didn't see you, Wolfe, out there in the thick of battle, either."

"I, sir, was out of town at that time. And if you remember, Miller . . ."—he had dropped the *Mr.*, which made Dooley think that maybe he had a friend in this room—". . . we hired Marshal Monahan so we would have little need of vigilantes anymore."

"If Leadville is to become respectable," the mayor began, but Miller cut him off.

"I am not certain that yesterday's bloodshed and destruction was an assault on our great city." He mocked Wolfe's description of the gunfight. "I think it was an assault on Dooley Monahan."

Dooley started to say something like: *It certainly felt that way to me, too,* or maybe an indictment of the county clerk: *Which you likely organized, you low-down cur.* But he figured neither statement, no matter how true, would help his cause.

"Mr. Miller," the mayor said, "Marshal Monahan and Deputy Sweeney deserve more than we can ever repay them. We do not know why those miscreants raided our fair city in another Northfield or St. Albans type of raid—the second such assault on this town—but they stopped the carnage."

"They," Miller interrupted. "Or let me just single out our town marshal, blew up a thriving business—completely destroyed the mercantile—left many other businesses in dire straits. Witnesses—as Mr. Pinkerton will be reporting in the *Telegram*—say they saw our great defender of Leadville hurl a horrible bomb of dynamite sticks into the once-thriving mercantile."

"Which," Wolfe said, "witnesses said a cold-blooded killer had lighted and was intent on doing ill will."

"If our marshal had any shred of human decency, he would have thrown himself down on that bomb. Sacrificed himself for the good of mankind, for the survival of Leadville, and not blown a great business—and a loyal citizen of our town—to smithereens."

"Are you calling Harley Boone a loyal citizen?" one of the councilmen bellowed.

Miller started to defend another gunman, but Dooley could tell by the expressions on the faces of everyone in the room—except Miller, the *Telegram* liar, and the bribe-taking federal lawmen—that he would find no defenders of the cutthroat Boone in this room.

"We have lost our best mercantile," Miller pointed out.

To which the mayor rose from his desk, walked to the window, and tapped against a pane.

"Have you not noticed the tent being erected? Men worked all yesterday and through the night carrying off the ruined timbers, shoveling out the ashes, hauling the ruined merchandise to the dump. Now a tent is going up and a new building—made of brick, by thunder—will be erected soon. Our great mercantile will be stronger, better, and more profitable!"

"At what expense to . . . ?"

Dooley stopped him. "No expense," he said. "Except to me."

Miller looked as if he had taken a blow from a poleax to his noggin. He gripped the back of his chair for support.

The mayor explained: "Marshal Monahan is paying to rebuild that great business, and restock the merchandise. We are certainly lucky to have as our marshal a man with charity in his heart. If only our other silver barons had such decency."

Miller still looked stunned, but the lying little scribe from Denver found another attack. "So your marshal admits his guilt." He grinned as if he had unearthed fodder for ten more articles of lies to be printed in the *Telegram*. "Why else would Marshal Monahan spend his own riches? Or have you negotiated a deal where the mercantile won't charge you a penny for all you buy there?"

"I rarely even doing my shopping there,"

Dooley said. "It just seemed like the right thing to do."

"Right?" the journalist scoffed.

"I have more money than I could spend in a lifetime," Dooley said.

"Well, if you're that generous, why don't you build a church? A school? An orphanage?"

"Maybe I will."

Mr. Pinkerton sat down.

The councilmen applauded Dooley's generosity.

But George Miller had recovered, as Dooley knew would happen, and found another way to attack Leadville's marshal.

"You fail to see the point," Miller said. "You don't understand how the hiring of this man"—he pointed the finger Dooley really wanted to snap off—under Dooley's nose—". . . how this man will lead to the utter destruction of Leadville, Colorado. For I—and I don't think I am alone in this belief—know that if Dooley Monahan remains our marshal, Leadville will see more violence, more destruction, and possibly—nay, I shall say with all certainty—its horrible demise as a town worth living in."

He had the floor. He had the councilmen's attention.

"We have seen several gangs of vermin attack Leadville, but do not believe they rode into our great city to rob a bank—or even two banks. They didn't ride here to destroy a mercantile, to blow it to smithereens. They came here for one reason." Again, he stuck his finger in Dooley's face. "This is the reason. This is why our city is doomed. As long as Dooley Monahan wears a star and owns a mine and lives in Leadville.

"You hired him as a lawman, but he is no man of justice. He is an infamous bounty hunter. He kills for his own profit. He shoots men down for he feels as though he is prosecutor, jury, judge, and executioner. He answers to no one. He is as cold-blooded as the victims he brings in, strapped over a saddle, the bodies still dripping blood— and from grievous, mortal wounds likely to be found in their backs."

Dooley fantasized about drawing his Colt and putting a .45 slug through George Miller's brisket. He had actually ridden with this horse's arse? He had actually maybe even thought of George Miller as a friend, or at least, as an honest acquaintance? He had somehow bollixed everything up so that a sweet kid like Julia Cooperman could have married this cad?

But he did not pull the revolver from his holster. He just stood there and let George Miller, the liar, have his say.

"We need law and order in Leadville, my good friends, my fellow citizens."

Mr. Pinkerton was busily writing all this down in his notepad, his pencil scratching furiously, even though he would likely rearrange George Miller's words into something even more inflammatory for the Denver populace—and even beyond Denver and Colorado. The *Telegram* was just a paper in a far-off Western state, but the editors had access to the telegraph, and eastern and California papers had a tendency to reprint many articles from the Denver *Telegram*. So did, Dooley had heard, papers in England.

"But when you hire as your head peace officer a man with Dooley Monahan's nefarious reputation, you bring in gunmen. Killers. The worst renegades in the West. That's why, I believe in all my heart, that we have seen murderous rogues ravaging our streets, dynamiting legitimate businesses, ruining every business in town except those of undertakers, coffin-makers, and gravediggers. If we keep Dooley Monahan as marshal, our streets will continue to run red, until our streets are flooded with blood, and we know what happens when rivers flood in these Rocky Mountains.

"Foundations," George Miller continued, and if he had not prepared this one, he was sure a smart thinker and fast talker on his feet, Dooley realized, "are unearthed, washed away with walls and merchandise and floors and ceilings. Buildings collapse. Lives collapse. Nothing will be left of Leadville except the graveyard in Evergreen Cemetery. The graves, I must remind you, filled with men who have been shot full of holes by your gallant, your notorious, your cold-blooded fiend of a town marshal."

He found his hat, said, "Good day, gentlemen, and thank you for your time. I hope what I have said, what I have warned, will sink in." He jerked open the door. "Before things are too late. For you. For Leadville."

Leaving the door open, he thundered down the hallway toward the stairs. Marshal Blue rose, nodded, and followed. Pinkerton, the lying snob of a reporter, scribbled over two or three more pages in his notepad before he stuck his pencil over his ear, closed his notes, shot out of his chair, and hurried out the door.

The editor of the *Leadville Ledger* switched the legs he had crossed and closed his notepad, too, but he had not written as much as Mr. Pinkerton.

"The *Denver Telegram* will print all that," the editor said, "and it won't be good for us."

Dooley waited for the mayor and even Mr. Wolfe to suggest that he, Dooley Monahan, tender his resignation and light out of town in a hurry.

But the mayor said, "I stand behind Dooley Monahan."

Mr. Wolfe, leader of the vigilantes, nodded his agreement. "As do I," he said.

Dooley didn't exactly feel relieved, or vindicated. They said they would stand behind Dooley. Which to Dooley's way of thinking meant: *So that I'll catch the first bullet.*

CHAPTER FORTY

Dooley didn't know if Paul Pinkerton actually got his pack of lies published in the *Denver Telegram*. Nobody in town mentioned it, and things sort of became close to normal in Leadville over the next few weeks. At least, no gangs of ruffians charged down Front Street trying to shoot Dooley dead or blow him to bits with dynamite.

The new mercantile slowly began to take shape as masons began doing their magic with bricks and mortar. Stagecoaches made their runs. Mine whistles blew. Dooley spent most of his nights merely guiding drunks to the Jail Tree and shackling them to a limb for the night, or just letting them bed down and sleep it off. Jarvis brought him some papers to sign, and every now and then he would pass Julia Cooperman on the street. She would smile, he would smile, and they would both keep walking. That proved to be the hardest part of those weeks.

Until August rolled around, and the first stagecoach braked to a hard stop outside the bank and Dooley's marshal's office.

Jarrod Dickinson was driving the stage, one of the new ones that had started up, making triweekly runs to Silver Plume and back. He was climbing off the old Concord, cussing up a storm, when Dooley came out onto the second-story landing.

"Marshal!"

Dooley saw the blood leaking from Dickinson's scalp just below his battered gray slouch hat.

"Some sons-a-curs held up my stage."

A plump, middle-aged woman bolted out of the Concord's door, her eyes red from crying, and holding a handkerchief drenched in tears. "The swine stole my brooch, the one my dearly departed husband gave me on our tenth anniversary."

Dooley started coming down the stairs. A gambler stepped out of the open stage and closed the door. He reached inside his pants pockets and pulled them inside out. "And all my winnings, as well."

Then everyone started talking at once, and Dooley raised his hands and started asking them to be quiet, to speak one at a time, that he needed a few questions answered. No one listened. Dooley saw Paul Pinkerton, that miserable scribe for the *Denver Telegram*, standing on the corner in front of the general store that was being built—at Dooley's expense and at Leadville prices—and frowned. The reporter was scribbling into his notepad again.

"Shut up!" Dooley snapped, and the citizens obeyed. Quickly Dooley apologized to the widow who had lost her brooch but explained that he needed some information and needed it in a hurry.

He looked at Dickinson.

"Where did it happen?" Dooley asked.

"Right at Chalk Creek." The old jehu took off his hat and allowed a prostitute—up early, Dooley thought—dab his head wound with a handkerchief that was not wet with tears.

Chalk Creek. That was the boundary of Dooley's jurisdiction, according to the papers he had signed and what the city council members had told him.

"Which side?"

"The fer side," Dickinson answered.

"Which way did they go after they held you up?"

"Away from here."

"On the road, though?"

"Yeah." He pointed to his shoulder and told the prostitute, "I fell on my shoulder, honey. It hurts here, too."

"Toward Silver Plume?"

The prostitute stuffed the blood-specked piece of cotton into her bosom and began massaging Dickinson's shoulders, the one that hurt, and the one that didn't.

"Yeah." Dooley guessed that the jehu was answering his question, but he might have been reacting to the woman's touch.

"How many of them?"

"Five," answered the gambler.

Dooley turned to him. "Did you get a good look at them?"

The man twisted his mustache and shook his head. "They wore flour sacks over their heads."

"Horses?"

The gambler shrugged. "No brands I could make out. Bays. Browns. Blacks. But I did not notice if they were geldings, stallions, or mares."

"Clothing?"

"Dusters. Spurs. Nothing that stood out."

"What are you gonna do, Marshal?" Dickinson asked. The prostitute had stopped rubbing his shoulders, and moved on toward one of the houses as more and more respectable men and women gathered on the street corner.

"How much money did they get?" Dooley asked.

"Five hundred or so from me," the gambler answered, "and a nickel-plated pocketknife, my Remington over-and-under derringer, and a fine hunter's watch of solid gold that once belonged to a young miner's grandpappy before he bet on his two pair against my three fours four nights back. A Seth Thomas," the man said, meaning the watchmaker and not the unlucky miner.

"The brooch, ma'am?" Dooley had turned to the woman who had stopped bawling. "Could you describe it?"

She did, in detail, peppered with memories of

her dearly departed husband and why she had found herself in a lawless town like Leadville. Dooley saw the pencil Paul Pinkerton held move faster.

"They also," the woman said, "took my purse, which contained fifty-four dollars and thirteen cents and a carte de visite of my poor, poor Seth." Meaning, Dooley guessed, her dearly departed husband and not another pocket watch.

"Jarrod?"

The stagecoach driver shook his head, grimaced, and gently touched the knot on his head that no longer bled. "Nothin' from me. I had just crossed and one of them rascals fired from the woods. Grazed my noggin. I managed to keep my mules from running off. Then they was all around us."

"What do you plan on doing about this heinous crime?" Paul Pinkerton, the low-down dog, had stopped writing in his notebook and had crossed the street. "Why aren't you forming a posse?"

Dooley sighed. "I'm going to ride out to the site of the holdup and see what I can find," he said. "After I send a telegraph to the marshal and county sheriff in Silver Plume. But I can't go chasing bandits after they cross Chalk Creek. That's out of my jurisdiction."

"Well, don't that beat all!"

Paul Pinkerton had someone else to back his play, Dooley realized, and he turned to see the bribe-taking federal deputy, Richard Blue, leaning against a column in front of the bank.

"A lawman with sand, I see. Sending a telegraph instead of a posse."

"I don't see you volunteering to lead a posse," Dooley fired back.

The man seemed unfazed. "I'm a federal lawman. I lack authority in this matter."

"I lack authority once they cross Chalk Creek," Dooley said. "In fact, going out there to look for sign is outside my jurisdiction, too."

"How convenient." The marshal turned on his heel and walked back down the boardwalk.

Looking around, Dooley found Adam Wolfe in the crowd. "Mr. Wolfe," he said, "could you do me a favor? Butch Sweeney, as you know, is on the stage coming in from Denver." He stopped, thinking, wondering, worrying if those owlhoots might try to hold up the Denver-Leadville stage, too. Yet there was nothing Dooley could do about that now. "If you could take down statements of these witnesses, I'll saddle up General Grant and ride out to see what I can find, after I send a telegraph to Silver Plume, Georgetown, Idaho Springs." Would they go west? Perhaps, Dooley thought. "And Glenwood Springs."

"Sure," the vigilante said.

"What do you expect to find at the scene of the crime, sir?" Pinkerton was on his soapbox again. "Other than a cold trail?"

Dooley wanted to punch that horse's hiney in his mouth, but he refrained. "They nicked Jarrod with a rifle. I might find the shell casing, see what they were firing."

The reporter snickered. "A spent brass casing is sure to send those culprits to the prison at Cañon City."

"Maybe it's a rare rifle," Dooley countered. "But if it—and it likely is—came from a Winchester or Henry, well, hammers strike cartridges at different points. That's a long shot, but it might become evidence in a court of law. But horses leave signs. Shod horses. Unshod. I can see what tracks the shoes left. A chip. A line. Or how a horse happens to be stepping. That's something I can telegraph lawmen across the state. And, most likely, they were waiting in the woods for a while. It was cold this morning. Cold for August, anyway. Maybe they dropped something. Likely they were smoking cigarettes. Maybe chewing tobacco. They might have even camped there overnight. And maybe I'll find nothing. But I'll definitely look for something."

He thought he sounded pretty good, like he knew what he was doing, even if he didn't. Yet he did know horses. And he could read sign pretty good when it came to horses. He left Paul Pinkerton with his notebook filled with lies, the witnesses, the crowd, and the victims of a routine stagecoach holdup. He sent telegraphs out, even one to Denver, hoping that might make its way to the *Telegram*'s next edition before Paul Pinkerton could file some outlandish piece of fiction. Then he rode out of town to Chalk Creek.

Those men were pros, though. Apparently, they had put canvas or burlap wrappings over their mounts' hooves to reduce any tracks, or signs. Either the gunman who had winged Dickinson had picked up his shell or had never cocked his rifle. They certainly had not camped, at least nowhere in the woods or general area, as far as Dooley could find. And had they smoked cigarettes, they smoked them down to nothing. Had they chewed tobacco, they swallowed their quids.

Even after all that, Dooley rode up and down the road for two miles, trying to figure out if the bandits had stopped to undo the bindings that hid their trail. At length, though, he gave up. Still, legally and ethically, Dooley figured he had done all he could do. He rode back to town, found the statements that Mr. Wolfe had taken and left on his desk. When the circuit-riding judge returned to Leadville, Dooley figured he could turn those over to him to get to the county solicitor at the county seat.

He gave General Grant some extra oats and a good rubdown, took Blue for a walk on his evening patrol, ate some Chinese food for supper, and, seeing things were quiet this evening, he retired early.

He got up, early, too, because someone was banging on the door and Blue was barking his head off.

It was the editor of the *Leadville Ledger*, but he wasn't here to get a story. He had news himself.

"Marshal. The Breckenridge omnibus has been held up!"

Dooley had just enough time to pull on his britches, boots, and a shirt. Back to his office he went, where he saw Jesus Gabaldon, the wiry one-time vaquero who had started the line that ran folks from Breckenridge to Leadville, and vice versa, one run one way once a week.

At least they hadn't shot Jesus. But old Gabaldon had been carrying six passengers, and none of them was happy at having their wallets and watches taken. No brooches, but no women had been on this wagon. The whiskey drummer had the biggest loss. The bandits had taken his case of samples.

The good news was that it was way too early for Paul Pinkerton to be standing on the corner, scratching his pad with his pencil, and thinking of new and devious ways he could make Dooley look bad.

"Did they take any mail?" Dooley asked.

"No, señor." Jesus Gabaldon's head shook. "Me no carry letters."

"Yeah," Dooley said, and muttered a curse under his breath. Those bandits were too smart to take any mail and have the deputy marshals on their trail.

They had hit the stage before the sky had even started to lighten, and the moon was new, so the only light came from the lanterns hanging from Gabaldon's coach. As an old vaquero and experienced cowboy and frontiersman, Jesus might have been able to tell more about the horses had there been more light. Still, Dooley felt certain of one thing.

It had to be the same gang, though, because they wore dusters and there were five of them, sacks pulled over their faces, and they had hit the stage just as it had pulled up to Chalk Creek—and had ridden back down the road toward Breckenridge or Georgetown or Idaho Falls or wherever. Away from Leadville, though, and out of Dooley's jurisdiction.

Still, after taking statements and sending out more telegraphs, once again Dooley made his way to Chalk Creek to find no tracks, no remnants of cigarettes, no clues whatsoever.

He rode back to town, did his marshaling duties, went over to a hotel café and met with Jarvis to sign more documents for the mine, and returned to his room, let Blue out, fed him, and waited till midnight before sneaking to the livery. He saddled General Grant and eased his way out of town. Payday was two weeks behind him and a little less than two weeks before him, so the town would likely be quiet. Dooley rode to Chalk Creek and found a good spot on the Leadville side of the stream that provided plenty of shelter. He would have a clear view, come morning, of the stage when it came in. And if anyone tried to shoot Butch Sweeney or rob his mud wagon, Dooley would be there to stop the robbery.

CHAPTER FORTY-ONE

Dawn crept up slowly in the high country, and cold. Dooley could remember waking up to temperatures like the hinges of hell when he had cowboyed in Texas and Arizona, but here he tried to warm his hands with frosty breath. Behind him, he heard General Grant unleashing about a gallon of urine. Frowning, Dooley wondered if any hidden bandit might hear the noise, for sounds traveled far in this country. That's why he had cautiously levered a round into the Winchester when he had first made camp, if you could call this a camp.

He shifted his legs to make himself more comfortable and get the blood circulating again. Without moving more than he had to, Dooley scanned the road and beyond. He studied the crevasses, the forests, the shadows, and the tops of rocks. He sought out where five men would have a good view of the road and might be able to ride out from their hiding places in a hurry.

Mostly, he waited.

That was one attribute he was glad to have. Patience. Men in a hurry did not survive long in this country

The sun rose. His breath lost its frosty accent. General Grant waited patiently, casually grazing on the shrub and mountain wildflowers nearby. No riders appeared. He felt pretty sure he was alone here, but he might be wrong.

He waited some more.

How much time passed he did not know, but well before the sun moved over his head, he recognized the sound of hooves pounding the hard-packed dirt that was the road to Leadville. Traces chimed out, and at length came the popping of a whip and the swearing of the driver of a stagecoach. The driver would be Butch Sweeney.

Dooley made himself move now, but slowly, not giving away his position to anyone who had less than a hawk's vision. He brought the Winchester up, eased back the hammer almost silently, and stared ahead. He did not look at the road, for Butch's mud wagon would show up in good time. He focused on the places he felt most likely could hide road agents on horseback.

He controlled his breathing, tried to keep his nerves at bay, somehow managed to steady his heartbeat.

The wagon topped the rise. Butch was easily recognizable in the driver's box. The mules did not look tired, and that was due to the driver. Butch Sweeney wasn't that green kid fresh off a farm and trying to learn to cowboy. Not anymore.

The stagecoach slowed as Butch neared Chalk Creek. Dooley sucked in a deep breath, held it, pressed his lips tightly. And watched the mud wagon ease across the creek into Dooley's jurisdiction. Still, Dooley did not move until Butch was cussing up a storm and working the whip, sending the mules back into a run. Dooley stood slowly, still looking this way and that, trying to see some sign of a gang of bandits. When none appeared, he moved quickly to General Grant, shoved the Winchester into the scabbard, tightened the cinch, and swung into the saddle. Once he put the spurs against the fine gelding's ribs, he, too, found himself back in his jurisdiction.

As he galloped after Butch's stage, Dooley decided that it made sense. The bandits had hit a couple of stages just outside of Leadville, so now they had decided to move on to some other town. Georgetown or Silver Plume or maybe they'd even leave Colorado for something new. No sense in pushing one's luck. Despite that thinking, Dooley kept his eyes sharp, half expecting those five desperadoes to appear out of the dust.

It didn't happen.

As Dooley drew nearer, he began shouting at Butch to rein up, although he knew with the wind blowing, the mules running hard, and the wheels rattling on the wagon, his young pard wouldn't be able to hear him. Eventually, Butch Sweeney looked over his shoulder and must have recognized Dooley—or at least General Grant—

because he pulled hard on the lines and the old coach eased to a stop.

Dooley reined up alongside the wagon, closest to the driver's seat, and let the gelding catch his wind.

"What's up, Dooley?" Butch asked.

Dooley looked inside the wagon, as Butch had rolled up the canvas curtains. Empty.

"You run into any trouble?" Dooley said once he had caught his breath.

"Nah."

"No passengers, eh?"

"Not this run, Dooley. You gonna answer my question and tell me what's happening?"

"Been some stage holdups."

"Here?"

Dooley thumbed down the road. "At the crossing. I thought they might hit you."

Butch grunted. "Well, don't that beat all."

"You didn't hear of any holdups between here and Denver, did you?"

"Truth is, I didn't make it to Denver this time, Dooley. Axle busted at Georgetown. The Swede there fixed me up, and since I didn't have much of a load and no passengers, I come back."

Dooley considered this. It didn't make sense that Butch wouldn't continue on to Denver, because passengers might be waiting to ride to Leadville, but, well, Butch Sweeney—like most cowhands—never had much of a head for business.

"But no one mentioned no stage robberies in Georgetown. And I didn't see anything out of the ordinary—no strangers, nothing like that—from there to here." He grinned widely. "You bodyguarding me, Dooley?"

Dooley smiled. "Let's get to town, pard. I'll buy you breakfast and fill you in on all that's happened since you left."

Back in town, the *Leadville Ledger* editor asked Dooley a few questions about the holdups and agreed with Dooley's assessment that the bandits had moved off to hit some other unsuspecting mining town. The journalist also asked Butch Sweeney about avoiding the holdups, but Butch just smiled and quipped how this time busting an axle on that miserable road near Georgetown might have done him some good. Since he had no passengers or anything worth robbing.

"Do you think Marshal Monahan is right and that the robbers have moved away?" the editor asked.

"Well, I wouldn't contradict nothing Dooley Monahan has to say. And it sure makes a lot of sense, if you ask me, which you did. The roads were safe for me, so I guess they're safe now. Hope so, anyhow."

That's what was printed in the paper the next day, and that's why Butch told Dooley that he didn't need any supper that day on account he had been eating his words all day.

Because the stagecoach from Georgetown was robbed at the exact same spot that afternoon.

Five men on horseback. Wearing dusters and some sort of masks. This time, though, the messenger had been able to describe the horses: two bays, a black, a chestnut, and a piebald. They had robbed the driver, the messenger—even taken the latter's Parker shotgun—and robbed the new schoolmistress, Miss LaDene Monroe, who was coming into town all the way from Chillicothe, Ohio. Taken her Bible, her volume of Shakespeare, and, most important, her complete set of Readers for the children of Leadville. She also happened to be young, thin, blond, and very, very attractive. An ugly schoolteacher wouldn't have aroused that much sympathy.

"What do you plan on doing about this wave of crime, Marshal?"

Dooley frowned. So George Miller had decided to do the stumping today instead of that crooked man from the *Denver Telegram*. Miller offered the schoolteacher a handkerchief, but she politely declined. That helped Dooley, he figured. At least it made him like the schoolteacher a lot more, especially when she stepped away from Miller.

"Same as before," Dooley answered.

"You mean *nothing*," Miller said.

"I'm sending a telegraph to the county sheriff, asking for a posse of deputies or at least one deputy sheriff, because these crimes are falling outside my jurisdiction. I can't lead a posse after those men because of that jurisdiction. The road agents haven't stolen any mail or broken any federal law so the U.S. marshal can't do anything for the time being. My hands are tied. I don't like it. But that's the way things are."

Miller's smile was menacing. Dooley knew he was up to something. The county clerk had an audience, and Dooley, as he had just said, had his hands tied. He had underestimated George Miller.

"I just think it's interesting . . ." Miller began, and Dooley swore underneath his breath as Paul Pinkerton stepped out of the crowd, pencil and notepad in his hands. "Yes, it's interesting that these lies happen to occur just a few feet outside of our town marshal's jurisdiction. And our marshal keeps making a note of that very fact. And what strikes me as even funnier is that only one stagecoach that makes a regular run to Leadville that has not been held up . . . happens to be . . . owned and operated and even driven by our town marshal's best friend, Butch Sweeney."

Dooley felt his ears redden. If only he, Dooley Monahan, was as corrupt as George Miller. Then he could just draw his pistol and put a .45 caliber slug in the liar's gut. Alas, Dooley had this thing called a conscience, and this belief that a man was supposed to do what's right.

"Mr. Odenkirk," Miller called out.

The shotgun-toting guard for the most recent

stagecoach holdup stepped away from the bank's front wall.

"Yes, sir."

"You said one of these brigands rode a chestnut?"

"Yes, sir."

Miller smiled. Dooley's stomach turned sour.

"If my memory is correct, Butch Sweeney owns a chestnut mare."

"And those first robberies happened while . . ." Dooley shut his trap, remembering too late, and George Miller sprung his trap.

"Yes. Butch Sweeney was conveniently out of town. Making his run to Denver. But Mr. Pinkerton of the *Telegram* has news, don't you, sir?" That was not a question.

The lying scribe from Denver flipped back a few pages in his notepad and told the crowd, "The Leadville stage never made it to Denver. No one in Denver saw it. A telegraph was sent from Mr. Sweeney saying that the stage would resume its run later. No explanation was given, except that a busted axle in Georgetown was to blame."

The crowd began to murmur. Dooley's temper began to boil.

Then Marshal Blue stepped out. He held something in his hand, and Dooley knew what it was: a warrant.

"I thought," he somehow managed to say, "that no federal crime had been committed."

The corrupt lawman grinned. "Miss Monroe told me that she had a letter from her fine mother as a bookmark in her volume of Shakespeare. A letter was stolen. That means this was a federal offense." He raised his voice. "I'm going after the leader of this gang of stagecoach robbers, Butch Sweeney! Who'll join me?"

CHAPTER FORTY-TWO

Dooley found Butch in the hotel room, unshaven, sitting on the bed, scratching Blue's ears. Quickly, Dooley closed the door. "What are you doing here?" he asked urgently.

"Julia told me what was going on," Butch said. "I saw the crowd, saw Miller and Marshal Blue, figured it was time for us to skedaddle." He hooked a thumb toward the wallpaper. "Got our horses tied up in the alley out back."

"Butch," Dooley pleaded, "you're innocent. Innocent men don't run."

"They do when they don't want to get lynched."

"They're not going to lynch you."

Butch stopped petting the shepherd. He hadn't been looking at Dooley all this time until now. "Dooley, they'll hang me twice."

Anger rising, Dooley fought back the urge to berate his friend with a litany of profanity, or to at least give him a firm punch in the nose. He opened his mouth, and shut it. Spurs jingled, boots pounded on the stairs, and excited voices easily sounded through the hotel's thin walls.

Butch heard the racket, too, and he understood.

Coming to his feet, Butch reached for his gun as Dooley jerked open the door and stepped into the hallway. A pistol barked, Dooley dropped to his knee and returned fire. He had never shot at a federal lawman before, and certainly did not want to hit the man, even though Richard Blue deserved to be at least grazed. The crooked peace officer dropped his pistol and dived toward the stairs. By then Butch had stepped outside and sent two rounds from his pistol.

The door slammed, trapping the barking shepherd in Dooley's room, the dog's paws scratching like a tiger against the flimsy door. Dooley hooked his thumb down the hall, and Butch took off toward the door that led to the outside stairs. There was a pretty good chance Richard Blue had some of his posse there, but Dooley knew he and Butch couldn't stay here. He sent another round that splintered the corner.

Dooley kept backing up, his gun trained at the men cowering behind the wall. He felt the breeze as Butch opened the door. No gunfire sounded outside, and Butch Sweeney was pounding down the stairs. That meant Richard Blue had not seen the horses. Maybe.

Dooley stepped onto the landing, slammed the door shut, and flinched as a bullet punched a hole just inches from his head. Butch had already swung into his saddle and pulled General Grant away. Halfway down the stairs, Dooley turned, fired a round through the door, then leaped over the rail, spread his legs, and landed in the saddle. He filled his left hand with the reins, kept his

Colt in his right, and raked General Grant's ribs with his spurs.

Both horses thundered out of the alley, the riders leaning low, as three or four bullets flew past them from Marshal Blue on the landing. Then the riders had turned the corner.

Butch Sweeney had once told Dooley that he had always wondered what it would be like to be an outlaw, riding hell-bent for leather out of a town, bullets chasing after him, seeing the frightened faces of citizens standing on the boardwalks or in the middle of the streets.

Well, now he knew.

"Hold up!" Dooley yelled as the horses splashed across Chalk Creek.

Reluctantly, Butch Sweeney brought his horse to a halt and turned angrily in the saddle. "A federal deputy's jurisdiction don't end at that creek, pard!" he snapped.

"I know that," Dooley barked back. "I also know that you didn't rob those stagecoaches . . ." He stopped. "Did you?"

"Of course not, Dooley. You know me better than that." He pulled on the reins to turn his chestnut around and started to spur the horse again.

"Hold it!" Dooley snapped. "We're both going to be put on wanted posters now. Unless we stop it!"

"Well, how the hell do you plan on doing that?" Dooley made himself smile.

"I got an idea," he said. "We've been following the wrong trail to nail George Miller's hide to the barn wall."

At this time of night, Dooley knew his mine would be empty. Jarvis had recommended that they quit paying men to guard the place at night, as the guards had been doing nothing except drawing Dooley's pay for months now. Dooley had always listened to his bookkeeper.

Dooley and Butch eased their horses to the shed, and Dooley dismounted. He found a shovel, and started digging, while Butch remained mounted, holding the reins to General Grant.

"I can't believe you bury your money in a hole in the ground," Butch said.

"Would you trust a bank in Leadville?"

Butch said: "You got some in Shaw's bank."

"Not as much as I got here."

"You sure no one's here?"

Dooley stopped digging. "There shouldn't be."

But he heard the noise, too. He leaned the shovel against a tree and pressed his lips together, as Butch dismounted and ground-reined both horses. They drew their rifles from the saddle scabbards and moved to the side of the shed. Dooley jutted his jaw toward the office, and they crept to the side.

They could hear the voices now, and a horse nickered. Freezing, Dooley felt his stomach tighten, fearing either Butch's chestnut or General Grant might answer, but the only sound was the rustling of leaves and limbs in the trees. Dooley peered past the wall and could make out the outlines of horses in the corral.

"Guards?" Butch whispered.

Dooley answered, "Shouldn't be."

They saw the glow of a campfire out behind where the worthless rocks were dumped. Dooley moved his left arm out and made a wide wave. Understanding, Butch Sweeney crept out that way, disappearing in the dark. Then Dooley crouched and began picking his path toward the fire.

He leaned against a rock slab and let his eyes adjust to the fire. Five men. Not miners. Not guards. They were drinking, laughing, and suddenly Dooley understood. He raised a hand to his mouth, covered it slightly, and gave his best impression of a hoot owl. One of the men laughed and said, "Who! Who! Who!"

Which told Dooley what he needed to know.

Those men were drunk.

So Dooley raised his rifle, eared back the hammer, and sent a round into the center of the fire. Sparks flew. Men fell backward, and Dooley leaped over the rocks, levering another round into the Winchester and sending another bullet into the center of the camp.

"Hands up, boys!" Dooley shouted. "You're surrounded!"

Butch Sweeney confirmed that with two shots from his rifle that he fired into the air.

"I better see hands reaching for air or we're killing everyone in this camp!" Dooley yelled. He felt relieved when he saw the men coming up to their knees, or simply staying on the ground, but all lifting hands.

"If one hand drops, we shoot you down!" Dooley growled.

"We ain't done nothin'," one of the men whined.

"This is my mine," Dooley said. "You're trespassing!"

"Son of a gun," one of the drunks whispered. "It's the marshal."

"But Miller said . . ."

"Shut up!"

Dooley stopped. He could make out Butch Sweeney's form off to his left. He could not see the men he had captured, but he had a pretty good idea what he would find in the corral. Two bay horses, a black, a chestnut, and a piebald.

They had just captured the stagecoach-robbing gang. But why would they be hiding out at Dooley's mine?

In the darkness of predawn, Dooley gently pulled open the front door to Mrs. Buxton's Boarding

House. He had no trouble finding the room he wanted. Mr. Buxton had told him two weeks ago that *"as soon as that drinkin', carousin', lyin' inkslinger left town, Dooley Monahan would be welcome to pay Leadville prices for a room with clean sheets and Mrs. Buxton's wonderful chicken and dumplings for supper every night."*

There were no keys to the rooms, Mr. Buxton had also told Dooley, because Mrs. Buxton believed that everyone had to be honest to live under her roof. Well, she had let this room to the wrong person.

Dooley opened the door, heard the snores, made sure that the lying inkslinger had not caroused a chirpy to the room—which would have sent Mrs. Bruxton into hysterics—and he pulled the door shut. He drew the revolver, walked to the bed, sat down, and placed the .45's barrel underneath Paul Pinkerton's nose.

The snoring stopped. The body tensed.

"Take off your eyeshades," Dooley ordered.

With trembling hands, the *Denver Telegram* reporter obeyed. Dooley struck a match on his thigh, saw the candle next to the bottle of bourbon on the nightstand, and lighted the wick.

"Monahan!" Pinkerton whispered. Tears welled in his well-rested eyes. "Please don't kill me."

Dooley eased the revolver away from the man's nose.

"I didn't come here to commit foul play,"

408

Dooley said, and found himself smiling, thinking that his crazy plan might just work after all. "I want to make an honest newspaper reporter out of you." Dooley knew, of course, that he had to speak in the language of a man like Paul Pinkerton. With his left hand, he brought up the pouch, unloosened the twine with his teeth, and dumped a handful of coins onto the quilt that covered the corrupt journalist's chest. "For a price," Dooley said. "Of course." He rattled the bag and let more coins topple onto the bed.

He waited until early afternoon, when the streets and boardwalks were crowded with citizens heading back to work or their homes after dinner. Then Dooley and Butch kicked their horses into a walk, kept their rifles in their arms, aimed at the backs of the prisoners who led the parade on their bay, black, chestnut, and piebald horses.

A driver pulled his freight wagon to a stop and stood in the box, holding the lines to his mules. Deputy U.S. Marshal Richard Blue reached for his revolver, but froze. His shoulders appeared to slump. The *Leadville Ledger* editor snatched the pencil from the top of his ear and ran down the street, past the freight wagon, and opened his notepad, which Dooley figured he would fill with truth, and not lies. Or at least just the lies Dooley might have to feed him.

"Marshal!" the man yelled. He turned around

and followed at the side of General Grant. "Are these . . . ?"

"The real men responsible for robbing those stagecoaches." He yelled at the men, slouched in their saddles, their hands tied in front of them so that they could hold the reins, their heads tilted forward, and their eyes bloodshot from their hangovers. "Rein up."

Dooley saw the new schoolmistress standing in front of the county clerk's office. The shades were open on this afternoon, and George Miller peered through the thick panes, his ears reddening in rage, in embarrassment. The man practically shook in his boots. Which pleased Dooley to no end.

"Miss Monroe." Dooley shifted his rifle to his left hand and used his right to remove his hat. "We have those Readers for your school, ma'am." He nodded at one of the sacks strapped to the horses of the robbers, this one on the chestnut that, now that Dooley could see, looked nothing like Butch Sweeney's horse. "And your Shakespeare. And the letter from your ma. Still unopened."

That's when George Miller reached up and pulled down the green shades.

"How'd you find them, Marshal?" the editor asked.

Dooley shrugged. "All those *Police Gazettes* I read in line shacks while cowboying, I reckon."

"Marshal Blue says . . ."

"Marshal Blue says a lot of things." Dooley met the crooked badge-toter's gaze. "He also shoots first, without cause, without identifying himself, like that fracas he started at the hotel yesterday. And he swears out writs of arrest without listening to reason, to the truth." He smiled at Miss Monroe. "But like the Bard says, 'All's well that ends well.' And I'm glad to have ended our stagecoach robbers' reign. If you'll excuse me, I need to take five outlaws to our Jail Tree."

CHAPTER FORTY-THREE

Dooley watched Butch Sweeney load the passengers on the stage to Denver the next morning, nodded at *Denver Telegram* reporter Paul Pinkerton as he climbed into the mud wagon, and smiled when Butch climbed up the coach and gave Dooley a knowing wink.

"See you in a few days, Marshal," Butch said as he grabbed the lines to the mules.

"Have a productive trip, Deputy," Dooley called back, and watched the old wagon rumble down the street and out of town.

He hired the guards who had been hired to guard his mine to guard the Jail Tree instead. Paid them better than Leadville prices, too, because he did not want those five stagecoach robbers to escape from the Jail Tree or to accidentally have their throats cut during the dead of night. Not that they would talk, or at least implicate George Miller and possibly Richard Blue . . . at least. Not yet.

Leadville turned peaceful, and Dooley enjoyed that, even though the shades to the county clerk's office remained closed. That worried Dooley a bit, because he knew that behind those green curtains, George Miller was planning something devious.

Plenty could go wrong, Dooley knew. His plan could backfire. George Miller could hire more men to rob stages, more men to rob banks, more men to assassinate Dooley Monahan. Pinkerton could not fulfill his bargain, but Butch Sweeney was supposed to stay in Denver to make sure that did not happen.

So Dooley just waited. He found time to chat with the pleasant schoolteacher on the streets, but kept hoping to run into young Julia on the boardwalk. Not that she could risk having a conversation in public with Dooley, but it would be nice just to see her face, see her smile, maybe catch her whisper as she said something nice as they passed each other.

Jarrod Dickinson's stage from Silver Plume made it into town without incident. So did Jesus Gabaldon's omnibus from Breckenridge. Yet that just worried Dooley more. Until he came down the stairs from his office on the afternoon and saw Butch Sweeney's mud wagon wheeling around the corner and heading right down the street. Butch rose to his feet and pulled hard, setting the brake, and the wagon skidded to a stop right in front of the bank.

Without a word, Butch wrapped the leather lines around the brake handle and bent forward, reaching into the boot. He came up with a stack of newspapers bound by twine. Smiling, Butch tossed those onto the boardwalk at Dooley's feet.

It was better than Dooley could have prayed for. It was the *Denver Telegram*, and stripped across that rag's front page was a boldfaced headline in all capital letters.

CORRUPTION, VIOLENCE IN LEADVILLE – UNCOVERED!

Even better was the next headline.

County Clerk Linked to Bribes, Stagecoach Robberies, Attempted Murder.

And below that:

Deputy U. S. Marshal
Also Involved in Immoral Actions.
STATE SOLICITOR VOWS TO BRING
CULPRITS TO JUSTICE.
EXCLUSIVE DETAILS!
Provided by OUR INTREPID REPORTER
On the Scene and on the Trail
for **JUSTICE!**

So Paul Pinkerton could write the truth after all. For $1,740 in double eagles.

The circuit-riding judge showed up on the stagecoach from Georgetown the next morning. By that time, Deputy U.S. Marshal Richard Blue had vanished for parts unknown. Dooley and Butch brought the five suspected stagecoach robbers from the Jail Tree to Dooley's office above the bank, and, as he expected, once they saw the *Denver Telegram* article—actually, after the two of them who could actually read told the other three what had been published—they opened their mouths. The *Leadville Ledger* editor was on hand to write down their confessions for his next paper, which he proclaimed would be an *extra,* a special edition. "News of this magnitude does not happen every day," he said.

That caused Dooley to wonder why something like two alleged bank robberies on the same day or the town marshal surviving assassination by blowing up a gunman and a general store to kingdom come was not considered news of magnitude.

When Dooley, Butch, the judge, and the editor went to confront George Miller, they found the shades up at the office, the door open, and Miller nowhere to be found. Mr. John Price, the banker, told them that he had seen the county clerk boarding the Georgetown stagecoach that afternoon.

"Was he alone?" Butch asked. "I mean, was his wife with him?"

"No," the banker answered. "I don't think he even had a carpetbag with him."

Butch Sweeney excused himself, and Dooley

spent the rest of the day learning about arrest warrants and taking depositions and other legal matters. He missed supper, locked up his office, checked on the guards at the Jail Tree, although by this time he figured he was paying them for nothing, just like Jarvis had told him he had been doing at the mine. Which reminded him to fire Jarvis, the crook, the next morning.

He checked on General Grant and hurried up the stairs of his hotel, almost cutting his right hand on the splinters he had caused by firing a warning shot at Marshal Richard Blue and the deputies he had sworn in. Once the door to his room opened, Blue the good dog, rushed into his arms, wagging his tail, licking his face.

"Sorry, Blue," Dooley told the dog. "Let's get you outside so you can . . ." His voice trailed off as he saw the note someone had shoved under the door. Reaching down, feeling that knot develop in his gut, he picked up the note and stood. Absently, he walked down the hallway, opened the door peppered with bullet holes, and let Blue run down the stairs to do his business in the alley. Then Dooley struck a match and held it up close to the paper. It was on Office of the Clerk of _____ County stationery.

IF YOU WANT TO SEE JULIA ALIVE, YOU WILL SIGN OVER OWNER- SHIP TO US. THEN YOU WILL BE

PERMITTED TO LEAVE TOWN, WITH OR WITHOUT THE WOMAN.
BE AT YOUR MINE BY MIDNIGHT TONIGHT. OR THE GIRL DIES.
WE ARE THE SILVER KINGS OF LEADVILLE & WE MEAN BUSINESS.

He didn't know what time it was, but he knew it was late. He knew the silver barons in town had not sent this threat. Whoever had done this, whoever had thought of this, was no smart silver king, but a demented fool.

George Miller.

Yet Dooley also knew that Miller would kill his wife—murder sweet Julia—if Dooley did not show up. He left the door to the upstairs open, the door to his room open. He left Blue outside sniffing the alley. Dooley ran down the hall, down the stairs, out the front door, and hurried to the livery.

At least the moon was full. Dooley followed the road to his mine, his heart pounding, palms clammy, throat dry. He prayed that he would not be late, that George Miller had not lost complete control of his faculties—that Julia was still alive.

Even before General Grant had slid to a stop, Dooley had dismounted, somehow keeping his feet as he staggered, found his balance, and ran to the office. The door had been kicked open. Light flittered from a candle on Jarvis's desk. Dooley stopped at the entrance and looked inside.

"Miller?" he called out in a whisper. Then, screaming, his voice bouncing across the empty mining property. "Miller! I'm here, Miller! I'm here!"

He heard only his echo.

A sickness entered his stomach, a cold fear that told him midnight had come and gone, and that George Miller had murdered Julia, that Dooley would find her body somewhere. Stepping away from the office, he felt as though he might vomit.

A voice brought him upright.

"Over here, Monahan." It was Miller's voice. Dooley walked toward the mine entrance.

"Drop your gun belt, Monahan," the voice called out when Dooley stood just ten yards from the mine.

"I didn't wear a gun," Dooley said, and held his hands away from his waist. He couldn't see Miller. Couldn't see Julia. He could catch the glow of a lantern from inside the mine, but far back. He could hear, though, and heard the hard metallic click of a revolver being cocked.

"Then come on in," Miller said, and laughed, "and welcome."

"Where's Julia?" Dooley asked.

"Why, Monahan, she's waiting for you. Come. Now."

Dooley obeyed.

When he stepped inside the opening—much larger, a real working mine entrance and not the hidden hole Ol' Ole Finkle had used—Dooley felt something he figured he had lost count of the number of times he had felt it.

A revolver barrel pressed against the small of his back.

"Keep walking, Monahan," the crazed clerk and dishonest schemer said. "Let's go see Julia. She's been waiting for you."

Dooley walked. Miller picked up a lantern from a wall hanger as they passed. It felt like ages since Dooley had first entered this mine. He remembered the feeling of complete darkness, and the consistency of the temperature. He recalled how he felt as though the cave went on forever. Then he saw Julia. A torch had been lighted over her head. She was in her nightshirt, hands and feet bound together, hair disheveled—but alive. Her head raised. Her mouth whispered Dooley's name.

"Touching," George Miller said, and shoved Dooley toward her.

He kept walking, anticipating the bullet in his back, but nothing happened. When he reached Julia, he waited, and George Miller said, "Go on. I want y'all to be together."

"I thought you wanted the mine," Dooley said. "I was supposed to deed it over to you. Remember?"

"I'm not a fool, Monahan," George Miller said. "I just wanted you to think I was mad."

That's when Dooley heard the hissing.

He turned, just as George Miller turned around and ran, the light bouncing off the black rocks, then disappearing. He saw the burning fuse—and he remembered the dynamite that had blown up the general store, along with Harley Boone. Only this time, Dooley understood that he had no time to run and save the day. George Miller had cut that fuse short.

Julia must have seen it, too, and understood everything. She screamed.

Dooley threw himself atop the young woman, just as the dynamite detonated. He felt the intense heat, the massive noise that he was certain would rupture his eardrums. He thought he felt rocks pounding against his back, legs, and head. He knew that George Miller had exacted his revenge. He had brought Dooley to the mine he had wanted for all those years. And now George Miller was burying Dooley, and poor Julia, in that mine.

Forever.

CHAPTER FORTY-FOUR

Coughing, bleeding, hurting, and madder than hell, Dooley rose from the rubble. The concussion had blown out the torch, but once the dust settled, he could make out Julia's face. So still. So lovely. Her eyelids fluttered, opened, and her mouth parted.

Dooley could breathe again.

Tears welled in her eyes, and Dooley worked on the knots on her wrists. He realized his fingers were raw, bleeding, and his ribs hurt, his head hurt, and he felt blood leaking from multiple wounds. But nothing seemed fatal.

"Dooley," Julia said, "we're going to die here."

"No," he said, "we're not."

"We'll suffocate."

Dooley tried to give her a reassuring smile. He wasn't sure it was reassuring, and, hell, he wasn't even certain he smiled, but now that he had her wrists untied and was working on the ropes that secured her ankles, he asked, "What do you see, Julia?"

She stared at him, confused at first, and finally managed to guess. "Dust. Smoke. You."

"It's after midnight," Dooley told her. "And the torch isn't burning anymore."

She understood, and began searching. Julia

gasped. Dooley got the last knot loosened, and she sat up and hugged him. That hurt, too, but somehow Dooley liked it. As he ran his fingers through her hair, he also looked up.

A man could breathe here.

Somehow, he remembered thinking that thought when he had first entered the mine, which then was more of a cave than an actual mine, but a cave filled with silver. Now he saw the moonbeams making their way through the holes in the ceiling. Back when he had first discovered this chamber, it had been daylight. He was happy the moon was full this evening.

"But," Julia reminded him, "we can still starve."

His head shook. "This is a working mine. It's Saturday night, early Sunday morning. They'll be here Monday at six o'clock a.m. for the first shift. They'll see what happened, and they'll start moving rock. All we need to do," he reassured her, "is wait. We can live in here for that long without any worries."

Reluctantly, he let her go, and stood, stepping over the rocks, and moving to the wall.

"But I'm not a patient man."

He began climbing up the wall. The explosion had loosened one slab, and a few smaller stones that could have crushed Julia and Dooley had they fallen a few feet closer. He moved with a purpose now, climbing up, bracing himself against the wall and the ceiling. He stuck his head through the largest of the air pockets.

Dooley Monahan began to dig.

Twenty minutes later, Julia was beside him. Determination chiseled into their faces, they worked with their hands and fingers, clawing, digging, wrenching out rocks and pebbles, even bits of silver and maybe even some copper. They did not speak. They barely glanced at each other. All they did was dig, dig, dig.

The moon had passed, though, so the only light filtering through the much larger hole now came from the stars. They kept digging. Dooley began to see clearly. The sky took shape. Despite the burning in his eyes from dirt, sweat, and grime, he could make out the forms of trees on the top of the hill. Dawn was approaching when they had managed to scrape out a hole big enough for Julia to be boosted through.

"Go," Dooley told her. "Quickly. Get to town."

"I'm not leaving you," she countered.

"I'll be fine. I don't want Miller to get away."

"I'm not leaving you," she belted out again, and began clawing the dirt once more.

Dooley started to curse, thought better of it, and he worked from the inside as Julia dug from the outside.

A circus had stopped in Iowa one year, and Dooley remembered the contortionist, or whatever she was called. That's what Dooley felt like as he squeezed his shoulder this way, craned his neck that way, moved his arm, and sucked in his belly. He felt Julia's mud-caked, bleeding, scarred fingers clawing at his shirt and tugging. Dooley grunted, cursed, groaned, and finally pushed himself through the opening. He felt as though half of the roof now resided inside his trousers, but he had no time to worry about such inconveniences.

He stared at the sky, breathed in the fresh morning air of the Colorado Rockies. They were out, safe, and then he heard the maniacal laughter. Dooley rose.

George Miller stood against a pine, holding a pistol in his right hand.

"You thought I'd just leave you here?" He stepped away from the tree and thumbed back the hammer. "You think I'm crazy? A fool? I just wanted you to *think* you had a chance."

Dooley came to his feet and stepped in front of Julia, shielding her body with his.

"Noble," Miller said. "But pointless. I'm going to kill you both."

Dooley tried to think of what he could do, looked on the dirt for some type of weapon. A rock he could throw, but all he saw were pine needles and pinecones. He'd have to charge, survive the bullets sure to strike him, give Julia a chance to run. And maybe he would have enough strength to break that criminal's neck before he died.

Just as Dooley broke into a run, a voice sounded off to his left.

"Miller!"

Charging with desperation, Dooley saw Miller turn, shift his gunsight down the incline, and then heard the roar of a rifle. Dooley stopped running and watched, uncomprehending, as George Miller was lifted off his feet and slammed against a tree trunk, then crumpled at the base and did not move, did not breathe, just died.

"Julia!"

Butch Sweeney climbed the hill, pitched the rifle aside, and Dooley felt something brush past him. He saw Julia running and leaping into Butch Sweeney's arms.

Dooley blinked. Sometimes, he could be a wee bit dense, especially this early in the morning, but not today.

Julia, he told himself, *loves Butch. Not you.*

He thought about that for a moment, and suddenly smiled. That was fine. Mighty fine.

CHAPTER FORTY-FIVE

Two weeks later, Dooley Monahan rode out of Leadville a wealthy man. Maybe not as wealthy as he could have been, or should have been. He had given the mine to the schoolmistress. Butch and Julia refused to take it, and Dooley had had enough of being a man of means.

He leaned over the saddle and shook the hands of the *Leadville Ledger* editor, of Mr. Adam Wolfe, and of both bank presidents. He smiled at Butch, and thought that marshal's badge looked fitting on his pard's vest. He tipped his hat at Julia, who wore black. She was a widow, and she'd be respectful right now. For a while. Then she and Butch would live happily ever after.

So would Dooley.

"We wish you would stay, Dooley," the mayor said. "Leadville won't be the same without you, sir."

Dooley smiled. "It'll be a whole lot quieter."

"What you did for Miss Monroe," the editor said, "giving her the mine, that was the most generous thing I've ever heard of. She will use the funds for an orphanage, a school, a hospital. Leadville will live on, sir, as will your memory, even if the silver boom ends."

Dooley looked around. "I've got all I need," he

said, and he knew it to be true. He had the best horse under his saddle, and a fine dog waiting patiently, ready to ride on, ride on.

All those years, Dooley had wanted to hit a mining town, strike it rich, but now he knew that he was rich. He had always been rich.

He straightened in the saddle, gave Butch and Julia a final nod, and rode out of town with Blue jogging along contentedly at his side.

There was no hurry in him. He rode south along the Arkansas River, climbing down out of the high country, through Buena Vista and Salida, and happened to be in Cañon City just as the prison wagon arrived with former deputy marshal Richard Blue in leg irons attached to a heavy ball that the corrupt man had to carry as he walked to the gate of the state prison. Blue had been arrested in Breckenridge, tried quickly, and sentenced to ten years. Paul Pinkerton had left the *Denver Telegram* for a new job at the *San Francisco Daily Caller*, turning down offers, according to the *Telegram*, from newspapers in Chicago, New York, and even London.

Dooley left the river in Pueblo and followed the wagon road south through Walsenburg and into Trinidad, where he tried his hand at a few games of poker, but didn't find the paste cards satisfying anymore. So he rode west, through the mountain passes, and into the western part of Colorado. Good country, he thought, where cattle could graze in the valleys in winter and the high country in summer. When he saw smoke, he smiled and turned off the little road to follow a path to a ranch. The bunkhouse and the main house weren't fancy, just roughhewn logs, but the barn was sturdy and he liked how the horses in the corral looked.

The door to the bunkhouse opened, and a man stuffed a muslin shirt inside his britches and stepped off the porch and to the ground. He was a wiry man, with a thick mustache, and a face bronzed from wind and sun.

"You ridin' the grub line?" the man asked. "Or lookin' fer work?"

"Food'd be welcome," Dooley said. "But a job would be better."

The foreman nodded. "That's a good dog you got with you, son, and I like the look of that horse, too. We pay thirty a month and found. Happens that an ol' boy decided he wanted to try minin' and up and lit out for Leadville. So I've got a job for a good cowboy, as long as he ain't got no interest in gamblin' and minin'."

"I'm a cowboy," Dooley said, and swung off General Grant and held out his hand. "The name's Monahan. Dooley Monahan."

This would determine everything, he knew. If the man knew of Dooley's reputation, he would tell him to eat and ride on. Instead, the man shook Dooley's hand.

"You look like a cowboy, son. My name's Dawson. Bitter Bob Dawson. Welcome to the Lazy Nine."

Blue barked a contented bark, and wagged his tail.

As Dooley led General Grant to the corral, he knew he had found his place in the world. For now, at least. Until he got the urge again to see something new. To drift, with Blue and his bay gelding. Riding North. East. South.

But most likely . . . West.

ABOUT THE AUTHORS

WILLIAM W. JOHNSTONE is the *New York Times* and *USA Today* bestselling author of over 300 books, including the series Preacher, the First Mountain Man, MacCallister, Luke Jensen, Bounty Hunter, Flintlock, Those Jensen Boys!, Savage Texas, Matt Jensen, the Last Mountain Man, and The Family Jensen. His thrillers include *Tyranny*, *Stand Your Ground*, *Suicide Mission*, and the upcoming *Black Friday*.

Visit his website at www.williamjohnstone.net.

Being the all-around assistant, typist, researcher, and fact-checker to one of the most popular western authors of all time, J. A. JOHNSTONE learned from the master, Uncle William W. Johnstone.

The elder Johnstone began tutoring J.A. at an early age. After-school hours were often spent retyping manuscripts or researching his massive American Western History library as well as the more modern wars and conflicts. J.A. worked hard—and learned.

"Every day with Bill was an adventure story in itself. Bill taught me all he could about the art of storytelling. *'Keep the historical facts accurate,'* he would say. *'Remember the readers—and as your grandfather once told me, I am telling you now: Be the best J. A. Johnstone you can be.'"*

Center Point Large Print
600 Brooks Road / PO Box 1
Thorndike, ME 04986-0001 USA

(207) 568-3717

US & Canada:
1 800 929-9108
www.centerpointlargeprint.com